Grounded Hearts

Grounded Hearts

Jeanne M. Dickson

Waterfall
PRESS

Published by Waterfall Press, Grand Haven, MI

www.brilliancepublishing.com

Amazon, the Amazon logo, and Waterfall Press are trademarks of Amazon.com, Inc., or its affiliates.

ISBN-13: 9781542045537
ISBN-10: 1542045533

Cover design and photography by Laura Klynstra

Printed in the United States of America

For Scott, the love of my life.

CHAPTER 1

10 February 1941
Ballyhaven, County Clare, Ireland

Dutch Whitney hit the bog hard, tumbling forward to smack facedown into the muck. The taste of dirt and the searing pain in his knee and arm signaled that the Canadian RAF pilot was alive. He'd survived the jump from the bomber. He looked side to side at the moonlit marsh for any sign of his crew.

He saw nothing.

His parachute floated down around him, the thin material glowing in the moonlight. He unlatched the chute and batted the silk away, but it fell on top of him like a giant spiderweb.

Don't panic, he told himself. Otherwise, he'd end up drowning in the bog like those RAF pilots in France.

Wind howled across the marsh, billowing the parachute. There. An opening in the material. Crawling on his elbows with his belly dragging through the mire, he managed to free himself. Icy mud and water sank into his boots, through his pants, and down inside his flight jacket. His old football injury, sustained in his days at McGill University, sent stabbing throbs through his knee. The shrapnel cut on his left arm burned with every movement, but he had to get out of the bog, find his crew, and then figure out where exactly in Ireland he'd landed.

Please, God, let it be the north. Not the south. Please. Or at least within dashing distance of the border. The crew had been briefed before the mission about Ireland's neutrality.

An RAF lawyer had swaggered into the briefing room, reeking of tobacco. "Right, lads," he'd said, picking up a pointer. His sneer lifted his mustache to his nose. "Seems our Irish friend, de Valera, has not only declined our requests to use Irish ports and landing strips, but Ireland has declared itself a neutral nation." He smacked the pointer at the map of Northern Ireland. "Land in the north or get your backside across the border, and you'll be debriefed and back in England in time for tea." He stabbed the pointer repeatedly across Southern Ireland. "Land anywhere in here, and you'll be arrested and shipped to an Irish internment camp to rot behind barbed wire for the rest of the war. Any questions?"

Dutch hadn't had any at the time, but now he had a million. Internment for the duration of the war would be unbearable.

Crawling through the slime, he inched his way to dry land. Exhausted, he spit the grit and the taste of mold out of his mouth before he rolled onto his back. He sucked in deep breaths and stared at the starry sky. If only the sky had been that clear three hours ago, when they had gotten separated from their squadron. Even with their navigation radio and antenna blown apart by shrapnel, they might have made it home.

Dutch struggled to sit upright. *Lord, help me,* he thought, peering at the bog as he tore off his flight helmet. The parachute shone in the moonlight, a dead giveaway of his presence. He'd have to go back into the bog to bury the evidence. Then relief edged through him as the silky material sank onto the earth.

Over his shoulder, he spotted a mound of hay about twenty feet away. He scooted to it on his bottom and then pressed his back against the haystack to help him stand.

He looked down at his leg and braced himself. With one swift chop to his knee, he sent the cartilage back where it belonged. A moan rattled in his throat, and he bit his lip to stifle a shout. Grabbing his throbbing knee with both hands, he squeezed. Needling pain shot through his wounded arm.

Heart thumping out of control, sweat dripping, he surveyed the moonlit surroundings. His stomach twisted. A red glow on the horizon had to be his aircraft. The Wellington bomber had crashed on land instead of open water.

Where was he? Visible in the moonlight, rolling hills and stone fences stretched for miles. A lone cabin stood tucked against a hillside, its windows flickering with golden light.

He was in the middle of nowhere.

The wind had scattered his crew in all directions like dandelion seeds. A sick feeling crept through his stomach. There weren't any other parachutes visible. God help his crew if they had dropped in the sea.

Dutch whistled a birdcall into the night, hoping to hear another back. Nothing.

He made the birdcall again.

In the distance, a dog barked. A cow mooed.

One more whistle, and he waited. Silence, grave-like, followed.

He blew his breath over his freezing fingers, trying to stop them from trembling. Deep down, this didn't feel right. Could he be the only survivor? Each of his crew members' young faces flickered in his mind. They were just kids and should be home, going to school and chasing girls, not fighting for their lives and country against a German madman.

Scrubbing a shaking hand over his face, he forced himself to focus. With slow, deep breaths through the nose that smelled of hay and damp night air, Dutch gradually slowed his pulse.

Think. Now what?

If he were in Northern Ireland, returning to England would be a piece of cake. He'd be home by dinner. But if this marsh was in the south, he was in deep trouble. The Garda and the Local Defence Force would be out looking for survivors. There was no way to determine how many LDF soldiers might be on patrol. Could be one or ten or a dozen. Either way, if found, he'd get hauled off to the internment camp.

He clenched his teeth; his destiny was to fight for freedom. Nothing would keep him here. He'd find his way back to England no matter what the cost. The RAF needed him. His crew would want him to carry on. He straightened up and kicked his fear into submission.

Okay. He could do this. All he needed was a plan.

He had to blend in with the locals, find out where he was, and, if necessary, head quickly across the border.

How did a brogue sound? He summoned up the way his Irish drinking buddies talked, tried to recall their pattern of speech. "Sure now," he whispered. *No. More lilt.* "Suuurre now."

He continued to practice the accent as he ripped off his RAF badges and insignia. *Get rid of the evidence.* If the Garda stopped him, he'd say he was visiting family in the area. *Yeah,* he got lost and stumbled into the bog. And that wasn't even a lie.

Ripping off the last RAF patch from his flight jacket, he winced as a searing stab shot through his left arm. Blood dripped down his fingers, an eerie purple color in the light of the moon.

He dropped the patch on top of the other badges and then stomped the lot into the soil, burying them in dirt.

Time to get moving.

Dutch set his sights on the cabin. Smoke trailed out of the chimney and looped around like a ghostly noose. As he made his way through a field, toward a stone fence, he caught the scent of a burning turf fire. It evoked memories of family campfires, of summertime in the Canadian mountains with his little nephews, of roasting marshmallows around the fire pit and telling bloodcurdling stories. He'd have a few to add after this war.

4

He thought about his brother, who wanted to but couldn't join the fight, because of his crippled leg. And his mother, at home organizing tin or cloth or food drives for the war effort. And of course, his sister-in-law, Rachel, a Jew who had converted to Christianity. Many of her German relatives were missing or deemed dead.

They all reminded him of why he was fighting. It was for their freedom. For peace.

Focus. How did that brogue sound? "Suuurre now . . ."

◆ ◆ ◆

Nan O'Neil gazed at the picture on her mantel of Jesus pointing at His Sacred Heart. She lowered herself to the slate floor in front of the roaring turf fire, the stone hard and rough and familiar against her knees. The flames warmed her, but inside, she sensed the coldness of death nearby.

The explosion and the afterglow on the hillside signaled another downed plane. Whatever side the airmen might have served on, they were all the same in the eyes of the Lord.

With her rosary beads wrapped around calloused fingers, she prayed, "Holy Father, watch over the men who fell to earth this night, and I pray You grant mercy to the souls who are at heaven's gate."

She blessed herself, stood, and rubbed her aching knees. Kneeling didn't used to hurt so much. Was she getting old? Today she'd noticed her first gray hair lurking among the red. Time moved on for everyone. Twenty-eight wasn't ancient, unless she was trying to have her first baby. Most women in town had six or more before their thirtieth birthday. She ran a hand over her flat belly, longing for the child she and her husband never had.

She ached for Teddy, for the chance to change the unchangeable. She was a nurse, a midwife, for heaven's sake. She helped everyone in town, especially the women, but she'd failed Teddy. And this failure bit at her insides, ripped away her peace late at night, when the shadows ought to be easing her to sleep instead of into regret.

She stared at the empty cane-back chair beside the fireplace. The image of him sitting there, reading his poems aloud, haunted her. If she closed her eyes, she could almost remember the deep sound of his voice. Prose had dripped off his tongue like diamonds and rubies. He would have been the next Yeats, scholars at the University of Dublin had all proclaimed. So young. So talented.

Her chest tightened. They didn't know about Teddy's dark moods, which would go on for hours, leaving him staring into the fireplace or pacing in the garden or pushing her away if she tried to help. He'd sit in the chair, hugging his knees and crying like an inconsolable child. Or rage at her, that she was the source of all his problems, and then go upstairs to his desk and drink himself to sleep.

She thought back to the day three years before, when she'd chased after him through the wind and rain to the craggy cliffs above the sea. Why had he gone against all that was holy and taken his own life? She feared for his immortal soul. At best, he was lost in purgatory for what he'd done. Why hadn't she been able to stop him? Now, all she could do was pray for her husband and hope the Lord would have mercy.

Clearing her throat, she found herself wondering if she'd ever be able to confess her sin to Father Albert. When the Garda had pronounced Teddy's death as "accidental," she'd remained silent. Her husband had been buried in the cemetery in town. He shouldn't have been. Suicide was a mortal sin. He shouldn't have been resting in hallowed ground.

The black rosary beads clicked as she placed them next to the oil lamp on the mantel. Maybe it was better she hadn't had his child, yet she could not ignore the empty ache, the loneliness of her cabin at night after she'd spent the day bringing new life and joy to the families in town. The hurting always surfaced again. Pressing her hand against her chest, she pushed away the grief. So much for not picking at those wounds. *Enough. Enough. Enough,* she told herself. *Stop.*

Staring at the portrait of Jesus, she whispered, "You are my shepherd. I shall not want." She closed her eyes, opened her palms, and invited the Holy Ghost to heal her heart and lead her to peace.

She looked down at her sleeping kitty and tapped him with her big toe. "We'll be grand on our own, won't we, Mr. Dee?"

Her tabby cat glanced up from his pillow on the hearth, meowed, flicked his tail, and then licked his paws. His purring filled the whitewashed room.

Stretching her arms above her head, she let out a yawn. *Time for a bath.* She couldn't wait to sink her tired body into a tub of hot water, and she'd be glad to get out of this wool dress, too. It smelled like hell itself.

And wouldn't music be lovely. She crossed the room to the radio, which sat in the recessed windowsill. With a click of the knob, the wireless crackled and static filled the cabin. An announcer said, "This is Radio Éireann. In the news, our leader, de Valera, came under attack today by British reporters for our neutrality policy in the European war, and he was lectured that our Emergency policies are ill-advised . . ."

Nan placed her hands on her hips. "Ill-advised, indeed."

Given the circumstances, there was little choice, but everyone in the pub the other night had argued over it. One Guinness-infused partisan had proclaimed, "If we join with England and the Allies, we're easy targets for the Germans. And how will we defend ourselves? Throw potatoes at them?"

While the other side, pint in hand, had argued, "If we join with the Germans and the Axis, England might finally do what they've wanted to do to us for centuries. Annihilate us."

De V was right—neutrality was the only solution.

But that solution had come at a cost. The LDF, formed to help the Garda patrol and keep the citizens safe, had backfired in Ballyhaven because they'd appointed that pig farmer, Shamus Finn. Finn had the legal power to question, follow, harass. Arrest.

He held this over the women in town. What exactly did he think he'd find in their undergarments hanging out to dry? He'd had the nerve to shove Nan aside after Mass last month, point his meaty finger at her nose, and say, "I'm watching you. Put a foot out of line, and I'll arrest you. You and your friends. I'll see you in jail, Nan. I'll see you run out of town."

All because she'd shunned his advances. Advances that made her skin crawl.

No more news about the Emergency, she thought, reaching to turn off the radio until she heard the announcer say, "And now for a few more bits and pieces from our featured composer, Cole Porter."

That was more like it.

Nan hummed along with Fred Astaire's sophisticated voice, held her skirt as though it were made of fine satin, and danced across the stone floor into a back room that she and Teddy had spent all their wedding money converting to a decent bathroom. Worth every pence, too. Plumbing and hot water was heaven on earth.

Perched on the edge of the claw-foot tub, she opened the faucets. The rush of hot water swirled steam into the room. She dipped her hand into the filling tub and then unbuttoned the front of her dress.

A soft rat-a-tat-tat sound at the front door stopped her from disrobing. She shut off the faucets. Who could that be at this time of night? Was there trouble with one of her mums-to-be? Maybe Kelly Halpin, the Garda's wife, had gone into early labor. Kelly might be shy of her twenty-third birthday, but Nan worried about her.

Hopefully it wasn't Shamus Finn. She wrinkled her nose. The downed plane would give Finn an excuse to bother her. Again.

She padded out of the bathroom into the cabin's main room and turned off the radio. Rebuttoning her dress, she called, "Who's there?"

"Top of morn . . . evening to ya. 'Tis meself, 'tis," a muffled voice answered.

What on earth? Who talked like that? She opened the door a couple of inches. A tall man covered in mud filled the doorway. Water dripped from his flight jacket and boots.

Her jaw squeezed so tight, her teeth immediately ached.

An airman. A bomber boy.

At the rumpled sight of him, a chill slithered down her spine. What had he already been through this night?

A million warnings sparked in her mind. *Get rid of him quick before Shamus Finn comes nosing around.*

"How'ya. What's wanting on this fine night?" She hoped all he needed was a glass of water and directions. Getting involved any deeper would only bring her trouble.

Straight white teeth gleamed from his theatrical smile. Even under the mud, he was a looker, with high cheekbones, a square jaw, and wide-set blue eyes. How much death had this young man seen tonight? What side was he on?

"Suuurre now, I'm sorry to bother ya, miss," he said, wiping a hand over his muddy forehead.

"Did you take a dip in the bog, then?" So he wasn't German. Or English. American, maybe? Canadian?

"I, ah—forgive my nasty appearance. I, um, fell into the marsh," he said, followed by a thin, nervous laugh. "I'm a bit lost, ya see, miss. I'm supposed to be meeting me friends up north. Where might I be? How far am I from the border?"

"You're in Ballyhaven, County Clare. You're two hundred miles south."

He turned his face from her and muttered several curse words.

Her gaze roamed over his broad chest, across his trim waist, and down his long legs. Then she saw his trembling hand.

"Lord help ya, you're bleeding on my threshold."

"Sorry. Just a scratch." He stepped back, wobbling from foot to foot. "Ah, if you'd point me in the direction . . ."

He slumped forward and gripped the door frame to keep from falling down.

Ah, she thought, *sweet Jesus, give me strength.*

Her heart sank, but she couldn't let him go off into the night in that condition. It wouldn't be right. She'd need to patch him up and send him on his way. Or turn him in if Finn showed up. She didn't want any trouble.

"Why don't ya come in and collapse a spell?" Nan wrapped her arm around his waist and pulled him inside. Beneath his wet clothing, she felt tight, lean muscles, and his heart beating faster than the woodpecker's jabbing on the apple trees behind her cabin.

And a gun.

The weapon pressed against her side through his sopping garments. She hated guns. She'd spent her childhood in the shadow of the Troubles. And then there was Teddy's obsession with pistols. She'd had enough weapons to last a lifetime.

Men and their guns.

"Sit here, so," she said, letting him down on the chair by the table inside the door. "Drink some water." She poured him a glass from the pitcher on the table. With her hands on her hips, she surveyed his face. Ah, but he had altogether gorgeous blue eyes. And the disheveled state of him aroused her pity and mercy.

"Thanks." He gulped the water, and she refilled his glass.

"What's your name?" She offered him a clean towel from the pile of fresh laundry on the table. His hand touched hers, sending a rush of heat over her skin.

No, she told herself. *Don't be drawn to this fella. No good would come of it.* "You have a name?" she asked again, her tone gentle.

"Dutch." He wiped the towel over his face. "Dutch Whitney."

"As in Amsterdam? That's an interesting name. How'd you come to get a name like Dutch?"

A pained expression flashed over his face as he shifted in the chair. "I liked Dutch chocolate when I was a kid."

She smiled. This warrior had once been a boy in knee pants. "And where might that be? Now tell me the truth, 'cause I know you're not of Eire."

He clunked the glass onto the table and gazed at her a few seconds before he admitted, "Toronto."

"Ah. You're an RAF flyer, then?"

"No," he said, struggling to sit straight. He grabbed his left arm and winced. "No. I'm here visiting a cousin."

"Sure ya are." And she was Ginger Rogers. "And how'd you get the wound?"

"What wound?"

"The one that's bleeding all over my clean floor."

He glanced down at the dots of blood. "Sorry. Fell in the bog."

"After you jumped from the plane that's burning over on Collins's farm?"

His thick brows came together, and his mouth tightened. When their gazes met, he pulled in a deep breath. "Something like that."

"All right, look," she said, cutting a piece of soda bread for him, releasing the scent into the air. "I don't want any trouble with the LDF, but I'll help you. I'm a nurse. I know how to patch ya up. And I've clean clothes for ya."

She paused to push down a sudden burst of pain that nipped at her from the bottom of her soul. Why she'd kept her dead husband's clothes, she didn't know. Perhaps it was the Holy Ghost's leading for this very moment in time.

"They'll be too small, but at least they won't be your uniform. Then you'd best be on your way tonight."

Chewing on the bread, he nodded. "Thank you."

11

"But first . . ." She held out her palm. "The gun."

Hesitation rode his features. "I don't—"

"Ya do. Give it, please. Or I'll not help ya." She wiggled her fingers. "No one walks around my home with a weapon." *Not anymore.*

They stared at each other. His hand crept toward the gun, his eyes growing tight. Wasn't he the stubborn one! But he was no match for her.

"I'm serious," she said in a low, deadly tone. "Or get down the lane, but you won't go far the way you're bleeding."

"Fine." He pulled the pistol from an inside jacket pocket and placed the cold revolver in her hand. "But I want it back."

"When you're on your way. Now, do you think you can stand?" She placed the weapon on the edge of the table.

"Of course I can," he said, lifting from the chair. "I'm not that hurt."

"And I suppose bog water smells like roses," she muttered. He slumped against her, and she led him into the bathroom.

"Sit here," she said, easing him into a chair beside the sink. "Let's get off your jacket and your shirt." She swallowed the knot in her throat. "Your pants, too."

She helped him peel off each layer until he sat in his undershirt and boxers. She didn't dare go the final layer or look too long at the man sitting in her bathroom for fear of descending into thoughts of a sinful nature.

Assembling her supplies from the medicine cabinet on the counter, she assured herself that having him sit there in his . . . underwear wasn't much different from being at the beach, but she placed a towel over his lap, anyway.

After giving him two aspirin, she sat him close to the pedestal sink, propped his arm over the rim, and flushed the wound with water, followed by a hydrogen peroxide solution. Then she sprinkled sulfanilamide over the wound.

The bleeding had slowed, but the three-inch gash on his left arm moved when she pinched the skin together. She pulled down on one side to see how deep the laceration went.

He moaned.

"I'm sorry," she said.

"It's okay." His flesh parted into a red slash.

Her stomach twisted. Wound care wasn't her favorite kind of nursing job.

"How did this happen? And no tales of bogs and fairies."

"Piece of shrapnel nicked me."

"I see. It's quite deep in places. You'll need stitches." She selected a sterilized needle and threaded it with a suture.

"This is going to hurt." She gazed into his eyes. Was he scared? He looked scared. "I'll take good care of you; don't worry. Can you be brave while I stitch you up?"

Staring at the sharp tip, he nodded. "Will I get ice cream later?"

"Ah. A sense of humor. No, but how about a nice cup of tea? Now, keep still."

The needle went into his cleaned flesh. His thighs tightened.

"You okay?"

"Peachy."

"So, are you a bomber boy? Or a fighter boy?" She sewed far away from the cut as the wound was deep, stitching his skin together.

"Flyboy," he said through gritted teeth.

"Flyboy? What is a flyboy?"

"It's what we Canadians and the Americans call a pilot."

"Ah. I see."

She made the final knot, cut the suture, and placed the scissors on the counter. "There, that wasn't so bad, was it?"

He frowned at the line of stitches. "I feel like a Christmas turkey."

She wrapped his arm in clean bandages. "You've lost blood, so you're probably a wee bit weak, but I'm sure you'll be fine if your arm doesn't get infected. Mind you keep it clean. Let's get you into the bath."

His gaze swept upward and down, lingering on her lips before it settled on her eyes. "You want me to strip?"

"You've stripped enough. Stay in your underwear. Come on. Up ya get. Slowly."

"I don't think I have any other speed."

It'd been a long time since she'd felt the hardness of a young male body, saw the bulging of powerful thigh muscles, or smelled the scent of a man in her house.

Dutch settled into the warm water, his underwear clinging to him. She tried not to look. Too much.

"Once you're out of the bath, I'll wrap your swelling knee."

"Thank you. What's your name?"

"Nan. Nan O'Neil."

His eyes went to her hand resting on the side of the tub. "Where's your husband?"

"My . . ." She twisted the plain wedding band, a symbol of her ill-fated marriage; yet, to take off the ring had seemed disloyal. "Gone to meet his maker," she said, for she didn't believe he'd be in heaven. "Go on, relax. You're safe for now. Close your eyes."

"Thank you." His dog tags glistened in the light from the oil lamps. He lay with his eyes closed, his head resting against the tub. He drifted into slumber. Or passed out, more likely.

Sitting on the edge of the tub, she dipped a washcloth into the bathwater. There was little chance that he'd be going anywhere tonight. Lying there in her tub, he seemed as weak as used tea leaves.

She ran the cloth over his muscular chest, down along his stomach, then back up to his neck.

He looked a great deal better all clean. Nan couldn't remember when she'd seen such a nice-looking fellow. Lovely thick, dark hair, with a curl dangling over his forehead. He had light skin with a touch of bronze where the sun had kissed his features. She moved the washcloth over his cheekbones, down his straight nose, and gently over his full lips. She teased the cloth over the scar that jagged across his square chin.

Ah sure now, he was a patient and she shouldn't have been think-ing of him in any other terms, but she was only human. And wasn't he all man?

Bam, bam, bam sounded at the front door. Nan slid off the edge of the tub. Her heart pounded, the noise pulsing in her ears.

Dutch's body jerked. His eyes opened wide as water sloshed over the sides of the tub.

"Who's that?" He grabbed her hand with a strong grip.

"Dunno. I'm a midwife, not a soothsayer. It could be a husband coming to fetch me for his wife."

His gaze bore into hers. "Or it could be the Garda."

She tried to look away but couldn't. Couldn't lie, either. "Yes."

He pulled her toward him, entwining his fingers with hers. "Don't give me up. I can't be interned. I must get back to England. Back to my unit. Fly more missions. Please?"

Nan swallowed hard. "I shouldn't help you. If I'm caught hiding you, there'll be repercussions. I could go to jail, lose my practice. The women in town rely on me."

Loud knocking struck again. She looked at the door.

His grip tightened, drawing her attention back. "Just for tonight. I'll hightail it out of here tomorrow. Ireland's freedom is at stake, too. The Germans will run you down like dogs. Look what they did to Poland. You want that to happen here?"

His words ignited the Irish patriot in her soul. He was on the right side of this horrible war. The danger was real.

Nan thought about her best friend, Tuda, and about Tuda's twin boys. They'd volunteered for the RAF and were out there somewhere. What if they needed help?

Dutch pulled her even closer. The heat of his body sank into hers. The set of his jaw, the intensity of his eyes weakened her resolve.

God forgive her. Saints protect her. "All right. Only for tonight."

"Thank you." He pressed her hand to his mouth. Sparks tingled up her arm to her cheeks. She stepped back, away from his grip. A sizzle from his kiss lingered on her skin.

Bam, bam, bam—the sound cut through the air with more impatience, more demand. She looked at her dress, covered in mud and blood.

She had to get out of the soiled garment, but she couldn't strip in front of him. Her pulse pounded. She hesitated. Had she left the curtains open in the cabin? If she had, she couldn't change out there, either.

"Look away from me, now. I need to change. And don't make a sound," she said, stripping off the dress. She grabbed a green bathrobe from a hook by the sink before she turned to face him. His gaze darted over her flimsy slip and down her bare legs.

"Dutch, for the love of Mary, are you listening? And I told ya not to look at me."

He blinked. With a sharp nod, he focused on the floor.

With her finger to her lips, she said, "Not a word."

She slipped on the robe, tied the belt, and headed toward the front door. Hopefully it was only a husband, fetching her for the wife's labor.

She pressed her palms against the red door, took a breath, and pushed out the words as calmly as possible. "The hour's late. Who's there?"

"Officer Finn."

Lord, please help me. She held the latch, the metal cold against her palm. Her lips twitched at the thought of last week's encounter with this moron, Shamus Finn—cornering her at the back of the church hall, putting his fat hand on her waist, demanding that she reconsider his offer of marriage.

She would have stomped his foot and slapped him if the priest hadn't strolled in. If Finn ever tried to touch her again, she'd take that gun of his and do something very unladylike.

But right now, she knew if she didn't show herself, he'd figure something was wrong. She cracked the door open a couple of inches. "Ah, it's yourself, Shamus. How are you this fine night?"

"Grand, grand. And it's Officer Finn when I'm wearing the uniform of the LDF." He puffed up his chest. The brown jacket fit tightly around his thick torso.

"Of course, Officer Finn. Why are you here at this time of night? Ya ma, is she all right then? Is she having the female trouble again? I was getting into my bath, but if she needs me, I'll only be a second."

His round cheeks reddened. "Not a'tall, Nan. Ma's grand. Sorry to disturb ya peace. Did you hear the plane go down earlier tonight?"

"I did, I did." She blessed herself. "What a terrible noise. Are they RAF? Did you find them?"

"Aye. RAF. We're looking for the crew. Have ya seen anyone, Nan?"

A beat passed between them. "No, indeed. Have you found any of the boys?"

"Belligerents. Combatants. That's what they are." His focus slid down her body to her bare legs, and he licked his lips, leaving a wet gleam. "If found alive, they'll be on their way to internment camp."

"I'll say a prayer for the airmen." Especially for the one in her bathtub.

"But you'll give me a holler if any come this way?"

"Of course I will."

His sharp brown eyes nailed her. "'Cause ya know it's an offense against the Free State of Eire to harbor a soldier."

"I'm knowing that, yes. I was at your meeting last week." Nan inched the door shut. Her knees trembled inside her robe, but she summoned up a smile that wobbled at the corners. "Good night then, Officer Finn."

"One more thing, Nan." His hand pressed the door back two inches. "I notice there's blood on the threshold."

Nan's stomach did a flip. "Disgusting, isn't it? Mr. Dee did that."

"Mr. Dee?" Shamus's eyes narrowed as his hand went to the rifle at his side. "Who might that be?"

"Ah sure, my tabby cat. He nabbed a mouse and chewed it on my doorstep. The blood was the cat's doing. Well, good night—"

The tip of his muddy boot stopped the door from shutting. "So what about the bloody fingerprints here?"

Nan squeezed together the neck of the robe. The cat rubbed against her legs, purring.

"Ah, that's a bit of my own doing. I couldn't stand the sight of the wee creature, all bloody there on my stoop. So I picked up the thing and then flung it over the hedge. Got my hands bloody and must have brushed them there while I was going inside. I'll clean it in the morning. Shamus, ah, Officer Finn, if you don't mind, my bath is getting cold."

"Okay, okay. I see."

Out of the corner of her eye, she glimpsed the cat jumping onto the table. He knocked Dutch's gun from the edge. The weapon fell to the floor and landed beside Nan's bare feet.

Her heart stopped. Maybe Finn hadn't noticed. Her gaze went to his.

Rubbing his double chin, he looked from the gun into Nan's eyes. "Well now, Nan. Is that the gun the cat used to shoot the mouse?"

CHAPTER 2

The quaking of Nan's feet rose to meet the sensation of dread in her belly. Her breath hitched and her legs turned heavy and dense as she stared at Finn, who filled the threshold with his girth.

She had two choices: come clean and betray the young man in her bathtub or continue the lies. The options raged in her brain. To do either would be a sin.

"Well, Nan?" Finn wiped a finger under his nose. With his chin he nodded to the gun, the metal barrel cold against her big toe. "What have you got to say now?"

Okay, here goes, she thought. She was about to say a lot, and it would be all lies. Everything she said would constitute a sin. And she'd use the only weapon she had at her disposal to defuse him.

Herself.

Pulling her shoulders back, she arched forward like a figurehead on the bow of a clipper ship. "Ah, Officer Finn. Sure, ya caught me," she said, words warm and smooth. "I admit I was afraid when I heard the airplane crash. I didn't want to tell you I had a gun, that I was worried."

She dropped to one knee, letting her robe open, revealing the bare skin of her thigh where the slip and robe parted. The gun, the steel barrel glinting in the light, felt cold against her palm. Heavy. Shivers raced up her spine.

Glancing up, she asked, "I suppose you wonder how I came to have this weapon?"

"Ah . . ." Finn's mouth hung open. His gaze was fixed on her leg.

Although she figured the gun wasn't on his mind anymore, she said, "I delivered a British soldier's child. He hadn't any money and offered this instead. A good exchange. After all, the Irish government can't always be here to protect me during this Emergency."

Slowly rising with the weight of the weapon pressing into her hand, she felt the damp air circle up her legs. Finn focused on the lacy top of her slip peeking out of her robe.

"Don't you agree?" Her smile deepened.

All he could do was bob his head up and down. She made sure the cat wasn't about before she placed the weapon back on the table.

And then, as though she were delivering the deathblow, she lightly touched the row of brass buttons on Finn's jacket and lingered on the one above his belted waistband, adding pressure, digging the button into his fleshy stomach.

Then she went in for the kill. "You needn't come around anymore. I can take care of myself."

With his slackened jaw and his mouth formed in the shape of a full moon, he wheezed in a sharp breath, and his narrowed eyes began to loosen.

It was time to release the spell. "Thanks for looking in on me. If a belligerent comes to my door, I'll send him packing."

His lips moved, but no words came out.

"Good night." She closed the door, flicked the lock, and held her breath until she heard the shuffle of his boots moving away through her courtyard, the squeak of the gate, and the clank of its closing.

Staying in place, she pressed her back against the door and found herself sliding to the floor. Her heart was beating so hard, she thought her ribs would rupture.

A crackle from the fireplace made her jump. She focused on the hearth. Jesus's portrait seemed to come alive. Surely, he was staring at her in disappointment.

To use her body in such a sinful way. "I'm sorry. Please forgive me," she whispered. She glanced at the gun on the table and hoped she'd never see another as long as she lived. Rising to her feet, she prayed no more pilots would knock on her door, either. She'd need to get the bomber boy out of the tub and healed enough to be on his way.

No need to make it easy for snooping eyes, she thought, racing around the house, closing all the heavy burlap curtains. She paused. The last time she'd closed all the window coverings had been after Teddy's death. She shook the memory away as she opened the bathroom door.

Dutch was biting his lip, his eyes wide. "Who was it?"

"Officer Finn with the Local Defence Force." Nan looked at Dutch's bandaged arm. Only a few dots of blood showed through the gauze, all on target for recovery.

"What happened? Does he suspect?"

"Oh, I believe so." She was too embarrassed to relay details. "Thanks to my cat. Don't worry. I got rid of the man. At least for tonight, but he'll be back like a shadow in the sunlight."

Dutch frowned. "Maybe I should go now. I don't want to get you into trouble."

"I'm already there."

Especially after her act with Finn. She reckoned he wouldn't forget the show she'd given him. In the pit of her stomach, she felt her supper threatening to come up.

"Let's get you out of the bath and into bed. What you need is sleep. You can leave tomorrow, once it's dark."

He gripped her hand and, with her help, stepped out of the tub. Water ran down his body to drip on the tiled floor.

Not any different from being at the beach with a young man, she tried to convince herself. She swaddled the towels around his shoulders and waist before he lowered himself onto the chair.

There was a bruise blossoming on the right side of his face. With her finger, she smoothed ointment over the scrape. "You're a sight."

He covered her hand with his, held on, and wouldn't let her go. With eyes raised upward to capture her gaze, he said, "I appreciate what you've done for me tonight." Pins seemed to rise up her arm as she took in his eyes. Fierce yet wounded. She couldn't look away.

"How can I repay you?"

Get down the road. Leave me in peace. "Return to your unit. Go be the hero."

"That's all I want. To be a hero," he said. "To save the world."

"That's a tall order." *So typical of a man,* she thought.

"It's my purpose in life."

"Is it? Well, ya purpose tonight is to get into bed. So let's bandage up your knee."

He released her, but she could feel him watching her as she gathered the bandages for his knee and unwrapped a new bundle of gauze. The wrapper fell on top of his jacket, turning the white paper pink from the bloody garment. The sight stopped her; the war was in her home. *Not for long,* she assured herself.

After dealing with his knee, she said, "Up you get. The bed's not far."

With her help, he limped into the bedroom. The mattress squeaked under his weight. "I need you to take off your wet things. Can you do that by yourself?"

"Yeah. Sure."

She turned away, crossing the room so she wouldn't be tempted to help. Or watch. The bed creaked from his efforts.

"It's cold in here." The hearth in the living room didn't warm the entire house so she placed more turf bricks onto the smoldering fire in the bedroom fireplace. The room warmed, then filled with the scent of smoke.

Out of the corner of her eye, she saw the towels and his undergarments on the floor. "Let me see if there's something for you to wear."

"Okay." His low voice felt like a caress. How long had it been since she'd had the feel of a man in her home? Her bed? The thought triggered heat to race through her. In the dresser beside the fireplace, she opened the bottom drawer.

Teddy's clothes. His clean nightshirt. The material felt soft in her hands. She sniffed it, half expecting after all these years for it to smell of her husband. It didn't. The vague scent of summer lavender she'd tucked into the drawer was all she could detect.

"Here," she said, shaking the garment out. She paused. He sat on her bed, the towel draped over his lap. "It gets cold in the morning," she said, focusing on his face.

Like a dutiful child, he let her ease him into the nightshirt. The garment barely fit. She left the five front buttons open; the nightshirt gapped across his chest.

"Is that comfortable?"

"It'll do," he said.

"Now, get inside the sheets and cover."

His head lay against her pillow, on the side of the bed where Teddy had slept. "I'll get you some water in case you wake in the night."

By the time she returned, he was already softly snoring. Pulling up the covers around his shoulders, she gazed at him.

Sweet baby Jesus. Please bring swift healing to my secret flyboy. And grant him safe passage to the north. Soon.

She shut the door behind her.

Inside the main room of her cabin, she spotted the gun on the table. Taking the weapon, she went back into the bedroom. Accompanied by the sound of his heavy breathing, she laid the gun on the bedroom's fireplace mantel and then counted down eleven bricks. With both hands, she struggled to wiggle the brick free. It slid out, revealing a deep hole. She put the gun inside, replaced the brick, and stepped back.

There. Safe until she returned it to Dutch. Folding her arms, she glanced at the far corner of the room. Behind the wood-paneled wall, there was a hiding place. She hadn't opened it in years. Perhaps she should air it out, bat away the spiderwebs. If Finn or the Garda came snooping, Dutch would need to hide there the same way IRA members had been hidden by her grandma when the authorities had come looking for resisters during the Troubles.

The cat strutted toward her, tail swishing. "And for you, Mr. Dee," she whispered. "No more interfering with the doings going on here. Dutch is our secret. Understand?"

Nan gathered her nightgown and the clothes she'd need in the morning and then left the room.

The cat followed her out. She closed the door, resting her hand on the wood for a second, wondering if she'd made the worst mistake of her life or if this was indeed her patriotic duty. Perhaps it was both.

The cat sat next to his empty bowl and meowed.

"Oh, all right. I did forget to feed you. You want your dinner, don't you?"

After she fed the cat, cleaned the bathroom, and took her own bath, she checked on Dutch before climbing the wooden staircase from the scullery to the loft.

She stood on the landing, the candlelight flickering, illuminating the room. Once a week she ventured up here to clean, but it was always during the day. Her gaze rested on Teddy's desk at the opposite corner of the loft. Tuda, her best friend in the whole world, had told her to pack up everything. Donate his books to the library, send his manuscripts to the Dublin publishers, take off her wedding ring, and get on with her life.

She couldn't. She'd left everything as it had been on that day three years before. Perhaps she was trying to make sense of something that made no sense, as though leaving his desk untouched might bring an answer to why he'd chosen to do what he did.

Leave her. Her and this world.

The candle's flame wavered from the wind that crept through the paned windows. She made her way to the other side of the loft, to the iron bed. She placed the candle on the nightstand, lay on top of the mattress, and pulled a heavy quilt over her.

When she blew out the candle, its smoky scent filled the air. Her eyes adjusted to the moonlight streaming in from the windows. Drawing the covers to her shoulders, she stared at the dancing shadows in the thatched roof ceiling. It had been a long time since she had slept up here. Twenty years, probably. With her ma, who'd visited the summer after her da, uncles, brothers, and cousins had perished.

All together, all at the same time, all in the basement of their house. *Such a waste.* Hatred had conquered them.

She'd never forget that day. She and her ma were at the market when they heard the explosion. From four blocks away, they could see smoke and flames rising to meet the gray sky.

Ma had squeezed Nan's hand so hard, she'd thought her fingers would break. By the time they arrived at their row house, there was nothing left. Ma picked up a fragment of a photograph of Da. Without a word or a tear or even a gesture of sorrow, her mother had opened her purse, dropped the picture in, and snapped the bag shut.

At her aunt's house that night, when Ma thought she was asleep upstairs, Nan could hear them talking.

"That's what comes of men and bombs," her ma had said. "Men and their wars."

"Would you prefer we live in a divided Ireland?"

"I'd prefer if we just live."

This place, Bramble Cottage, her current home, wasn't supposed to have come to her. It should have been handed down to her oldest brother. When the time came, Nan was the only one left to inherit the old farm.

She snuggled into the warmth of the quilt. Tuda had been the last person to lay her head on this pillow, after that awful ordeal, the night when Tuda had lost her unborn baby. She'd come to the door, bleeding, but Nan hadn't been able to save the child. After the news, Tuda's husband had gone mad. He drank himself into a stupor. Accidentally set fire to their home. Then managed to land in jail, near death after picking a fight with the wrong fellow.

The bed shook. Nan gazed at the foot of the mattress. She could barely discern the outline of the cat in the moonlight, circling around, stepping on and over her legs.

"If it isn't himself, the troublemaker."

Mr. Dee settled at the bottom of the bed. Nan was glad for the warmth of the wee beast. With a sigh, she shifted onto her side.

Forgive me, Lord. Forgive me my sins. Give me strength and confidence to continue in spite of my shortcomings. Grant me courage tomorrow. I'm going to need it.

She cringed. Had she really touched Finn's buttons? Shown him a bit of skin? How could she have? She rolled onto her back. Because there was a wounded pilot in her bathtub.

Dutch. He was far more injured than she'd first thought. He couldn't pedal out of here tomorrow, not with his arm and his knee in bandages. Walking would be impossible, too.

She rolled onto her stomach and felt the cat stroll along her back. *No.* There had to be another means of escape. She searched her mind for a solution.

Her eyes opened. The Ford. Her car. It hadn't run for almost a year, but Tuda had said it wouldn't take much to get it going again. Her best friend would know what to do. She was a better auto mechanic than her husband, especially now that Paddy had taken to the drink again.

When the car had died last year, Nan decided that with the cost and scarcity of petrol, riding her bike would do her fine.

The trick with Tuda would be keeping the flyboy downstairs a secret. Nan didn't want her friend knowingly involved, in case something went wrong. Finn had warned everyone: help a belligerent, face jail time. No exceptions on his watch.

She should have never opened her door tonight, to either man. Both had brought trouble. Deep trouble. Drumming her fingers on the mattress, she weighed the possibilities.

Okay. This was the plan. Get Tuda to fix the Ford. Get Dutch healed. Get back to normal.

Normal, she laughed. *What was normal anymore?*

If only she could fix her past, fix what had happened with Teddy, as easily as Tuda could fix the Ford.

The ache at the back of her throat grew as she looked across the moonlit room to her husband's desk, everything in its place, as though he might climb the stairs again, sit down, and start typing. If it were anything else, she could face the priest, confess her wrongdoings; but she'd tightened her lips around the half-truths for so long, what actually happened that day had to remain locked in her heart. For Teddy's sake.

Nan tried to sleep, but she tossed and turned and repositioned herself until the cat finally jumped off the bed. She smacked her pillow several times before she flopped facedown into its feathers.

Finally, she started to drift into sleep, mumbling the Lord's Prayer, hoping for peace, comfort. "Forgive us our trespasses . . ." She paused, eyes open in the darkness.

How could she seek forgiveness through Father Albert or from God for her sins if she couldn't bear to even talk about what had happened that horrendous day Teddy died? The shame and guilt poked at her soul.

She rolled onto her back, stared at the shadows. With a swipe to her face, she tamped down her resolve. Best to leave it alone. What good could come from disturbing the dead? She should leave it be, let it go; but like a tick burrowed under her skin, her conscience would not let her rest.

CHAPTER 3

The faint morning light filtered through the drawn curtains in Nan's bedroom. She set a tray with tea, brown bread, jam, and a slice of ham on the nightstand next to her medical supplies.

She stood, hand on the iron headboard, watching him asleep in her bed, his chest slowly rising and falling.

A rustling noise from the yard made her flinch. She stepped to the window, her boots clicking over the tiled floor, her knees shaking. She knew Finn would be back, snooping around, trying to catch her.

But so soon?

The scuffling, tapping noise grew louder. She parted the curtain and gazed through the wavy glass. Across the way, the tin roof of the calf house dripped moisture onto the cobblestone courtyard.

Crows. Five of them. The gangsters of the farm, waddling along the stone fence as though they owned the place. They even intimidated the cat. Too bad she couldn't train the birds to attack Finn when he entered her yard.

Tuda had been insisting for years that Nan should get another dog, but somehow it didn't seem right. When old Hamme—the mutt that she and Teddy had raised from a puppy—died, she couldn't bring herself to get another dog. Father Albert had apologized profusely for running over the pet with his car. He was a notoriously bad driver.

After the incident, the priest no longer drove. Mrs. Norman, the housekeeper shared by the town doctor and the priest, took over chauffeuring duties, but her driving was no improvement. Mrs. Norman smashed the vehicle six months later and mowed down four chickens in the process. Father Albert gave up on a car. He rode a bicycle instead. Now it was the village dogs that terrorized him.

Another pair of crows landed on top of the calf house, their claws tapping loudly on the tin roof. One smack of her palm on the window sent the crows flapping away with angry caws.

"Dutch," she whispered, approaching the bed. "Wake up." Her hand went to the stubble on his cheek.

His eyelids flickered, and he looked up at her.

She smiled. The sensation of his stubble lingered on her fingertips and echoed up her arm. "Good morning. How are you?"

After a brief confused expression, he adjusted his position, grabbing his injured arm as though he'd forgotten about the wound. Pain rode his chiseled features. "I'm dandy. I'm ready to go."

Sure you are, she thought. "We'll talk about that in a minute. First, I have your breakfast. Are you hungry?"

"Famished." He grimaced as he rose to a sitting position, her husband's nightshirt stretched across his brawny chest. A rip below the open buttons provided additional room for him to move. She glanced at the dark chest hair that peeked out from the nightshirt's gap. The sight stirred a part of her she barely remembered.

He leaned forward. "I'll get out of bed. Eat at the table."

"You won't." With her mere push on his firm chest, he slumped back. The sensation of touching his skin and seeing his chest hair and the depth of his dark-blue eyes had her tongue-tied for a second.

She shook her head. "Stay put. You need time to heal."

"No, I have to go."

"Ah, you mean to the bathroom? Sure." She reached for a walking stick she'd placed against the nightstand. The cane was made out of wood, with a stag-horn handle and a silver cap at the end of the slender shaft. The face of a fox, carved into the end of the handle, had always given Nan the willies.

"Here, use this." She offered him the cane.

Dutch looked her up and down, then settled his gaze on the cane. "What's that for?"

"What do you think?"

"To beat Finn with? Just give me my gun."

"Don't be daft. I'm in enough trouble without you beating the tar out of an LDF officer."

"Then what's the cane for?"

She held it out, waiting for him to take it. "You're the one who said he needs the loo."

"Well, yeah. Later, but . . ." He frowned at the cane. "I don't need that to get around."

"Dutch. You do. You have a knee that's swollen to the size of a melon, plus you've sliced open your arm. Aren't you in pain?"

He shrugged, glanced at his bandage. "Nay."

"Oh, stop. I know that's not true." She set the cane back against the nightstand, within his reach, and then she handed him a cup of tea. "Careful," she said. "It's hot."

Their gazes locked, and her breath caught deep in her chest. Ah, but he was a good-looking man. She drew away, stepped back. *Trouble.* He was trouble.

He glanced at the cane. "Where'd you get that thing? Is that a horn handle? Doesn't look like a peasant—eh, country type of cane."

Peasant. He thought she was a peasant. A washed-up, old peasant midwife. She supposed the description fit.

"Indeed it is. The cane came from Lord Harry. He owns the big house a couple of miles from here. My cottage used to belong to the manor, but like most of the Irish ascendancy, the Harrison family fell on hard times. They've sold off most of their property, including this patch."

"You bought the cane from him?"

"Not a'tall. About two years ago, Lord Harry's butler knocked on my door. There was an emergency. A servant girl was about to give birth. She'd kept her pending motherhood a secret until she went into labor."

"Why would she keep it a secret?"

Nan shrugged. "To save her job. The maid wouldn't say who the father was, but the evidence pointed to Lord Harry's son, Tipper. He's a nasty bit of work."

"He fess up?"

"No. The maid delivered a healthy baby girl. Lord Harry supposedly gave her money and sent her back to her family in Wicklow. On top of my fee, I got this cane as a gift for my troubles."

"Your troubles?"

"To keep my mouth shut in town, but everyone knew." Everyone would know about Dutch, too, if she wasn't extra careful. Telephones were not needed to spread news, especially if Mrs. Norman got wind of the flyboy in Nan's bed.

"What happened to Tipper?"

"Nothing. He joined the RAF. He's serving in Africa. He managed to marry a Royal Ballet ballerina, Margot Dorian."

"Margot Dorian? I know who she is. I saw her dance once. Sort of."

Nan tilted her head. "You did?"

"My mom, sister-in-law, and a couple other ladies dragged me to a ballet performance in Canada a while back. She was the star."

"What did you think?"

He shrugged. "I fell asleep."

Nan laughed. "I'm surprised you'd go to the ballet."

A curve of a smile formed as he said, "The ladies needed an escort, and my brother and I tossed a coin. I lost."

"How many brothers do you have?"

"One. He's the best."

"So, you're close?"

"I'd do anything for him. Or any member of my family. How about you?"

"I would, too, except I don't have any family."

He stopped, his lips on the edge of the cup. "Isn't that unusual for you Catholics? I mean, big families, right?"

Nan sank to the corner of the mattress. "I had three brothers, but they all died when I was a kid."

"I'm sorry. Your mom and dad?"

"Gone to meet the angels." She waved her hand as though it didn't matter. Waved her hand to wipe the memories away—away for good, if only she could.

He waited a beat, watching her. She steered the conversation to present day. "Margot . . . Lady Margot is one of my clients now. She lives at the manor house and is expecting a child. Boy oh boy, she must have been shocked when she arrived and found herself in a crumbling mansion. I'm afraid she learned too late that Tipper's title doesn't carry much of a bank account. They have no money a'tall. I'll be lucky to collect my fee."

"Yeah, a title doesn't give a person money or class. Or happiness."

"That's true. Lady Margot is unhappy. She's gained so much weight, she might be expecting twins, except I know she's not. Poor creature."

He steadied his gaze on her. A flipping sensation in her stomach made her look away. She stood, cleared her throat. "Eat, please. You need to regain your strength."

"Thank you. I know this isn't fair to you. I know—"

"Not another word. This is for the cause, right?" She stumbled over the uneven slate floor, in the spot she normally remembered to avoid. She added turf to the fire and then poked the embers into a burning glow.

"This is good," he said. "The best bread I've ever had. You make this?"

"I did. Not the butter or jam, though."

"I thought butter and jam were impossible to find with rationing."

"Not in Ireland. We ladies have an informal exchange system."

"Black market?"

She grinned. "Green market. I make apple butter to trade, but I can't get jars so far this year. Tin is near impossible to find these days. Are you done with your breakfast?" she asked, although she could see by the empty plate that he was. Only a few crumbs remained. *Good.* He had a healthy appetite.

The dishes rattled as she took the tray. "I need to check your knee and re-dress your wound before I go."

"Go where?"

"Town. I have patients to visit and supplies to pick up. Let's have a look at my handiwork."

"Be my guest."

She resisted returning his smile, but in the end, her lips betrayed her. She pulled back the covers, hitching a breath. The too-small night-shirt was hiked halfway up his muscular thighs. He tried to pull down the shirt, but it barely budged. The top ripped again. She made a note to herself to buy a new one in town. She would need a logical reason for such a purchase. She'd think of something.

Focusing on his swollen knee, she laid her hand over the bandage. Heat filtered through the gauze. No improvement. "Does this feel tight? Uncomfortable?"

"Not particularly."

"Okay." With a flick of the wrist, she threw the covers over his lap. "We'll leave that be. Mind you don't put any weight on that leg today. Use the cane."

He saluted her.

"Funny. Let's inspect your arm."

He glanced at his shoulders. "You want me to wiggle out of this? Is my T-shirt dry?"

"It had blood on it. I had to burn it this morning, with the rest of your clothes."

He pressed back into the pillows. "Are you kidding?"

"Do I look like I'm kidding? I saved your . . ." She hesitated at the memory of washing them last night. "Your underwear."

"How the heck am I supposed to get over the border? In my boxers?"

"Don't be daft. I have my husband's clothes. Remember?"

He pulled at the torn nightshirt. "I probably wore this-size shirt when I was twelve."

Teddy had been on the short, slender side. Fine-boned, like a porcelain figurine. Masculine, though, not effeminate. At least in her opinion. Every bit the poet.

Certainly, this pilot sitting in her bed, wearing a nightshirt that stretched across his manly form, had nothing of a poet in him. Hemingway, perhaps.

Nan considered the dilemma. Either Dutch had to take off the nightshirt and he'd be naked, or she'd need to cut the sleeve and expose the wound.

Naked in her bed. *Nope.* That didn't work. An image of Father Albert with his acne scars, thick glasses, and thinning hair came to mind. He'd surely wag his finger at Nan.

"I'm going to slit the nightshirt up the arm," she said, reaching for the scissors on the tray. "It'll be easier than trying to take the garment off and get it back on again. I'll get you a new nightshirt in town. How does that sound?"

"Snip away."

The snapping sound of each cut filled the air until she had the sleeve trimmed to the shoulder. Blood had seeped through the bandage. Not a particularly worrisome sign. Carefully, she unrolled the gauze. She was so close to him, she could feel the heat of his body against hers. His moist breath teased her skin.

She saw his eyes tense. She knew the wound must hurt worse than stepping barefoot on a beehive.

"I'm sorry this is painful. It's necessary."

"I'm fine." His voice dropped to a deep bass tone that resonated in her bones.

A yeasty scent rose from the bandage, immediately setting her on alert. *Shouldn't smell so strongly.* Her lips tightened. There was swelling around the edges of the sutured wound, but the cut remained stitched together.

"How's it looking, Doc?"

Don't get ahead of yourself, she thought. Some redness and swelling was normal. "I'm only a nurse, but you're doing grand. How painful is this? Tell me the truth."

"Hurts a little."

"I'd be worried if it didn't." She cleaned the area with a hydrogen peroxide solution, sprinkled more sulfanilamide over the wound, and then wrapped his arm with clean gauze. "There."

She picked up the soiled bandages and threw them into the blazing fire. White smoke circled up the chimney.

"Right." Returning to his bedside, she poured him more tea and handed it to him. Their fingers connected, making part of her want to jump back and another part want to slide her hand over his. Sit next to him. Keep him company.

"I'm off to town. I'll be back soon."

Stepping to the mirrored wardrobe, she gazed at herself and combed her fingers through her hair. She stared at her dry lips, wishing she had some Tangee lipstick and rouge to make herself look prettier. Ah, what was she thinking? Who cared about her appearance? Certainly not the patient in her bed.

He cleared his throat. "If you can, will you find out what happened to my crew?"

"Did they bail out, too?" She gazed at him in the mirror.

He stopped midsip and lowered the cup. "Of course they did. Do you think I'd leave them in a doomed plane? Go off by myself? What kind of officer do you think I am?" His voice was sharp with an undertone of anger. Frustration.

With a shake of her head, she opened the wardrobe door. "It was only a question, not an assault on your character."

He let out a breath. "We all got out. I was the last to bail. I didn't see any of them after I landed. The wind scattered us."

Nan opened the wardrobe, selected a soft wool scarf, and placed it around her neck. The knit brought out the blue in her eyes, not that anyone cared. Closing the wardrobe door, she asked, "Were any of your men injured before they jumped?"

His jaw twitched. After a sip of tea, he said, "No. Just me."

"That's a relief."

"Yes, but sometimes . . . stuff happens when you reach the ground."

"Or the sea?"

"Do you have to bring up the worst-case scenario?" His words snapped. He squeezed his eyes shut, seeming to regroup.

"Sure now, I don't mean to worry you."

His forehead was creased with lines that seemed beyond his years. "I feel responsible for those kids."

Kids? "I'll find out as much as I can. I promise. By the way, how old are you?"

"I'm an old guy. Twenty-six."

"Old?" She was two years his elder. What did that make her?

"Old for the RAF. The rest of my crew were . . . are under twenty-two. Kids. Please find out what happened to them?"

"Of course. I'm sure it's the talk of the town."

He placed the cup on the nightstand and lay back on the pillow. "I promise I'll be out of here tonight. Is there a back road I can take? A bike I can borrow?"

"There's my husband's bike, but . . ." She stood at the foot of the bed. "I've got a better plan to get you safely on your way. I have a car."

"What?" He sat up, eyes wide. "You do? Why didn't you give it to me last night?"

"Last night? When you were bleeding and passing out?"

The edge of his mouth pulled to the side. "Yeah, you have a point. So I can leave tonight?"

She raised her hand. "The car isn't running."

"Then you have the *potential* of a car. That's pretty much useless. What's wrong with the vehicle?"

"I . . . I don't know. Tuda—"

"Who?"

"Tuda. My best friend. She's the best auto mechanic this side of Limerick."

"Can you trust him?"

"*Her.* Yes. She's like a sister."

"A *girl* mechanic?"

"Don't underestimate her. She took on the garage twenty years ago, when her husband took on the bottle. Unfortunately, she's away in Dublin."

"So, this is just a tease? You have a useless car and an absent mechanic? Is this some sort of Irish joke?"

"Then the joke's on me."

He rubbed his chin. "What's your plan?"

"She comes back tomorrow. I'll say I've decided to fix the car, have her come over and look at it. Mind you stay put. I don't want her mixed up in . . . this." She bit her lip, the full impact of her deeds swirling around in her mind, especially the odious way she'd gotten rid of Finn. She shuddered at the memory of her fingertip on his cold brass buttons.

"How long of a drive to the border?"

"About six hours."

He frowned. "That far? Listen, I know a lot about cars," he said, his gaze traveling up her legs to her eyes.

What was he looking at? Her old-lady black stockings? Did he notice the run up the side?

"Do ya?"

"One of my hobbies. Where's the car? I'm sure I can figure out what's wrong with it."

"In the calf house."

"You have cows?"

"No. It's a garage now, across the courtyard, but the name stuck."

"Okay. I'll get on it."

"It's going to stay undisturbed until I get back from town. Understand?"

He lifted his chin, squinted. "Why wait? I can get started right away. It's my mission to get out of here as soon as I can."

"Your mission is to stay in bed and heal. Understand?"

"That's ridiculous. Why waste the time?"

"Because I need to be here in case Finn or someone else looking for bomber boys shows up."

"I'll be careful."

"You'll stay in bed and not move from the house. Promise?"

He wouldn't meet her gaze. She folded her arms and summoned up her best imitation of Sister Mary Catherine, a nun at school who could send a girl into panic with one glare.

"You'll do as I say, Officer Whitney. Or I *will* kick you out. You'll get about as far as town before Finn finds you, limping along the lane. And if you get caught, I get caught, because when they see how you're patched up, they'll come looking for me."

"Then why would you kick me out? That makes no sense."

She worked her logic through again, but it didn't add up. He had her there. None of this was logical, though. "Just stay in bed. We'll figure out the details and get you out the door soon. You'll have to work with me, not against me. I'm sure you're used to being in charge, but you must take my lead in this adventure."

He nodded. "All right."

"Do you need anything else before I go?" She softened her tone, adjusted the pillows behind his head. His legs moved under the covers. He clutched her hand, stopping her from walking away.

"Why are you doing this? Helping me?"

His touch sparked a wave of goose bumps up her arm. "You came in need of medical assistance; I was obliged to help."

"How can I ever repay you?"

She squeezed his hand. "Consider this my contribution to the war effort. But you must do what I say. Stay in bed. Keep the curtains drawn. If Finn comes sniffing around, you are out of sight. Do not answer the door to anyone."

"Sure. And if someone breaks in, I can defend myself with the cane."

CHAPTER 4

Nan searched in each direction before she stepped out of the house. She darted across the cobbled courtyard. The misty day barely cast a shadow as she reached the calf house. Heart pounding, she swung open the faded-red door.

This must have been what it was like for her grandmother twenty years before, when she'd hidden members of the Irish Republican Brotherhood from the English during the war of independence. The irony wasn't lost on her; today, she was hiding a soldier from the Irish authorities.

The damp air smelled of rotting hay and mold. To the left, the Ford Model A was covered by a thick burlap tarp, as though she'd tucked the car in for a nap. A Saint Brigid's cross made of reeds and straw, the corners of the diamond pattern chewed by something, hung on the wall above a workbench. She hoped the old cross still had power to safeguard them.

Pulling her bike from the docking place, its handlebar scraping along the stone wall, Nan proceeded to the lane that led to town.

Haze shrouded the tops of the rolling hills. Carpets of green stretched in every direction, segmented by gray strips of stone fence. The lane dipped down between identical walls of greenery. Within the gloomy tunnel, the temperature dropped.

She sped toward the crossroads, the pungent scent of marsh mixing with salty sea. The bog stretched down the valley between barren cliffs. Looking the other way, she watched the roll of the dark sea beyond the black sandy beach.

The sounds of chirping reminded her of happier times, when young people would meet at this spot for a moonlit dance. A man would play the fiddle, another the drum. Couples would dance, laugh, kiss, drink. Some nights, Father Albert would ride in on his bicycle to scare the couples off in all directions.

The next Sunday, the congregation could count on a sermon regarding the evils of dancing, of giving into carnal desires.

Those nights, she and Teddy would stroll home arm in arm. He'd recite poetry or sing in his rich tenor voice. Toward the end, though, he'd tell her some tale of how the world should be, not how the world was. He'd given up hope. And then he'd given up dancing at the crossroads.

The cold breeze whistled inside her scarf. She twisted the bike wheel one direction and then the other, trying to decide which way to go. She could either take the shortcut along the bog or go the long way to town, past Collins's farm, where she'd seen the billowing smoke of Dutch's bomber.

She headed north, toward the crash site. Maybe someone would know about the other airmen.

Thank you, Lord, for sparing Dutch. I'm sure You have something grand in mind for him to do, for I know You take no one before their time.

When Nan neared the crash site, she noticed a dozen or so bicycles lying in the grass. The odor of ground-up dirt, mixed with petrol and oil, hung in the air. At the top of the hill, the mangled bomber rested like a child's no-longer-loved toy. The wings were broken off, while the rest of the airplane had burrowed into the ground.

Nan let her own bike drop. A herd of boys in short pants ran around the craft, poking sticks into the rubble. She was about to yell at them to get away when she heard the sound of creaking metal. Several men dressed in tweed jackets and flat caps, cigarettes dangling from their lips, pulled a piece of the wing from the craft.

"That's the ticket," one of them said.

"Mind ya don't cut ya hand," replied another.

They dragged the sheet of metal toward a wagon hitched to a horse. One of the men tipped his flat cap to her.

"'Lo, Nan. How are ya this fine morning?"

"Grand, Peter. Better than the boys who flew this airplane, that's for sure. Collecting souvenirs?"

"Not a'tall. We're going to make gates out of the metal." He placed his dirty hands in prayer, bowed his head, and said, "May the Lord have mercy on their brave souls."

Nan felt the blood drain from her face. Her balance swayed. A wave of dizziness hit her. Gripping her jacket collar, she barely noticed the spray of mist that splattered across her face. *Dutch's crew. Lost.* How would he take the news? How would she tell him?

"It's a Vickers Wellington," ten-year-old Sean, a round-cheeked, red-haired boy, offered. "Are ya all right, Nurse Nan?"

She shored up her shoulders and nodded. "Just sad for the airmen. The plane, it's so big. And crumpled."

"The Krauts who caught their bombs, they're the crumpled ones now. When I grow up, I'm going to pilot a Wellington bomber, too. I'm gonna save the world!"

Hmm. Where had she heard that before?

The boy spread his arms out like airplane wings and made a roaring sound. He ran after another boy who did the same.

"Let's hope the war is over before he's out of knee pants," Peter murmured.

If men would only come to their senses. "Yes. Please be to God. Tell me. Do you know for a fact the crew was lost?"

Peter adjusted his cap. "Ah, that was just a prayer in advance should there be tragic news. Where you off to, Nan? A baby being born?"

More like a flyboy almost dead. "Not yet. How is Josie?"

"The wife couldn't be fitter. She's hoping for a girl this time. I told her that's okay, since she already gave me five strapping sons."

A Ford sedan filled with LDF officers came thundering down the road. One of them leaned out the window with a megaphone, shouting, "Get away from there. This is government property now. You're all stealing. Do you hear me? We'll arrest ya all."

"I'd best be off. If ya see the missus, tell her I'll be late for tea." Peter tipped his hat, ran to the other side of the airplane, and hopped onto the back of a horse-drawn cart filled with scrap airplane metal. He laughed along with the other two men beside him. The horse galloped down a lane, too rough and narrow for the army car to follow. Everyone else scattered.

Back on her way to town, the road curved and twisted, Nan's stomach following the motion. Thatched and slate roofs of Ballyhaven loomed ahead as she sped down a hill into the village.

The muddy lane gave way to wet pavement. Saint Patrick's Church soared to the sky with a steeple that leaned to the right. Father Albert had warned, once the war and the Emergency were over, there'd be a massive building fund drive to repair the structure, advising everyone to save their pennies.

She slowed near the churchyard. The gravestones resembled teeth as they poked up from the unkempt grass. Teddy was in there. He shouldn't be after what he'd done. She squeezed the handlebar grips and pushed down the throb of guilt rising from deep inside. What she'd done was wrong. Truly wrong.

Focusing on the bike wheel as it bounced over Ballyhaven's cobblestone streets, she joined a busy stream of bicycles, men pushing handbarrows, and horse- or donkey-drawn carts that snaked their way past the numerous shops and houses, all crowded together like a deck of gray playing cards.

She steered around a slow-moving cart carrying a load of turf, managing to miss the many animal offerings on the road.

At the beep of a horn, she guided her bike to the side of the road. A new Guinness lorry, its bed filled with barrels, thundered past her. The driver parked at the corner pub, cut the engine, and swung open the door.

Mrs. Odin, the pub owner, stood outside her establishment, rubbing a cloth over the multiple windowpanes. A scarf tied over her ears, her salt-and-pepper curls piled on top of her head, she offered a coy smile to the driver, Brian Monaghan, a short man with a bulldog face.

Everyone knew he was sweet on the widow. Or perhaps he was sweet on her bountiful breakfast. He always stopped at Odin's Pub before delivering his other shipments.

More cynical villagers thought it wasn't only the widow's bacon he was sweet on, but also her curves. Nan refused to pass judgment. They were both adults, and what happened inside the pub was between the two of them. And the confessional booth.

Nan scooted around another horse-drawn trap and then slowed to a stop outside Mikie's, one of Ballyhaven's biggest general stores. She stationed the bike, grabbed her basket from the back rack, and let herself inside the dark, crowded shop. It reeked of smoke, cabbage, and dried herbs.

She hoped that the men hanging around the fireplace would let her get on with her purchases and not ask her too many questions.

"Morning, Nan," the owner called from a bench where several men sat around a glowing fire. They smoked pipes or cigarettes and held cups of tea. It was too early in the day for a Guinness, but after lunch, the back room would open.

"Margaret," Mikie yelled to his wife, who was behind a beaded curtain that led to their private quarters. "Margaret. Nan's here. Get out here, woman, you have a customer."

"Keep ya pants on, Mikie. I'll be there in a minute."

"Take your time," Nan called out. *Please don't,* she thought.

An old man wearing a fedora winked at her, shuffling toward her with open arms. Muddy tracks lay in his wake. "How are ya, me beauty?"

"Morning, Thomas." She braced herself for the hug that Thomas Carlow, the vegetable man, always gave her.

He placed his hands on her shoulders and then kissed her on the right cheek. "Ya remind me of my dearly departed daughter."

Nan knew what came next.

He kissed her left cheek. "Ya remind me of my dearly departed wife, too. May she rest in peace."

Unexpectedly, he kissed her right cheek again. "Don't ya have the same lovely spirit of my mother, gone to be with the angels."

His mother? That was new. Maybe she was getting old. She wondered if Dutch thought she was some dried-up Irish biddy. He had indicated he was past his prime at twenty-six. She glanced at her black stockings. Old-lady stockings. Old-lady laced-up shoes. She hoped she didn't smell like one as well.

She stepped away before Thomas could plant another kiss. This had to end before he invoked her likeness to his grandma.

Returning to his stool by the fire, Thomas asked, "Did you hear the airplane go down last night, darling? I almost got out my horse and came to ya house to make sure you were all right."

"I was fine."

"No bomber boy at your door?"

She gripped the basket to her chest, the rough weave pressing through her coat. "Of course not. You needn't check on me. I can fend for myself."

"Fend for yourself? Nan, you need a man. If I were ten years younger, and you ten years older, well. We'd be a pair."

Her groan tickled her throat. Placing the basket on the counter, she craned her head to see if Margaret might be on her way out.

"What about Shamus Finn?" Mikie packed tobacco into his pipe with a stained thumb. "Did he check on you last night?"

"Yes, but he needn't have been concerned." *Thank you, Lord.* "I saw the crash site today. Peter thought the crew had all been killed." She rubbed her collarbone. "Is it so?"

Mikie lit a match on the bottom of his boot, then swung the flame to the pipe that jutted out of the corner of his mouth. After a couple of puffs, smoke looped from the pipe. "They're not dead," he said, flicking the match into the fireplace. "Lord Harry found them hiding in his barn. He gave them supper and delivered them to the Garda. They spent the night in jail."

Nan let out the breath she hadn't known she held. "Thank you, Lord, for protecting those brave young men, fighting for our freedom," she said, blessing herself. The men nodded and someone muttered, "Amen."

Mikie perched on a wooden stool, its seat worn from countless mornings around the fire. "The Garda's looking for the new doctor to take a peek at them."

A toothless man pushed up his flat cap. His cigarette dangled between two fat fingers, the smoke twisting upward to the beamed ceiling and disappearing into bundles of dried rosemary. "Tell me, Mikie. Have ya met the new doctor?"

"I did, Liam. I did. Dr. Mann."

"What's the doctor's name?"

"Dr. Mann."

"I know he's a man. What's his name, then?"

Mikie shook his head, his comb-over slipping the wrong way. A fringe of hair swayed around his ear. "Dr. Mann is not a man. Dr. Mann is a woman. Her name is Dr. Mann."

"A woman doctor? A woman who calls herself a man?"

Thomas Carlow wrinkled up his nose. "No woman doctor is gonna get a look at me private parts."

Poor Dr. Mann, Nan thought, *whoever she might be.*

Parting the beaded curtains, Mikie's wife entered the shop. Margaret wore a flowered apron over her brown dress. Her hair was pulled into a tight bun, making her ears stick out.

"Sorry to keep ya waiting. Have a cup of tea." She plunked a full cup onto the counter.

"Ah, thanks. That's very kind of you." Nan picked up the rose-patterned mug, the heat warming her icy-cold fingers. But the inner shaking that chilled her had nothing to do with the climate and everything to do with the hot-blooded pilot in her bed. "How are you, Margaret?"

"Still married to the brilliant one over there." Her friend let out a low hiss toward the men around the fireplace.

Margaret had been married to Mikie for forty-plus years. From what Nan could tell, they tolerated each other. At times the couple could be heard in heated arguments, their shouting echoing down the lane.

Margaret rubbed the counter with a rag. "What can I do for ya this fine morning?"

"You know. Bits and pieces." Margaret wouldn't think it was so fine if she knew Nan had an injured pilot sleeping in her bed. The thought made Nan blush. Not that there was anything to be ashamed of.

Except all the lying. Nan reached into her basket and handed over her shopping list and ration book.

The outline of Margaret's tongue pushed through her cheek. "What's wanting with you this morning?"

"Whatever do you mean?"

"Ya seem a bit off."

"Do I?" What was giving her away?

"Your fingers have been shaking like a piano player's."

Nan shoved them into her pockets. "I'm cold is all."

"I've known ya long enough to know when ya out of sorts," Margaret said, grasping her reading glasses. She wiped them with the corner of her apron before balancing them on the bridge of her bulbous nose. "What's doing?"

"Nothing."

"Okay. If you say so." Margaret returned to the list. Looking over the rims of her glasses, she inclined her head. "Why do ya have 'one large men's nightshirt' on ya list?"

Nan shrugged. "Actually, I changed my mind. I want a pair of men's pajamas. It's a birthday gift for my cousin up north. Do you have any?"

"I do. I didn't know you had a cousin up north."

"He's a distant cousin, and he's in need. I want to help."

"Ya a good girl that way, you are."

Well, Nan thought, *I'm getting good at lying.*

Margaret looked her up and down. "What's the matter?"

There was no hiding the state she was in, at least not to Margaret. "The truth is . . ." Nan glanced side to side.

"Yes?" Margaret leaned forward.

"I suppose it's the plane crash. It was close by. It could have crashed on my head."

Margaret smiled, revealing a dark spot where her eyetooth once was. "But it didn't. And the Lord doesn't bring anything to ya door that ya can't handle."

"Do you really think so?" The idea was reassuring.

"I know so."

"Of course. You're right." Nan hoped. Prayed. "Tell me, have you heard from Tuda? Is she back yet?"

"Tonight, I think Paddy said." Margaret adjusted her glasses. "'Tis sad the Lord called her da home, but we all get called home someday. Let me see; I have most everything on ya list."

"How about the canning jars?" Nan was glad to get back to mundane items.

With a shake of her head, Margaret measured out three scoops of flour into a bag. "It's a shame they haven't arrived yet. I hear the factory is having a devil of a time finding tin. And this is probably the last of the white flour for a while."

"Ah, that's too bad." Nan tucked the bag into her basket.

"Will the apples keep? The customers are asking after your jam."

"The fruit will be good a bit longer." As well as the sugar she'd been stockpiling for three months. Sugar supply was very unreliable these days, but she was glad to live in a farming village where vegetables, eggs, and dairy products were available without a problem. At least for now. Who knew how desperate things would get if the war dragged on.

"Over by Christmas, that's what the English had boasted." Margaret faced the shelves and stepped onto a footstool. "That was over two years ago, and there seems no end in sight." Her friend sorted through bundled garments on the top shelf. "Size large, you say? I've two styles of pajamas. Would ya like to look at them? Give them a feel?"

Nan thought about Dutch, wearing the bitty nightshirt. Heat rose in her cheeks. "No. I'll take the cheaper one."

Margaret frowned. "Don't you want to get a feel for the pajamas that will grace your young man's body?"

"He's not my young man. He's not even a close relative. Just wrap it up."

"Okay." Margaret selected a navy-and-white-pinstriped garment, wrapped it in brown paper, and set it in the basket. "I'll run the jars over to you as soon as they come."

"No, I'll pick them up." She might have said that too quickly, because Margaret's forehead turned into rows of lines.

Hooking her finger for Nan to lean in closer, Margaret pressed her ample chest into the counter. "I'll run them out to ya. I'd like a bit of an outing, ya see. Get away from those meatheads over there. And I'll bring ya a cup of sugar."

Nan's mouth went dry. What if Margaret happened by and saw Dutch?

"When do you think the jars will come in?"

"At least a week. Maybe two."

Dutch would be long gone before the jars came in. Over the border and back to his RAF base. *God willing.* "All right, if it's not too much trouble."

"Not a bit. Tell ya what." Margaret ripped coupons from Nan's ration book. "I'll give you a discount on the pajamas, seeing how you delivered my lovely grandson last month. Shall I put everything on your account today?"

"Yes, thank you. How is baby John?"

Margaret smiled. "Still has them lungs that would wake the dead. And isn't my daughter recovering without a care?"

"She's grand. If only all my mums and babes were that easy. I'll pop up to see them right now."

The door swung open, followed by a chorus of hellos from the men sitting around the fireplace. Sergeant Paul Halpin, the village Garda, tipped his hat to them. His uniform fit his trim figure with precision. Just like the man, not a detail out of place. He had a broad forehead, a refined straight nose, and keen dark eyes. He set his gaze on Nan. "Ah, I've been looking for you."

Had he been to her home and discovered Dutch? "Oh? Is it Kelly? She's not due for a month, but first babies can be unpredictable."

"Kelly's grand. I was about to go round to your house, so I'm glad I stopped here first."

Me, too. Nan lifted her basket from the counter. "What can I do for you?"

"It's a matter of some importance. Have you heard we found most of the bomber crew?"

"Yes."

"I've tried to find Dr. Mann—"

"Did ya know Dr. Mann isn't a man a'tall, he's a woman?" Liam shouted.

Halpin pulled a half smile. "That I know." He focused back on Nan. "I can't find the doctor. The bus for the internment camp will arrive shortly. Would you mind looking after the RAF crew?"

"Not at all. Are they badly injured?"

"Scrapes and bruises. They're extremely lucky to be alive."

"I'd be happy to examine the lads. Are they in jail?"

"At my house with Kelly."

Nan leaned back. "Alone with your wife? Is that wise?"

"Hardly alone. There's a vast number of the village girls hovering about, along with an armed army officer. They're just scared kids, really. They know there's nowhere to go. I'll meet you at the house?"

"I'll be along. I need to check on Margaret's grandson."

"Yes. That's fine. Oh, and Nan. There are two airmen unaccounted for. Finn is searching for them now."

She hoped Finn wasn't poking around her cabin again. And if he was, she prayed Dutch had stayed in bed. She'd be glad when her secret flyboy was on his way. She wasn't made for all this Mata Hari intrigue.

Halpin moved closer. With a lift of an eyebrow and a low tone, he said, "Have you seen anyone?"

With gaze steady, she said, "No."

He studied her. She could feel her stomach tightening, her throat squeezing, but she didn't falter. She remembered the instructions her ma had given her as a child. "If the authorities come looking for your da or uncles, you look the blaggards in the eye, say nothing, or deny everything."

The sergeant nodded and exited the shop with straight shoulders and perfect posture. She didn't notice Thomas Carlow until the old man stepped in front of her.

"Here, darling." He shoved two fat potatoes into her basket. "Here's a little something to give ya lots of strength for the journey."

"Thanks, Thomas."

If only he knew the journey she was on, and the weakness, the pure uncertainty, that plagued her heart and weighed down her soul, he'd probably give her a few more spuds.

CHAPTER 5

Perched on the edge of town, Ballyhaven's Garda station mounted the cliffs like a fortress of Irish justice. A two-story residence was attached to the left side of the low building, where Paul and Kelly Halpin lived.

Nan opened the gate that led to the backyard. The sun broke through the clouds for a brief moment to wash the residence in sparkling light. Daffodils in flower boxes outside the windows seemed to lift their heads to the sun. The lace curtains that hung inside gleamed as white as a girl's first-communion dress. The embellishments were Kelly Halpin's influence. Seemed she could do anything with a bit of this or that. Then clouds consumed the sun again, shrouding everything back into dullness.

There wasn't much cause to use the jail, but certain town drinkers, Thomas Carlow in particular, were well acquainted with the facilities. Many nights, Thomas would be found passed out in his cart, the horse circling the Celtic cross in the town square. Paul Halpin would wake up Thomas, take him to the station, and give him a bed to sleep it off.

Kelly told Nan that after a night in lockup, Carlow would stroll into her kitchen, hat in hand. "Me home away from home, clean and warm. Any chance you might pour me a cup of tea and feed me a bit of your famous bread?"

Nan hoped she wouldn't wind up in the cell next to Thomas some night. She buttoned down her nerves as she strolled over the brick sidewalk, around to the backyard. Her medical bag's contents tinkled with each stride.

A lame Irish wolfhound padded toward her, tongue hanging out the side of his pink mouth.

"Hello, Lugus. How's yaself?" Nan patted the dog's huge head. His breath stank like an ancient tomb. "How ya keeping?"

Lugus nuzzled Nan's palm, then started sniffing her with so much force, she rocked back on her heels. Did the hound whiff Dutch? Good thing the Lord hadn't granted dogs the gift of language.

"Ah, ya after my cat, Mr. Dee, aren't ya?" she said for the benefit of anyone within earshot. After a slurping lick of her hand, Lugus hobbled away, back to his spot on an old mattress inside a doghouse.

"Ah, there you are, Nan." Kelly Halpin waved from the far end of the yard, where she stood knee high in cabbages. She wore Wellies and a heavy knit sweater, and she held a bunch of carrots she'd just grabbed from the soil. Her blonde hair was French braided and tied with a pink ribbon. Unlike some expecting mums, Kelly looked lovely in her natural state, her middle budding with new life.

When Paul Halpin's first wife died four years ago, no one in the village had a dry eye. His wife had passed one fall morning when the wind had whistled down the chimney like a banshee. Rain had hit the earth so hard that day, it had ripped the leaves off Nan's apple trees and tossed the remaining fruit around like miniature bombs.

Heart attack, the doctor had declared. For months, Paul had moped around the town in a state of grief, heartbroken over the loss of his wife, yet he never let his emotions interfere with his work.

After Teddy was laid to rest, some thought she and Paul would make a fine couple. He was attractive, intelligent, educated, and a good sort of person. Nan refused to even consider a man who carried a gun for a living.

But God was good and merciful. The village women's prayers for Paul were answered when young Kelly Maloney arrived for a visit with her cousins two summers ago. On her way into town, the twenty-year-old had blown out her bicycle tire and found herself tumbling into a ditch. Paul happened to see the accident and helped her out of the gully.

"'Twas love at first sight," Kelly later declared.

The following Christmas, no one was happier than Nan to see the couple wed. She liked Kelly straightaway and considered her God's new match for Paul. No matter the circumstances, if Nan needed her, Kelly was one of those few friends who would be there. Not that Nan planned to involve Kelly in the Dutch situation.

Nan walked along the brick path. "How are you?" she asked Kelly. "Not overdoing work in your lovely garden? You know what we discussed."

"Oh, go on with ya. I'm fit and ready to pull carrots all day." Kelly dropped the vegetables into a basket at her feet. "I'll be in directly. Go meet the lads."

To the sound of laughter and conversation, Nan climbed the stairs to the back door that led into the kitchen. Her medical bag banged into her thigh as she swung open the door. Four young men in RAF uniforms, along with numerous village girls, crowded around a long kitchen table. Nan's throat tightened. Dutch was right. They were only kids. Is this what the Allies were fighting the Nazis with? Children? They looked no older than twenty. Then again, the bored LDF soldier standing in the corner with a cup of tea didn't appear to be much older himself.

Several teenage girls surrounded the crewmen, sitting next to them or standing behind them. All were batting their eyelids and giggling with admiring gazes.

"Good day to you. Ah, you must be the RAF crew," Nan said.

"And who else would they be?" A sassy girl of fourteen, with chubby cheeks and legs to match, drew on a cigarette and sent the smoke toward the ceiling. Her girlfriends laughed.

The future mothers of Ireland. Heaven save them. Saints preserve them. "I'm Nurse Nan O'Neil," she said to the boys. *Men,* she corrected herself. "I'm to examine you."

The crewmen rose. The tallest of them attempted a smile with his bruised lips. He straightened, squeezed his eyes shut, and dropped the smile for a second. Then, in that "What, what?" stiff-upper-lip way of the English, he smiled, showing twisted front teeth. "We're all fine, miss."

"I'm so glad, but Sergeant Halpin insists I examine you. Please, sit. Finish your tea first. And conversation."

They returned to their chairs, and the girls continued their banter.

"Hey ya, Nurse O'Neil," Siobhan called over the sizzling of frying breakfast meat. A thick-waisted girl with freckles covering her face, Siobhan was the daughter of the town's solicitor. She'd set her heart on studies in London. The plans, like so many others, were on hold for the duration of the war.

The Halpins employed Siobhan as their housekeeper, and Kelly claimed she couldn't function without the girl's help.

Nan placed her bag on the floor and stepped to the cooker, where Siobhan was flipping pieces of blood pudding. "Siobhan, how are you? What are you up to?"

"We're giving our heroes a proper Irish fry before they're off to internment camp." In another pan, she poked tomatoes with a fork. They, too, sizzled in the cooking grease.

"Where on earth did you get tomatoes at this time of year?"

"They're from the Harrisons' hothouse."

"Oh yes?"

"A consolation prize, I think. Lord Harry found the bomber boys in the stables last night. He gave them a grand meal and then called the Garda. The boys spent the night in jail. He brought the tomatoes when he came to check on them this morning."

"Nice of him, I suppose."

56

"Would you fancy one?"

"Of the boys? Of course not." It made her think of Dutch lying in her bed. She couldn't shake the vision of him in the too-small nightshirt.

Siobhan laughed. "Don't be daft. I mean a tomato."

"Ah, no thanks." Food, in any form right now, would be impossible to keep down.

She glanced at the lads. Why hadn't Lord Harry helped them to escape, the way she was helping Dutch? Too many in number, perhaps. Or too smart to take such a chance with Finn nosing into everyone's business.

Kelly strolled into the kitchen with a basket of root vegetables. "Get out of the way, girls. And give the airmen some breathing room."

The crowd of girls parted to let Kelly reach the counter. She placed the basket in the sink, then rubbed the small of her back.

Nan joined her. "Does your back hurt? Didn't I tell you to be careful? The muscles and joints aren't stable when you're so far along."

"Don't worry. I'm grand." Her green eyes sparkled, and a smile dimpled her cheeks. She tied an apron around her swollen waist. "Ah, Nan. Have you met our guests?"

"Guests?" one of the airmen asked in a spiteful tone.

The room went silent.

"That's right, Pilot Officer Ryan. As my husband explained, you'll be guests of the State of Ireland for the duration of the war. I'm terribly sorry you're all so disappointed."

The young men grumbled.

Kelly turned on the tap, and water gushed into the sink, splashing the windows that looked out over the garden. She glanced at Nan. In a low voice for Nan's ears only, she said, "Why do these boys so itch to get back into the fight?"

"Because they're warriors," Nan replied. "And men."

"I think it's because they're eejits who enjoy playing with their big-boy toys."

"That's an interesting comment coming from the Garda's wife."

Kelly winked. "Isn't it, though? Let me introduce you to the boys."

"Men."

"If you say so, but they look barely old enough to be out of knee pants."

She introduced Dutch's crew one by one. Each gave a polite nod. How Nan wished she could tell them their flight officer was alive, recuperating, and—if all went according to a plan yet to be hatched—rejoining the RAF in a couple of days. She knew they'd all cheer.

"Now, sit, boys. Eat your breakfast before your bacon gets cold." Kelly dumped the vegetables from the basket into the sink. "Then gorgeous Nurse Nan here will have a good look at you. Tea, Nan? Something to eat?"

"Tea, thanks."

"Bridie, get up and give Mrs. O'Neil your seat."

The skinny girl pouted but did as she was told.

"They're too old for you anyway," Nan heard Siobhan say to the girl before placing a plate of hot tomatoes on the table.

"Are not," Bridie said. "Me ma was sixteen when she married me da."

"Then come back in three years, Bridie, and maybe then you won't have to stuff ya bra with tissues."

The comment sent the girls into fits of laughter. Bridie's face turned bright red. She folded her arms and backed away until she stood against the wall.

The pack of girls poured tea, replenished eggs and rashers for the men, and yattered on.

Nan surveyed the airmen. Bruises, nicks, and abrasions seemed to be the main problem. "Does anyone have an injury besides cuts and scrapes?"

They shook their heads.

"How many of your crew are still missing?"

The room went silent. They glanced around at each other.

"Is this the entire crew?" Of course she knew it wasn't.

Kelly placed a pitcher of milk in front of Nan. "They won't admit it, but there should be six of them. Isn't that right, lads? Six crew members to fly the Wellington?"

The tall crewman rubbed his mouth with a napkin. On his plate were half-eaten patties of blood pudding. "Yeah, that's true. We're missing two crew members. Ouch!"

Someone had kicked him under the table.

"Shut up, Curtis," a boy with a thin mustache said.

Curtis sneered at the man next to him. "They're not daft, sir. They can count."

"Yes," Nan said. "I saw the accident site today. What a shame. I hope everyone will prove to be all right."

"They're probably dead." Officer Ryan stared at his plate. "My mum has a teapot like that. Back home. But we're never going to make it home again."

The tea in Nan's stomach burned. She knew that look. Teddy had worn the same chewed-up, desperate expression. It was as though someone had pulled the plug and all the joy and promise of life had drained.

Her thoughts spiraled back. There'd been nothing physically wrong with her Teddy. Nothing a doctor could do or fix or even diagnose. It had been spiritual. She heard the inner voice that accused her of not soliciting help from Father Albert. Teddy wouldn't hear of it. He'd turned his back on God the last few months of his life, and nothing Nan could say would change his mind. Or his heart.

"Shut your trap, Ryan. We're sick of your gloom and doom. Aren't we?"

The rest of the airmen agreed.

Nan longed to help him. "What's your first name?"

"Rich," he sniffed.

"You'll be fine, Rich."

His eyes went to her. "You don't know that. How can you know that?"

"Because God doesn't give us anything we can't handle."

He scoffed. The same way Teddy had.

"It's true," Nan said.

The kid rolled his eyes.

A young girl with a robust chest and hips to match placed her hands on his shoulders. "There, there. It'll be all right. Have another rasher."

He looked into her chest, then stared at the meat on his plate. "We're good as dead. We're going to rot in prison camp."

"Ah, will you shut your trap, Ryan," the mustached officer said. "These good ladies don't need any more of your remorseful grumblings, and we don't, either."

The sound of footsteps sent their attention to the back door.

"What have we here?" Kelly held the door open.

Sergeant Halpin stood behind a young man with a muddy face, curly dark hair, a torn pant leg, and scrapes across his unshaven jaw. His jacket was turned inside out, but there was no disguising the RAF uniform.

Dutch hadn't fooled her yesterday, either.

"Williams! We thought you were dead!" a pilot shouted.

"No, just caught."

The boys got up and gathered around their comrade, patting him on the back and shaking his hand.

Williams looked around. "Where's Whit—ah, our . . ."

"Still unaccounted for," someone said. "No one's seen him." The conversation died.

How Nan ached to tell them he was asleep in her bed. Instead, she folded her arms around herself, rocking from side to side.

"Cheer up, men," Halpin said. "We'll find him."

Kelly gestured toward the crowded table. "Sit down, lad. Enjoy a proper Irish breakfast."

Nan stood and offered her chair. Williams slumped into the seat. "Before you send us to prison."

"Internment camp," Halpin corrected. "It won't be too terrible. You'll see."

The girls hovered around Williams. One of them ran a wet washcloth over his face. Another wiped his hands with a damp towel.

Williams seemed to enjoy the attention. A grin began to spread across his young face.

Paul joined Nan and Kelly at the sink. "Thank baby Jesus you found him alive," Nan whispered. "After seeing the wreck this morning, I prayed they all got out safely."

"Where did you find Williams?" Kelly handed her husband a peeled carrot.

"Walking the railroad tracks toward the north."

"No sign of the other pilot?" Nan asked.

Paul shot Nan a quick glance. She stared back without twitching a muscle, but her insides were jumping around like circus animals with their tent on fire.

"Not yet. I hope we find him alive and not washed up on the shoreline."

Nan's shoulders tensed. She hoped they didn't find him at all. At least Dutch would know his crew had made it through, even if they were on their way to internment.

Halpin chomped on the carrot. "Nan, you seem a bit tense. Are you in a hurry somewhere? A babe coming into the world?"

Her smile came in a jerk. "Not a'tall. I've all the time in the world for these lads. And I need to do a proper inspection of your wife before I go, too."

"Don't say it like that. You make me feel like a cow." Kelly patted her stomach. "I'm fit as a heifer."

"Yes. You've turned into a bovine beauty." Paul grinned.

"Ah, you'll be sleeping on the couch if you say that one more time." The couple exchanged a gaze born from the intimacy of their marriage.

Looking at the young men, Nan said, "Don't they resemble birds who know they're about to get their wings clipped and be locked in a cage?"

Kelly placed a carrot onto a cutting board beside the sink. "I've heard some Allies are given escorts to the border."

"Where did you hear such a thing?" he asked.

Kelly glanced at Siobhan, who poured hot water into a teapot. The scent of freshly wetted tea leaves filled the air.

"Siobhan's father. He has friends in Dublin who are solicitors, and there's been talk."

Nan perked up, trying not to show it. "Is that true? They let the RAF pilots go?"

"Only if their mission was noncombat. A training mission or transport." He chomped on the carrot.

"So, we can let them go?" If Halpin planned to release the boys, a world of problems would be solved. She could come clean about Dutch.

"The crew has clearly been in combat. I've been informed the LDF found magazines full of bullets, and their mission log. These airmen are internment bound."

Siobhan swatted a fly with a towel. It fell to the floor, dead. Just like Nan's hope.

Nan glanced over at the boys. "Can't we turn a blind eye?"

He stopped midbite. "What you're suggesting violates our Emergency Act. If word were to get out—"

"Who'd be daft enough to tell?" Nan's voice boomed louder than she'd intended.

Paul's face tightened, sending lines like twigs around his eyes. "Finn for one. He's bucking to get full membership in the Garda after the war, so he's trying his hardest to make points."

Kelly dropped her paring knife into the water, wiped her hands on her apron, then placed them on her hips. "That's not all he's trying for, is it, Nan? He still after you?"

"Unfortunately, yes." Regret for last night's encounter stewed through her.

The sergeant wiped the back of his hand over his mouth. "He's a good officer."

"He's a rotter," Kelly huffed. "First class. And he's sweet on Nan. Won't give her a moment of rest. It's enough to make any girl sick."

The women exchanged a glance.

"Is he so bad?" Halpin asked. "He's better than most. Owns a farm. May have a good job as a Garda after the war."

Kelly smirked, then looked to the young women crowding the table. "Girls," she said above their chatter, "what do ya think of Shamus Finn, our eligible village bachelor?"

The teen pack made gagging noises. Turned their thumbs down. Someone let out a raspberry sound.

"I'd sooner marry one of his pigs," the sassy girl said.

"Better looking," Bridie added. The teens' laughter filled the kitchen.

With a satisfied expression, Kelly turned her palms upward. "See?"

"Oh," Halpin said. "I thought you liked him, Nan."

Kelly smacked his arm. "Are ya blind? You men are so dense sometimes. Where did you get an idea like that, Paul?"

"From Finn."

"Of course he'd say that." Kelly shook her head.

"Is he giving you a hard time then, Nan?"

"Always," Nan muttered. "Nothing I can't handle." Nan knew she shouldn't, but she found herself saying, "He came by my house last night, looking for the bomber crew." She hesitated. "What if, say, a citizen were to help one of them get across the border? What then?"

Halpin looked her up and down. "Why do you ask?"

She shrugged. "Curious is all. Wondering what our Free State of Ireland would really do."

Folding his arms, he seemed to assess her like the nuns at school had, but this time it wasn't for hopping out the window late at night to smoke or smooch with a local boy.

"You know this, Nan. Under the Emergency Act, the guilty party would face jail time. It's imperative we remain neutral. Show no leniency to either side. Allies or Axis. They're all deemed belligerents and combatants for the purpose of our official stance."

"Is that a fact?" Her mother's outlaw training kicked in. She held her gaze on his. Let her facial muscles slacken.

He looked away and focused on his wife as she chopped carrots. "Afraid so. We're all in this together. We all have to do our part to keep Ireland neutral."

"Oh, enough now. Enough politics." Kelly gave her husband a gentle push with her hip. "Both of you sit down and have your tea. When will the army be here to pick up our RAF heroes?"

"I got a call. They've had a flat tire. They'll be along before nightfall."

Kelly carried a plate of chopped carrots to the table. Before Nan could advance a step, the sergeant stopped her by the elbow. It was a gentle yet firm hold.

"I'm telling you this because you're one of Kelly's best friends. If the opportunity arises to help one of these combatants, resist. Don't underestimate Finn's ambitions. He's out to make a hero of himself. He wants that Garda post, and he'd give up his mother if it suited his purposes."

"A regular hero." She hoped he couldn't hear her heart pounding. He let go.

Halpin joined the troops at the table. If she didn't know better, she'd think the young men, the "belligerents," were the Halpins' nephews come for a visit. Not RAF pilots on their way to internment. That's where they were headed. No mistake there. Was she completely daft to help Dutch?

A voice within reminded her of what Margaret had said today: *God doesn't bring you anything you can't handle.*

She trusted the Lord with all her heart. In a couple of days, no one would be the wiser. And then life would return to normal.

As long as Dutch kept out of sight.

CHAPTER 6

Dutch sat with his bare legs stretched out over the patchwork quilt. He balanced the cane across his palm and looked at the cat, who sat at the foot of the bed, mildly interested in Dutch's balancing act. "You believe in destiny?"

The cat stopped licking his paw, stared at Dutch, and then resumed his cleaning.

"I do. Oops." The cane dipped to the right. He counterbalanced to the left. "I believe in trusting the Lord with my destiny. The hard part for most people is figuring out what the Lord has in mind. I'm lucky; I know. I'm supposed to save the free world. But I can't do it from this bed."

He glanced at the recessed bedroom window. Beyond the heavy burlap drape, a Ford Model A sedan waited to be fixed. He itched to open the hood and poke around, get the car working.

He'd read somewhere that Ford had opened a manufacturing plant in Cork for the Irish market. The steering wheel position would be different, but he hoped that Ireland's Fords were basically the same as the American versions. Fords were cars he knew how to fix.

The cane dipped right, the evil fox face on the handle staring up at him. Then left and right again. He felt so useless. How swiftly their victory mission over Germany had ended in defeat. His chest tightened at the thought of his crew. Were they alive? Captured? Free across the border?

The cane tipped and rolled off balance. Instinctually, he righted the stick with his other hand. Burning pain shot from his wound to race over his arm and across his shoulder. "Ouch. Ouch. Ouch." He dropped the cane. It smacked against the floor, bounced, and rolled away.

"Great." He looked at the cat licking his orange-colored paw. "I don't suppose you'd like to get that for me?"

The cat yawned, then flopped onto his side.

"No, I didn't think so. A mutt would at least try."

The tabby stretched his lanky body across the quilt.

"Yeah, you're a real tomcat, eh? Bet you have a female at every farm. Me, I'm more of a dog person. Loyal. To a fault."

Loyal. He knew what that meant in every part of his body and soul. His mind slipped back to home. He wondered what his older brother, Simon, was up to right now. Probably sitting at his newspaper desk, studying war reports, trying to decide what story to lead with tomorrow.

Perhaps Simon knew that the bomber had gone down. His brother had a finger on what was happening overseas. Best investigative reporter on either side of the pond. If Dutch was reported missing, he was sure Simon would be on the case, trying to figure out what had happened. *Poor Mom.* She'd be going out of her mind. *Thank you, God, for sending Rachel.* His sister-in-law had a calming effect on his mother.

"If I could fight, I'd go with you," Simon had said at the train station. They'd hugged, and then, as Dutch stepped onto the train bound for New York and the war, Simon had limped away.

Mother had been too upset to see Dutch off, but if Father were still alive, Dutch was sure his dad would have been there.

"Fight injustice wherever you see it" had been his father's motto, especially when it applied to family and those he loved.

Dutch had always protected his big brother from bullies. A fight in secondary school, after a bully had shoved Simon down the stairs, had gotten Dutch expelled.

"The price you pay sometimes for standing up for justice," his dad had said. "Proud of you, kid."

Mother wasn't so happy about the brawl. Dutch had to leave one of the best prep schools in the city and take an hour-long train ride to his new school.

Dutch thought the price was worth it. The bully he beat up would forever have a crooked nose, and the kid had also been expelled. No one messed with Simon after that day.

His father had fought in the Great War. Lost the use of his left hand. "Mark my words," he would say, positioning his useless hand in his jacket pocket. "The Hun will rise again. When they do, we'll fight to the death. Freedom is worth dying for."

Dutch nudged the cat with his big toe, the soft fur a reminder of all that was good. "For what does the Lord require of me? To seek justice, and love mercy, and to walk humbly with the Lord."

The cat strutted over Dutch's legs and jumped off the bed, sniffing at the cane on his way out of the room.

"Thanks for picking up my cane." Dutch lay back onto the pillow with a groan. He stared at the window and tapped his fingers over the patchwork quilt. What kind of condition was the Ford in? At the very least, the car would need a battery charge. Parked in the barn for so long, the vehicle had probably had its wires and tubes chewed through by mice.

The cat sashayed back into the bedroom, jumped onto the bed, and lay at Dutch's feet.

"Did you do your job and keep the mice away?"

The cat shut his eyes and licked a spot of milk from his lips.

"No, I didn't think so. Nan feeds you too well, right? Why bother with scrappy field rodents?"

In his periphery, Dutch noticed the torn sleeve of the minuscule nightshirt. Hobbling around today, he'd ripped the back, too. Teddy must have been a shrimp. There was no way her dead husband's clothes would fit. They'd figure that one out later, but something had to be done or he'd be driving to the border in his drawers.

He'd found his cleaned underwear hanging in the room off the scullery, still damp, and had put them on. They were wet and clammy, but he deemed his discomfort better than being in the natural beneath the shirt.

The only glimmer of fortune in this situation was Nan. Brave girl. And the prettiest he'd ever met. He liked her taking care of him, her cool fingers over his forehead, down his neck, gently across his shoulders. Gazing into her deep blue eyes, he felt a million miles away from the war. And he felt connected. Connected to something worth the fight.

Pain throbbed through his arm, stabbing and burning. Being stitched up by her hadn't been much fun though.

Where was she? What was taking her so long? Perhaps "back soon" in Ireland really meant hours.

Or maybe she was turning him in. She'd given her word, but could he trust her? What would he do in her situation?

He leaned back and covered his eyes with his good arm. His crew had trusted him. Look where it'd landed them. In Ireland. In trouble. Or even dead.

He tried to quiet the jumble of thoughts about the night before, but they would not be silenced. The sequence of events spun through his mind. With a sharp inhale, he felt searing pain lash through his arm.

"Bail out, bail out, bail out!" Dutch had yelled to his crew. Each one had jumped out the door, the tops of their parachutes disappearing into the night.

"Go on ahead, Williams," he'd said to his flight officer. "I'm going to reset the tabs."

"See you down there." Williams had stepped out the door and into the night.

Dutch scooted back into the cockpit. He must have read the winds wrong. The bomber was supposed to crash into the sea, not a cow pasture. Certainly not in Eire, either.

Course set, he'd jumped, drifting in silence toward the Irish soil. So serene, and the moonlight so brilliant, it'd seemed unreal. Peaceful. But hitting the bog had grounded him back into reality.

If he'd been a better pilot, he might have corkscrewed the aircraft out of harm's way, far from the flak, from the ribbons of purple, yellow, orange, stretching up and exploding around them. One burst had rocked the front fuselage, destroying the loop antenna.

It had been his fault, getting separated from the formation. They'd headed back to the base without a radio, the navigator's only guidance in the darkness a compass and watch.

He was responsible for his crew. What had happened was his fault. His. Fault.

His stomach lurched at the sound of footsteps and laughter. Heavy footsteps that couldn't belong to the beautiful, young nurse. A child's laughter rang over the sound of crows.

Who was out there? The LDF officer? Had Nan turned him in? The LDF wasn't going to take him without a fight. Why hadn't she given him the gun?

He focused on the cane, slid off the blankets, and stood. A razor-sharp burn struck his knee. Groaning, he grabbed his leg. Pain needled down his left arm, flaming, aching. The fox face seemed to mock him as he picked up the walking stick.

The front doorknob rattled. He straightened. His pulse raced fast and hard, as though he'd just run down the football field. Whoever it was, he was trying to get inside.

Where had she put his gun? He'd poked around the cabin looking for it earlier, but she'd squirreled it away somewhere. How could she leave him without protection? He squeezed the cane. That was her idea of defense?

Overriding the aches that ripped through his body, he padded barefoot over the slate floor to the window.

The doorknob rattled again. He froze, cane in hand.

His heart pumped as hard as bullets shooting against his ribs. From outside, he heard a female voice say, "Mind ya don't take too much turf, or Nurse Nan will know we've been here."

What? Parting the curtain a little, he surveyed the yard. A barefoot boy, wearing a muddy RAF-aviator flight helmet and dressed in shabby clothes, helped himself to the turf piled in a shelter built against the calf house. The kid took the bricks in such a way as to disguise the theft, loading them into a bucket.

Dutch gaped. The aviator helmet. He bet it was his. His name would be written inside.

The woman who accompanied the child wore a multipatched dress that hung down to her dirty, oversized men's shoes. She adjusted the shawl around her shoulders, then jiggled the door handle one more time.

Without any luck, she stepped away, turned on her heel, and strolled into the calf house. A minute later she returned, her apron pockets filled. She bit into an apple and then handed one to the boy. The two lumbered off after leaving a dent in Nan's fuel supply and probably her apple barrel, too.

Lowlife thieves. Why didn't Nan have a dog? A nice big, ferocious mutt who could scare away the likes of those two. The cat rubbed against Dutch's calf, then passed in and out of the space between the man's legs. "Think you could meow or something to scare them away?"

Dutch hobbled into the main cabin room, the cane tapping along with each step. He lowered himself to a chair beside the fireplace. Stretching his legs out, he inhaled slowly, taking in the scent of the burning turf. He let the air escape in one powerful puff.

He'd placed his wet boots beside the fireplace, in the hopes of drying them, but they still appeared to be soaking wet. With this cold, damp climate, they'd grow mold first.

He scratched his eyebrow. Nan had scrubbed the boots clean and had left them in the laundry room to air beside his cleaned underpants. He shifted in his seat as the damp boxers clung to his skin.

This was no good for Nan. She shouldn't have agreed to hide him. There was too much at risk. If he was discovered, they'd take him into custody, and her, too. The longer he waited around, the more his odds of being found increased.

He smacked his hand against the armrest. Time to stop being a wimp and take decisive action. His escape training kicked in. No time to wait for Nan to get back. He resolved to inspect the car, get it operational, and save her further entanglement.

Standing, Dutch wobbled. The floor's coldness penetrated his bare feet. No telling what he might encounter in the barn. Adding cuts to his injuries seemed unwise. He remembered a pair of men's Wellington boots in the laundry room beside the back door.

He considered picking up the cane, but after staring at the creepy fox-face handle, he decided to leave it beside his drying boots.

When he got to the back room, he saw a rack holding the dress she'd worn the night before, along with her bra and panties. He ran his hand over the soft wool. The dress was damp. He resisted touching her drying undergarments.

He wasn't supposed to look at her last night, but he hadn't been able to help himself. The image of her standing there in only a slip was burned in his memory.

He wished she hadn't burned his clothes. He felt ridiculous wearing this tiny nightshirt. And cold. *Never mind,* he told himself. *Buck up. Carry on with your mission.*

He yanked on the rubber boots. They were too small, but they had to do. Cramped toes beat cut feet. He limped to the recessed window in the main cabin, pulled back the curtain, and peered outside. It seemed clear, so he unlocked the door.

The cat stepped over Dutch's feet and ran into the yard, disappearing into a row of hedges. Dutch closed the door behind him and dashed across the cobblestone courtyard, the boots pinching his toes and sending smacking sounds into the misty air. Every step sent a stab to his knee. He swung open the faded calf-barn door and stepped inside. His knee burned, and pain throbbed up his hip, but he tried his best to ignore it.

He waited for his eyes to adjust. The barn smelled of hay, earth, mold. And apples. Three barrels stood to his left, under a window. The shuttered window was the only one in the barn.

Sweat poured down his face. Catching his breath, his gaze lit on a hulking form covered with a tarp. "There you are. Let's see what's going on."

He spotted a lantern in the recessed window, along with a box of matches. After adjusting the dilapidated barn-window shutters to a closed position, he lit the lamp.

From the corner of his eye, he spotted the cat wiggling in through a broken board in the double doors at the other end of the barn.

"So, you going to be my lookout? Pretend you're a dog?"

The cat hopped onto a barrel and glared at him.

"Right. Sorry for the insult. Any help accepted," he said, scratching the cat behind the ears.

Dutch placed the lamp on a tool bench, illuminating the car and the concrete floor. The tarp came off without a struggle. The black Ford sedan appeared solid enough, no missing doors, headlights intact. The windows were all there and mostly free of cracks. The tires needed air but seemed sound.

"Not bad," he muttered. On the surface, at any rate.

Now the fun part. He set the oil lamp closer to the edge of the tool bench and opened the car's hood. It creaked and protested at being lifted, but he fought to raise it with his good arm. When it started to close, he grabbed the edge with his injured arm. Pain burst down his limb, but he powered through until he set the hood prop. He stepped back, holding his arm. After he took a few long gulps of air, the pain receded and he continued to inspect the engine.

He raked a hand through his hair, peered into the straw-stuffed engine. The mice had done considerable damage. He found a wrench on the tool bench and poked out a giant nest. Two tiny mice jetted from under the car and scurried between the barrels where the cat sat. The tabby stood on all fours, then sat back down, continuing to lick his paw.

"Like I said, Nan feeds you too well."

The cat jumped off the barrel and poked his nose around in a disinterested fashion. Then he began stalking. The mice were in for it.

Pulling wires, inspecting hoses, Dutch lost himself in the rhythm of diagnosing each element that needed to work together with precision. The constant ache in his knee he ignored, but a searing pain in his arm stopped him. Twice.

Push through, push through, he demanded. *Now is not the time to whine about pain.*

Back in the rhythm again, he had to admit he loved working on cars. The wires, the mechanical parts, the smell of oil and gasoline. It'd been a while since he'd had to dig in and get his hands this dirty. Or hand, in this case; the wound on his arm kept his left hand pretty useless. Now he knew what his father must have endured all those years with only the use of his right hand.

When was the last time he'd worked on a car? Oh yeah, about three years ago. His sister-in-law's Chrysler Royal coupe. Two-door, five windows, the color black as her eyes. He'd had two assistants that day, his then seven- and five-year-old nephews.

Dutch stooped and wiggled a tube. His mood darkened. The Nazis had become real last summer, when some of his sister-in-law's Jewish relatives had shown up at their doorstep with only the clothes on their backs. The rest hadn't shown up at all.

Rachel kept asking, "Where is Grandpa? Grandma?" No one knew.

The war had become personal that day, when Rachel had been inconsolable. Simon, through his newspaper connections, had discovered that her grandparents had been taken from their home, whisked off on a train, and sent to a concentration camp in Poland.

The Nazi machine had taken away her loved ones. Dutch could no longer ignore the brutality, the suffering due to the war. The next day he signed up for the RAF. His mother refused to talk to him for a day, but she finally resigned herself to the fact that—like father, like son—Dutch was going to join the war effort.

Fight for freedom.

Right now, though, all he fought for was a way out of Eire.

After a few minutes more of tinkering with the car engine, he stepped back. Hands filthy, he searched the tool bench for a towel, found a bit of yellow terrycloth, and wiped his hands.

Not too bad, he decided. Mostly worn or chewed hoses and wires. What he needed next was a battery, and then maybe he'd get lucky and the engine would turn over. Nan would be pleased he had started the process. He could give her a list of parts tonight. Be on his way all that much sooner.

At the sound of the gate creaking open, Dutch froze. Probably Nan. The cat hopped onto the bench, meowing.

"I know. I hear it."

He turned off the lamp and limped to the window. Through a gap in the shutters, he peered out. And gulped.

Some fireplug in a green uniform was at the cottage, his fist banging on the door. Waiting a second, the man banged again. Then he pushed down on the latch.

Dutch's stomach kicked around like a rotary fan. His throat tightened, and his breath turned rapid and shallow. *No, no, no.* He'd left his boots beside the fireplace. And that stupid cane. Game over if the officer walked in. But if Dutch went out there to stop him—

Nan rode her bike into the yard. "Why, Officer Finn. What brings you out here again so soon?" She dismounted, wheeled the bike to the house, and leaned it against the whitewashed wall. Her smile could melt a bowl of ice cream. It seemed to daze Finn.

"Trying to keep you safe is all. One RAF pilot is still unaccounted for, and I want to make sure you're safe."

"Ah, isn't it grand, you stopping by and all, but I can take care of myself. I have a gun. Remember?"

"Then I hope your cat is around and ready to take aim at a combatant pilot if he happens by." He stepped closer to her. "I do remember the gun. And everything about last night. In fact, I keep thinking about it. All night. All day. How about you invite me in for tea?"

His fat hand moved toward her shoulder.

She backed away before he touched her. "Sure now, I would, but sorry. I've a birthing to attend. I must get ready. Some other time. Maybe in a week or so." Nan reached into her pocket and pulled out a key. "Good-bye. Be on your way."

"You won't be needing that. You left the door open."

Nan swung around to face the door. "Did I? Oh dear."

"I'll go in first, check everything out," Finn said.

She turned, pressed her back against the door, blocked the entryway. "Ah, no, you won't. I've . . . put my underthings by the fire to dry. My unmentionables. I don't want to embarrass you."

Dutch swallowed, thinking about his boots. Set on the hearth. *Lord, help Nan explain that one away, please. Please.*

Finn seemed stunned, his hands quaking at his sides. "I'm only doing my duty. I can go in if I want. The Emergency Act gives me the authority to investigate as I see fit."

"No need, but okay." Still facing Finn, she opened the door. "Wait here a second. I'll check. And yell if I need ya."

She bolted into the house, slammed the door behind her. The window opened. "All clear. Thanks. Now, be on your way. Give my regards to your sainted mother."

Finn stroked his double chin. "Who's having the baby?"

"Mrs. Kennedy."

He pulled down his jacket. "I'll give you a ride. My car's down the lane."

"No thanks. It'll only take a few minutes on my bike."

He stepped closer to the window. "I could give you protection all day and all night. Just say the word."

"I'm knowing that."

"You need a man around, Nan. You're only a bit of a girl. There's no one else in town like me."

"Thank God for that."

Finn fingered his gun. "I won't wait for you forever."

"Grand. Duly noted. Be off with ya. I'm sure other ladies need your protection from that big bad RAF pilot, but you'd think by now if the fella is alive, he'd be across the border."

Dutch wiped his hand over his dry lips. This wasn't about a downed pilot. Finn had other motives. He wanted Nan.

Leaning closer to the shutter for a better view, Dutch hit his knee on the stone wall. Pain radiated up his leg. He parted the shutter wider.

Finn went to the cabin window. "Unless the belligerent is hurt. Bleeding." His hand ran down the doorjamb. "I see you cleaned the doorjamb."

"He's not here. Hasn't been here. Now, off you go. I'd love to chat, but if you hold me up any longer, poor Mrs. Kennedy will have her baby without my assistance. And you know she's great friends with Father Albert. You'll have him to contend with."

Finn shuffled away. "I'll be on my way, but I'll be back to check on ya."

"I've no doubt you will." She slammed the window shut.

Finn paced over the cobblestone entry and took one long look at Nan's cabin before he strolled away, whistling.

How had Nan done that? Dutch wondered. *Kept so cool. Unflustered. No surprise that fat lump was in love with her.*

A shiver snaked down his spine. What had she done last night when Finn had come to the door? How did she get rid of him? It worried him.

Dutch moved away from the window to lean against the stone wall. Pressing his hands to the cold surface, he decided he'd wait a couple of minutes before he traipsed across the courtyard, in case Finn was lurking in the hedges.

Nan would be happy that he'd made so much progress with the Ford.

At the sound of her footsteps, he moved away from the wall. The door swung open, and light fused around her as though she were some angel captured by the earth.

"You stupid article. Didn't I tell you to stay put?"

CHAPTER 7

Nan stomped toward him with a glare that could scorch ice. The cat darted outside through the crack in the double doors.

Dutch wished he could follow, but instead he backed against the wall. Her mouth opened, but he preempted her tirade with "I'm sorry." His eyes darted to the car. "I wanted to work on the Ford. The sooner I'm gone, the better."

"You got that right. I told you to stay put. And to use the cane." She stabbed the cane toward him with each word, the fox face appearing to grimace. "If I hadn't come home when I did, Finn would have gone inside and seen your boots. Two seconds later, you'd be off to internment and I'd be off to jail. How could you disobey me? It wasn't a suggestion to stay inside."

"Ah . . . God blessed us with perfect timing," Dutch offered. He took the cane from her. The fox-face handle spooked him enough that he'd stopped looking at it.

She folded her arms, her mouth a slash of disapproval. "That's as good as you got?"

"No. Yeah." His arm burned. "I'm stupid." His mouth tasted like tin. "I won't do it again. I promise."

"If you do, you're gone. Understand?"

"Understood."

She straightened her jacket, seeming to compose herself. "Well? Did you get my car started? Figure out what was wrong?"

With a shake of his head, he said, "The mice had moved in. They chewed the wires and hoses. I need time to investigate."

"Tomorrow. Not a second before then."

"Why not now?"

"Because I have a birthing. Mrs. Kennedy really is having her baby." She glanced at her wristwatch. "I have an hour before I have to go. We better eat something, and I need to change your dressing. I probably won't be back until morning."

He was pushing his luck, pushing her temper and patience, but he had to ask. "Did you find out what happened to my crew?"

"They're all accounted for. I attended to them. Minor injuries. Cuts and bruises."

The tension in his neck relaxed, and the tight spot between his shoulder blades released. "Where are they?"

Her red curls swayed over her face. "At the Garda station, waiting for transportation to an internment camp."

He pulled away from the wall, ignoring the blasts of pain vibrating in his arm and knee. "We have to break them out."

Her laugh rang through the barn. "You and what army?"

"Me, myself, and I. Whatever it takes."

"It'd take more than the likes of you. And how far do you think you'll get, dressed like that?" She gestured at his getup. "Think you'll blend in with the locals?"

Not likely, he realized. Ripped nightshirt and rubber boots. Maybe he'd blend in if he were in Paris. Or Berlin. Pre-Nazi Berlin. "I do look a sight." It was humiliating.

"I'll find you clothes that fit, more or less."

He looked down at the rubber boots, at the dirty concrete floor, the scraps of hay and muddy boot prints. "The authorities are still searching for me?"

"Of course they are. They won't give up until they find you. I'm afraid Finn can smell ya."

Nan wasn't safe until he was gone. The thought punched him in the chest.

She wrapped her arm around his waist. "Come on. We have a lot to do before I leave."

She peered in both directions before they scurried across the courtyard. Nan helped him inside to the comfortable chair beside the fireplace. "I hope you didn't split your stitches."

"I'm okay." His arm hurt something awful, though.

He watched her put a kettle of water on the cooker. Her movements were graceful, smooth, supple.

She kneeled before him to tug off the rubber boots, her hair falling around her shoulders in a cascade of curls. His fingers trembled for want of touching them.

Placing his feet on the needlepoint footrest, he asked, "Tell me about the creep in the green uniform. Finn." Even saying the name left a disgusting taste on his tongue.

"Shamus Finn. Our village LDF officer. All we women hate him." She placed a knitted throw blanket over Dutch's lap. "I need to re-dress your wound."

He watched her walk to a tall cabinet with open shelves that held blue-and-white dishes.

"What'd you do to Finn last night?"

"Do?" She opened the lower cabinet drawers, pulled out clean linens, and stuffed them into her medical bag.

"Yeah, I heard him say, 'everything about last night . . .'"

"Ah, nothing to concern yourself about."

Was she not aware? Or ignoring Finn's expectations? That man would not settle for a brush-off forever. "Tell me about him. What's with the louse?"

"Long story."

"I'm listening."

"I'm not telling. Not right now, anyway. Don't worry. It's not important. I can handle him." She paused, holding a bundle of cotton bandages. Gliding toward him, she focused on his arm.

"Men with agendas can be deadly in their pursuits. Finn doesn't impress me as the sort of man who plays parlor games. At least not for long."

"He's a brute and an arse but not dangerous. Don't give it another thought." She stood before him, her eyes widening. "You've done it. You've ripped your stitches."

Dutch looked down at the stain of red weeping through the bandage. "No wonder my arm hurts so much."

"Yes, no wonder." She pressed a wad of gauze to the wound. "Keep pressure on it. I'll be right back." She was off to the bathroom. The sound of opening and shutting cabinet doors, the whoosh of water, and the tinkling of bottles came through the rhythmic song that was her cottage. She was humming. Softly.

She padded back with a medical kit, flipping it open with her long, slender fingers. Her wedding ring glinted in the lamplight. With expert movements, she snipped the gauze and removed the soiled bandage.

A nauseating odor rose from his arm. Foul and yeasty. The wound wept with pus and blood through the sutures. His stomach turned aerial rolls. "Is it supposed to look like this?"

"It's not uncommon." Her voice was calm, soothing. She seemed undisturbed by the wound's appearance.

"Your crew fared much better. Little cuts and bruises, but otherwise in good health. Except one boy, Rich Ryan. Physically he's fine, but I worry about his state of mind."

"He should have been shipped back to his mother after the last mission, but the RAF is pretty desperate for gunners."

"What happened?"

"Nothing out of the ordinary." He didn't want to tell her they'd lost one of the crew in a particularly harsh way on their last mission, and Ryan had been inches from that death. The ground crew had tried to clean up the blood, but Ryan had turned green when he spotted the red pattern still clinging to a wall. "He's a sensitive kid. Too sensitive for this war."

"We're all too sensitive for this war. This might sting."

Whatever she poured on the oozing wound sent a current of stabbing pain through his arm. He clamped his teeth. Each dab felt like exploding miniature bombs. His teeth hurt from clamping his jaw.

"I'm sorry. I know it hurts. Almost done."

He willed himself to ignore the pain. Conversation, that's what he needed. The cat swaggered in from the scullery, sniffed Dutch's boots, and flopped down beside the man.

"Your cat's a pal."

"I'm glad you've made friends."

"Yeah. We've had quite the conversation. What's his name?"

"Mr. Dee. Short for Mr. De-Lovely. He showed up one day when the song was playing."

"Why don't you have a dog?"

It was a tiny pause, one that would have gone unnoticed except she'd exerted extra pressure to his wound.

"I only ask because I heard someone trying to open the door. A dog would have chased the intruders away. Would alert you to unwanted visitors."

"Like yourself?"

"Yeah. Like me."

"Maybe someday." She held the used bandages in her hand. "Did you see who was here? Was it Finn?"

"No. Some ragamuffin kid wearing my flight helmet. He was with a woman in a long dress, maybe his mother. They stole turf and apples."

"The Tinkers. Irish gypsies. It's okay. It's their way."

"Thieving?"

She shrugged. "We don't look at it that way. We help them out, that's all."

"You mean they help themselves."

"They're not bad people. They just have a different code of ethics. They claim to be the last descendants of Irish royalty." Her slow-moving smile nearly snatched his breath away.

"You're okay with Irish royalty raiding your supplies?"

"I don't mind is all." She pulled in a deep breath, motioned with her chin toward his arm. Her eyes, such a deep blue, almost purple, reminded him of lobelia flowers from his mother's spring garden. How did Nan have such light, perfect skin? He didn't think she wore makeup, yet her lips were pink. Pink like tulips at Easter.

"I'm not going to lie to you," she said. "Your arm is borderline bad. Your escapade in the barn and tinkering with the Ford was far from helpful."

"I know. Now."

Their eyes met, and neither of them spoke, moved, nor reacted to the screaming kettle. She looked away first.

"The kettle is boiling." She stood. Touching his cheek so lightly, it might have been a butterfly, she said, "Fancy a cup of tea?"

He grabbed her hand. "I fancy . . ." He thought for a second to say "you" but instead said, "getting out of your hair as soon as possible."

"As do I." She went to the sink with graceful, powerful movements. Opening a canister, she dipped a spoon in, measuring out two spoons of black tea.

The cat jumped onto Dutch's lap, purring and rubbing his head into Dutch's palm. "She's really something, isn't she, Mr. Dee? No wonder you decided to park yourself here."

"You say something?"

"Talking to your cat."

She rewarded him with a smile. "Are you hungry a'tall?"

"Yes." But the hunger he felt would never be satisfied by food. He craved her kind words. Intimate sentences. Her touch.

"I'll have something ready in a minute. In the meantime . . ." She glanced at his chest before she reached into a basket and produced a package wrapped in paper. "Here. This is for you."

"What is it?"

"A pair of pajamas that will fit you better than the nightshirt you're wearing."

"Oh. Thank you."

She strolled toward him, the parcel pressed against her chest, her dress swaying with each step. The wrapping made a crinkling sound when she handed it to him.

Their fingertips brushed. They stayed there, connected. She paused, sucked in a breath. The air rushed out of her mouth with an almost-silent groan as she withdrew. "You've shredded my husband's nightshirt."

"Sorry." The garment hung on his shoulders by a couple of threads. He opened the package and smiled at the navy-and-white-pinstriped garment. "It's really nice. Thanks."

"I hope it fits. Why don't you wash up?" She returned to the kitchen counter. "And put on your pajamas. Do you need help?"

"I think I can get myself to the bathroom and back." He rose, decided it best to rely on the cane.

"Wait." From her medical bag, she retrieved scissors. "I'll cut you out of the nightshirt. No one will ever wear it again."

The blades felt cold against his skin as she snipped along the collar until she'd cut deep enough into the garment that it folded back, flopping open so much, he had to hold the edges together or it would fall.

They were eye to eye, a heartbeat away. She stepped back, the scissors against her chest, pointing down. His gaze followed the motion, then rode up her slender figure to her face.

"There," she said. "That should do it."

That did it all right. He was dizzy from her nearness and glad he had the cane to support his wobbly walk into the bathroom. He washed up, put on the pajamas—which fit perfectly—and ran a comb through his hair. Five o'clock shadow covered his face. As though she read his mind, she knocked and said through the closed the door, "If you'd like to shave, there's a razor under the sink. And a bar of shaving soap."

"Thanks." Must have belonged to her husband, he decided, finding the razor and soap in a shaving cup. He felt a lot better once he'd rid his face of hair.

"Dutch, are you almost done in there? Come to the table. I haven't much time."

They sat at the table, eating potato-and-bacon soup, sliced bread with butter, and chopped carrots. She poured tea.

He stared at the weeping-willow pattern on the teacup. "I've put you in an impossible position, haven't I? I wouldn't blame you if you turned me in."

Her spoon clanked against her empty bowl. "I gave my word. I will not betray you. And I'll be fine as long as you do as I say. Tuda will be back tomorrow. You make a list of the auto parts you need."

"Okay." He hoped he could fix the car with only one good arm. Somehow, he'd manage. Maybe with the help of the Lord.

"I'll bring it to her. In the meantime, I'll show you a hiding place in case Finn noses around here again, and I'm sure he will. Think you can stand? Walk into the bedroom?"

She reached a hand to help him up from the table. Her touch ignited a spark that could have powered up his bomber.

"Lean on me," she said, wrapping her arm around his waist. He really didn't need her help, but he took it. She was soft and warm and smelled mysteriously like Irish heather.

"My family owned this farmhouse," she said, leading him into the bedroom. "It was used as a safe house during the Troubles and the civil war. The Black and Tans used to search the houses for IRA members. We built the cubby to hide them."

She let him down to sit on the corner of the bed. He felt a rush of cold air when she stepped away.

She ran her hand along the boards until she found a large knot in the wood. With a forceful jab, the wall made a clicking sound. The door opened, revealing a dark space large enough for two people. Skinny people. Short people, like her husband.

"There's a place inside where you can slide a panel open. See what's going on in the other room."

"Ingenious."

"One had to be to survive during those times."

"These times, too." He'd heard some of his sister-in-law's stories of running and hiding from the Nazis. Here, he was running and hiding from the Irish government, but he doubted that if he were caught they'd put a bullet in his brain. They wouldn't free him, either.

"I planned to remove the doors and put in a linen closet, but I dunno. It's a bit of history, I suppose." The door shut with a cracking noise.

"I hope I'll be long gone before I need to hide in your wall."

"Just in case."

All this hiding made him feel like a coward. "Where's my gun?"

"I told you. You'll get it when you leave."

"More hiding places?"

"What do you think?"

"Come on. I *need* it."

"Well, I don't *need* dead Tinkers or LDF officers in my yard." The clock in the other room chimed. "I'm off."

"I want my gun."

"It's my Christian duty to take care of you, but you'll not get the gun."

"And it's my Christian duty to fight for God and country."

Her expression turned hard. "Men and their guns. Violence never solved anything."

"Hey, we didn't start this thing, but we're going to end it, with or without your country's help." With a shake of his head, he muttered, "If your country would just let us use your ports—"

"If we let the British back, they'd never leave."

He clicked his tongue. "How do you know that?"

"Eight hundred years of British oppression."

"We're the only ones taking the fight to the Nazis."

"We're helping. Hundreds of Irish boys are fighting with the English and her allies."

"Rumor has it your people are sympathetic to the Germans. In fact, I hear they're helping them. I hear they're letting them refuel their submarines in the bay."

"Don't be daft. That's not even feasible. We don't have fuel."

"Churchill claims it's true."

"He's pouting like a little boy because he didn't get his ports back."

"Are you calling the British prime minister a liar?"

"Isn't that another definition of politician?"

She folded her arms over her chest and looked down her nose at him. "There are some Irish who side wrongly with the Nazis, but we're with the Allies. We simply can't forgive and forget what the Brits have done to us. Can't openly support the crown."

"The truth comes out. Isn't that what the Lord tells us to do? Forgive and forget?" He slumped into the pillows on the bed. His arm ached, as if a hot poker were jabbing it over and over and over.

"If men did as the Lord told them, if we all obeyed the Ten Commandments, we wouldn't be at war a'tall. And you're not killing wooden soldiers. They're humans, too. With families. Loved ones."

Her words stunned him. Left him searching for a response, but he had none. She threw several bricks of turf onto the fire.

Memories of the pounding of guns and images of the burning earth below his plane—and of the rubble left behind—after they'd dropped their bombs collided with the emotional armor he held to protect himself. He ran a hand over his face as though to melt the reality of the situation.

War. This was war.

Them or us.

He shifted, his knee reminding him he was still oh-so-human.

"I'm off." She wiped her hands over her slender hips, leaving bits of dried turf clinging to her skirt. She brushed off the dust. "I'll be back. I don't know when. Get some rest. In the morning, I'll go with you to assess the Ford. Promise me you'll stay put tonight."

Dutch looked at his throbbing arm. "Once I drive over the border and abandon the car, will you get it back?"

Her eyes sparkled in the soft cabin lights. "Fifty-fifty. The government may claim it's their property even if I say you stole it. If I don't get it back, I'll consider it my contribution to the war effort."

Dutch struggled with the urge to get up and hug her. Not in a lusty sort of way, but not in a brotherly fashion, either.

With her hand on the door latch, she pointed at him. "And if you go outside this cabin tonight, if I don't keel over from a heart attack because you did, I'll murder ya. Understand?"

He saluted. "Sir, yes, sir."

"Get some sleep."

In the other room, he heard her snap her medical bag shut and then lock the door. He listened to the sound of the bicycle ticking off into the distance.

He stared into the amber glow of the fire and watched a spark shoot up the chimney. A lot of guys fell in love with their nurses. He was no exception, he guessed. But the last thing Nan needed was another unwanted advance from an "eejit" military man.

CHAPTER 8

Nan climbed down the stairs and into the Kennedys' main room, where a party roared. One man played the pennywhistle, another a drum, and the extended Kennedy family, numbering at least two dozen, crowded the cabin, celebrating. Huge pots of stew simmered over a turf fire, and cooked oatcakes leaned against a metal stand to dry out.

Mr. Kennedy approached Nan with a smile that revealed a grand set of straight teeth, yellow as butter. He offered her an oatcake and a shot glass full of whiskey. "Thanks, Nurse. You delivered a seventh son of a seventh son. Now, that's something to celebrate. This boy is special. He'll have grand powers and make his mark on our sweet earth. Seventh son of a seventh son. Ah, but he's got the angels smiling tonight."

"Is that what all the ruckus is about out here?" She refused the whiskey and chomped into the oatcake, the flavor deep and satisfying. Someone passed her a cup of tea.

"Will ya not stay?" Mr. Kennedy gulped the whiskey shot and then yanked down his wool vest. He was the kind of man who thought every event deserved a good celebration, from cradle to grave and everything in between.

He lived on what the locals described as a "strong farm," passed down to him through several generations. It comprised a large two-story house, several outbuildings, and a few dozen head of cattle and sheep that roamed the substantial fields.

Nan placed her hand on his arm. "I'm sorry. I must be on my way. Your son's a lovely babe. Healthy and strong. I thought he might climb out of the bassinet and walk down the hallway."

"That's my boy. No problems with my wife?" He swiped a hand through his thinning hair.

"None a'tall. One of the easiest births this side of heaven." *It might prove to be the easiest night of the child's life, too,* she thought. Who wanted the sort of pressure that his da or perhaps fate had bestowed on him?

As she left the house, she was patted on the back for a job well done. Cycling home, she let herself drift into imagining herself as a mother.

And Dutch the father.

Her stomach churned. Was she being disloyal to Teddy?

When she got home, she checked on the flyboy in her bed, sleeping, thankfully, with the cat by his side. She pulled the quilt up around his chest and noticed how well the new pajamas fit.

Lingering longer than necessary, she chided herself to get a move on. There was no medical value in observing him further. It only brought about a strange mixture of want and fear to her heart. She gathered her things for the night and closed the door behind her.

When she'd gotten into bed upstairs, she found herself tossing and turning, thinking about what Margaret had proclaimed. *God doesn't bring anything to our doorsteps that we can't handle.*

She stared at the thatched roof, the neat rows of reeds running the length of the ceiling. *Let that be true, heavenly Father. Let that be true.*

◆ ◆ ◆

After breakfast the next morning and having re-dressed Dutch's wound, which seemed no better or worse, they set out for the calf house. While Dutch tinkered with the Ford Model A's engine, Nan gazed out the dirty window, on alert for any visitors.

Please, Lord, keep Finn from my door.

Nan glanced over her shoulder at Dutch. He was bent above the open bonnet, reaching into the engine. Ah sure, the pajamas fit him nicely. Hung and nipped in at all the right places. Her face heated at such cheeky musing, but didn't his backside look . . . muscular. Manly.

She might have heard a cuss word, but she couldn't be sure. He looked up and caught her staring. His blue eyes were sparkling.

"How long before you make the list?" Nan asked.

"Not long." His jaw muscles tightened as he continued to probe the engine.

She returned her attention to the window. Sunlight broke from the morning clouds. Behind her house, the rocks that littered the hillside shone like medals in the sunshine. A brilliant day. The Lord had blessed them with good weather. Sure now, wasn't that a sign that all would be well?

The cat jumped onto the outside window ledge, and Nan gasped. She jumped back, kicked a pail at her feet, and fought to keep her balance.

He bolted upright. "What is it? What?" he asked.

"Nothing." She shook her head. "The cat frightened me. That's all. I'm a bit jumpy."

Mr. Dee bumped his nose on the glass before he leapt down. With a grin, Dutch set his focus back on the car. "You sure your cat's not working for the Garda?"

"Wouldn't put it past him."

They shared a smile.

He reached for a tool on the bench. "Promise me you'll get a dog." Dutch tapped the wrench on the car's bumper, waiting for an answer. "Aside from security, a dog is a great companion."

"Okay. I promise I'll give it some thought."

He winked at her, then returned to tinkering with the car's engine.

Nan approached the Ford. The car had sparked so much marital discord. "Let's get rid of it," Teddy had suggested after he'd driven it into a ditch. "No," Nan had insisted. "I'll be the driver in the family. Besides, I like the freedom." Teddy had grabbed his notebook, stomped over to his spot on the cliff, and sulked. Her driving seemed to threaten his manhood.

Nan stood beside Dutch and peered at the engine. "What do you think? Can you get the car running again?" She pressed her hand on the car door, the cold metal soothing her hot skin.

"Piece of cake if your pal can get me the parts."

"Once you have them, how long to make the fixes?"

"A few hours. Maybe." He winced, grabbed his arm, but then seemed to shrug off the pain.

"Be careful with your arm."

"I'm fine."

Fine as a boil on the backside of a priest. "How's your knee?"

"Fine."

Liar. She let it go. "You sure you can do this?"

He frowned at her. "Like I said, piece of cake if I get the parts."

"And if you don't?" She bit her lip, not wanting to tell him there was a possibility the parts might not be available. The war made anything connected with autos nearly impossible to find.

"Plan B."

"Which is?"

"Working on it. I'm open to suggestions."

She pulled in a breath. The scent of apples mixed with the smell of motor oil. He'd shaved again today, making him even more handsome. Off-limits, too, if she knew what was good for her. And she did.

His hands were covered in grease, his fingernails embedded with black grime. She grabbed a towel and handed it to him.

"We'll think of something," she said. "Mind you wash up before you touch anything in the house. Don't leave any fingerprints, or I'll have to tell Finn the cat was fixing the car."

He laughed. Sunlight sifted in, spotlighting the union of their hands on the towel.

If Nan didn't know better, she'd think it was the Lord, shedding light on the situation. Dutch stepped closer to her, so near that she could feel the warmth from his body. She could smell the soap he'd used. He smelled downright dangerous.

"You've given yourself a grease spot." She touched her forefinger to his chin. The mark smeared across his skin and onto her finger. There was a snap of energy connecting them. A need for him swelled through her like the rise of a high tide.

He closed the distance between them. Everything in the calf house faded when he placed his hand against hers and pressed it into his chin. He guided her hand to his mouth. The tip of her pinkie brushed the soft outer line of his lip. Nan felt her insides spin, sliding out of her control.

The sound of a bicycle bell woke her from what seemed a dream. They both shuffled away from each other.

"Who's that? Finn? Where can I hide?" he asked, dropping the towel.

"It's not Finn. He'd never announce his presence."

"This is why you need a dog."

"What I need is for you to be on your way. Get in the car and stay out of sight."

She raced to the window. When she peered through the dirty glass, she let out a breath filled with relief. "It's only Kelly Halpin."

"Who's that?"

"The Garda's wife."

"Garda's wife? What do you mean, 'only'?" His eyes flashed as though he was looking for an escape route, one that didn't exist. "Can she be trusted?"

"Yes." She hoped. "As long as I act normal-like." *Whatever that was when you were hiding a flyboy.* "Lie down inside the car. I'll come get you after Kelly's on her way."

Nan paced out of the building, shut the calf house door behind her, and called across the courtyard, "Hello, Kelly. How are ya? What brings you to my door on this lovely morning?"

"I'm grand. Out for a bit of ride in this fine weather. I miss the weather reports, don't you? As if the RAF and Nazis listen to our weather reports. Doing our part for the Emergency Act, my husband likes to say."

Nodding, Nan said, "A bit daft in my opinion. It's not as though the reports are terribly reliable, anyway."

"Now, isn't that the truth?" Kelly wheeled her bike to the side of the whitewashed cottage. She wiped a stray blonde curl from her forehead.

"I'm glad to find ya home, Nan. Have ya a few minutes?"

"Sure, Kelly. I've a few before I start my rounds." Nan frowned. Kelly's eyes were red and puffy, with dark circles, and creases outlined her mouth. Nan hadn't seen any of this yesterday.

She placed her hand on her friend's shoulder. "Are you feeling all right? Are you spotting again?"

"Not a'tall. I'm grand. The baby is kicking like a football player. I wanted a bit of away time from the doings in town is all. Fresh air."

No. There was more going on. Nan glanced at the calf house, where Dutch waited inside the car, and then back at Kelly. Instead of making an excuse and sending Kelly on her way, Nan listened to her gut and invited Kelly in. "Have you time for tea? I'll put the kettle on."

"All right then, Nan. If you insist." Kelly's weak smile validated Nan's suspicion there was something wanting.

A few minutes later, Kelly picked at a slice of bread and nibbled a bit of sliced apple. She was indeed eating for two, but not today, God love her.

"I've news," Kelly said, spreading blackberry jam on her bread.

"What might that be?"

"Paul thinks they've found the last Wellington pilot."

Nan's throat tightened around a chunk of apple. She sipped her hot tea and burned her tongue, but she managed to get the bite down without choking.

"Is that so?" She forced herself to steady her gaze on Kelly, just as her mother had taught her.

Kelly lifted a piece of apple to her lips. "Poor lad. His body washed up a few miles away."

Nan's muscles relaxed. "What a shame. I knew I felt the coldness of death the other night. May he rest in peace, and God help the family he left behind."

Both women blessed themselves and said in union, "Amen."

"They're sure it's him?" Nan poured milk into Kelly's tea.

"Not completely, no. His dog tags were missing, and the poor fellow's face was quite destroyed. The Irish Army is working with the RAF to figure out who he is." Her lip quivered. "Was."

Nan closed her eyes, picturing Teddy's faceless body washing up on the shore three years before. Paul Halpin had been there, had let Nan sob into his shoulder. He'd declared Teddy's death an accident.

Nan blinked away a tear, for her husband and for this poor lost soul as well. "How will they identify him?"

"His jacket insignias and things found in his pockets. They'll let Paul know when he can officially stop looking."

"He's still looking?" Nan asked. "Why?"

"Something about it doesn't feel right to Paul."

Nan knew the feeling. "And why is that?"

"He didn't go into any details."

"I see. Have they called off the search for him or not?"

"Suspended for the time being."

Nan lifted her teacup and relaxed into the cane-back chair. "Then no more midnight visits from Finn."

"Ah, ya poor darling. Is he still bothering you?"

"What do you think? I wish he'd find another woman to pursue, but I wouldn't put that on anyone."

Kelly grew quiet as she stared at the turf blazing in the fireplace. She wiped a tear from the corner of her eye.

"What is it, Kelly? Something is bothering you."

Her friend let out a sob. Nan's hand went to her throat. "You're bleeding, aren't you?"

"Please don't tell Paul."

Nan slid to the edge of her seat, reached across the table, and placed her hand over Kelly's. "When did the bleeding start?"

She shook her head. "I'm not. The baby's fine, please God."

"Then what is it?" A million possibilities ran through Nan's mind. "Tell me."

"I hope . . . I hope I have a daughter. I couldn't bear my son going off to war. Can you imagine the poor mum when she reads the telegram that her son was lost in battle? Washed up on our shore? I can't bear it. I can't."

"A terrible, terrible thing." By now, Dutch's mother must have received that telegram. *Missing in action.* The poor woman. Nan wished she could tell his mum Dutch was fine and fit and fixing up his escape route.

Kelly blotted her eyes with a handkerchief. "Do you think maybe this will be the last war?"

"That's about as possible as Ireland turning into a desert. The day men stop fighting is the day we're finally in heaven."

"Ah, but wasn't there a war in heaven, and that's how the devil came to earth?" Kelly rested her elbows on the table and held her face in her hands. "I know it's wrong, but I've prayed and prayed and prayed. I've asked the Lord for a daughter. Do you think He'll punish me for my brazen request?"

"It's not brazen a'tall. We are the Lord's children. He likes to hear our wants and needs. Doesn't mean He'll grant them, of course. He knows what's best for us."

Kelly nodded, her hand squeezing Nan's. "Please don't tell Paul. He so wants a son."

"Don't all Irish men?"

"I suppose they do. But I don't." Kelly dabbed at her mouth with a linen napkin. "I better get back before he worries."

She rose, her belly skimming the edge of the table. They strolled outside into the warm sunshine.

"Thanks for the tea, Nan. And for calming my jumpy fears." Kelly mounted her bicycle.

"An expectant mother always has them. You'll love the baby, no matter what. And if it's a boy, you'll raise him to love peace. I'll check on you next week."

Nan stood at the edge of the courtyard, watching Kelly ride away. Why did Irish men think a son was the sun, the moon, and the earth? While the woman was there to fetch him his tea? With a shake of her head, she turned on her heel and ran to the calf house.

She swung the door open. "Dutch. She's gone. And I've got news." He sat up as she slid into the backseat beside him. "It'll buy us a few hours more to get the car going."

"What?"

After she told him about the dead pilot, she expected he'd be relieved, but instead he leaned back against the cracked leather seat and stared ahead.

"I wonder who he was? If I knew him."

She brushed her hand over his knee. "He's someone else's heartbreak, unfortunately. Such is war."

With a nod, he reached toward the floor. "Hey, I found these."

He held up a pair of black suede shoes with rhinestone buckles on the toes. "Yours?"

"Would you look at that? I wondered what had happened to those." She held up the shoes, remembering happier times. New Year's Eve at Gilmour House, where she'd laughed in the massive dining room by candlelight. In the dimness, the dented walls and their peeling paper had receded into the shadows. The house had seemed romantic.

"They look like dancing shoes."

She smiled. "I wore them to a New Year's Eve dinner two years ago, but it seems like forever ago. I was called to a birthing that night. Had to leave the party before the dancing. I threw these in the backseat and put on my nursing shoes before I went to work."

He held a shoe and ran a finger over the rhinestones. "Bet they looked real pretty on you. Bet you had a great dress to go with them, too."

"It was a velvet number with a bow in the front and a low back."

"Wish I could have seen you, all dressed up. Bet the men in the room couldn't take their eyes off you."

"Or hands after a few bottles of wine."

"You're beautiful."

Nervous laughter spilled from her throat. "In an Irish-peasant sort of way, right?"

"In a beautiful-woman sort of way. If I took you home to Canada, you'd knock 'em dead."

"Ah, go on with ya." His knee pressed into her thigh, and she returned the gesture with equal power. The energy between them could have started the car.

No. She scooted away along the crinkled leather seat, to the door. Away from him. He was toying with her.

"If I don't go into town, I won't be getting your parts. Did you write them down?"

"On the bench."

"Let me help you out of there—"

His gaze went from her outstretched hand to her eyes. It felt like a sword through her heart when he said, "I can do it on my own." He opened the other side of the car, made his way out. If he was in pain, he didn't show it.

She was glad she didn't need to touch him in that instant. Glad he'd been given this gift of time, even at the expense of some other poor sod. Glad he'd be gone before the next church service in town.

Lord, please. Look after him. Bring healing to his body. And a grand escape to the border.

She stood next to him at the bench, and he gave her the list. "You should probably rewrite this in your own hand."

"Good idea. Yes. I will." Their gazes met. She wondered if his heart was beating as fast as hers. Would he take her into his arms? Did he want that? Did she?

He coughed and smiled, uncovering a dimple in his cheek. "Mind if I take a bath while you're gone?" he asked.

"I think you should." She could use a cold dip herself. "Just mind you stay out of sight this time."

CHAPTER 9

After checking on Mrs. Kennedy and her baby boy, now named Thomas, Nan rode her bike up the long driveway to Gilmour House, Lord Harry's estate. The Georgian manor appeared majestic from afar. From the portico, though, as she knocked on the faded wood door, it was apparent—in the cracked windows, the crumbling plaster details, the dead plants in the chipped urns that flanked the entrance—that the house's heyday had passed some fifty years before.

The door creaked open. The butler, who had been there for at least that long, attempted a smile. "Nurse O'Neil. Lady Margot is waiting in the conservatory."

"Thank you, James. How is her ladyship today?"

With a grimace, a result of age and serving her ladyship, he said, "Same as usual."

Nan stepped inside and was met by the dank odor of mildew. If ghosts existed, she could imagine them roaming the cold hallways. Rumor had it the house was home to at least one poor trapped soul, a maid who had fallen to her death on the treacherous back stairs. The apparition reportedly appeared on dark mornings to light the fires in the master's bedroom.

Nan would take her warm cottage any day, even with a flyboy hiding in its shadows.

"I heard you had some excitement here yesterday with the RAF pilots," Nan said, trying hard not to look at the heads of the unfortunate stags mounted on the foyer's walls. "And Lord Harry sent them to the Garda."

"Indeed we did. It's the law of the land, and Lord Harry decided it was best to turn the lads in. This way, Nurse."

Too bad Dutch hadn't happened upon Lord Harry's barn instead of her cabin. She'd be minding her own business right now, instead of turning her life upside down.

She slowed her pace to match that of the butler. He inched toward the double-paned glass doors leading to the conservatory and then made a grand gesture for her to enter.

Lady Margot lay on a chaise longue in the corner of the room, under three gigantic ferns. An open tin of biscuits and a pot of tea graced the wicker table beside her. She wore a turban over her dark hair and a long scarlet dress with buttons down the front, left open across her bulging stomach. A glimpse of her satin slip showed beneath.

"Ah, there you are." Her face, thick with stage makeup, seemed more pimpled and swollen since Nan had last seen her.

"How are you today?" Nan placed her bag on the table beside the tin. Empty tin. Only crumbs remained.

"Horrible. Fat. And I'm desperately mad at Tipper."

"Why is that, now?" Had Margot heard rumors about the unfortunate maid Tipper had ruined?

"He hasn't written me in a week. I'm going mad with worry." She placed her arm over her forehead and groaned in a gesture worthy of *Swan Lake*.

"You would have heard something from the War Office if there were a problem," Nan assured her.

Lady Margot swept her arm over her bosom. "I almost wish he was dead, so he'd have an excuse for not writing. What if he's carrying on with some beautiful African girl? Leaving me here in this cold climate like a beached whale?"

"Now, now. Enough of that. Let's get a look at you." In fact, Nan wouldn't be surprised if the woman's imaginings were the case.

Lady Margot struggled to sit upright. "Why do men do it?"

"Do what?" Nan opened her bag for a blood pressure cuff.

"How can he run off to war like it's some grand adventure? Leave his unborn child and me in this rotting, old house? Is that fair?"

"That's life. 'Tisn't fair. Don't give it another thought, Lady Margot. Let's have a look. Have you felt the baby kick yet?" She slid the pressure cuff around her patient's arm.

"Like she's dancing *Sleeping Beauty*. Do you think I'll dance again after having a baby?"

"I don't see why not."

"I'll tell you why. Because my life will be different after the baby."

"But that's a grand thing. A baby is a wonderful joy." Nan wondered if she'd ever know that joy. Didn't seem likely. Her chance had passed.

"What's so grand about being fat?" Lady Margot huffed. "Did you hear the news? Did you hear we had RAF pilots in our barn?"

"I did, indeed. I met them yesterday and examined them."

"Oh . . . you mean with their clothes off?" She licked her lips, and her eyes sparkled.

"Wasn't necessary. They only had a few bumps and scrapes. I understand you gave them a grand dinner?" Nan squeezed the blood pressure bulb for the reading.

"Yes, chicken and mash, green beans, and cake. It was desperate fun to have them here. We hadn't had guests . . . young guests . . . young *male* guests in so long, I was beginning to think only old men and women live in Ireland. Of course, they didn't pay a bit of attention to me in my horrid state, my belly sticking out like a tugboat. What did you think of the pilots?"

"They were very lucky."

"I mean, what did you think of *them*?"

Nan read Lady Margot's blood pressure and then slid the cuff off. "They are very young and brave. Your blood pressure is a wee high. How much weight have you gained?" Nan took out a measuring tape and laid it across Lady Margot's belly.

"I don't know. I don't care."

"You need to. It's not good for you or the baby. Unless you're carrying twins—"

"Oh, bloody hell! I hope not."

"You're not, but at five months, you're rather—"

"Fat? Tell me something I don't know."

"I suggest you lay off the biscuits and eat salads. Take more strolls around the estate gardens. You're putting on too many pounds, and they're not easy to lose after the birth."

Lady Margot's upper lip curled. "How dare you! Who do you think you are?"

"Your midwife."

"You're not telling me what to do. I'll eat as many biscuits as I want to. James," she called to the butler who lingered at the doorway. "See the nurse out."

"I'm not done with my examination."

"Yes, you are. James, escort this woman out. And bring me a cup of hot chocolate and the pie we had for lunch."

"Does my lady mean a slice of pie?"

"Not you, too, you old . . . the whole pie. Now. I'm famished. I'm eating for two."

More like twenty-two. There was only so much Nan could do to keep her patient healthy. She placed her instruments back into her bag and snapped it closed. "It's all right, James. I'll see myself out."

At this rate, there'd be no fitting into tutus after Lady Margot's child was born, or into anything else in her wardrobe.

Nan rode her bike toward Quinn's Garage. Tuda and Paddy Quinn owned the only petrol station in the village. It was Tuda who did everything, from filling up cars to fixing them to keeping the books.

She was the sort of woman Nan admired. Being a "girl" never stopped Tuda from anything. Why she had married Paddy Quinn could only be left to speculation. Stately and tall, Tuda, even in her midforties, was a raven-haired beauty with eyes as green as castle moss.

Paddy, well, he'd been a man. Perhaps Tuda had panicked and thought she'd never get married if she let this one go. But once an Irish woman wed, she stayed married. Didn't matter what her husband turned out to be. In Tuda's case, at least he was a happy drunk without a mean bone in his flabby body. And he'd been a good da, always doing things with the twins.

Paddy was so proud the day the boys had joined the RAF. Tuda had cried and cried. Paddy took the boys down to the pub and got them drunk. And Tuda cried some more.

Nan wondered if Dutch might know the boys, but there were hundreds of young men who had joined the RAF. And many had gone to their graves, may Jesus have mercy on their souls.

Nan's bicycle wheels bounced across the humpbacked bridge. The water below raged, sloshing over the boulders on either side of the banks. Beyond the bridge, several men sat on the banks, their fishing lines swaying in the stream.

Quinn's white garage with red trim came into view. She thought back two years, when Tuda had discovered she was with child again. Seemed a miracle since she'd only been able to have the twins, who were by that time nineteen.

Tuda had wanted that late-in-life baby so much, but unfortunately, at four months along, Nan had helped her friend through a miscarriage. Tuda had gone into shock, followed by a deep depression. Very dark days. She knew the Lord would not give her another baby of her own to hold.

After Paddy's drunken bender, and the fire, Tuda had moved in with Nan for a few weeks, waiting for the Quinns' house to be repaired. And waiting for her husband's release from jail. She'd cried herself to sleep every night for over a month.

Nan would see her during the day, climbing the hills behind the house, sobbing, screaming out loud, "Why? Why, Lord?"

All Nan could tell her while they sat up nights, drinking tea and finding comfort in their friendship by the glow of the fire, was that there were no answers, merely friends who could help each other through the rough times.

Tuda's Paddy had stopped the drink for a couple of months after their troubles, but his sobriety hadn't lasted.

Arriving at the garage, Nan spotted her friend taking money from a lorry driver. She waved, slowing her bike to a stop beside the petrol pump. Tuda gave Nan a hug. "'Lo, Nan. How's yaself?"

In desperate need of a running car for Dutch's escape. "Grand. How was your da's funeral?"

"A sorrowful affair. I miss him something terrible. He was a good man." She sniffed and then adjusted the kerchief she wore over her head. Her wavy, dark hair added an attractive depth to her still-beautiful features. "But he's in our Father's house now, sitting with Ma, having his tea."

"Saddest part of life is the parting. Do you need to talk about it a'tall?"

With a shake of her head, Tuda said, "He was old. Had a good long life. It was his time."

Nan reached into her pocket for the piece of paper with the auto-parts list. "Am I interrupting your work?"

"Not a'tall. I've promised Dr. Mann I'd have her tire repaired by four. Will ya talk to me while I finish the job? I've only got to mount the beastly thing."

"That'd be lovely." *Inspirational, actually.* Nan could start her car and drive, but that was as far as her mechanical talents went.

"I dunno how lovely it'll be in my grease pit, but you're the sort of woman who doesn't shy away from strange situations."

If Tuda only knew the half of it.

"Park your bike and follow me inside."

The brick-walled interior of the garage was ten degrees colder than outside. It smelled of oil, grease, and burning rubber. Tools hung neatly on the walls, above wooden cabinets with multiple drawers.

A calendar with an advertisement for Tangee lipstick hung above a box of bolts. A beautiful young woman wearing a smile and a military hat beamed, beckoning Nan to read the caption that highlighted the services of the Navy, Army and Air Force Institutes: "The 'Uniform' lipstick for individual loveliness. Tangee Natural. Available on request at your NAAFI Canteen."

Nan had a tiny bit left of the tube she'd bought before the war. Maybe tonight she'd put some on. She did have a visitor, after all. Perhaps she'd even put on those dancing shoes.

Tuda grunted as she lifted a tire from a workbench. The tire thudded to the concrete floor. With expert handling, arm muscles flexing, she rolled the wheel toward a Ford Model A, a much newer version of the car Nan had parked in the calf house.

"Have you met our new doctor, Dr. Mann?" Tuda asked.

"No, not yet." Nan grinned, remembering the exchange between the men at Mikie's.

"She's causing quite a stir." After leaning the tire against the car, Tuda brushed her hands together, then returned to the workbench for the hubcap.

"Is she, now?"

"The men are afraid of her."

"Afraid of her?"

"She's quite the looker, you see. American, so she's bold as brass. The men claim they don't want her to examine any secrets under their belts."

"Ah please. Say no more."

Tuda cocked a grin. "I understand you tended to the pilots yesterday. Is that true, Nan?"

"Yes, I did." She perched on a stool.

"Were they hurt?"

"Cuts and bruises. No worse than a hurling match."

"Am glad for that." Tuda struggled with the tire, got it into place, and then picked up a bolt from the hubcap she'd placed on the floor beside the car. "Did you hear they found the last poor fellow dead on the beach?" she asked, putting a bolt into position.

"I did. Very sad."

Tuda took a tool and began tightening the bolt. "A sad end to a bright young life."

"RAF pilots are the bravest of the brave." Nan almost didn't want to ask, but it seemed more disrespectful not to. "Have you heard from your lads?"

Tuda's compressed lips revealed the anxiety Nan figured all mothers must feel with their boys off to war. Allied or Axis. When Ballyhaven's telegraph boy rode his bicycle down the lane, families waited nervously until he had passed their doors.

Staring off toward the windows, Tuda said, "They're doing well. Thanks for asking after them."

"I remember them in my prayers every night."

"Thank you." Tuda shut her eyes for a brief second, then continued to bolt the tire into the wheel. "So, what brings ya out to see me?"

Nan reached inside her tweed jacket for the list. Her stomach did a flip when she opened the paper: it was in Dutch's handwriting. She'd copied his list down in her own hand but must have taken the wrong piece of paper.

Needling tension tightened her stomach.

No, wait. What a silly goose you are, Nan O'Neil. How would Tuda know this was his writing?

Nan took a deep breath and then shot the words out. "I've decided to repair the Model A."

Tuda banged the hubcap into place. "Have ya, now? Well, it's about time. And you being a medical professional, you can get petrol rationing. I'll come out directly and have a look. We'll get it going in no time a'tall. I'm dying for a project."

Nan was just dying. "That won't be necessary. Here's the list of things I need. Do you have such things?" She slipped off the stool.

Tuda rose, her expression inquisitive. "My, Nan. You have such strong handwriting."

"All the better for you to read."

Did that sound too much like a fairy-tale answer? Nan's fingernails dug into her palms. She slid her fists into her pockets. "Do you have all the parts in stock?"

"Most of them. I'll have to send for a few things. All doable."

"How soon?"

"A couple of days for the parts."

"Can you make it sooner?"

Tuda tilted her head, holding Nan's gaze as if Nan were a kid caught by the priest with her hand down her pants. "What's your rush?"

Nan shrugged. "You know me. Once I get something into my head, I have to go forward in an altogether rapid fashion."

"No, I didn't know that about you. I always thought of you as a patient sort. Cautious." She read on, frowning. "What makes you sure you need these parts?"

"Ah, well now. I have a book."

"A book is it?"

"Yeah, a book." *Please, God, let her drop it.*

"This looks very detailed. Tell me, how is it you diagnosed the problem with the car?"

"The book." Nan waved a hand, smiled. She hadn't used such a fake smile since she'd lied to Sister Mary Teresa at nursing college, when she had told the nun she'd been at the library instead of at the pub with Teddy. "It's a fine book. Very informative."

"Is it?" Tuda flicked her gaze from the list to Nan's eyes.

Looking around the shop, anywhere except at her friend, Nan shifted from foot to foot. "Yes. A great book."

Tuda's eyes narrowed. "Are ya sure it's a great book and not a great bloke?"

CHAPTER 10

The garage walls seemed to close in on Nan. "A bloke? And where would I be getting myself a bloke?"

"Good question. Where?" Tuda placed the list on the workbench and waited.

And waited.

Nan's knees were shaking. If these encounters regarding Dutch didn't stop making her heart beat faster than seemed humanly possible, she would meet the new doctor sooner rather than later. She'd be having a heart attack.

Apparently, she was out of practice with her fake smile; Tuda wasn't buying it. Nan tugged the scarf around her neck. "Is it hot in here? I feel hot."

"I bet you do. Well?" Tuda's eyebrows rose, leaving enough horizontal lines to write a musical score. "Is there something you want to tell me?"

Want to tell you? "No."

The garage door that led into the shop creaked open. Paddy held the phone receiver to his chest. His curly white hair was plastered down with Brylcreem. He winked at Nan. "Tuda, I've got Shamus Finn on the line. He's wanting to know if his auto parts came in?"

Nan swung around. Finn's car was parked on the other side of the garage. *Please, don't let him come by. Please.*

Even above the pounding sound of her heartbeat, Nan could hear Tuda's guttural growl. "Ya tell Finn, for the fiftieth time already, when the postman delivers his parts, I'll let him know. Until then, tell him to stop calling and shut his piehole."

Paddy shook his head and rubbed the phone receiver up and down his chest. "I can't tell him that."

"Then tell him what ya want, but don't be bothering me with Finn again." Her words had increased in volume.

Looking toward the ceiling, Paddy said into the phone, "Sorry, Shamus—I mean, Officer Finn. The parts are still in transit . . ." Paddy closed the door behind him.

"That Finn. If ever I wanted to throw someone under a bus."

"He's the worst," Nan agreed. "He's been snooping around my house, looking for the flyboy, but it's only an excuse to bother me." Her pulse pounded in her ears. She'd used the word "flyboy." What a stupid mistake. Perhaps Tuda hadn't caught it.

"He still after you? Still asking you to marry him?"

"I'd sooner marry one of his pigs."

"There wouldn't be much difference, except the pig wouldn't come with an ailing mother."

"I pray he stops annoying me."

"Tell me, Nan. What on earth is a flyboy?"

Nan shrugged. "Oh, it's American slang for a pilot."

"Ya don't say. Where did you pick up such a word?"

"The BBC."

"Right. The BBC." Holding a tool, Tuda asked, "Now, Nan. What's this thing called in my hand?"

"A tool." She felt the collar of her sweater sticking to her neck.

"What sort of tool is it?"

"Why is that important? Don't you know?"

"Because for me to believe you wrote this list," Tuda said, "that you diagnosed your car with only the aid of a book, I'd have to believe you knew the difference between a socket wrench and a screwdriver."

Fifty-fifty chance of being right. "It's a socket wrench."

Tuda smiled. "Not even close. This is a tire iron."

Nan focused on the grease spots on the floor. "Look, if you don't want to help me, that's fine."

The tire iron clanked onto the bench, startling Nan. "Level with me, or you won't get a blessed thing."

Nan let out a sigh. "Best you don't know."

"Not helping unless I do."

Nan glanced around to be sure no one was listening before she whispered, "That poor fellow that washed up today, you know the one?"

"The bomber boy from the Wellington crew?"

Nan crossed her arms over her chest. "That's just it. He wasn't from the Wellington crew, at least not the one that went down on Collins's farm."

"How do you know that?"

"I've got the wounded pilot in my bed."

Tuda's hand went to her mouth. Her eyes widened. "No."

"Yes. He came to me in the middle of the night, bleeding. I promised to patch up his wounds, and then he was supposed to be on his way." She paused. "I decided to help him escape over the border. He's planning to fix up my car. Now, you can turn us in to the Garda or LDF or the Irish Army—"

"I'd sooner have a bad rash on my face. How badly is he injured?"

Nan sucked in a breath. *That arm.* She didn't like the way the lacerated edges pulled away or the pus or the smell. "I think he'll be fine. Just a cut to the arm that required stitches. And he jarred an old injury to his knee."

"You can count on me for anything, Nan. Anything. Including helping him. Did he really think he'd be able to install all these hoses and whatnots with an injured arm?"

"Optimistic. But what if we're found out? There's jail time for citizens who violate the Emergency Act."

"In theory, I suppose. No one's been brought up on charges yet."

"Yet." Nan wished there were some other way besides dragging Tuda into her scheme. "No one's been caught, yet. What if Finn catches us? He's angling for a permanent Garda post. He'd do anything to make himself look good."

"We can outsmart that lard-arse." Tuda hooked her thumbs into the back pockets of her overalls. "Besides, I'd like to think that if one of my twins were in need of escaping, there'd be women like us to help him. But tell me, Nan. One thing."

"All right."

"Are you sharing your bed with the bomber boy?"

Nan slapped her arm. "The cheek on ya. No, of course not."

"Is it because he's ugly?"

"It's because I'm a good Catholic girl. Please, don't tease me about him." The thought of Dutch between her sheets caused a ripple of goose bumps to trickle down her spine.

"Okay, okay. Tell your pilot—does he have a name?"

"Dutch."

Tuda grinned. "The Flying Dutchman?"

"Just 'flyboy.'"

"Flyboy is it? So, he's your secret flyboy?"

"Not mine." She felt her body smoldering like a turf fire. No man since Teddy had even lit a match in her heart. Why did Dutch Whitney manage to stoke her soul?

Tuda's eyes gleamed and sparkled. "You tell Dutch I'll get his parts quicker than my husband can drain a Guinness. I'll be out to your place early tomorrow morning, by six."

Nan frowned. "I thought you had to send for them?"

A grin—*no, more of a smirk,* Nan thought—split across Tuda's face. "Sure now, I have the parts. Finn's order."

"Finn's order? Didn't you say they hadn't arrived yet?"

"He takes his time paying his bills, so I take my time fixing his car. I'll help get Dutch on his way in no time."

Nan put her hand on Tuda's. "Thank you."

Tuda winked. "It's my pleasure. I'm glad for a bit of excitement. And it's about time you found yourself a new love."

"Don't be daft." Yet her body suddenly ached to be held. Held and kissed. Cherished by his touch, his words, his gaze upon hers.

"Did I hit a chord?"

Like an Irish harp, but Nan wasn't about to admit it. At the sound of footsteps, Nan turned, gaping at the woman entering the garage.

"If it isn't herself, our new doctor. Hello, Dr. Mann."

"Hello, Mrs. Quinn," the doctor said in her American accent. She had wavy, shoulder-length mink-colored hair, clear skin, and deep-brown eyes. She could have been one of those American movie stars, a real looker with a magazine-worthy figure. "Is my car ready?"

"Indeed it is, and if you'd please, call me Tuda. I'd like you to meet our extraordinary midwife, Nan O'Neil."

"Juliet Mann." She held out a manicured hand. Nan wondered if the lovely American had brought nail polish with her; she'd be hard-pressed to find any in Ireland these days.

"A pleasure to meet you, Dr. Mann." The doctor's hand was soft, her handshake firm.

"Just call me Juliet. I've heard so many great things about you. My uncle said he counted on you more than his stethoscope where the women of the town were concerned."

"Ah, go on ya. Dr. Glennon is too kind. Juliet. What a lovely name."

The doctor smelled like an expensive Dublin perfume counter—lilies and vanilla. "Mom thought it best to give me a girlie name to go along with 'Mann.'" Juliet smiled.

Americans had such grand teeth. All straight and white. Nan tongued the space at the back of her mouth, where a molar used to be.

The doctor must be in her late thirties, she thought, though Juliet could have passed for Nan's age, maybe even younger. There were no wrinkles branching out from her eyes. No parentheses around her mouth. No furrows feathering up from her lips.

Nan brushed her drab hair behind her shoulders. Juliet was probably the sort of woman Dutch would be drawn to. Not plain like Nan, a small-town girl who smelled of antiseptic and turf, with a missing tooth.

Juliet touched the pearl necklace that dangled over her silk blouse. "I hope we'll be good friends as well as medical colleagues. I'm going to rely on you to keep doing what you're doing. You only call me in if a case needs extra help. Then I'll be there. Okay?"

Nan took an instant liking to the tall American. "Okay, same as with your uncle. Call me Nan."

"Sure, love to. Hey, you need a ride? It's getting dark."

"No, I have my bicycle. I best be on my way."

"Yes." Tuda's lips spread into a mischievous grin. "The night is young and so are you."

"You got yourself a fella waiting?" Juliet inspected the tire with a kick of her polished high-heel shoe.

More like a headache. "Not hardly in this town." And if Nan wasn't careful, if she didn't pray hard enough for strength against her fleshy self, he might turn into a sinful heartache.

CHAPTER 11

Dutch drummed his fingers on the mantel, beside the picture of Jesus pointing to the Sacred Heart.

Where had Nan hidden his gun?

He scanned the room for the hundredth time. He'd been through the cabinet where blue-willow-patterned plates and teacups hung, searched the spotlessly clean scullery, even poked between the pans. He'd started upstairs to the loft, but halfway up, a wave of nausea overtook him. Sinking to the steps, he focused on the cat at the bottom of the stairway. Mr. Dee couldn't be spinning. It had to be him.

Stay calm, he told himself. *This will pass.* He held his head in his hands for what seemed like an hour, but couldn't have been more than five minutes, until the dizziness finally stabilized. The pain shooting through his arm did not go away, though.

When he rose, his knee cried foul. He looked up the steps that led to the loft and decided maybe he'd try going up there following a bath.

After soaking in the tub for thirty minutes, he did feel better. The gun had to be in the loft somewhere. Or not. He hadn't had any luck in the hiding place in the wall, but perhaps there was another secret hiding place for weapons. That gave him an idea. He'd poke around the fireplace.

He got out of the bath and dressed. Shaved. And then, he stared at the massive fireplace and hearth in the main room of the cottage.

Perhaps in the hob, the seat within the hearth, there might be a hiding place. "Excuse me, Mr. Dee," he said to the cat sitting there, enjoying the warmth of the fire.

Dutch skimmed his fingers over the fireplace stones, stopping to wiggle and nudge the stones that seemed promising.

A throbbing ache ripped through his arm. He withdrew, stepped back, and tried to ignore the burn shooting up to his neck and down to his fingertips. He clamped his teeth against the surge. The pain always came in waves, like the tide, pounding and then receding. *This one would pass, too. Eventually.*

He'd tried to keep the bandage dry in the bath but hadn't been careful enough. The stitches must have been disturbed; when he'd taken off his shirt, blood had blossomed through the gauze.

He felt relief as the pain subsided. At least no blood had seeped through the material. There was a seed of worry inside him, but he followed the advice he'd given to his crew: *Don't fret about the possibility of German fighters appearing from nowhere. Focus on the mission.*

Pain was normal. *Had to hurt before it healed.* "Right, Mr. Dee? Carry on?"

The cat stared at him.

Dutch rubbed his clean-shaven chin. What had she done with the weapon? It wasn't so much that he wanted to use the gun; he merely wanted to locate it. Just in case he had to defend himself. And Nan.

The cat strutted across Dutch's bare feet. Rubbing against the back of the man's calves, Mr. Dee filled the room with his purr.

"Yes, I want to protect you, too. I don't suppose you know where she hid my gun?"

The tabby bounded away into the scullery, followed by the sound of the cat door flapping closed.

He wished he could do that. Get out of this cabin. He wanted to be working on the Ford, figuring out how to escape over the border, not rummaging through Nan's belongings, hoping to run across his gun.

A grin stretched his lips. She had nice things, though. Simple. But nice. Clean. Uncomplicated.

Not like his family home in Toronto, where antiques and gold-framed art cluttered every inch of space. He'd cleared his bedroom of unnecessary stuff, much to his mother's confusion. To her, the possessions symbolized security, a connection with her ancestors. To him, they spoke of generational burdens.

Dutch approached the mantel and studied the silver-framed wedding photo beside a chipped statue of Saint Patrick. The couple stood together, smiling, the sea behind them. Nan was only five foot two or so, her husband no taller. With his thin, fine, elegant features, Teddy reminded Dutch of a porcelain figurine his mother had displayed in her living room curio cabinet.

Nan didn't say much about her husband. Dutch wondered how he'd died. Had she been there? Nursed him through an illness that claimed him despite her efforts? The man wasn't exactly a picture of robust health. Delicate seeming. *Bet a wind could have knocked him over.*

Was that the type of man Nan preferred? A poet with a pen? If so, Dutch didn't stand a chance. He was more of a warrior with a gun. John Wayne, not Cole Porter.

"Wrong thinking, old chap," he muttered with an English accent, trying to mimic his commanding officer, who, at that minute over in England, must have been thinking Dutch was dead.

A stab radiated through his arm and coiled around his heart. He wondered if his CO had contacted Dutch's mother. What would the telegram say? *MIA?* Or *killed in action? Poor Mom. Getting that telegram would be her worst nightmare.*

Dutch steadied himself against the mantel. He was dizzy again. *Better sit down. Drink water.* Only dehydrated. *Only.*

Pivoting too fast on his good leg, he felt pain pierce his other knee. He limped across to the table and lowered himself onto a chair.

He poured a glass of water from an earthen pitcher, downing the liquid in one deep pull. He'd sat here the first night. He peered down. She'd cleaned his blood from the floor.

A flash of heat washed over him. He wiped a bead of sweat from his forehead. *Funny.* A few minutes ago, he was shivering. A metallic taste overcame his mouth.

Fever.

He had a fever. And his heart was pounding, pumping against his ribs. *Mild fever. That was all.* The aspirin he'd taken before the bath hadn't kicked in yet. *It would,* he assured himself. *It better.* Some stupid fever wasn't going to stop him.

His teeth began to chatter. He felt frozen, from his bare feet all the way up to his shoulders.

Best to get moving, get the blood circulating. Maybe he'd make the trek back upstairs to the loft. His gun had to be hidden somewhere up there. This time, he'd use the cane.

He reached for the walking stick he'd propped against the table. It skidded from his grasp and fell. The smacking sound echoed about the cabin. Reaching down, his arm revolted with a sharp, stabbing pain. Swallowing hard, he pushed down the ache.

He drank the rest of the water in the glass. *Forget the cane. Later for the loft.* He was too cold.

He stood, stumbled to the chair next to the fireplace, and landed on the drooping cushioned seat. He grabbed the throw from the chair arm and positioned the knitted blanket over his legs.

It smelled like Nan. *Sweet. Lavender. Soap.* He inhaled deeply, his heart responding with a swell of emotions that nearly sank him. His teeth were chattering, and he clamped his jaw shut, sending his body into spastic quivers.

The cabin door swung open. Nan stood there, the dark room barely revealing her features. Even in this light, he could make out the curves of her slender body. She'd cinched the waist of her raincoat with a belt. Red hair flared from under her beret.

"What's this? Didn't you think to light the lamp?" Her pleasant smile drifted away, and her eyes carried concern. "Dutch? Are you all right?"

"I'm fine. Just wet. You know. Took a bath. Now I'm cold." His words came out far too clipped. He wished he could turn off the shivers and turn on the calm. The chattering of his teeth left him no choice but to clamp his mouth shut again. Took all his strength to resist the shakes. He lost. His body shook.

"Ah, don't be alarmed with the shivers. Let them go. It's your body fighting off an infection."

He cut a glance to his arm. *Good. Still no blood seeping through.* "I don't have an infection. Cold from the bath is all."

"What you need is rest. The fever will pass. Get in bed."

"Bed? No. I'm fine. Now that you're home, maybe we can look at the car again." The prompt he sent to his legs, and the rest of his body, to stand up and declare he was more than capable of working on the Ford, fell short of actual movement. Instead, his arm replied with a sharp stab, and his knee froze like water poured over ice.

"Not tonight. Bed. Rest. The car will still be there tomorrow."

"What are you, my mother?"

She placed her hands on her hips. "Do I look like your mother?"

"Only the frown." His lips quivered. "I'm sorry. I'm sorry for everything. I shouldn't be here. You shouldn't have let me in. Shouldn't have let me stay."

"Hush. We're in too deep to stop now, but please, Dutch. If am to help you, do as I say."

"Yeah, yeah. Okay. I need to rest."

"All you need."

"The parts. Did you get them?"

"They'll be here tomorrow. Tuda will bring them along with her tool kit. We'll have the Ford off and running to the border in no time a'tall."

"You told her about me? Can you trust her?"

"She figured it out, I'm afraid. And yes. We can trust her with our lives. Up you go." She offered her hands. Her touch warmed his skin, sent waves of prickling sensations up his spine. She helped pull him out of the chair. They stood together, peering into each other's eyes. She looked away, bit her lip, and then snuggled her body against his.

A groan rattled up his throat.

"Are ya in pain?"

"Something like that."

She reached her arm around his waist and pulled him into her to support him. Dizziness fell over him. This time, he needed her help to walk.

"What if I'd been a German pilot come to your door?"

"I would have shooed you away."

Somehow, he didn't believe she'd have the heart to turn an injured pilot away into the darkness, but he hoped for her sake she would have.

Entering the bedroom, he gazed at her. Her red hair framed her face and cascaded down along her long pale neck, which led to an opening in her blouse where a gold Celtic cross peeked out. Her lips were perfectly proportioned to her wide-set eyes.

"You have a really pretty profile," he blurted. Wished he could take it back. What happened to his control? First his body, now his mouth. A bead of sweat dripped down his back.

A smile dimpled her cheek. "Ah, go on with ya, big fella. Enough with the blarney."

"How come every time I give you a compliment, you accuse me of blarney?" They paced to the edge of the bed, where she let go of him. The mattress squeaked under his weight.

"You don't have to say such things to me. I'm your nurse, not your girl. What's this? You made the bed?"

"Force of habit. Always makes me feel better." He felt disappointment pound through him. Of course he wasn't even in the running for anything besides a nuisance. Or a cause. The Irish and their causes.

She threw back the bedcovers. "Get in," she said.

He was aware of her gaze as he inched his way along the edge of the bed into the open sheets. Moving seemed such an effort. Even the weight of the blankets hurt his arm. His flesh felt on fire.

"I'll make your tea and have a look at your arm. You rest."

Dutch gave in to her warmth. Tomorrow, he'd find his gun and get the Ford running. Tonight, he'd let her spoil him.

◆ ◆ ◆

Nan shoved so much turf onto the bedroom's roaring fire, the room felt as hot as an Italian summer day, yet Dutch continued to shiver. She stood beside the bed, dipping another clean towel into a bowl of steaming water. She'd folded his pajama sleeve up to keep the material dry, providing access to the wound.

Wringing out the towel, her hands stung from the heat and the wet, and her fingers were raw. She tried to push down her panic, but if his fever didn't break soon, Dutch might die in her bed this very night.

"Here we go." She positioned the hot cloth over his wound. The technique ought to have brought down the swelling, but so far, her efforts had failed. The wound smelled yeasty, and the angry red line oozed with a yellow discharge.

Altogether very bad, indeed. She summoned her most pleasant expression, the one she'd perfected over the years when a patient's situation called for prayer. Leaving the cloth on his wound, she moved to the foot of the bed. "Let's get this quilt on top of you, and you'll be grand as new come morning." She unfolded the bedspread and tucked it around him, leaving his arm exposed so she could continue to soak it.

"Colorful," he mumbled. "You make it?"

"No, I'm not that talented. It was my grandmother's."

She returned to the washbasin, laid another cloth into the hot water, and replaced the cooled towel with the hot one.

Please, sweet baby Jesus. Let this work.

Dutch gave her a weak smile. It settled deep inside her. She turned away and stared into the blazing turf in the fireplace.

No way could she allow this man into her heart. She'd resist. And within a few hours, he'd be on his way. Lord willing.

As long as that poor, unfortunate pilot who'd washed up yesterday remained unidentified, they had time. The Irish Army must think they had the last pilot from the Wellington. She didn't know how closely the Irish Army and the RAF were working together. Eventually, the two countries would have to reconcile who was missing, who was captured, who was dead. She looked over at Dutch. *Dear Lord, don't let him die.*

"Nan," he whispered. "Do you have another blanket, maybe?"

The mattress trembled under his shivering. Wringing her hands, she shuffled away from the bed. There were no more blankets. "Let's put something else over you." She opened the wardrobe and pulled out a thick coat made of heavy English tweed, with a fox-fur collar.

She held the coat, sniffed the fur. Teddy had bought her the garment when they'd been freezing in London on their honeymoon. Despite the weather, those had been happy days. He'd signed a book contract with a publisher there. The future was shiny as dewdrops in the morning sun. They'd planned to live here, in Grandma's cottage. No farming—neither of them was cut out for that—but she'd continue being a midwife until they had their first child; he'd write brilliant volumes of poetry. It was a life lost to her now. A life impossible to recapture.

"Here you go." She settled the old coat over Dutch and sat beside him, placing her hand over the coat. "Does that help?"

He shivered but nodded.

His face was a Valentine-rose red. With the turf roaring in the fireplace, blankets piled high, she didn't know what else to do next except pray. She faced the portrait of Jesus above the mantel.

Dear Lord. Please. Thy will be done, but please don't let him die of infection. Dutch is in your hands, but make my hands help. Tell me what to do.

She closed her eyes, launched into the Lord's Prayer, and repeated it over and over and over. A spark from the fire, as loud as a gunshot, jolted her. A quiet whisper, more an awareness than a voice, seemed to come from her soul, telling her that the only way to warm him now would be to get next to him in bed.

He needed her. There was nothing shameful here. *Nothing.* It was only herself being his nurse.

Nan wrapped his arm in gauze, then pulled off her shoes and slid into the bed beside him.

"What's this?" His eyes opened.

"'Tis nothing. Your virtue will remain intact. I'm getting you warm, that's all. You behave, you understand? Or I'll be out of here quicker than children running from the classroom for summer holiday."

He laughed, a shaky sound that chattered through his teeth. "I'm in no condition to do anything except shiver."

Her toes found his calf, her hand his belly, and her cheek his shoulder. Pressing her body against his, she felt his muscles, his soft yet hot skin, and his silky dark hair against her forehead.

He shook and groaned. His body tightened.

"It's all right, Dutch. I'm going to take good care of you," she said in her most soothing voice, hoping her words would calm him.

Turning his head to face her, he gazed into her eyes. He clutched her hand in his and held them both against his chest. "Do you think maybe the good Lord sent me here?"

"Ah, maybe."

"I think He did."

"Why did He send you?"

"I don't know yet."

His warm breath drew across her forehead. A whirling sensation tingled in her stomach. His look seemed to soar through her, to a place the nuns had always deemed sinful outside the marriage bed. *Or even in it.*

The weakest of smiles lit her lips. "Close your eyes and sleep."

His eyelids flickered, then closed. Heavy, uneven breathing followed. She knew she should untangle her fingers from his, but she didn't want to wake him. It was a massive lie; she liked holding his hand.

Closing her eyes, she recalled the sensation of her husband's arms around her. It seemed like yesterday they'd shared these sheets. She'd never even kissed another man since her husband, and here she was, beside a flyboy who couldn't wait to get his hands on his gun and return to the fight.

"Ah, men." Tears traveled down her cheek to the corner of her mouth.

With a meow, the cat jumped onto the bed, settling on top of Dutch's feet.

She sighed. She'd turned into an old crone with a cat for a companion. *Some life.* "Thanks," she whispered to Mr. Dee. "He needs your furry warmth."

The cat's purring lulled her to sleep.

The next morning, barely dawn, Nan woke to the mattress shaking. Dutch was dreaming, kicking his legs. She climbed to her elbows and gazed at him in the dull light. "It's okay, darling." He quieted back into slumber.

She stared at the man in her bed. Did she ever have a lot to confess to Father Albert once Dutch was back in England. Until then, she'd do whatever she needed to keep him safe. And herself.

A hand on his cheek was enough to check his fever, but she kissed his forehead. He tasted salty and hot. He'd stopped shaking, though his fever still raged.

Best start soaking his arm again, she thought, sliding out of bed. Maybe he'd eat something. She needed a cup of tea like a dog needed to bark. Padding into the main room, toward the cooker, she prayed that the Lord would take mercy on Dutch and bring him healing. *Fast.*

She went through the motions of making breakfast, frying bacon and cooking oatmeal, but was dreading what she'd need to do if his fever didn't break; she'd have no choice but go to the doctor for help. Dr. Mann—Juliet—might well turn them in. It was, after all, the law.

Nan delivered breakfast to the table beside the bed, along with fresh hot water and towels. "Dutch. Wake up."

His eyes opened wide. "Where am I? Where's my crew?"

"You're safe. They're safe. Remember?"

He looked around the cabin, and his expression softened. "Nan. Good morning." A smile swept the corners of his mouth, though pain was in his eyes.

"Have your tea. And I'll see to re-dressing your wound." She placed a tray beside him. He sipped the tea and watched her.

She cut the gauze around his arm, but it stuck to the wound, prompting her to place a wet towel over the bandage until it loosened.

Her insides pinged as she inspected his gaping, swollen laceration. *Terrible, awful.* This wound was beyond her capabilities to heal, and she knew it. Her attempts to bring down the swelling with more hot towels seemed futile, but she had to at least try.

"Are you in much pain?" she asked, placing a clean wet cloth over his arm.

The teacup rattled as he set it on the tray. "No."

"If you're not hurting a'tall, that means you've got nerve damage or your arm is dead. So don't go all Hemingway on me. Be honest."

He glanced at the wound before pinning his focus on her. "It hurts like someone stomped on it, lit it on fire, and then a mad dog got ahold of it."

"That's more like it."

"If you say so."

"You know what I mean." She couldn't recall being more afraid for one of her patients than this one. Disaster all around if he succumbed to his fever.

The blast of a car horn broke their connection.

"Who's that?"

"Probably Tuda." She repositioned the hot towel over his arm, then strode to the window. Outside, heavy rain banged against the glass.

"She's here. I'll be right back." Nan paced out, intending to unlatch the gate, but Tuda had already opened it. She roared the van into the yard, barely missing the cat as she skidded to a stop.

"You nearly flattened Mr. Dee. What's the rush?"

"I'll tell ya. I passed Father Albert on his bike. He said he's on his way here to talk to ya."

The slice of bacon Nan had eaten for breakfast lurched in her stomach.

"What about?"

"I dunno, but it can't be good. He's not one for a friendly visit, especially in the rain. If ya got the flyboy inside, I suggest we hide him. Now."

CHAPTER 12

Nan led Tuda into the bedroom. The cat sped past them, jumped onto the bed and sat next to Dutch's head, then meowed into his ear.

Dutch opened his eyes and looked up. "What's going on?"

"We're hiding you, or Nan's midwife days are over. I'm Tuda, by the way. Out of bed," she instructed him.

"The girl mechanic?"

"I've been called worse. Can you please get your handsome young self out of bed?"

Nan opened the hiding cubby and batted the cobwebs with a towel. "Get in here."

Dutch angled his legs off the mattress. His feet trembled, hovered above the floor.

"Do you need help?" Nan asked.

"No. I'm fine."

But he wasn't fine. His eyes were glassy. His face was red. He shivered. He stretched his hand toward the headboard, missed, and fell back onto the mattress.

Nan sucked in a gasp. Her hand went to her throat.

"Ah, for the love of Mary. Don't pass out," Tuda said, lifting him up.

He got up and stumbled toward the open hiding place. "I'm fine."

"Fine as snow in a volcano," Tuda said, helping him across the room. He leaned into her, seemingly incapable of making the journey on his own.

"Finn? Is he here again?" Dutch asked.

"Worse." Nan grabbed her robe from the peg beside the door. "Father Albert."

"Your priest? How is that worse?"

"Finn can send us to jail, but Father Albert can send us to hell. In you go." Nan swung the robe over Dutch's shoulders and slid her arm around his back. "I can take him from here. I've got him." Tuda slipped away.

He leaned on Nan with so much weight, she fought to keep her balance. A drip of sweat streamed from his forehead and trickled over his cheek, yet he still shivered. *A very bad sign, indeed,* Nan thought. The gauze around his wound was seeping, the stitched area bulging.

"In you go." She guided him through the small opening.

He stopped. "I won't fit. It's too small. You won't get the door closed."

"In my grandmother's day, she'd stick three men in there, no problem."

"They must have been leprechauns."

"Just get in. There's a panel that slides open beside the seat. You can see inside the cabin. But not a sound out of you. Understand? Sit." She released him, pressed him down on the bench.

Before he had a chance to agree, she shut the door. From inside, his muffled voice said, "Hey, it's pitch dark. And cold."

Nan grabbed the coat from her bed. "Don't be such a baby," she said, opening the door. She threw the coat in over his lap. "Let me open the viewing hole." She climbed in and the back of her legs squeezed against his knees. He let out a groan. She fumbled around, searching for the secret panel. "Do you suffer from claustrophobia?"

"No. I only suffer."

"Don't we all?" She found the panel. Sliding it open, a small amount of light filled the compartment. She patted his chest. "You going to be okay?"

"Peachy."

"Not another sound. You understand?" For once, he obeyed without comment. "Be careful not to knock your arm."

"You mean don't move?"

Backing out and then closing the door, Nan spun on her heel. Tuda had already made the bed and stuffed the medical supplies beneath. "The poor lamb. He's really sick, isn't he?" Her voice was a whisper.

"Yes. And I'm worried."

"We'll sort him out later."

A fist beat on the door three times. Each knock sent a hit to Nan's gut. "Father Albert."

Tuda nodded. "I'll make the tea. We'll act real natural-like."

"Like I hide a flyboy in my closet every day."

"Just like your granny and the IRA. It's in your blood."

They hurried into the main room of the cabin. Tuda seized the teapot and dashed a load of new tea leaves in before filling it with boiling water. Her motions were so fast, it was like watching a sped-up film.

"Will ya open the door already, Nan O'Neil? I'm getting a soaking out here, waiting."

Nan squared her shoulders and opened the door. "Sorry, Father. I was making myself decent." The comment struck her as an odd choice of words, considering what had just transpired. Was still transpiring. Oh, how the confession booth beckoned her.

"Welcome, Father. Come in. May I take your coat? And what brings you to my door? Will you take tea?"

Nan helped the priest take off his sopping coat. While she hooked the garment onto a peg, Father Albert removed his wet trilby, shook the water from it, and placed it on a hook beside the coat. He slicked back his thinning hair with a wet hand.

"I'm not here on a social visit, but I'll take tea. And bread if you have it."

"Hello again, Father." Tuda sliced the soda bread Nan had left on the counter.

"What are you doing here, child? Don't you have a petrol station to run?" He rubbed raindrops off his thick glasses with a handkerchief.

"She's fixing up my Ford," Nan said. "I've decided, after last winter, a car may help me move about more quickly."

"Getting old, are ya?" He shook his head.

"I suppose I am, Father. Will you sit by the fire?"

He made a clucking sound with his tongue. "You ought to marry again, Nan." He sat in front of the fireplace. "Will ya give us some privacy, Tuda?"

"Of course, Father." She had almost made it outside into the downpour when he said, "By the way, are you planning to buy Mass cards for your da?"

"Of course, Father. I will."

"May he rest in peace."

"Amen." They all blessed themselves.

Tuda closed the door behind her. Nan delivered the tea, plus a slice of bread on her finest china, the plate with the pink roses and the golden rim.

"That soda bread looks dry. Have you your apple butter?"

"No. I'm sorry, Father. I know it's your favorite, but I'm still waiting on the jars. Will strawberry preserves do?"

He waved his hand. "Just the tea. Sit here, my child."

She sat on the chair opposite him. "What brings you out here, Father?"

"I'm on my way to give last rites. The fancy lady doctor told me Pat Connor is a goner. But I have business with you, too."

"Have you?"

He sipped his tea loudly. "I've heard some salacious gossip concerning you."

She felt guilt pouring through her. She'd been a very bad girl indeed, all cozy in bed with her flyboy last night. But how could the priest know? Or did he realize Dutch was hiding in her wall? The tea burned the roof of her mouth. "Oh? And what might that be?"

"It's come to my attention that some of the women in the parish are practicing the rhythm method."

"Are they?" Nan knew they were. And still conceiving.

"And I hear you've taught them how it works. You know what we call people who practice such things?"

"Parents."

"Sinners." Deep wrinkles appeared at the corners of his eyes. "Don't make a jest of it, Nan O'Neil. This is very serious church business."

And so was having ten children when the poor mother could barely find the means to raise two. "I'm sorry, Father. You're wrong. I haven't taught the method to anyone." She'd merely explained how their bodies function, how each month they have a cycle. For some, she had to read the pamphlet aloud, not because the women couldn't read, but because they were too ashamed to talk or think or even read about such things.

Someone must have overheard and gone running to the priest.

He nailed her with an accusing glare. "Are ya telling me not a one? Not a word regarding the sinful practice?"

"Father, if a parishioner comes to you, confesses her wrongdoings, do you go and tell the Garda?"

His lips pinched together. "What are you getting at?"

"I'm sworn to confidentiality as much as you are. I will not betray my patients."

He pointed his finger at her. "So you are."

She leaned back and said nothing.

"Practicing the rhythm method is a sin." He jabbed his finger with every word.

If he only knew what she was really up to, he'd slap her. "That may be true, but that's between themselves and the Lord and you. I swear on the cross, I have not given anyone instruction on the rhythm method." *Only confirmed a thing or two.*

"See that ya don't." His nose twitched. "And you tell them, if they ask, that married people are to have sex with the full expectation that children could result each time. A married couple should in no way interrupt God's plan for them to have lots of children. To do anything else is a grave sin. Tell them to confess to me promptly."

"Perhaps that's your place to say, not mine."

"Ah, the cheek on ya. Mind, Nan. I may not be able to see what you're up to, but the good Lord does." He pointed skyward. "There's no hiding from Him. You understand your immortal soul is at risk?"

More than he knew. "I do, Father. I didn't mean any disrespect or disobedience."

He set the teacup on the stand beside the chair. "My sermon on Sunday will touch upon this very topic." He stood. "I've got to be on my way. I'll see you in church on Sunday."

"Of course, Father. Unless the good Lord decides it's time to provide another member to your flock."

"I'd be happy if for once a member of my flock would do me the favor of dying when there isn't the storm of the century brewing."

"Thanks for stopping by."

"One more thing," he said as Nan helped him back into his rain slicker. "Don't cross me on this matter. I will not tolerate insubordination."

She nodded. "I know, Father."

"And why haven't you been to confession lately?"

Because she was heaping up the sins, and would come clean all at one time. "I'll go to confession soon, Father."

She breathed a sigh of relief as she watched him ride his bicycle out of the yard and through the pouring rain.

Tuda swung the barn door open. She ran across the courtyard and into the cottage. "What did he want?"

"The village women to stop sinning. Stop using the rhythm method."

"If men could get pregnant, they'd make the rhythm method a holy sacrament."

"Tuda, you'll surely go to hell for that remark."

"Probably. But you'll be beside me. We best get the source of your damnation out of the closet."

Nan carried clean towels into the bedroom, her nerves fraying like a used wool sweater. Tuda placed a hot towel over Dutch's festering arm. He gave her a weak smile. "Are all Irish women beautiful?"

"You must have bit the Blarney stone on your way down to earth."

"He did." Nan dipped a cloth into the water, running it over his neck and chest.

His gaze settled on hers. "I should never have worked on the car yesterday."

"You're a man on a mission. Today, your mission is healing."

"Easy. Especially with two Irish angels nursing me."

Tuda signaled for Nan to join her in the other room.

Nan stood. "You rest now, Dutch. We'll be back in a second with your tea."

"I'm not hungry," he said. His voice sank into her heart. She'd seen mums in a bad way, infections setting in after birth. The doctor was called in, and sometimes he'd been able to rouse the pink back into their cheeks. Sometimes not. This was no different. Something had to be done, or Nan risked losing him.

Perhaps it was worry, or the raw sense of doom, but she felt numb. The doctor needed to be called, but Nan feared it'd be the end of her. She followed Tuda into the main room, recognizing, deep down, the only choice was to heal him.

Her friend rested a hand on the mantel and peered at the picture of Jesus. "Nan, he's in an altogether bad way. You better get the doctor."

"Yes, I must." She bit her lip. "I don't know if I can trust her, but if she turns me in, so be it."

"She's one of us." Tuda threw four bricks of turf onto the fire, stabbed it with the poker, and then tossed on two more bricks for good measure. "You can trust her."

"How do you know?"

Tuda bowed her head to the statue of the Virgin holding the baby Jesus, mumbled a prayer, and then clapped her hands clean.

"I saw her in action at Mrs. Odin's pub last night. I was there with the mister. Dr. Mann was enjoying the fiddling music, and having a grand old time. Mick Hart sat next to her at the table. Did ya hear what happened to him?"

Nan shook her head. "What now?"

"That mean old cow of his succeeded in stomping on his foot. Broke it this time."

"Ah, the poor unfortunate."

"He had no choice but to seek Dr. Mann. She fixed him real good. She laid a big old smacker of a kiss on the cast, leaving a lovely red-lipstick stain. Then she took him to Mrs. Odin's pub and bought him and everyone there a pint."

"You trust her because she drinks and kisses casts?"

"Let me finish. We're all enjoying a bit of the craic. Some grand songs last night, when who should come swaggering in like he owned the place?"

"Let me guess. Finn."

"Himself." The corner of her mouth slipped into a mischievous smile. "He took one look at Dr. Mann and made a beeline for her. Intimidated the bloke sitting next to her into giving him his seat. Juliet nodded to him, then returned her attention to the lads fiddling and drumming. A few seconds later, Finn whispered something into her ear."

"What do you think he said?"

"I dunno, but it was enough to change her expression from enjoyment to absolute disgust."

Nan covered her mouth with her hand. "The blaggard."

"So she got up, strolled over to the bar, ordered another pint, and who do you think followed her?"

"The blaggard himself."

Tuda nodded. "He got real close to her, backed her against the wall with that belly of his. She listened for a second before she said something to him. He got that cocky look. You know the one?" Tuda made a face.

Nan laughed. "Ya have him down."

"Dr. Mann threw her drink in his face."

"No." Nan laughed. "You're joking."

"Ah, she did. She did. If you could have seen the look on Finn's face. I'm afraid the doctor made herself an enemy last night. But she showed herself to be one of us. You can ask her for help. She's no fan of Finn's."

"But there's still Sergeant Halpin to contend with."

"Paul? Don't be daft. He's far too focused on Kelly. Do you know what he did?"

"What?"

"He filled up his car yesterday, and he paid me twice. His mind is elsewhere. Isn't the baby due soon?"

"About two weeks."

"Go get the doctor. I'll stay with Dutch."

"I'll have to take the risk," Nan said. Even if Dr. Mann turned her in and she ended up in prison for a couple of years, at least Dutch would have a chance to survive.

Prison. The thought chilled her. Not that her family members hadn't seen their share of jail cells. But what would the expecting mothers of Ballyhaven do with her locked up? Yet how could she put herself before the sick lad in her bed? She'd made him a promise.

"Shall I go into town and fetch the doc?" Tuda asked.

"No. I can't let you do that. I don't want you to be involved."

Tuda laughed. "Then what am I doing here?"

"If this goes wrong, I don't want you to go down the drain with me. You must remain innocent."

"Innocent, indeed. As innocent as a fox with chicken feathers in its mouth."

Wind bucked the window, causing the curtains to sway. Rain pelted the glass and the thatch roof. The fire sizzled from drops slanting their way down the chimney.

"It's raining something fierce. If you won't let me go, then at least take my van. I can stay here and look after him. What sort of name is that, Dutch? Has he a brother named English? A sister named French? If you two have a child, you can name her Eire."

The thought of having his child sent a shiver dancing across Nan's skin. "He goes by 'Dutch' because he liked hot chocolate as a lad."

"Then good thing his ma didn't nickname him 'Coco,' like that godless woman shacking up with a Nazi general in Paris. I'll never buy another dress from her as long as I live."

"You have a Chanel dress?"

Tuda reached into her pocket. "No, but I won't get one now, either. My purse is more suited to Limerick tweeds, anyway."

Tuda pressed the van's key into Nan's palm. It felt warm against her skin.

"Get him to drink some water, but I think he'll sleep." Nan took her coat from the peg.

"Go on. I've nursed boys before. Watch for reverse. The gear's a bit sticky."

Like the situation. "Thanks. I'll hurry." She buttoned her raincoat. "I'll be back soon."

"I'll pray for you." Tuda stood in the door, the rain splashing on the threshold.

And Nan prayed also, all the way into the village.

CHAPTER 13

Amid the vicious downpour, Nan pulled up in front of River House, the doctor's three-story Victorian at the border of town, where the river split in two directions. It was a place Nan knew well. Dr. Glennon had lived about three miles from River House, but he'd converted it into his office, with guest rooms upstairs. The first floor contained examination rooms and a surgery.

Glennon was the sort of Irishman who made every girl in the county swoon. There'd been tears when he wed a rich American girl, but no one could fault him. Kate Glennon was generous with her money. She even turned the town's one-room library into a wonderful place for adults and children alike. Over her husband's objections, a ruined chapel had become a lovely wedding venue.

Paul and Kelly Halpin had been married there. Nan had lost hope of ever having a wedding in the cozy chapel. Seemed the good Lord had other plans for her. A needling sensation circled around her brain. If circumstances were different, maybe she and Dutch . . .

Am I daft! With a shake of her head, Nan pushed the thought away.

When the war broke out, Glennon volunteered for the Royal Army Medical Corps, which caused a squabble with his wife. In the end, Kate packed up their three sons and returned to New York. The doctor was on surgical staff in a military hospital outside London. Both he and his wife vowed to return to Ireland once the war ended.

Juliet Mann was Kate Glennon's niece, and with doctors in such short supply, she'd offered to fill in. Regardless of being "only" a woman and all such nonsense, everyone in town knew they were lucky to have her.

Nan parked the van and saw a warm light glowing in the windows. She also noticed Mrs. Norman—on that day working for the doctor instead of Father Albert—peering out at her through the parted lace curtains.

She hoped the nosy housekeeper wouldn't think too much of her visit. It wouldn't do to get her curiosity up.

The wind blew through Nan's raincoat as she hurried up the steps to the porch, not that it provided much shelter. The cold air found a path up her pant legs. There was no escape from the damp tentacles of an Irish gale.

Mrs. Norman opened the door with a smile, revealing her overlapping front teeth. Gray hair escaped from the tight bun.

"Morning, Mrs. Norman."

"Well, if it isn't Nan O'Neil. Come on in out of the cold."

"Thanks. Is Dr. Mann in?"

"She is. She just went into her office."

"Can I see her?"

"Go down the hall, turn left, and knock on the door. If she answers, you'll see her, so. 'Cause she's not invisible." She laughed at her own quip.

Nan obliged with a chuckle and moved on. She drew a deep breath before she knocked. "Come in," she heard Dr. Mann respond.

"Have you a minute to consult about a patient?"

The doctor stood at a coatrack. She tugged a white lab coat on over her sky-blue dress with black trim that matched the row of buttons down the front. "Yeah, of course. Come in."

Mrs. Norman stood behind Nan. "Shall I bring some tea?"

"Have you time, Nan?" The doctor went to her desk. She signaled for Nan to take the chair across from her.

"No, thank you, I don't." Nan sat on the leather chair and clutched the edge of the seat.

"Shut the door, Mrs. Norman," Juliet said.

"All right then." Mrs. Norman grinned, then closed the door behind her.

Juliet buttoned the lab coat. "I half expected to see you today. I know why you're here."

Nan's mouth went dry. "Oh? And how are you knowing that?"

"Doesn't take a genius. Listen, I think it's a bum deal."

"You do?" Nan heard her heart pounding.

"Sure I do. It's not right."

"You don't think so?"

"Of course I don't." Juliet's mouth was a lipstick line of disapproval.

Nan focused on her feet. Why in heaven's name had Tuda thought Juliet would understand? Perhaps Nan needed to bolt before it was too late. Or had the doctor called the Garda already? She imagined Officer Halpin finding Tuda at the cottage, nursing the flyboy.

Nan pushed back into the chair. "Did you tell anyone?" The words came out choked.

"I'd never. Patient privilege, kid. It's sacred. Didn't they send you notice? They said they would."

"Not yet." Nan shook her head, confused. "The Garda or LDF?"

Dr. Mann squinted, lifted her chin. "Why would the Garda send word that Margot Dorian has asked me to deliver her baby, instead of you? Is it against the law in Ireland to change medical practices?"

Nan's mouth gaped. Then she laughed. "Not a'tall. And did she, now?"

"I'm sorry. It's not my style to poach patients."

"You can have her with my blessings, but don't count on getting paid. They don't have two pence to rub together."

"A charity case? Great. Just what I need. So if you're not here about the stuck-up deadbeats in the stinky house, what can I do for you?"

"I have a sick patient, Dr. Mann—"

"Oh, good heavens, *Juliet*. We're colleagues."

"All right, Juliet. My patient is burning up with fever."

"That's too bad. How far along is she?"

"Ah . . . well . . . it's not a she."

"She's a he?"

Nan glanced around the tidy room, its bookcases loaded with volumes, glass-front cabinets overflowing with medicine bottles, walls advertising the doctor's many diplomas. "Definitely a he," she answered.

"Okay, kid. Spill. Who is this mystery man?"

"I'd rather not say. Could I just give you the details and ask for a course of action?"

Juliet crossed her legs. "Can't help you unless you tell me everything. Including who he is."

The scarf around Nan's neck suddenly felt as if it were strangling her. "I don't want to tell you too much. You'd be implicated should things go wrong."

Juliet studied her with dark, intense eyes. "If it's not a woman who's done something illegal to, say, end a pregnancy, I don't see why you won't tell me about the fellow." She looked Nan squarely in the eyes. "If I didn't know better, I'd say that flyboy who washed up wasn't from the Wellington crash. You hiding someone?"

Nan's chest tightened like a tourniquet.

Juliet slapped the desk. "I'll take that as an affirmative. Don't worry; on my mother's grave, I won't tell a soul, especially not that meathead Finn. What are the man's symptoms?"

The tension gripping Nan's neck released. She went into detail about the wound and what she'd done so far. Juliet listened and jotted down notes.

"I don't know what else to try," Nan pleaded. "Can you help him?"

"You did everything right, Nan. I wouldn't have done anything differently. He fell in a bog, after all. Worst place in Ireland for an open cut."

Nan's heart sank. "Is it in the Lord's hands now? Should I kneel in prayer at the church, begging the Lord for mercy?"

"Prayers? Why not, but I didn't say he's beyond help." Juliet opened a desk drawer and took out a key. "I have something new, a very powerful drug." She stood, crossed the room to a locked supply cabinet. Opening the glass door, she said, "This will do the trick. I'm not supposed to have it. Can you keep a secret?"

Nan nodded. "Of course. What is it?"

"More precious than gold. It's called penicillin. Don't ask how I came to have it, except to say there's a research scientist who's still grinning. I'll get my bag."

Nan shook her head. "You can't come. You can't afford to be involved. Please, just give me the medicine and instructions."

Juliet rooted around the cabinet. "I can't prescribe medication if I don't examine him. Let's get a move on. Time is of the essence." She found a bottle and put it into her medical bag.

"Did I wait too long?" Nan asked. An agonizing thought picked at her: Was she to be condemned for not having been bolder?

"He'll probably be fine. Infections come on quickly, but this drug is a downright miracle." Juliet put a raincoat on over her lab coat. She topped off her outfit with a fedora. "Shall we?"

Nan arrived at the door first, opened it, and Mrs. Norman jumped back. The blood drained from Nan's face. "Were you listening?" The entire town would know by noon.

Juliet pushed past Nan. "What did I tell you about listening at the door?" Her words came out low and angry.

The housekeeper backed away. "I didn't hear a word. Not a word. But I'll say a few prayers for him."

Juliet closed the distance between the two of them. In a deadly tone, she said, "Breathe a word about this to anyone and it'll be the last word you say. *Capisce?*"

The woman nodded, her double chin jiggling, fear in her eyes.

Juliet's charming smile returned. "Mrs. Norman, go make a big pot of your chicken soup for the patient. Can you do that?"

"I can. Do you want the pleasure of killing the chicken yourself?"

◆ ◆ ◆

Juliet sashayed into Nan's bedroom like some American movie star and stood at the end of the bed. "Hey, good-looking. Hear you took a tumble out of a bomber and into the bog."

Dutch tried to smile. "Like I said, all the women in Ireland are beautiful."

Juliet's laugh slid into a snort. "Something wrong with your hearing? Do I sound Irish?"

"No, but you look like an angel."

Juliet groaned, rolling her eyes upward. "Is he always like that?" she asked Nan. "Full of bull?"

"He is," Tuda answered. She sat on a chair on the other side of the bed, with Mr. Dee curled up on her lap. "He bit the Blarney stone on his way down to earth."

"Dutch, this is Dr. Mann." Nan laid a pile of clean towels on the nightstand.

Dutch's gaze went from Tuda to Juliet. "A girl mechanic and now a girl doctor? This place is upside down."

"Only if a female priest walks in," Nan said.

"Get with the twentieth century, flyboy," Juliet added. "We're not gonna be barefoot and pregnant anymore."

Nan felt a rush of heat to her cheeks. Americans were bold as brass. *Imagine saying "pregnant" out loud in mixed company.*

Juliet sat beside the bed. She raised the wet towel from his wound. "Wow, that's a beaut. How'd this happen?"

"Gift from the Nazis. Flak."

Juliet's upper lip curled. "Vermin," she uttered. "We can't rest until we rid the world of the fascist scum."

"Hear, hear." Dutch winced as she investigated his wound. "Get me across the border so I can return to the fight."

"Agreed," the doctor said. "I'll do whatever I can to help you."

"You'll help me get to Northern Ireland?"

"Yeah. Of course. I don't want to see you interned, either. How you going to get there?"

"I've a car that Tuda's fixing up," Nan said, feeling useless.

"Sounds like a good plan. How about papers? And a map?"

"I'm just figuring out clothes at this point," Nan said.

The doctor continued to raise issues Nan hadn't even considered. She, in turn, searched her mind for how and where to find everything Dutch would need. Her muscles tightened into knots.

"Will you let me help?" Juliet asked Nan. "I can get all those things. Don't ask how, but will you leave it to me?"

"Yes. Thank you." Nan's hands relaxed at her sides.

Juliet lifted Dutch's arm for a closer look, making him flinch.

"Why won't the Irish join the fight?" he asked. "What's the matter with this country?"

"Nothing," Juliet said. "Neutrality is a perfect solution for the Irish. They have no defenses. It's the only way they can manage to keep their newly founded country intact. Quite brilliant, actually. Nan, hand me a clean towel."

Nan put the towel into her grasp. "What do you think?"

Juliet laid Dutch's arm on the cloth. "I think it's a good thing you had the courage to call me, but we'll get him back on his feet in no time."

She glanced over her shoulder at Nan. "Nice job on the stitches. Couldn't have done better myself. But they'll have to come out. I'll sanitize the wound."

"Then stitches again?"

"Nope. Not after it's been infected. Best to let it heal on its own. You're gonna have a great scar there, kid." She winked at Dutch. "A good story for the family back home."

"Thanks."

Juliet snapped her bag open and began taking out supplies.

"You really a doctor?" he asked.

"You really a flyboy?"

"I've got the shrapnel wounds to prove it. What do you have?"

"This." She shook the thermometer, the glass gleaming in the lit oil lamp. "Let me stick this in your kisser. Will that be proof enough? Or do you want to roll over and I'll do the alternative method."

"Option one, Doc." With the thermometer in his mouth, he looked more like a child than an officer with a long list of bombing kills.

Nan's thoughts were racing. When the war was over, just or not, how would these young men face themselves in the mirror, knowing what they'd done? The lives they'd shattered.

"Tuda," Nan said. "You can go. I think we have it under control."

Her friend put the cat on the floor. She stood and stretched her long arms above her head. "I'm going to unload those auto parts and see what's wanting with the Ford. I've got about two hours; then I best be off before Paddy starts drinking and giving away petrol without ration books again."

Nan pulled her into a hug. "Thank you." Tears burned in her eyes. "How will I ever repay you?"

"Funny. I thought I was repaying you."

150

"You're my best friend in the world, Tuda. You know I'd do anything for you."

"I feel the same."

"Ladies," Juliet said, filling a syringe, "I hate to break up your moment, but I need boiled water. And empty bowls. Now."

"Kettle's on," Nan said. "Soon as it whistles, I'll get it."

Dutch blinked at the doctor. "What's that for?"

"What do you think?"

"Is that really necessary?"

"Afraid of needles?"

"No." His frown betrayed his apprehension.

"Don't worry, flyboy. This time you won't feel a thing. You ever have morphine?"

"Can't say that I have."

"You'll like it. It'll take the edge off. Then we'll get some penicillin on board, and you'll be good to go before you know it. Nan, pull down his pants. I'm gonna give this big boy a shot right in his rump."

Nan hesitated. "Pull down his pants?"

"I'm waiting." Juliet's impatience was clear. "Well?"

Nan's fingers trembled. "Ah, Dutch. Have ya underwear under there?"

Juliet let out an exasperated breath. "Are you kidding me? Didn't you bathe him? Stitch him up? Haven't you seen the flyboy naked?"

A hot prickling sensation coursed through Nan. "Certainly not."

"What kind of nurse are you?"

Tuda shoved Nan out of the way with her hip. "The kind that thinks about sin before medicine." Tuda tugged down Dutch's pajama pants. Nan stood behind her, sneaking a look over Tuda's shoulder.

He had underpants on. The ones she'd washed the other day. Now she felt stupid. She'd seen him in his underwear before. *Like a bathing suit, right?*

Juliet flicked the needle with her finger. "On your side, big boy. Tuda, do the honors."

He rolled onto his hip, and Tuda pulled down his drawers to expose his rump.

A gasp escaped Nan's lips.

"I'll say." Juliet grinned. "He's quite the young specimen."

Nan's entire body heated, a mix of embarrassment and desire.

The needle prick made Dutch wince.

"There. That'll do the trick. Until the next time."

Tuda rearranged his underwear. She started to pull up his pajama bottoms, but the doctor said, "Leave the pants off. This won't be his last rodeo ride."

"I'll pull up the blanket, so." Tuda flicked the covers up to his chest.

"All right, kid. Swallow this." Juliet gave him three round pills along with a glass of water.

"Thanks."

"Don't thank me yet." She opened her medical bag and reached in. "What are you two waiting for? Isn't the kettle whistling?"

Nan and Tuda stepped out of the bedroom. Nan reached for the kettle, steaming away on the cooker.

"Nan? Ya look flushed. Are you all right?"

"I'm not sure if I called the doctor soon enough. What if he takes a turn for the worse? What if he dies in my bed? Ah, it'll be my fault." *Again. Like with Teddy.* "How will I explain it? I can't dig a grave for him. Bury him behind the apple trees. He'd have no rest. Nor would I."

"You mustn't worry. Juliet will fix him up."

"It'll be on my head if he dies."

"You're wrong. You've done your best. You have only so much control over his recovery. Without you, he'd already be dead."

Dead. She squeezed her eyes shut, then opened them. *No time for thoughts like these.* She poured steaming water into a steel bowl. "I want things to be the way they used to be." More boiling water was sloshed into the next bowl, smarting as it splashed over the back of Nan's hand.

"And how far back do you want to go? Three years? You think you could have changed what happened on that day?"

Nan's heart was aching. "Please, don't."

"Or maybe twenty years? To that day in Cork when your life and your ma's changed forever."

"You're tormenting me!"

"Teddy's death was not your fault any more than it was your ma's fault what happened to your da. If this young man dies in your bed, that'll be tragic. That's all. Not your fault."

"It'll be my burden. My cross to bear."

"Only if you take it up like you have for Teddy."

Nan turned her back on her best friend. Right then, she wished she'd never confided a single, blessed thing to Tuda. Nan set the kettle back on the burner; it hissed from the lack of water. Empty. Like herself.

Tuda stood close enough that Nan could smell the faint scent of petrol and motor oil from her friend's overalls. "The past cannot be reclaimed. There are no do-overs. Why don't you accept it? Stop torturing yourself. What happened with Teddy can't be changed."

"In my mind, I know. In my heart, that's another situation."

"Nan, love." Tuda hugged her.

Nan let tears roll down her cheeks. "I'm sorry. This whole situation has me frayed."

"Of course it does. Give it over to the Lord. He has a plan."

"Yes. I suppose He does." *But had He a plan when Teddy went over the cliff? What kind of a plan was that?*

"Hey, sorority sisters out there," they heard Juliet call. "How about some hot water and empty bowls?"

CHAPTER 14

After Dr. Mann left, Nan spent the rest of the day and evening at Dutch's side, doing as the doctor had instructed.

The sight of his skin no longer jolted Nan when she gave him a shot. At least not too much. He was a patient needing her services. That was all. She was only his nurse. And she made sure to pull down only enough of the underwear to expose his bottom. Nothing more. Nothing more or she'd be wondering and thinking and dreaming.

Ah, but a practically naked man was sleeping in her bed.

She looked skyward. *Did He really have this in mind when He sent him to my door?*

Nan fed the fire in the fireplace, turned down the lamps, and then sat in the chair beside the bed. He was asleep, twitching occasionally, his feet kicking as though he were walking. She snuggled into a blanket. Dutch opened his eyes, blinking at her a couple of times, then slipped in and out of sleep. She slipped in and out of prayer, snoozing beside him.

Thank you, Lord, that the good doctor happened upon the penicillin, and if she had to sin to get it, please have mercy on her soul.

The sound of the gate opening and closing woke her early; the morning sun barely peeked in between the burlap curtains. She stood, rubbed her aching back, and hurried to the window, adrenaline waking every fiber of her being.

Please don't let it be Finn, she thought. Her breath rattled in her throat with relief as she parted the curtain and saw the doctor, carrying her medical bag and a box. Nan rushed to the front door and swung it open before Juliet could land a knock.

"Hey, kid." She shoved the box into Nan's arms. "How's the flyboy?"

"Resting."

"I was in the neighborhood, thought I'd take a gander." She nodded toward the box. "Actually, that's a lie. I wanted to see how he's doing. Here are some of my uncle's clothes. They should fit your pilot. He's what? About six foot? Slender like my uncle, too. I hope the shoes fit. He can't go around wearing RAF-issued boots. It's a dead giveaway."

"*My* pilot? Hardly. Well, perhaps for a few more hours. Thank you." Nan placed the box under the table. "It was very thoughtful of you. The clothes. Won't Dr. Glennon miss these fine things?" Juliet's uncle always had the best clothes. His heiress wife had them custom made in London, or so Mrs. Norman claimed.

"Nope. He's got more where that came from." Juliet hooked her wet raincoat onto a peg beside the door. "Listen, don't ask how I got any of this, but in the envelope, there's a detailed map to the border, a fake ID card, and a ration book for gas along the way. Follow the map. It's a good escape route. It leads to a ruined abbey where he can ditch the car, then walk across the border. It's all in here, but seriously: Warn him not to attempt crossing at night. The cliffs are treacherous."

Nan was taken aback. *Who was this woman? How did she get this?* "Detailed map?"

"Yeah, as in where the LDF and Irish Army have their roadblocks. Like I said, no questions."

Nan held the box. "There's more to you than just being a doctor, isn't there?"

"I'm not at liberty to say. Whitney still sleeping?"

"Yes." Nan ached to ask more questions but figured Juliet wouldn't or couldn't answer them. Whatever the good doctor was up to, she was on the right side of things. Hopefully not too-dangerous things.

"Let's wake him up, shall we?" Juliet's hips swayed as she paced toward the bedroom. She looked crisp and attractive in an expensive tan-colored ensemble, stockings with seams running down the back, and high-heel shoes that somehow resisted the Irish mud. They weren't even wet.

"Morning, sunshine." Juliet knuckled Dutch's shoulder with a tap-tap-tap.

His eyes opened, and he blinked several times, adjusting to being awake. "Ireland is full of angels."

"And you're full of something, all right. How are you feeling?"

"Groggy."

"That's the morphine. Let's take a look-see at your arm."

Nan stood near, watching the doctor unwind the gauze.

"Much better," Juliet declared. "How's your pain level, on a scale of one to ten, ten being—"

"I'm forced to have dinner with Hitler?"

Juliet smiled. "Sense of humor back; I'm glad." She opened her bag. "Number?"

"Why? You wanna call me after the war?"

"I don't date children. Pain level, lover boy?"

He gave her a lopsided grin, and Nan felt a stir of jealousy. He wanted to date Dr. Mann.

And why in-all-that's-holy not? She was a beautiful woman. Educated. Sophisticated. Wore couture clothes. Dr. Juliet Mann looked like a movie star.

Nan caught a glimpse of herself in the wardrobe mirror. *The very opposite.* Where had she even gotten the mud-colored sweater she was wearing? She tugged the rough brown garment down and frowned at the row of crooked green stripes at the bottom.

Homemade. Free. From Mrs. Norman.

It had belonged to the daughter Mrs. Norman was so proud of, the middle one with the missing front tooth. The girl had become a nun and left her clothes behind. Mrs. Norman had bundled them up for Nan, saying, "Ya can leave your nursing outfit at home. What you need is good, honest country clothes for stomping around Ballyhaven."

They all fit Nan, more or less. And they'd been free. With a quick glance at herself, she decided she'd paid too much.

Juliet put on a pair of glasses, the lenses so square and tiny, they looked like a pair of child's spectacles. "I'm pleased," she said, holding Dutch's arm and inspecting the wound. "Much improved. No fever?"

"Just when I look at Nan."

Nan's insides sizzled like water in a hot tail pipe, until Juliet laughed. Nan stared down into her lace-up boots. They were making fun of her. Yeah, she was a good Irish joke.

She looked back at Dutch. The way he was staring at her, his eyes so relaxed and dark—perhaps he wasn't making fun of her a'tall.

"I'm still waiting for your pain-level number, kid."

Dutch moved his arm. The skin seemed to be healing, and the pus had vanished. "Oh, I don't know."

"If you don't, no one does."

"Okay. A weak four," he said.

"Excellent." She glanced at Nan. "After I'm gone, wrap his arm again. One more shot, kid." Juliet tore off the covers. "Okay, flyboy. You know where I'm headed. Onto your hip."

Nan bit her lip. There he was, clad only in his underwear. Unlike herself, the good doctor left nothing to the imagination. Juliet pulled down his underwear. His bottom was bruised from where Dr. Mann had already stuck him with the needle.

"Like what you see, Doc?" he asked.

"You're just another boy who needs my expertise. Only a patient. Right, Nan?" Juliet prepared a shot.

Nan took him in from head to toe. "What else would he be?"

She returned to the fireplace, poked the turf and wood, added a few bricks, and turned the flames into an inferno. She probably ought to get used to infernos, considering where she might be headed if she didn't get to confession soon.

Juliet continued her examination of Dutch. "Even through the bandage, I can tell your knee is swollen like an orange. Oh, how I miss oranges."

"What else do you miss?" Dutch asked.

"The list is as long as the night. There's not much I can do for your knee. Keep it tightly wrapped, take some aspirin, and try to stay off your leg as much as possible."

"Can't do that. So I'll ignore the pain."

The doctor nodded. "Okay, tough guy. When you get back to your base in England, be sure you have the doctors check your knee. How's your appetite? You hungry? I want you to eat."

"Yeah. Actually, I am."

"A good Irish fry coming right up," Nan said. "You'll be right as rain in no time a'tall."

The doctor touched Dutch's forehead. "Nice work, even if I say so myself. Penicillin is a twentieth-century miracle."

"Thank the Lord you got your hands on the drug," Nan replied.

"I had to get my hands on more than the drug." Juliet hooked her hair behind her ear; a grin spread across her lips, and a sparkle lit her eyes. "And I'd do it all again in a second."

There was something so lascivious about the response, Nan found herself blushing.

Juliet turned to her, all business again. "Keep the wound clean and covered with gauze. It'll heal without any more intervention from us. Make sure he finishes the medication. No need for more morphine. Let the wound air for a couple of minutes, and then bandage it up loosely." She snapped her bag closed.

"Can you stay for breakfast?"

"Very kind of you, but no. I best get a move on before someone bangs on your door and wonders why I'm here. I'll leave him in your expert hands." Juliet gave Dutch's shoulder a mock punch. "I'll be seeing you, kid. Dip a wing over Ballyhaven for us next time you pass by."

"Once I'm outta here, I won't be coming back."

The comment shouldn't have caused Nan's stomach to twist, but her insides knotted like a Celtic cross. He couldn't wait to get out of Ireland. She understood. She was nothing, after all. Just a country midwife. A means to his escape.

She followed Juliet to the door. "Thank you. For everything."

"A pleasure." Juliet buttoned her raincoat. "Doing my part for the war effort. Like you. See ya around, kid."

Nan stood in the doorway. *There goes a patriot, a saint, and a sinner,* she thought.

The cat jumped onto the table and nudged his head against her hand. "But aren't we all sinners, Mr. Dee? By God's amazing grace, aren't we also forgiven?"

She closed the door and held on to the cold latch, the metal warming in her hand. Lingering there, she thought about her sins. She had to admit, she still hadn't forgiven herself for a marriage that had ended on a cloudy day over an argument. So how could God?

CHAPTER 15

Nan sat on the chair beside Dutch, opening a fresh package of gauze. His face had a peachy glow, a hue she hadn't actually seen before. Made him look even more handsome. Now his blue eyes stood out and complemented his skin tone.

She wondered why Juliet had told Dutch she didn't date children. This was no child in her bed. What did the good doctor prefer? Middle-aged men? Men old enough to be her father?

"Let me ask you something," Dutch said, adjusting his position.

Nan wrapped his wound with clean gauze. The angry red lines around the gash had subsided. Healthy new skin filled in the gaps. "What might that be?"

"Did you like being in bed with me the other night?"

She stopped encasing his arm for a second, just long enough for her face to grow hot. "The cheek on ya. Why do you ask? Do you think I did?"

"I don't know. I was wondering."

"Why?"

"'Cause I liked it. A lot."

"I bet you did." Her fingers trembled over the soft gauze. His question stirred needs in her.

Yes. She'd liked it, but she would never admit this, not in a million years.

She kept dressing the wound. "I needed to get you warm, nothing more. As innocent as it was, don't you go telling anyone. Stories can harm a girl, even if told from afar. Please. You promise? You'll ruin me, you will." Her voice squeaked out the last sentence.

"Relax. It's a joke."

She was a joke to him. This man brought out her insecurities. "Yes. Joke. Just."

"I promise. Our secret. Forever."

He smiled at her, his gaze roaming over her face. It was an intimate look, one that alarmed her. They'd been in bed together. Ah, but that sounded so much worse than it actually was.

Hussy. Sinner. A decent man had to be half-dead to get into bed with the likes of you.

She flinched. Shook her head. Dismissed the charges, knowing it was only the devil stealing her resolve. Nothing to confess. Not a thing. A healer's business.

Healer? But you failed with Teddy, didn't you? Let him die. And lied. If the doctor hadn't stepped in, your flyboy would be dead. Was this any different from Teddy?

"Satan get behind me," she muttered.

"What?" Dutch turned his head.

"Nothing."

After she reconciled with Father Albert in the hot, stuffy confessional booth, and he heard her sack of sins, her knees would ache from the penance he would dish out. But that was fine. Do the sin. Do the atonement. The correct order of things.

Looking at Dutch, the correct order of things had been turned upside down. Had the Lord led him to her? Was this His will? A test?

Nan positioned the final layer of gauze around his arm, ripped the end, and tied the bandage into place. "How's that feel? Not too tight?"

"Rotten."

"Does it hurt? I can reposition the bandage—"

"It's fine, really."

"How about we put your pajama top back on?"

She reached for the garment at the foot of the bed, then helped him into the shirt. "That's better." For both of them.

"Your family must be worried sick about you," she said.

"Probably."

"Tell me about your home. Have you a large family?"

"Not really. We live in Toronto. My father's long gone, but my mom is still rattling after her cause of the month. Since the war, it's been victory gardens and collecting metal for the war effort. My older brother runs the newspaper. It's our family business. He's married with two great little boys."

"Have you a girl back home? Sure now, a good-looking fella like you, you must have one. Or more."

He shrugged his shoulder. "I had a fiancée. We were going to get married, but . . . ," he hesitated, "she died of pneumonia about three years ago."

"Ah, that's terrible. I'm so sorry for your loss."

"Thank you."

"Are you still heartbroken?"

He looked shocked by the question. "No. We had our time together. In the end, she got called home. I got called to war."

So matter-of-fact. Nan had been absolutely gutted when she'd lost Teddy. Dutch didn't seem torn up a bit. Perhaps, being a man, he found moving on easy. Or perhaps he hadn't loved his fiancée deeply enough.

Or maybe there was a coldhearted man behind those smoldering eyes. A womanizer. She could not stem her curiosity. "What was her name?"

"Beatrice. Bea." He teased a thread that hung from his pajama top. "Truth is, she turned out to be someone I didn't know. Our relationship ended before she passed on."

"How so?"

"We were very young when we got engaged," he answered. "I met her at university. We'd shared football games and dances. Everything was fun." He shook his head. "Seems like such a long time ago."

"So, you two grew apart?"

The button thread he toyed with unraveled. "Yes. In a way we couldn't repair. She went to Germany for the summer, to visit relatives, and came back a different person. Buying into the whole Nazi nonsense of a master race. Made me so mad. My dad fought in the Great War. Lost the use of his left hand." He hesitated for a few seconds, then went on, "We had a huge fight. I told my mom that we were over, but not why, and she invited Bea to dinner, thinking we could patch things up. Halfway through the meal, Bea started in with her Nazi garbage. Clearly, she had forgotten that my sister-in-law was born Jewish."

"Oh my."

"Rachel converted to Christianity. My brother met her at church. She's a living doll. Their kids, my nephews, are the best. They're eight and ten now." He shifted in the bed, a pained expression overtaking his face when he moved his leg. "Rachel's relatives started showing up at the door. They'd escaped from Nazi Germany. Mom took them in. Found them apartments. Work. Then, they stopped showing up. It's why I joined the RAF. Hitler and his death machine had to be stopped. I promised my dad, if the Germans came to power again, as he predicted, I wouldn't sit on the sidelines and let them run us over."

Now she knew why the war was so personal to him. "What happened after Bea put her foot in her mouth?"

"My sister-in-law is a class act. She asked to be excused from the table. Took the boys with her."

"What did Bea say when you told her what an eejit she'd been?"

"She declared that my sister-in-law would not be welcomed in our future home."

"Oh, Dutch. What a terrible, awful thing."

"I broke off our engagement for good. A couple of days later, she caught the cold that led to pneumonia, and she was gone within a week."

"I'm sorry."

The curve of his cheek glowed in the golden light. "People make their own decisions. We can't always agree. I grieved for the person she used to be."

"It's so sad."

"You Irish aren't the only ones with tales of woe. You have your own sad story, don't you, Nan?"

"My marriage was happy." The words shamed her heart. *What a lie.* "Teddy's life ended too soon, of course." *Truth there.*

"How about you now? You have a boyfriend?"

"Don't be daft. I'm a widow."

"I didn't realize you were still in mourning. You lost him recently?"

"Three years ago."

He frowned. "The Irish mourning period is long."

"I'm not in the mourning period." *Not technically, anyway.* "Last week was the anniversary of his death."

"It must have brought up painful memories."

The memories are as raw as the day it happened. "Yes. Teddy was my love. He was enough to last a lifetime." Of course, it was the guilt she carried for failing to help him that would last a lifetime.

He took the glass of water she offered, drank half of it, then peered at her over the top of the glass. "Won't you marry again? There must be a hundred guys out there wanting to court you."

"Go on with ya. I'm no tart." She took the glass from him and set it on the nightstand.

"That's not what I meant. I think you'd be quite the catch. That's all."

She snorted a laugh. "I prefer not to be caught by anything that might be roaming around this town."

His grin sent a dimple to his cheek. "Best ones taken?"

She folded her arms against the wisp of loneliness she felt. "More like gone. The men left in town are too young, too old, or too odd."

The cat jumped onto the bed and dropped down beside Dutch.

"Hey, buddy." Dutch ran his hand over the cat's orange body.

"Besides," she said. "I have Mr. Dee to keep me company."

Both Dutch and the cat stared at her. "Oh no," Dutch responded. "Pets are great, but they're not people. Don't you want family around you?"

She twisted her wedding ring around her finger. "I have family galore. Babies everywhere I turn."

"But not yours."

His words tore at her. "Sometimes the Lord uses us in ways we don't plan. My role is to bring other women's babies into the world. It's enough for me."

"Really?"

"Yes. Really." It was time to redirect the conversation. "Tuda worked on the Ford yesterday. Said she nearly got it started."

"Did the engine crank over?"

"She got a couple of moans out of it, but no, she couldn't coax it into life. She wasn't sure why."

"Figures. Too much for her."

"Meaning what? A girl can't be a good mechanic?"

"Don't get your Irish up. I'm sure she missed something that I can figure out."

"Confident, aren't you?"

"Yes. Besides, two heads are better than one at reviving something dead."

The words sliced through her. A dozen people couldn't revive her heart.

"Is she coming back today?" he asked.

"Tomorrow. She's getting more parts. I'm sure the two of you will get the old thing started. We'll send you on your way tomorrow night.

You rest, now. You'll need your wits about you for the journey across the border."

She looked at him before going to the door and closing it behind her.

The cheek of him, she thought, *asking if I enjoyed being in bed with him.* The sensation of lying beside him flooded her senses, and her pulse sped.

With a sigh, she dismissed the thought. Once he was back in England, he'd forget her in the flicker of a smile. Men couldn't help themselves, God love 'em.

The morning proceeded with a thankful respite from visitors. Nan went outside to greet the rare sunny day, climbing halfway up the hill to see the ocean in the distance. The air smelled clean with a hint of sea breeze. She felt invigorated. On days like this, she wondered why people lived anywhere else.

Later, she fed lunch to Dutch, insisting that he rest afterward. Amazingly, he made no protest, drifting off before she'd even removed the tray. The cat jumped onto the bed and settled at the man's feet.

Her cat had jilted her. She wondered if her feline would wander about the cottage looking for Dutch, once he was gone. She might, too, she realized.

After a nap in the chair beside the fireplace, marred by a nightmare about Finn, she woke with a start, relieved to find herself safe in her comfy chair. The day had drifted into twilight, and the lanterns needed to be lit.

After lighting the cabin, she headed to the pantry. She would make a loaf of bread for their evening tea. *Their* evening tea. They would share one more evening meal. She poured the milk into the well of brown flour, thankful for a normal activity that would ground her back into reality.

Lord, thank you for Dutch's continual healing, she prayed, working the dough on the floured board.

The cat trotted into the room. "Ah, Mr. Dee," she said. "About time you were up and about."

"So am I." Dutch appeared in the doorway. His clinging pajamas showed the definition of his chest muscles. "May I sit by the fire?"

"Of course. Let me help you."

"No need. I feel so much better."

"You look . . ." *Amazing.* "Better."

His smile warmed her as he wobbled to the big chair. The cat hopped onto Dutch's lap, and Dutch patted the animal with tender strokes. "Hey, Mr. Dee. Thanks for keeping my toes warm."

Her heart softened. Hadn't Teddy always sat there to stare into the fire, the dog at his feet, a cup of tea within reach? Why did it seem so natural to have Dutch there now? She never thought another man would occupy the chair, conversing with her. Sharing a pet.

Their gazes met, and the room grew hot and small around them. She wasn't aware she'd stopped working the dough until he asked, "What are you making?"

A mess of things, she thought, *especially my heart.* "Soda bread."

"Like the night when I first arrived?"

"The same." She patted the spongy dough into a round cake, then cut a cross into the top.

"Why are you doing that?"

"It's tradition. Supposed to excise any devils hanging around the house." She glanced at her roof. She was sure there were a few still dancing up there.

She set the bread on a greased pan and shoved the loaf into the oven.

"Nan, I want to ask you something."

"Yes?"

"Will I see you again, after the war?"

"I hope so. I'll pray for you every day."

The image of a bomber in flames, spinning down to the sea, sent stabs of worry plunging through her. His next mission might be his last. She couldn't bear the thought, but only the Lord knew if he'd survive. *Please, God, protect him.*

She sat across from him just as she used to do with Teddy. His foot, in her late husband's sock, slid across the slate floor toward hers. She expected him to say he wanted to see her again, too. To say anything kind.

She sank against the back of her chair.

"When the war's over," he said, "will you visit me in Canada?"

"That'd be lovely."

She slid her foot in the direction of his, until their feet almost touched. Instinct demanded she recoil. It was too intimate. Too bold. Instead, she turned her foot to the side, exposing the curve of her instep. His big toe touched her arch and meandered up to her ankle, making her melt like butter left too close to the hearth.

"What will you do when peace returns?" She shifted forward, bringing her knee near his. The heat from his body radiated to hers. Or was it merely the turf fire? Perhaps she was reading too much into this.

"Besides celebrate, I'll continue flying. I love airplanes. Maybe I'll be a test pilot or run an airport."

"What do you like about flying?"

"Sailing up in the clouds feels so free."

She smiled. "Free? How can that be? Stuffed in a steel cage, enough petrol in your tanks to take out a city, and whirling propellers the only thing keeping you up in the clouds?"

He sat up. "When you put it that way, it doesn't seem so great."

She'd offended him, and he removed his touch. *For the best,* she thought. "But you love flying."

"I do."

"How about being at war? Dropping bombs?" As soon as the words left her mouth, she regretted them.

He winced. "Do you hate me for what I do in the war?"

"Not a'tall. I hate war is all."

"That's a sane position. I hate war, too, but I can't think about the destruction we render. It's them or us. Freedom or oppression."

Instead of spinning into an anti-war tirade, she said, "Then you're doing what God intended. Does your family support your career choice?"

"Not really. I'm supposed to follow in the family business, but I'd be miserable working at a newspaper."

"When you get back, don't let them bully you into doing something you don't want to do. My ma tried to do that." She stopped. "Out of love," she quickly added.

"How?"

Nan focused on her hand, on Teddy's ring. She looked at Dutch's left hand. His ring fingernail was black. She wondered how he'd bruised it. When he hit the bog, perhaps, or before.

"Ma didn't want me to marry Teddy." She felt a sharp pain in her heart.

"Why not?"

She gazed up at the shadows flickering on the ceiling. "Irish mothers never think their daughters marry boys who are good enough for them. But I married Teddy anyway," she said, skipping the full story, folding her hands onto her lap. "Once I married him, she wanted me to quit my job, because a good Irish wife stays home and has beautiful Irish babies. That wasn't in the cards for me. Or for Ma to be a grandmother."

"How did your husband . . . ah . . . ?"

"Die?"

"If you don't mind telling me."

A lump formed in her throat. No one knew the whole truth of that day, not even Tuda. How she'd run after him, chasing him to the cliffs. Pleading with him to put the gun and the bottle down. He'd cursed her with such vile language. To this day, she blushed when the words came to her in the dead of the night.

She'd failed Teddy. She should have done something besides scream like a helpless eejit.

"You don't have to tell me." His hand brushed across her knee, leaving a dazzling awareness.

She willed the scene back into the depths of her soul. "There was an accident. Teddy fell off the cliff into the sea."

"I'm sorry," he said.

She shrugged. "The good Lord doesn't take anyone a minute before his time, or a second after." Those were the empty words she used when babies passed. And it was true. But what about the people who took the decision out of the Lord's hands?

Their conversation dwindled. Wind bucked the windows and stirred the ashes, sending the turf fire into a fierce blaze. Rain pelted the windows, loud as pebbles; then came the sound of water draining from the roof into the rain barrel outside the back door.

"Storm's returned," she said.

"Big one." His gaze traveled over her body to rest on her eyes. She felt as though he were touching her, but of course that was completely daft. "How did you end up here?"

"The property was left to my mother, and I inherited the place. Teddy and I decided to live here."

"How long ago?"

"Three years. The town needed a midwife, and Teddy thought this would be a wonderful place to write. Much better than Dublin."

"He was a writer?"

"A poet."

"I could have guessed." He glanced at the honeymoon picture on the mantel. "He looks like a poet."

"And how might that be?"

"Sensitive."

Beyond sensitive, she thought. She longed to tell Dutch the whole story, but she held back. She didn't want to talk about Teddy or that day or what had happened.

His knee touched hers. She inhaled his scent, woodsy and manly, and she knew she'd never forget him.

"Were you there when the accident happened?"

"I don't like to talk about it."

"You can tell me." He placed a hand on her knee and gazed into her eyes with perfect kindness.

She couldn't tell him. It was none of his business, how Teddy had gone from being a lover to a hater.

At the sound of the gate opening, he straightened, moved back into his chair. "You expecting someone?"

"Never expecting. Always receiving." The sound of car wheels and a motor filled the cottage. Car headlights shone through the burlap curtains. She sprinted to the window and cracked open the heavy covering.

"Lord have mercy. It's the Garda. Sergeant Halpin."

CHAPTER 16

Dutch stood and his knee locked. The pain momentarily paralyzed him.

"You need to get in the closet."

"You think?" He dragged his leg along, biting down the burning torture of each step. His knee hurt more than his arm. *Progress,* he supposed.

Letting go of the curtain, she bit her bottom lip. "It's probably about Kelly. It's a wee soon for the baby, but they have a way of being born on their own schedules."

Halpin knocked. Nan waved her hand at Dutch and whispered, "Don't just gape at me. Go on with ya."

"I'm moving as fast as I can," he said. Every step brought a sharp stab to his leg, but he had no choice.

The knock at the door grew louder. "I'm coming," Dutch heard her call as he closed the closet door behind him.

His heart threatened to explode out of his chest, and he gulped for air. He ran his hand up the wall until he found the panel that slid open. From this vantage point, he could see Halpin.

"Come in out of the rain, Sergeant Halpin."

"Ah, Nan. I was about to give up on you." Halpin's wet raincoat glistened in the soft cabin light.

"Sorry. I was in the, you know." She gestured toward the bathroom. "What's wanting?"

"Kelly. It's her time."

"Ah, is it? Grand. A wee early, but not to be alarmed. I was just saying—"

"To whom?" he asked, peering around the room.

"My cat, of course. Babies have their own timetable. Wait in the car while I get my things."

Dutch grinned. She was quick with the tongue.

After Halpin stepped back outside, she gathered her medical bag.

"It's Kelly's time," she said out loud. "I probably won't be back until morning. Be careful. Please eat and get some rest. Wait a few minutes before you come out. When the timer goes off, take the bread out of the oven. Oh. And there's a box of clothes and things for you under the table, from the doctor."

With that, she grabbed her coat and left.

He leaned his back against the cold stone, his hand touching his throbbing knee. It was hot, puffy. *Doggone it.* He'd done it again, injuring his knee. He had to get that car running and himself out of Nan's life before their luck burned out.

And while she was gone, he was going to hunt for his gun. *Ridiculous.* How was he supposed to protect himself? He pressed the door open and sucked in clean air as he limped to the table by the door.

He reached under the table for the box and set it on top. *This is better,* he thought as he dug through the contents. There was a complete outfit, shoes even. Nice ones, lace-up Italian leather. Seemed more his size, not like Teddy's tiny nightshirt.

Nan had been on the verge of telling him what had happened. Maybe later she would. But he wouldn't push her, lest he send her deeper into her funk.

At the bottom of the box, he found a nine-by-twelve envelope.

Wow, he thought while opening it. He found phony Irish identification papers—with a picture so blurry it could be anyone—money, and a ration book for petrol. How had Dr. Mann done it?

The same way she got the penicillin, he thought with a grin. *Good woman.*

Then he unfolded the map. "Astonishing," he whispered. Roads with LDF and Irish Army checkpoints were flagged. Dr. Mann had to be MI6 or the American equivalent. So what on earth was she doing in this Irish bog of a town? What was there to spy on?

He shrugged. *Her business.* Yet the good doctor had not only taken him from the brink of death but had figured out an escape route that would make the journey a piece of cake, provided that hunk of metal in the garage was operational.

Seemed odd to him, though, why Nan hadn't mentioned the map and papers—rather important items. The cat jumped onto the table and stuck his nose in the map.

"Even you're curious." Dutch scratched behind Mr. Dee's ears for a moment and stuffed the papers back into the envelope. "I don't always understand women." The cat meowed several times as though agreeing, then jumped to the floor.

Dutch glanced at his swollen knee. If Nan didn't get home soon, he'd need to go against her rules again and work on the car.

The timer pinged, so Dutch opened the oven and took out the bread. It smelled so good, he was sure he'd remember the aroma forever. His stomach grumbled with hunger.

After two cups of tea with bread and jam and a long study of the map, he decided to rest on Nan's bed for a few minutes. The quilt smelled of lavender. And Nan. He closed his eyes and drifted into sleep, thinking about the deep blue of her eyes against the creamy color of her skin, her hair curling around the curves of her cheek. He couldn't bear leaving her, but he had to.

◆ ◆ ◆

The next morning, he woke when the cat jumped on his stomach. "Good morning, Mr. Dee."

He sat up. The cottage was silent. Nan wasn't home yet.

Home.

He wiped the sleep from his eyes. Interesting he'd thought of this as "home."

So much for finding his gun last night. He moved his arm back and forth. It hardly hurt . . . at least not very much.

It was time to tinker with the car. Tuda should show up soon, too.

After a quick bite to eat, he dressed in the clothes the doctor had provided. Almost a perfect fit. Good-quality garments, too. Brown wool slacks, a white button-down cotton shirt, a tweed vest, and a deep-blue wool tie, which he put loosely around his neck. He'd leave the tweed jacket with leather patches for later, but it fit. The shoes were a size too big, but who cared? He could pass for a proper Irish gentleman in this gear, as long as he kept his brogue to himself.

Dutch glanced in both directions before he slipped out the door and dashed across the cobblestone yard. With each step, his knee throbbed.

The calf house was freezing and damp, but the Ford's hood was open, tools and parts arranged on the bench with precision. Tuda was meticulous, a good sign.

The cat jumped onto the bench, sniffing the tools.

"You going to be my lookout again today?"

Dutch scratched behind Mr. Dee's ears. "You know, you're more of a dog than a cat. So that makes you what? A *dat*?"

Then he picked up a wrench and peered under the hood at the engine. The connections, the new hoses, and the general condition of the engine met with his approval. "Nice work."

Impressive, even. Tuda knew what she was doing. Together, they'd get this hulk running.

Grounded Hearts

He fiddled with the spark plugs, tugged on the wires. Checked hoses, connectors, bolts. He lost himself in the rhythm of work and ignored the pain in his arm and his knee.

His fingers scraped over a sharp edge. "Ouch." He pulled out his hand. Red blossomed across his knuckles.

The sound of a car approaching sent him to the dirty window to peer outside. Not Tuda.

The Garda's car.

The passenger door opened, and Nan stepped out. "Stop worrying. You're not the first man to have a baby. Kelly and your new daughter will be fine," she was saying. "Go rest. You've the town's women taking care of her. I'll check on Kelly and baby later today."

Nan. He waited until the sound of the Garda's car faded before he stepped into the courtyard.

She was about to discover the door was unlocked, and he braced himself for a lecture. He almost called out to her when he heard another vehicle approaching. Probably Tuda, but he wasn't going to take any chances. He slipped back inside the barn and peeked through the cracked window.

Doggone it. It was Finn, parking his beat-up sedan. The car appeared to have already been through a war.

Nan stood in the open doorway.

Dutch watched the big lug step out of the car. "I'm glad I caught you in, Nan."

"Ah sure. So you did. Have you heard the news? Paul and Kelly have a new little girl."

"Well, she's young. She can try again."

"For what?"

"A boy, of course."

She looked skyward. "All that matters is that the child is healthy. What brings you to my doorstep so early?"

"I've news."

"Do tell. Have you managed to catch some Nazis?"

"How about a cup of tea first? That'd be grand."

"I'm sorry, Finn—Officer Finn. I'm tired as the sunset. I can barely stay standing. Will you tell the news and be on your way, please?"

The smile she sent Finn left him gaping for a few seconds. His boots crunched over the cobblestones as he approached her. "Seems the lad who washed up down the beach wasn't from the Wellington crash after all."

Her eyebrows lifted. "What a sad bit of news for the lad and his family." She cut the sign of the cross over her body. "I'll remember him in my prayers."

"Have you seen anyone suspicious lately?"

"Besides yourself?"

Finn's eyes narrowed. "You and the women in town might think this is all fun and games, but I assure you it isn't. That RAF pilot is hiding somewhere close by. He's armed and dangerous. No match for a girl like yourself."

"I can take care of myself, but why do you think he's still about? Wouldn't he be across the border by now?"

"Not if he's injured."

"Why would you think he's injured?"

"I caught a Tinker boy yesterday. He was wearing a flight helmet. I grabbed it off the lad's head. It was bloodstained and labeled."

Oh no, Dutch thought.

"With what?"

"His name. 'Dutch Whitney.' He's the missing bomber boy."

Nan didn't show the tiniest crack of composure. "And how are you knowing that?"

"Because the poor sod who washed up onshore has been identified. We found his name sewn into his jacket. And his insignias marked him from a different sort of crew, not a bomber a'tall."

"Is that a fact?" Nan crossed her arms and arched an eyebrow.

"It's been confirmed by the RAF. So. We still have one Wellington pilot missing. And we know his name—Whitney. Thanks to the Tinker boy."

"Doggone it," Dutch whispered.

Nan said only, "Wasn't that clever of you, finding the Tinker?"

Finn puffed up his chest, fingered the gun at his side. "I'm good as hired for the Garda position. I'd best go inside and see that you're safe."

Dutch placed a hand over his mouth. Dread washed over him. He'd cleared all his things off the table. Made the bed. Tucked his pajamas into the hiding hole. He sucked in a breath. The box of clothes. The map. He'd put them under the table.

Hadn't he? His heart pounded, beating hard.

Nan closed the door, stood in front of it, and blocked Finn's entrance. "Do you think that instead of hiding, this fellow might be dead?"

"No way of telling. He's still deemed missing by the RAF."

"Is he, now? I'll tell you what. If I happen to be strolling down the beach and see a dead pilot, I'll come looking for you."

"I'm counting on ya to do the right thing. Your country is, too." He stepped into her, reached his hands for the latch. "Move aside, Nan. I'm going inside."

"You're not. No need a'tall."

"I am. It's my duty to keep you safe."

"There's nothing in there except my things."

"You're not knowing that unless I check. And I have the authority to investigate as I see fit. Do ya mind? Step aside."

Dutch held his breath.

"I do mind, but all right then. Don't linger on my panties, set out to dry. In the back room off the scullery."

He licked his lips, which disgusted Dutch.

Nan moved out of Finn's way, her hands locked in prayer and head bowed.

Dutch tapped his thumb against the window until she opened her eyes toward the sound. Her jaw dropped and her eyes flashed. Finn stomped out of the house. "You're all clear. Why do ya have so many dishes in ya sink?"

She crossed her arms, turned to him, didn't miss a beat. "Not that it's your business, but Tuda and I were having tea when I was called away to deliver the Halpin baby. Did you touch my panties?"

Finn blushed.

"Ah, ya did, didn't ya? Did you find the bomber boy hiding behind them?"

Dutch grinned. The woman was a master at redirecting conversation.

The wind howled across the courtyard, and the calf-house door slammed shut, then popped open again.

Finn spun around, stared at the barn.

Startled, Dutch stepped away. His foot hit a shovel, and he grabbed for the tool but missed. Crashing to the ground, the shovel hit a pail and sent the bucket rolling away, making loud clanking sounds. Deep pain tingled down his arm, and his knee quaked with painful spasms. He pressed his back against the cold wall. Now he'd done it.

"What's that?" he heard Officer Finn say. "Is someone in there?"

"Who would be in there?"

"A bomber boy."

Dutch's heart pounded. Where should he hide? Would he fit under the car? The hay bale? *No.* Not enough time to kick it apart.

It'd come down to his clumsiness. The lads at the internment camp would have a hoot when they learned his big banana-boat foot had given him away.

Lord, if you're watching, send me an escape route. Tell me what to do. Protect me, please.

The cat trotted out of the narrow opening of the barn door.

"Good kitty," Dutch whispered. He looked skyward. "Thanks."

"Pay no mind," he heard Nan say. "Sure, it's only the cat, knocking things over in the pursuit of a mouse, no doubt."

"So, he didn't pack his gun today?"

Nan let out a musical laugh. "Aren't you the joker? Please, Officer Finn, I've been up all night. Be on your way, and I'll have you for tea at a later date."

Dutch couldn't help himself. He peeked through the broken blinds again. Hands on hips, and a sly smile, she was flirting with Finn.

Dutch rubbed a hand over his mouth. That wasn't a good strategy with a jerk like Finn. It might come back to bite her.

"I'll hold you to it." Finn slicked back his thinning hair. "You and me, Nan. We've got things to talk over. When this war is over, I'll be an even more important man in town. As important as Sergeant Halpin."

"Well now, won't that be grand for you?"

"All the girls will be after me. But you're the one."

"What would make me happy today is a nap. Be on your way, so." She pointed to the open gate.

Dutch clenched his hands. He half wanted to go into the courtyard and beat the tar out of Finn. And he worried about what Nan would need to endure once he escaped.

The cat jumped on top of Finn's car and made a low hissing sound.

"Go on with ya," Finn yelled, swatting the side of the car.

Dutch felt a grin rise through him.

Maybe the cat was MI6, too.

CHAPTER 17

Dutch waited a few minutes before he returned to the warmth of Nan's cabin, although the look she gave him froze him on the spot. She was on the comfy chair, glaring.

Trouble seemed to be his middle name.

He wiped the rain from his hair. "I'm sorry."

"Oh, you're sorry. Again? You near gave me a heart attack. Didn't I tell you to stay put?" Her voice came out shrill.

He presented his open palms. "Mea culpa."

"Mea angry. You'll be the death of me yet."

His stomach clenched as though a wrench were tightening the bolts. "Don't say that. I can't stand to think of you that way."

"Nor can I stand thinking of you dead. Going back to England, hopping into a bomber." She covered her eyes with her hands.

Dutch crossed the room, sat in the chair opposite her. "Nan. I'm sorry."

She knocked his hand away. "I promised you I'd put you out if you did that again."

He nodded. "You did. I'll get my things. I need my gun."

"And go where?"

"Toward the border. I'll walk. At least I have decent clothes now."

"Thanks to me, Tuda, and Juliet. We've put ourselves in danger for you. Are you so self-involved you can only think of yourself and your mission? You gave me your word."

"My pledge to God and country overrode my promise to you."

She stood, slapping her hands on her hips. "Isn't that nice? We're expendable down here so you can get back into the air and save the world. Do you care a'tall that you might destroy our world?"

He'd always thought of his mission in terms of the broad picture of victory, not the day-to-day lives of his victims. The words shook him. *His victims.* With a shake of his head, he hardened his emotions, took up his armor. "It's them or us."

"Don't give me that load of garbage. From where I sit, it's you or us, too. We're helping you, taking the risks, but you're not helping."

For the very first time, he began to understand the impact of war on real people. Real heartaches. Real risks that carried real consequences.

"You truly disappointed me. You gave me your word."

"I did. I'm sorry. I should have waited for Tuda."

"Yes, you should have. You heard what Finn said? They know you're not dead."

"Yeah. Listen, I also heard what you said to Finn. You're giving him the wrong impression."

"Finn? Oh, I can handle him."

He stood and looked her in the eye. "It's a dangerous game you're playing."

"What game is that?" She matched the intensity of his gaze.

"Leading him on."

"You mean getting rid of him? It works."

"For now. He's going to want his pound of flesh."

"He might get a cup of tea if he's lucky. That's all he'll ever get from me."

"I worry about you."

"I'll be fine." Her eyes softened.

"Will you come with me?" he found himself asking.

She laughed. "To England? Are you daft?"

"I don't see how you can stay here anymore. Finn—"

"He's a buffoon. I'm not leaving my home. Don't ask me again. Come back after the war and visit if you wish."

"Will you at least think about it?"

She gave him a stubborn stare. "My place is here. What you ask is impossible."

The sound of bicycle wheels rolling over the cobblestones interrupted them.

From outside they heard, "Hello in there. 'Tis I, Tuda, the girl mechanic. Are you decent?"

"Why is Tuda riding her bike?" Nan asked, leaving Dutch feeling like a little boy whose puppy had run away. He followed on her heels to the door.

"Why are you on your bike?" Nan called out as she opened the door. "If ever there was a need to keep dry in the van, today would be the day."

"Exactly what I said to my Paddy when he walked in last night, covered in mud, with a black eye, no less," Tuda replied as she entered. "Seems he had a wee bit too much to drink and ran the van into a ditch. He smashed the whole thing. It'll be ages before I can get it running again."

"Oh, Lord have mercy. Is he all right?" Nan closed the door.

"Yes. God protects drunkards and fools, so he's got double protection." She looked at Dutch. "Don't you look grand? Much better than the last time I saw you. Those clothes do you justice. They can't be Teddy's. Doesn't he look grand, Nan?"

"He looks passable," Nan said. "Juliet brought them. They belonged to Dr. Glennon."

Dutch straightened the vest. "You think I'll blend in? Go unnoticed?"

Tuda laughed. "Not a chance. You're far too good-looking. You'll turn every woman's head."

"Come on. That's not true," he said.

Nan rubbed her hand over his arm, the heat penetrating through his shirt. A ripple of goose bumps scurried up his arm to his neck. "You'll pass. Just don't try and use your brogue."

"Good advice."

"The next time I come, I'll bring you some maps," Tuda said.

He hooked a thumb toward the box under the table. "I have maps. The doc brought them."

Nan's hand pressed against her chest. "I'm such an eejit. I forget to tell you."

"That's okay. I found them." He looked into her eyes, and their gazes locked. The rest of the room crept into the shadows. For the first time since he'd crash-landed in Eire, a spark of regret that he'd be leaving pinched his heart.

"Hmm. That doctor is clever." Tuda coughed, breaking their concentration. "Nan, you look like a spent penny."

Nan stepped away from Dutch, her cheeks blooming pink. "Up all night delivering the Halpins' baby."

"All's well?"

"Ah sure, she's got lungs on her like a gale."

"She had a girl," Tuda said. "I'm so glad. Kelly wanted a girl."

"She did. And the da couldn't be more pleased."

Dutch listened. The ladies slipped into a sort of conversational shorthand he didn't completely understand. But it was a nice change to hear women talk, instead of the cursing and leering he was used to among the men in the barracks.

"And who do you think was here when I got back?"

"Ah, the lard-arse, himself. I saw him speeding down the lane. He'll give you no rest, Nan."

"That's what I tried to tell her," Dutch piped up.

A crease deepened between Nan's eyebrows. "You needn't worry. I know how to give him the brush-off. Once you're gone, he'll have no cause to come around."

"You think that'll stop him?" Dutch touched Nan's arm.

Tuda shook her head. "Not likely. I worry about you, too, Nan."

"You're both wrong. He's nothing a'tall but a bully. A lot of hot air. Unfortunately, Tuda, they discovered the dead pilot's true identity. Our time is running out."

"Come on, let's get that Ford running. I brought some petrol and a couple of extra parts."

Dutch gave Nan a lingering look before he followed Tuda out into the rain. His mission to save the world paled. How could he leave her here to face Finn?

◆ ◆ ◆

Dutch and Tuda worked together on the car, and he was impressed by her technical knowledge. They reached across the engine from opposite sides of the open hood. "You ever think of joining the RAF as a mechanic?"

"I've my boys in the service. That's enough. Have you met them? Aidan and Barry Quinn?"

"Wish I did. Are they pilots?"

"Mechanics. Taught them everything they know." She grinned. "Except about airplanes, of course. They wanted to fly, but they're grounded. Too valuable to lose, their commanding officer told them."

"He's right. We flyboys are a dime a dozen. Good mechanics, they're worth their weight in gold."

Tuda got misty-eyed. "They are to me."

"I'll keep an eye out for them. They must be special if they're *your* sons."

"They are."

"Can I ask you something?"

"About what?"

"Nan."

"You can ask, but I probably won't answer."

He nodded. "About Teddy. He didn't really fall off the cliff, did he?"

Tuda stopped tightening a bolt and stared across at him. "All I know is that he washed up on the beach. Dead."

"All you know?"

"Pretty much." She returned to her bolt.

"It's just that, well . . . I don't know." He searched for the right words. "I know about losing someone you love. I lost my dad ten years ago and my fiancée three years ago. It hurts. Deeply. But with time, I got over my grief. It seems so fresh for her. Why can't she move on?"

Tuda set the wrench on the bumper and took a long drink from a bottle of water. Wiping her hand across the gleaming drips on her chin, she shrugged. "Because you're applying logic to a heart problem."

"What do you mean?"

"When she's ready, she'll talk about that day. Now, what do you think is wanting with this spark plug?"

❖ ❖ ❖

Nan fell asleep on her bed. When she woke, she breathed in his scent again, sending her insides into a spin.

Had he really asked her to go to England with him? That was completely out of the question. He only asked because he was sorry for what he'd done. There was no way she could justify leaving Ballyhaven. The women of this town needed her. And she needed them. Besides, like her family before her, she was not a runner.

A hider, yes. But not a runner.

She glanced at the clock. "Good gracious," she muttered, slipping out of bed. She'd better get a move on or she'd lose the light.

After a conversation with Tuda and Dutch, Nan headed to town to check on Kelly Halpin and her baby.

She found mother and child recuperating well. The set of lungs on that baby would be the envy of the banshees. Assured all was on the right path, Nan left them to rest, although as she watched Siobhan hover around Kelly, Nan realized that might be near impossible.

Nan leaned her bicycle against Mikie's shop, grabbed her basket, and went inside. The usual group of men sat around the smoldering fireplace, a cloud of cigarette smoke floating above their heads. Mikie was holding his pipe in one hand, resting his elbow on the mantel.

"'Lo, Nan. How are ya this soft Irish day?" he called.

"Grand. Yourself?"

"I could complain, but I won't."

"That'll be a first," Margaret muttered. She strolled in from the private room, the beads clicking as she passed. She sat behind the glass counter, the *Irish Times* open in front of her. Her reading glasses slid to the tip of her rounded nose. She pushed them up and said, "How's yaself?"

"Grand."

Old Liam lifted a mug of tea. "Ah, it's yourself, then, Nan. I hear Officer Halpin had a wee one. A girl or boy?"

"A lovely little girl," Mikie said. "Where has ya mind been? We've been talking about it all morning."

"Is that a fact, now? Me hearing is none too good these days. A girl?"

Mikie shook his head. "Ya ought to have the doc take a look at them ears."

"Dr. Mann? No way. I'll not give that woman doctor the chance to look at me nasty bits." Liam grinned. "But Nan can."

Margaret huffed. "In ya dreams, ya old goat! She's got the pick of any man in town. Why would she bother with the likes of you?"

Liam shoved tobacco into a cigarette paper. "Finn. That's the man for Nan."

Mikie nodded. "Ah yeah. He'll be a Garda after the war if he plays his cards right. Wouldn't that be grand, Nan? Be a Garda's wife?"

Placing her basket on the counter, Nan let out a sigh.

Margaret flipped the paper to the next page. "She'd sooner marry a potato. She'd have more intelligent conversations and a much better love life."

Nan blushed but laughed. "Ah, Margaret. What a thing to say."

Mikie pointed his crooked finger at his wife. "Ya a nasty bit of work, woman. Add that to the sins you're gonna confess this week to Father Albert."

"Go stuff ya pipe, Mikie." Margaret winked at Nan. "Tea?" She didn't wait for a reply, pouring the liquid into a white mug. "Wish I had news about them jam jars. Alas, I don't, but I hope to see them next shipment from Limerick."

"Okay." Making apple jam was the last task on Nan's mind. She splashed some milk into her cup. "Thanks, this is just what I need." She sipped the familiar tea as though it were a passage from earth to heaven.

"So tell me, Mikie," Liam said. "Why aren't we celebrating the birth of the lovely babe born to our most revered Sergeant Halpin?"

"'Cause the back room doesn't open until . . ." Mikie glanced at his watch. "Now, lads."

"What are we waiting for?" Liam tucked a cigarette behind his ear and pushed down his flat cap. "Let's go."

A stampede of booted men bolted toward the keg of Guinness in the back room.

"Mind you don't make a mess," Margaret bellowed after them.

"Ya bet, missus," someone replied. "We'll have Mikie clean it up."

"It'll be a dry winter in Ireland when that happens," Margaret said, folding the paper.

Nan finished her tea. "They make a good case for spinsterhood."

"A good case for the rhythm method, too. Don't mind the eejits, Nan. Aren't you a sight?"

"Am I?" Did it show how nerve-racking the last few days had been? "I'm tired."

"You're a hero, a hero," Margaret whispered, even though no one was in the shop. "We're all behind ya and your RAF pilot."

Nan's heart pounded against her rib cage. "I'm only a midwife. I know nothing about an RAF pilot."

"Not from what I hear." Margaret winked so many times, Nan thought she might have something irritating her eye.

"What are you hearing? From whom?" The blood rushed so fast through Nan's veins, she was sure she'd start bleeding through her nose.

"I just hear things."

Nan mustered a breathy whisper. "Who's saying what?" That nosy Mrs. Norman, no doubt. A sieve could hold water longer than that old woman could keep a secret.

"Not a thing. Not a word. Not a thing. And from no one." Margaret set the paper into Nan's basket. "Some entertainment for himself." She added a package of Woodbine cigarettes. "That, too. Now, what can I do for you?"

From the back room, a roar of laughter penetrated the shop. Nan glanced over her shoulder. "Have the men been spreading rumors about me?"

With pudgy hands on her hips, Margaret lifted her chin. "Are you daft? That lot? They're the last ones to figure anything out." She grinned. "Tell me, Nan. Is he as altogether gorgeous as I hear he is?"

Nan placed a supply list on the counter. "I have no idea what you're talking about." She longed for escape. "Here are the things I'll be wanting."

Margaret grinned. "Now, what's on your list for today besides denial?"

Nan wasn't sure her legs would keep her standing. "Who else knows?"

"Only the Shamrocks."

"All of them?" The vast network of women who named themselves the Shamrock Sisters stretched across the surrounding area. They bartered their goods and services, most of the time aboveboard, yet sometimes stretched the legality of things, especially now, during the government's "Emergency."

"Don't worry, Nan. On our mother's graves, we'll keep ya bomber boy a secret. And if ya needing any help, you can count on us."

Nan considered the woman. She probably wanted to help, but Margaret was making Nan regret her deepening involvement. "Yes, I know. Thank you."

A few minutes later, the wheels of Nan's bicycle bumped along the wet cobbled street. The buildings, turned dark gray by the rain, seemed to close in on her. Smoke from the chimneys added to the fog. The rain had slowed to a drizzle.

She nodded to several villagers as they went about their activities. A band of teenage girls loitered on the steps of a walk-up flat, smoking, cursing, and talking loudly until the arrival of Father Albert sent them scurrying away like giggling mice.

"Ah, Nan. How are you?" he called as she passed by.

"Grand, Father. Grand."

"Will I see you at confession this Wednesday?"

She glanced over her shoulder without stopping. "Ah, you will, if there isn't a baby being born." She set her eyes on the road. Too many sins were piling up.

Turning the corner, she slowed. She was nearing the Guinness lorry parked outside of Mrs. Odin's pub. The woman herself was leaning against the multipaned window under an awning, chatting with the short truck driver, Brian Monaghan. A Dublin man, he was a bachelor, and from the sparkle in his brown eyes, his status might be changing. Or maybe he had a barkeep in every town.

He didn't seem to mind being soaked while he was getting a bit of conversation with Mrs. Odin. From the sly grin on her face, Nan thought he'd probably gotten a bit more from her besides.

"Ah, Nan," Mrs. Odin called with a wave. "Might I have a word?"

Nan slowed to a stop. "Of course."

"Good-bye, Brian." Mrs. Odin smiled, swaying her hips from side to side.

Brian took a long drag on a cigarette and nodded. "Next time, then?"

"Oh yeah. I'll have some lovely blood sausages. Do stop by for a bit of a fry on your way back into town."

"See you soon." He slanted a look at Nan.

Nan slanted one back.

Mrs. Odin squeezed Nan's hand so hard, it smarted. "I was hoping I'd find you."

"What's wanting?"

"Get off ya bike and come inside."

"I really don't have time. Is there something you need me to attend to?" Nan couldn't help but sweep a glance below Mrs. Odin's belt.

"Don't be making assumptions," she said. "No worries a'tall. That boat sailed a long time ago."

"There are other things."

"Ah, go on. He wears a French letter."

Nan's throat tightened. She didn't want to hear about Mrs. Odin's love life.

"Inside. Quickly, before that buffoon Finn shows his ugly mug. He's been prowling the streets. I've something to give ya for you know who."

Of course Mrs. Odin knew, too. Why wouldn't she? Wasn't she Mrs. Norman's sidekick? The two of them always discussing the comings and goings of the townsfolk.

Inside the pub, the air smelled of lemon oil, bacon, and the stale scent of beer, an aged smell that proved impossible to scrub clean, even for Mrs. Odin, who knew how to do just about anything.

The woman went behind the bar and then carried a wrapped bottle to Nan.

"What's this? You know I don't drink."

"It's only to warm the belly. Maybe there's a certain someone who might need it on a cold Irish night. Unless, of course, you're keeping him warm."

It was impossible to keep a secret in this town. She and Dutch were doomed.

The sound of the back door opening made Nan jump.

"Don't worry; it's just Mrs. Norman."

The woman came plodding toward them, her Wellies flapping on the wood floor. The scarf over her gray hair sat on her head like a wilted piece of lettuce.

"How did ya get here, Mrs. Norman?" Mrs. Odin asked. "Through the fields? You're leaving a trail of mud on my freshly scrubbed floor."

"I spotted Finn hanging outside the doctor's house. He'd only be asking me questions, so I took the path down by the river and went under the bridge."

"Have yourself a glass of water," Mrs. Odin said, pouring a tumbler from an earthenware pitcher.

Mrs. Norman gulped down the water. "Here you are, Nan. Am glad I ran into ya and didn't have to make the trip out to your house." She held a pot with a snap top.

"What's this?" Nan frowned.

"My special chicken soup."

"Why might you be giving me that?"

"Ah, go on with ya. You know why. Remember? Dr. Mann told me to make a pot."

Nan stared at the two women. "Does everyone know?"

"Only them that's important." Mrs. Odin handed her the bottle. "Me. Mrs. Norman here. Margaret. Tuda. Kelly—"

"No, not Kelly. She's the Garda's wife."

"That's to your advantage."

Nan couldn't imagine how. But it appeared that Kelly had been welcomed into the Shamrock Sisters club. Not everyone made the cut.

"That's right." Mrs. Norman placed the pot of soup on the bar counter. "Did ya see the baby yet, Mrs. Odin?"

"I did. A beauty. Her cries could fill an opera house." She pushed the wrapped bottle into Nan's chest. "Ya don't need to look so alarmed, you poor blessed girl. We can keep a secret. If you only knew what we knew about this town."

"So true," Mrs. Norman agreed. "Make your red, curly hair white and straight."

Did they suspect about Teddy? How he shouldn't be buried on hallowed ground? *No.*

"Don't frown, dear, or those lines across ya brow will be etched there, and how will ya get another man then?" Mrs. Odin threw a towel onto the floor and, with her foot, wiped the wet spots.

Mrs. Norman smiled at Nan. "We know how to keep our pieholes shut. What you're doing is the most noble and romantic thing we've ever heard of. Isn't that so, Mrs. Odin?"

"'Tis. Ah, to have a man such as yours."

"He's not mine. He belongs to the RAF." The truth hurt. He'd never be hers even if she dreamed of it some lonely night after he was gone.

"Not his heart. That's yours."

Nan was about to argue the point when Mrs. Norman said, "And his soul belongs to Jesus."

The women crossed themselves as though they were joined at the hip. For good measure, Nan made the sign of the cross as well.

Mrs. Norman held out the soup. "And, dear, if you need any help, you just come asking. There's nothing we wouldn't do for you and that man of yours."

That man of mine.

There wasn't even any point in trying to set them straight. The ladies herded Nan to the pub entrance. Mrs. Odin held the door open. The rain splashed on the sidewalk and dripped down the sides of the buildings.

Nan positioned the gifts in her bicycle basket. "Thanks," she said.

"Now, be on your way. Feed him my soup. Pour him a whiskey. You'll make him a proper Irishman before he hops the fence to the border."

"And kiss him like it's the last kiss he'll ever get on earth, 'cause it just might be." Mrs. Odin let out a sigh.

"I'm not kissing him."

"You're a fool if you don't," Mrs. Odin said.

"Ah, I agree," Mrs. Norman added. "You're only young once. And sins can be confessed and forgiven when you're white on top and the smoke has gone out below."

Nan heard the ladies cackle as they returned inside the pub. Part of Nan wanted to take their advice.

She winced at the thought of the Shamrocks discovering Dutch. They had the goods on everyone in town, and now this included Nan.

But how could it have been the most "romantic thing" they'd ever heard of? Hiding a flyboy in her house? Playing cat and mouse with Finn?

Lord, if you're listening, please bring a peaceful end to this dangerous situation.

She pedaled home, repeating her prayers over and over again.

The rain stopped after a few minutes. Sunlight streamed over the emerald landscape, double rainbows stretching across the water.

A sign from the Lord that He was with her. He was watching over the situation. All she had to do was have faith. He would do the rest.

This notion was tested the moment she pulled into the courtyard. Finn skulked around the side of the house, keeping his chubby hand on his gun.

"Officer Finn. What are you doing here?" Nan leaned the bike against the whitewashed wall. To hide her trembling hands, she shoved them into her pockets, then plastered on the charming smile that Dutch had warned her about.

Finn came toward her. His heavy breathing echoed around the courtyard.

"Well, cat got your tongue?"

"Your cat seems to have a lot to do with the goings around here, but no. The cat hasn't been successful in getting my tongue."

Not yet. "Why do I have the pleasure of another visit so soon? What do you want?"

His gaze flicked from her chest to her eyes. "To make sure you're safe."

"Thanks. You have done your duty today. Twice. Now, be on your way. There's nothing here that needs your attention."

He closed the distance between them, smelling like last night's cabbage. And whiskey. "You need a man around the house."

She stepped back, her foot slipping on the wet cobblestone. "I don't. Be off with ya. Have you been drinking?"

"Nan," he said, his hand reaching for her shoulder. "You're making a mistake, not trusting me."

"Be on your way, Finn, before I send word to your ma that you've been drinking on the job."

He froze, panic on his face.

Mama's boy.

"What's doing out here? I thought I heard someone rumbling about the place." Tuda walked from the garage onto the courtyard, wiping her hands on a rag.

"Hello, Tuda." Nan waved, hurrying toward her. "How's my car coming along?"

"Just grand."

"He's been drinking," Nan whispered.

"I can tell."

"Mrs. Quinn," he said, "I've been looking for you. My car won't start again."

"What a shame. Bring it back into the shop."

"I did. Left it with your husband. This is the third time in two months. Why can't you fix the blasted thing? This is what happens when a woman tries to do a man's job."

Tuda widened her stance and glared at him. "Ah, cars are complicated things altogether. Maybe, Officer Finn, you ought to take your vehicle to Limerick from now on."

"Maybe I should. Tell me, Mrs. Quinn, what brings ya here?"

"Fixing Nan's car so she can speed along in comfort this winter."

"I'll let ya use my car." Finn slurred his words. "Anytime ya want. Say the word."

"Thanks, Officer Finn, but I understand ya car's not working. Did you find anything suspicious round my house?"

"Not a thing out of order. I've checked the perimeters, and all is clear."

"Could have told you that," Tuda said.

"How could you tell me that, Mrs. Quinn? You not being here?"

"Not here? Am I a ghost or something?"

"I mean with your head under the bonnet. And where is your ne'er-do-well husband? Why aren't you with him like a good wife should be? I heard he drove the van into a ditch after taking too much drink. Again."

Tuda straightened her shoulders. "If that isn't the pot calling the kettle black. I can smell liquor on ya from here."

Finn fingered his gun. "You'd be an expert at that, wouldn't you?"

Nan could tell her friend was about to deliver a rash of fury on Finn, who, goodness knows, deserved it. But she squeezed Tuda's elbow.

"I don't want any trouble. Leave him be."

Tuda sucked in a breath. "Finn, are you done here?"

"You'll address me as 'Officer Finn' when I'm wearing the uniform. I'll be around again to make sure Nan's safe."

"Please, don't bother," Nan said.

"No bother a'tall." He spun on his heel and made his way to the bike leaning against the gate. Nan couldn't be certain, but she thought the cat might have left his calling card on the wheel.

"Get away, cat." He kicked toward Mr. Dee, lost his balance, and hopped sideways into the gate. Then he righted himself and grabbed his handlebars.

Love that cat.

Finn winked at Nan, then pedaled away.

Tuda shook her head. "You poor creature. You've really got a problem with that one, don't you? Maybe what Dutch warned you about is true."

"Finn is about as dangerous as dandruff on my shoulders. Annoying, unsightly, and gone with one brush of the hand. Where is Dutch?"

"He's buried in dirty hay in the garage. I'm glad he isn't allergic, or he'd have sneezed his way into captivity."

"We better rescue him." Nan walked over to the calf house.

"You're getting good at that." Tuda glanced around the yard. "Why don't you have a dog? It would give you a bit of a warning. You could train the dog to bite Finn's thick arse."

Nan's heart tightened. "Ah, after old Hamme went to heaven—I don't care what Sister Katherine claimed, I believe pets go to heaven—I haven't had the heart to replace him."

"Sounds a lot like how you feel about Teddy."

Nan's hand went to her throat. *That hurt. Deeply.* But she wouldn't show it. She stared at Tuda. "How could you say such a thing?"

"Ah now, Nan, darling," Tuda said. "I'm sorry. Paddy tells me my mouth is big enough to swallow the Irish Sea."

"How does one replace the irreplaceable?" Nan blurted.

"You could put his memory to rest and move on."

"Maybe someday, but right now I can't afford another heartbreak."

"How is it living if you don't reach out to love? Even Mrs. Odin has found herself a fellow."

Nan decided it was better to ignore the subject. "Where did you say Dutch is?"

She followed Tuda into the garage. The car's bonnet was open as though it were in the middle of a surgery.

"Dutch," Nan called. "Coast is clear."

Tuda's tongue pushed out her cheek. "Yeah, come out, come out, wherever you are."

"Very funny," his muffled voice replied.

The pile of hay in the corner of the building came to life. Dutch was covered in straw. He coughed, sneezed, then coughed again. "Awful stinky stuff."

"Fast thinking, Tuda."

Tuda lifted her chin in Dutch's direction. "It was himself. First thing he did this morning was break up a bale of hay in case he might need a hiding place."

He stood there, brushing himself clean. A sigh caught in Nan's throat when he ran his hand through his thick head of hair to comb away the debris.

"Turn around," Tuda said, pushing Nan forward. "Nan will brush off your back."

Nan picked straw from between his shoulder blades, then plucked at the hay on his calves.

"Get the stuff across his shoulders, so." Tuda kicked the straw back into a mound, ready again if necessary.

Nan's palm smoothed across Dutch's broad shoulders, the muscles tight beneath her touch. The light from the window sent shadows to caress his cheeks.

Tuda muttered out of the corner of her mouth, barely loud enough for Nan to hear, "He'd be worth the risk of breaking that heart of yours."

"Shhhh."

"I had a feeling Finn might return. He has a nose for things not being quite right here," Dutch said as Nan's hand traveled along his back. With a slow turn, he faced her. "Thanks."

"Welcome." Nan focused on her muddy boots. "How's the car coming along?"

"Good." He picked a piece of straw from her hair, and his touch sent tingles up her back. "Tuda here is pretty good for a girl."

"I'll arm-wrestle you later if you want."

"No kidding, I'm grateful to you both."

"Okay, flyboy," Tuda said. "Don't get sappy on us. We've got work to do."

"Did you get the Ford started?" Nan asked.

If so, maybe he'd leave tonight. Her stomach twisted at the thought.

"Nope. There are a couple of items we still need. Right, Tuda?"

"Yes. If the parts don't come in, I'm going to borrow them from Finn's car. You'll be off by tomorrow night."

"Yes." He had been looking at Nan but now turned his attention to the cat. "Hey, Mr. Dee. Where'd you go?"

Ignoring Nan, the cat bounded toward Dutch.

"That cat's in love with ya," Tuda said, grinning.

Dutch smiled. "The cat and I have an understanding. Mr. Dee is doing his part for the war effort, too."

"I'll say. He piddled on Finn's tire wheel," Nan said.

"Good kitty." Dutch laughed. "I wish I could take you back to England with me. You could be the airfield's mascot."

His smile sank Nan's stomach to the floor.

But she hung around for a moment, watching Dutch tinker with the car and also taking in the muscles in his arms, exposed by his rolled-up sleeves.

"Are you here to help?" Tuda asked.

"Me? Ha. You two have things to do. I'll make the tea. Mrs. Norman has sent along her famous chicken soup. Tuda, will you stay?"

"Thanks, but I better go home to my Paddy. No telling what he might get into. Besides," she paused, settling her gaze on Nan. "I wouldn't dream of intruding on your last night together."

CHAPTER 18

After a bowl of Mrs. Norman's delicious chicken soup, served with bread, Nan settled Dutch into the chair close to the fireplace. The cat lay over the man's feet in perfect comfort, in a way that spoke of ownership—the cat owned Dutch, of course.

"Shall I read aloud?" He held a book of Yeats's poetry.

"Please," she said. He looked so comfortable in the big chair, the cat at his feet. And so handsome.

He began to read, and listening to him nearly broke Nan's heart. The words were sublime, but it was his voice that sent shivers through her. *Gentle. Articulate.*

"Wonderful, don't you think?" he asked, looking up at her.

"Oh yes. Read another."

He flipped through the book until he landed on another poem. The words registered in the musical part of her brain, but it was the fact of Dutch sitting there just as Teddy used to, reading poetry to her out loud, that made her heart race.

He finished and closed the book. "I'd forgotten how beautiful Yeats's poetry is."

"Yes. You've read him before? Certainly sounds like you know your way around a poem."

"I was a literature major before I switched to engineering."

"No future in poetry?"

"Not if I want to eat."

"That's not true. My husband . . . did you see that Yeats signed the book?"

Dutch's eyes widened. "Really?" He flipped to the front pages and smiled as his finger traced the signature. "Did you meet Yeats?"

"No, not me. My husband did. He and his family were part of the Dublin arts and intellectual crowd, the literary bunch. His mother was an actress. A Dublin player."

"And you? You ever acted? You're certainly pretty enough to be an actress."

"Go on with ya."

He placed the book on the side table. "You're the most beautiful girl I've ever met."

"Then you haven't met many girls."

"Stop underestimating yourself. You're beautiful, brave, and smart. And not just on the surface. You're beautiful inside."

Nan focused on the fire, her cheeks blossoming with heat. "Thanks," she said. "You're not so bad yourself. I bet the girls line up back in England."

"I don't know. I'm not really good at that sort of thing."

"What sort of thing?"

"Chasing skirts. My RAF pals have a saying, 'You get your wings, you get the birds,' but I don't go in for that. I mean, what's the point if you don't love the girl? It doesn't sit right with me. I have to care."

What's not to love about this man? "Your buddies must think you're odd."

"I don't care what they think."

She crossed her legs and saw him glance at the underside of her thigh, despite the fact that she was wearing trousers.

He set his attention back on her eyes. "Where did you meet Teddy?"

"Dublin. When I was in nursing school. He taught literature and English at the University of Dublin."

Even now she could visualize Teddy, stunning in his black robes, white chalk dust drifting down his sleeves. All the girls were after him. To this day she wasn't sure why he'd chosen her. Her mood darkened as she remembered more: The day he began to blame her for all his troubles. Her fault they were in this cottage. Her fault he couldn't write. Her fault he'd drink himself to sleep every night.

Her fault he no longer wanted to touch her.

She forced herself to go on. "We met at a tea shop. He invited me to his lectures. I used to sit in the back of the auditorium and watch him. He had a brilliant mind." *A mind that betrayed him later.*

"What happened to him?" Dutch asked.

"I told you. Terrible accident. He fell off the cliff. Bashed his head on a rock below. Washed up like that poor RAF pilot."

He waited for her to continue, but she was lost in her memories. In that chair beside the fireplace Teddy would sit, slapping his head, crying that the voices wouldn't leave him be.

He refused to see a doctor, telling her to get away, as though she was some annoying pet. She had felt as if her heart would split open.

"Must have been terrible for you, Nan."

She lifted a hand, waved it. "Such is life."

"And death. No man since then?"

"No." A void that deep couldn't be filled.

"Why?"

She wanted to say "none of your business," but instead she shrugged. "You've seen the local talent. Why haven't you dated anyone since your engagement?"

He shrugged. "The war."

They sat without speaking for a few minutes. Death and her love life were not topics she wished to expound on. Apparently, Dutch didn't, either.

"The map the doctor gave you, was it a'tall helpful?"

"Immensely. I have a question for you, though." He stood up, displacing Mr. Dee. "Can you fill me in on one area? It looks like it could be a shortcut, but the route goes around it. Maybe it's bog land?"

"Let me see." She stood as well and followed him to the table.

He pulled the map out of the envelope and spread it open on the table. "Here, this area. Bog? Or lake?"

Her shoulder pressed against his arm as she leaned over to study the map. "Ah, I dunno. I've never ventured down that way. But this road, the one the doctor has mapped, I know is fine." She pointed along a black line that snaked around a lake. "There's the abbey. Last stop before freedom."

His hand covered her fingers. "Here?" His voice looped around her chest as his palm covered hers.

He lifted her hand to his lips. Nearly caused her knees to buckle.

He's going to kiss me.

She closed her eyes and slid her hand up to his chest as he wrapped his arms around her, pulling her into his strong body.

Soft lips touched her forehead, then the sides of her mouth, finally her lips.

Her body seemed to turn to liquid. She melted into him. The kiss deepened, making her feel as if they were swirling around the room.

Bells were going off, like the chimes of heaven.

Bells.

Like . . . a bicycle bell!

The dream broken, she pushed away from him. "Dutch. No. Someone's coming."

He turned toward the sound. "Again?"

"What do you think?"

"I think someone has the worst timing in the world."

Or maybe the best. "Go." Nan's lips were aflame, her body shimmering. She hoped whoever was at the door couldn't tell.

Dutch walked to the bedroom, tripped on his own feet, then stopped. "Nan, I—"

"Please, just go."

He disappeared into the bedroom, and she heard the pop of the hiding-room door opening.

She parted the curtain to peek and felt a stab of panic.

Officer Halpin.

She folded the map, dropped it into the box, then kicked it under the table. She threw the front door open. "Officer Halpin. What brings you here so late?"

Deep lines creased his cheeks, and there were bags under his eyes. "I've come to fetch you. Kelly is having a hard time."

"What's wanting?"

He looked uneasy with the question. "Ah, well, ya see . . ."

"There's no shame in talking about what's going on with your wife's body."

"She's bleeding something fierce."

Nan sucked in a sharp breath. "Did you call Dr. Mann?"

"Can't find her. Besides, Kelly wants you."

Nan wished Paul had found the doctor, but she was getting ahead of herself. Maybe it was nothing. Nothing much. Something Nan could handle.

Please, Lord. Nothing a'tall.

"Who's with Kelly and the baby now?"

"Mrs. Norman."

"Then they're in good hands." She frowned, remembering the bicycle bell. "Why didn't you drive your car?"

"No petrol. I went by the garage earlier, but Paddy Quinn was out."

Out cold, no doubt. "Didn't Tuda come to the door?"

"She did, but Quinn is out of petrol altogether. Seems the Irish Army filled their tanks today. There won't be another shipment for a long time."

Where would they get fuel for the escape? she wondered. Tuda probably had some scheme. She would take care of getting whatever they needed. Tuda had better.

"Ah, this war," Nan said. "Wait one minute. I'll get my things."

"Where's your bike?"

"In the garage." Nan pointed across the courtyard.

"I'll get it while you put your coat on. We'll travel together over the dark lanes."

Her heart broke for the sergeant. There was no worse hurt than that for a loved one in trouble. "I'll be out in one second."

Her pulse was pounding. She sprinted to the bedroom, grabbed her coat, and placed her hands against the closet wall. Her fingernails scraped the wood. "I've an emergency. Kelly's in need. Wait a few minutes; then you can come out."

"Okay," she heard his muffled voice respond. "Will you be back tonight?"

"Honestly, I don't know. I hope so." For everyone's sake.

With that, she snatched her medical bag and raced to her bicycle.

The storm had moved on, leaving the cold air slapping against her cheeks. There were so many things to pray for as she traveled, she could hardly get them all in.

First, Kelly.

Next, Dutch.

Last, she prayed for her immortal soul—all the lies she'd been telling, and that kiss. Her thoughts spiraled to the sensation of Dutch's lips upon hers.

No, don't, she told herself, yet inside she was screaming, *Yes.* It was no mistake that he'd come to her door; the good Lord had led him there.

Not for you to kiss him, you eejit. To heal.

Her bike dipped into a rut, throwing her off balance. She struggled for equilibrium, gripping the handlebars so hard, she was sure she'd bruised her palms.

Ahead of her, Halpin looked back and called, "Are you all right, Nan?"

"Dandy."

When they neared town, the sight of the church bell tower against the moonlit night was comforting. Yet foreboding.

Nan felt a bone-chilling coldness.

Death. Nearby.

She shook off the sensation, refusing to believe it could be Kelly. Tears bit the corner of her eyes at the mere thought. But the feeling, the creeping darkness, did not go away.

They cycled down the quiet streets, the moonlight casting eerie shadows on the two-story buildings. Upstairs windows were mostly dark. Only the barking of dogs creased the night air with sound.

Finally, they reached the town square. The Celtic cross in the center seemed to slant backward, but perhaps that was only a trick of light. A horse pulling a cart meandered around the square, the cart's occupant slumped over and clutching the reins. Paul paused for a second but continued on.

He looked back at Nan. "Carlow will have to wait."

They pedaled past the rectory house. Nan pictured Father Albert in his private quarters, no doubt preparing Sunday's sermon. From the father's open window, the tender voice of John McCormack penetrated the night air in a sorrowful song.

A sigh escaped her throat at the thought of the confession booth. She'd rather not confess, but then again, she didn't want to burn in hell for all eternity. Once Dutch was on his way, she'd square things with God. Receive absolution for her sins and do her penance.

She gazed at the moon and the silver clouds.

I promise, Lord.

Although that wasn't true, was it? She couldn't tell Father Albert about Teddy, rotting in his grave in a place where he shouldn't be.

She'd go to her own grave with that secret. And doom herself to purgatory, too.

She stopped the mental spiral before it sank too deep. *Not now,* she told herself. *Worry about your fate later.* She had to concentrate on those still on earth.

◆ ◆ ◆

Dutch waited for what seemed an eternity before he came out of his hiding place. Nan's absence left the warm cottage feeling cold.

His knee was aching and swollen as a football. His arm stung, but the wound reminded him of why he'd happened upon her door, of how much Nan had helped him. He'd kissed her. And he wanted to kiss her again. His lips burned. His fingers trembled over his mouth.

It certainly hadn't been his mission to find romance when he'd knocked on her door. And it was the worst-possible time to find a girl he was sure he could love forever. That is, if she'd give him a chance.

He stared at Teddy's portrait on the mantel. She clearly hadn't put her husband to rest. What was the hold this dead man had on her? It was as though he was reaching up from the grave, still keeping her at his side.

But Dutch had kissed Nan. And she'd kissed him back. It wasn't his imagination.

He wondered what would have happened if Halpin hadn't turned up. The heat between them might have carried them in a direction neither of them intended to go before marriage.

Seated on the comfy chair, he stared at the fire. This was torture. His mission was to get out of Ireland, to return to the base and win the war. Why did he feel he needed to save Nan when she didn't even want to be saved? That creep, Finn. He was trouble. Dutch smacked the arm of the chair. Why didn't she see the danger?

He had a few hours to convince her, he supposed. Time to get back to business. Noticing the edge of the map peeking out of the box, he got up and returned to the table. He spread the map out, but his concentration drifted back to what had happened right on this spot.

He'd kissed her. And she'd kissed him back.

Yes, he was sure, she'd kissed him back. The fact filled him with an ache.

He pushed away the sensation and instead thought about his escape route. After several minutes, he folded up the map, praying it was accurate.

He closed his eyes. "Lord. Please be with me during my escape and grant me traveling mercies. And protect the women of Ballyhaven who have helped me." Taking a breath, he savored the scent of fresh bread and tea. He gazed around the simple, clean room. It was comfortable here. A shelter from the real world.

Well, he realized, the house might be simple, but Nan wasn't. Part of him wanted to keep hiding, but his unit called. Duty called. The war called.

Ah, Nan. What would happen to her? When would he see her again? And would there be room in her heart for another man? He looked again at the picture of Teddy. "What did you do to her?"

He had to stop this, had to do something productive or he'd go mad. His gun. He'd go on the hunt again. Maybe his gun was hidden in the loft. He picked up a lit lantern and headed up the steep stairs.

He paused on the landing. The loft was cold, tomb-like, a startling contrast to the warm rooms below. Or maybe it was merely the dead man's desk, the typewriter, and the manuscript, all left there undisturbed. Seemed unlikely Nan would stash the gun in one of the drawers and violate the mausoleum she'd erected in her husband's honor. Nonetheless, Dutch pulled out the desk chair and sat.

He opened the top drawer, then another and another. All packed with pens, ink, paper, but no gun. A silver hip flask with the initials

"TOO" engraved in curly script was wedged among the letters in the bottom drawer.

"Too?" He muttered. *Yeah. Too much.*

Out of nowhere, the cat jumped onto the desktop.

"What's going on, Mr. Dee?"

The tabby meandered over the surface, knocking manuscript pages to the floor.

"If I didn't know better, I'd say you did that on purpose." He picked up the scattered pages.

Teddy's poems. A genius, the next Yeats, wasn't that what Nan had proclaimed?

It felt like snooping, but Dutch started reading. As he read, his blood pressure soared. Didn't take much scrutiny to realize what old Teddy boy was all about. He slapped the pages back into a messy pile. Self-indulgent, misogynist garbage.

The poet wasn't a genius; he was a complete disgrace, with his venom aimed at everything and everyone. Especially Nan. "The whore wife who sucks the life out of me." It made Dutch's stomach churn to read such rubbish.

He'd like to take Teddy out to the woodshed and give him a few whacks, something Teddy's parents should have done.

His thoughts softened. The guy was mental. For him to hate women so much, perhaps Teddy's mother had done something unspeakable to him. Not that it was an excuse. Teddy had choices. Drinking himself into a daily stupor had been a choice. Marrying Nan had been a choice.

The way his life ended—Dutch suspected that had been a choice, too.

He wondered what he ought to do, if he ought to say something to her. How could Nan continue to give her heart, her life, her entire being to this dead creep? Hadn't she read the poems? Didn't she grasp their meaning? "No love hath I other than the drink for my wife is a poor excuse for being married."

Nan shouldn't be suffering over this man. She was squandering her time and energy. Throwing pearls at swine.

Straightening the pile of papers, Dutch wondered if he ought to let it go. It wasn't his business. Nor was it his place. Yet if he didn't talk to her, who would?

He yawned, made his way to the other side of the room. After checking under the bed and the nightstand, he sat on the mattress. Just a nap, he told himself, settling into the comfort of a wool blanket.

Tossing and turning, his mind would not rest. He couldn't leave without talking to her. She was too good to mourn a man who didn't deserve her love.

She wouldn't like it, though, being presented with the naked truth. Might cost him their friendship. The cat jumped onto the bed and settled next to Dutch's head.

He didn't want to, but he had to talk to her. It'd be worth the pain of losing her if he could free her from her emotional prison.

CHAPTER 19

The wind buckled the Halpins' upstairs window, startling Nan as though she'd been slapped on the cheeks. She stared at her reflection in the multipaned window. Had she missed something after the birth? What? What could cause a young, healthy mum to slide toward an early grave?

Nan packed up her medical bag, unable to shake the feeling of doom. She went over and over the details of the delivery in her mind. Two weeks early, but that was no cause for alarm. Or harm. Nothing out of the ordinary. *Nothing.*

So why, less than forty-eight hours after the birth, was Kelly bleeding out?

The situation was grave, and there was nothing Nan could do for Kelly besides hold her hand and wait. The ambulance would be there soon to take her to hospital. As fate would have it, Dr. Mann had finally been found, but Nan knew it was already too late.

Mrs. Norman entered the room. "Here's your tea, Nan. Drink some before ya fall on your face from thirst." The cup clanked onto the dresser top beside Nan's medical bag.

"Thanks."

Nan's turmoil must have been obvious, as Mrs. Norman squeezed her arm and whispered into her ear.

"Sometimes explanations remain in the hands of the Lord," she said.

"I know." The painful truth seared Nan's heart.

Paul. How would he cope with the loss of another wife? She trembled at the mere thought of the coffin being lowered into the village graveyard.

"Nan. Sit next to me and my daughter." Kelly's voice was barely a whisper. Baby Maeve cuddled next to her, asleep against the warmth of her ma.

Nan held Kelly's wrist, checking her pulse. Weak but steady. "You're going to be fine."

"Then why do I feel the life draining from me?"

"Now, now. You'll be fine."

Kelly looked toward the ceiling. "You're being optimistic."

"You're being pessimistic. After an operation—"

"I won't have any more children." The words sounded desperate.

There was a painful knot in Nan's throat. "Thank the Lord that you have a lovely daughter."

"I wanted to fill my house with children."

"Then you'll love Maeve all the more." Nan brushed her hand over the dewy head of the child.

Tears ran down Kelly's cheeks. "If I don't come back, Maeve, don't you worry. Your da is a wonderful man, and he'll look after you. And I'll be waiting for ya in heaven."

"Stop talking such nonsense." This time it was Mrs. Norman. She adjusted the pillow behind Kelly's head. "You'll give the poor dear child nightmares."

The young woman's face was as pale as a wedding veil. Deep lines etched her forehead and around her eyes. Life itself seemed to be dripping out of her.

"You be a good girl for your da, Maeve."

"Of course she will." Mrs. Norman winked. "Maeve is one of us. An honorary Shamrock Sister. I promise."

A clamor of footsteps stomping up the stairway sent Nan to the door. It was the ambulance crew.

"About time you showed up," Mrs. Norman said. "You're in a motor ambulance, aren't you? Not some horse-drawn cart?"

"That we are," the burly driver said. "We're not completely in Victorian times, ya know."

"Yep," the second added. "When we kicked dirty-drawers Victoria and her lot out of Eire, we gave her back her horse-drawn ambulances."

"Shame you gave back your manners, too." Mrs. Norman scooped up the baby.

"Ah, ya got a mouth on ya, don't ya, missus?" With hearty laughter, the men lifted Kelly from the bed onto a stretcher and headed out of the room.

Baby Maeve must have sensed her mother's absence. She let out a howl.

"There, there, there." Mrs. Norman dipped a washcloth into a glass of whiskey that she'd poured for Officer Halpin. She placed the cloth into the baby's gaping mouth.

"Mrs. Norman, what do you think you're doing?"

"It's how I calmed my own six boys. Worked every time."

"You'd get your babies drunk so they'd pass out?"

"Taught them to be good Irish drinkers."

"I don't know if that's something to be proud of." Nan rummaged through her medical bag until she found a pacifier.

"Ah sure. They're all good lads, every one of them. Even if they all left Ireland for other parts of the world."

"Here, let Maeve suck on this instead," Nan said.

"A dummy? Well, aren't you the smart one, carrying this in that bag of tricks ya got there."

"I am a midwife, after all. I'm going to insist Sergeant Halpin go to hospital with Kelly. You can take care of Maeve for a while?"

"Like I was her grandma. Will they be long?"

"They will." The reality sank deep into her bones. This might be Kelly's first night in eternity. "I'm trusting you with the baby."

"Of course ya can. Anu Collins can wet-nurse her, don't ya think?"

Nan nodded. "If she'd be so kind."

"Ah, she will. She told me she has enough milk to feed the Irish Army. I told her that was disgusting."

"Agreed." Nan watched the baby drawing on the dummy, the infant's sucking noises filling the room.

Mrs. Norman swayed back and forth with Maeve. "Tell me so, Nan, will Kelly be coming back?"

"In God's hands" was all she could say.

"I'll get the Shamrocks together for the rosary. And we'll light candles. Call on Holy Mother Mary and all the saints and angels in heaven to see our Kelly through."

Nan touched the baby's soft cheek. "That'd be grand. I best be off. Please don't teach Maeve any dirty Irish tricks while she's in your care."

"Ah no. Maybe a bit of the jig, though. What do you say?" Mrs. Norman smiled at the baby as she rocked her side to side.

"Nurse Nan?" Paul Halpin called from the bottom of the stairs. "May I have a word?"

His forehead was creased into a million lines of concern, leading Nan to wonder if Kelly's emergency had dug up memories of his first wife's passing.

How could it not?

"Will she be all right?" he asked when Nan reached the bottom of the stairs.

"We're doing everything possible. You should go with the ambulance, Paul. Ride in the back with Kelly. Hold her hand."

"What about Maeve?"

"Mrs. Norman will take good care of her."

"Are you sure?"

"She raised six of her own. Now go." She guided him outside into the snapping cold air.

"In you get," she said.

He climbed aboard the ambulance and took Kelly's hand. "How you doing?"

His wife burst into tears. "I'm sorry."

"I'll hear none of that," he whispered to her in a loving tone.

The driver shut the doors.

"Take good care of Mrs. Halpin," Nan urged him.

The vehicle sputtered down the moonlit street, and Nan went back inside to gather her things and check on the baby once more.

As she rode toward home, she had the feeling of death in her soul. *Tonight, everything might change for the Halpins. Forever.*

Nan approached Thomas Carlow's horse-drawn cart. All these hours after she had passed by on her way to help Kelly, the horse was still pulling the cart around the town square, with Thomas slumped in the front seat. Not an uncommon sight.

"Mr. Carlow," she called, getting off her bike.

No response. Undoubtedly gone into the deep well of alcohol-induced sleep after too much Guinness, she figured.

"Ah now. Mr. Carlow." She didn't know what worried her so, yet she found herself reaching out for the horse's reins. "Whoa, whoa," she cried.

The horse obeyed, and Nan came up next to the cart.

"Mr. Carlow? Mr. Carlow? Will ya not wake up?"

He didn't move.

Nan climbed onto the cart and shook his shoulder. He flopped backward, his eyes fixed ahead.

Nan gasped. No, he would not wake up this time.

"Ah, you poor unfortunate thing. May the Lord have mercy on your soul." She looked across the street at the lights in the rectory. *Good.* The priest was still up.

The lights went off.

Poor Father Albert, she thought, shaking her head. He believed he was on his way to dreamland, but instead, Nan was about to wake him to take care of the dead.

The clacking of her boots echoed down the moonlit lane as she walked to the rectory gate. She paused, inhaling the scent of newly turned garden soil.

Her feelings had been right. Death had come tonight. Perhaps death would not come for Kelly, then.

"Please, God," she whispered.

Nan rang the bell several times before the lights clicked on.

"There better be someone dead to wake me at this hour," she heard Father Albert yell before he opened the door.

"There is."

"Who?" He tightened the belt of his robe. The light behind him lit his matted gray hair, reminding Nan of a halo.

"I'm sorry to disturb you, Father."

"One of your patients needs last rites?"

"Unfortunately, he's beyond that. I'm afraid Thomas Carlow is dead."

"Ah now. Are ya sure? He's probably just dead drunk."

"I recognize death when I see it."

Father Albert stretched forward to get a better look at the horse, who was once again clomping around the cross. "He could have had the decency to wait until morning. Why are you waking me? You ought to tell Halpin. Wake him. He'll take care of things."

Nan jabbed her hands into her coat pockets. "You should know, Father, that Paul—Sergeant Halpin has gone to hospital with Kelly."

"What's wanting?"

"Your prayers, I'm afraid. Something has gone terribly wrong in the aftermath of birth."

"Will she recover?"

Nan looked down at the nightshirt peeking out of his robe, then met his gaze. "I can't predict, I'm sad to say."

"A sad thing, indeed. Is Dr. Mann on the case?"

"She is."

"Grand. I hear good things about her abilities, even if she is a woman. And an American. Well, it doesn't look as though I'll get much rest tonight. Without Halpin, I suppose I'll need to call that lard-arse Finn to help."

Nan suppressed a grin. "If you don't need me—"

"Why would I be needing you? You bring lives into this world, not escort them into the next. That's my job."

"Yes, Father. I suppose that's true."

"There is no supposing," Father Albert said. "You and I play our God-given roles, but the start of life and its end is not up to us."

Ah, but wasn't that the worst thing Father Albert could have said? "What if it's not up to Him? What if someone takes another's life? Or their own?"

"A mortal sin, but that's a discussion for another time, Nan O'Neil. Now, be on your way. And God bless you, child."

"Thanks, Father."

She began down the brick walkway.

"And Nan," Father Albert called.

"Yes?" she answered, looking back.

"You haven't been to Mass the last two Sundays, nor have I heard your confession in a month."

"Sorry, Father. Duties have called me elsewhere."

"See that you come to church this Sunday. If you don't, I fear for your immortal soul."

"I will." She, too, feared for her soul.

She raced home, trying to beat the sunrise. The moonlight had succumbed to storm clouds that scurried in from the sea. When she rounded the lane to her house, the cottage stood a black shadow against the dull morning light.

Inside, it was cold; the turf fire had died.

She discarded her coat and medical bag before peeking into the bedroom. Dutch wasn't there, but he'd made the bed. The bathroom door was open, the room empty.

Her heart pounded. Had he left without saying good-bye? Or maybe Finn had captured him? Could Dutch have decided to take his chances on foot?

Her last hope was the loft.

Last hope? She must be daft. It'd be better if he'd hightailed it out of there, as he had promised six nights ago that he would.

She climbed the stairs, an oil lamp casting a yellow glow of light. At the top, she froze, from both relief and dread. Dutch lay on the twin bed. His heavy breathing spoke of a deep sleep.

He was still here. But he should have stayed downstairs, close to the hiding place. She'd take it up with him tomorrow. Or rather, later this morning.

The floor creaked. She turned toward the noise and held the lantern high. The light cascaded over Teddy's desk. The unfinished manuscript sat in the exact spot Teddy had placed it the day he died.

She stepped lightly toward the desk and ran a finger over the typed words as she set the lamp next to the stack of papers. Slumping onto the chair, she stared at the stack of poems. His poems. Why had his work careered into dark, hateful places? She knew his daggers were aimed at her. Teddy must have really come to despise her, but to this day, she didn't understand why. She had been a good, obedient wife. She'd never betrayed him. Tears stung behind her eyes. These days, she realized, there always seemed to be a flood waiting to burst forth.

She felt sorrow for Teddy, and worry for Kelly, whom she'd also failed. Sadness for Mr. Carlow.

She looked across to the bed. Anxiety for Dutch.

She could no longer bear the load. She tried to stifle the sobs, but then she surrendered, burying her face in her hands.

CHAPTER 20

Dutch woke to the sound of Nan's sobbing. She was so sad and beautiful in the lamplight, sitting at the writing desk. The whitewashed walls, pink and shadowy, faded into corners of darkness. Her reflection in the window seemed almost ghostlike.

He watched as she wiped her cheeks and combed her fingers through her hair, tears on her face glistening in the subdued light. She straightened the stack of papers on the desk, then slowed until she stopped moving. Her sobs wafted softly through the room and seemed to be absorbed into the thatched ceiling.

His heart ached for her. Those awful poems her late husband had penned would make anyone cry. *She ought to burn them.*

He sat up. "Are you okay?"

She swiveled around in the chair to face him. "Did I wake you?"

"No. I mean, yes." He threw off the heavy blanket he'd lain under, and it fell to the wide-planked wood floor. Mr. Dee jumped from the end of the bed and pranced toward Nan, then leapt onto her lap.

"I'm fine. It's been a rough night." She wiped the corners of her eyes. "You ought to be downstairs, closer to the hiding place."

He thought about telling her some story or another but instead admitted, "I was looking for my gun."

"You won't find it up here."

"I figured that out." He put on his shoes and approached her, his footsteps sounding like thunder on the bare wood floor.

"I'm good to my word. You'll get it when you're on your way. You might as well stop looking."

"I'm sure you're right. I have a feeling you're a woman who knows how to hide things."

"Things? Like yourself?"

"Yeah. I guess."

"Sorry I woke you." The cat jumped from her lap and strutted down the stairs.

"It's okay." He pulled up a cane-back chair and sat beside her. "How is Kelly? The baby?"

"She's in the hands of the Lord." Her voice reached deep inside him. Again, death, hand in glove with life.

He touched her knee. "I'm sorry. She died?"

Nan rested her hand on his, and heat radiated up his arm. There was a tingling sensation across his jaw. "No. I didn't mean that. She's at hospital with Dr. Mann, but she's in a bad way."

"What happened?"

Her hand slid away from his, but the sensation of her touch lingered.

"I'm not sure. I've asked myself that question a hundred times. Gone over every detail. Everything was fine after the birth, but last night she started bleeding and I couldn't stop it. I pray Dr. Mann can save her."

"This must be very difficult for you. How's the baby? Her husband?"

"The baby is grand. Paul Halpin's heart is breaking. Worse than the first time."

"First time?"

"His first wife died suddenly. One minute she was making tea; the next, she was gone."

"A double dose of hard."

"There's more. Mr. Carlow, a local farmer, I found him dead in his cart tonight."

"Oh, Nan. I'm sorry." No wonder she was crying. It wasn't merely her husband's morbid poetry. "Does his family know?"

"Mr. Carlow has no family. He's the last of his tribe. A bachelor."

The thought stung. Dutch had family, but Nan seemed to be alone. "Who's with the baby?"

"Mrs. Norman, although I hope she doesn't feed the child whiskey again."

"What? Are you joking?"

"An old folk remedy I don't approve of." She crossed her legs. "This is what happens when you dare to love again. Paul should have left well enough alone."

Dutch frowned. "You really feel that way?"

"Yes." The word was a sharp rebuke.

He sat back. "He chose to go on. He made his life fuller by loving again. It's sad that he faces another loss, but he has a daughter now. A new love."

"She might grow up without a mother."

"She has a father."

"She has a broken home."

He shifted his weight, and the chair creaked. "Their home isn't broken. She has a loving parent."

"It's not enough."

"It's never going to be perfect."

"It can be." Her statement came out more of a question.

"Life is messy. It doesn't make sense." He thought about Teddy's sordid pile of excessive gloom. His self-proclaimed "dissipated Irish shame." He would not mention it to Nan.

But she must have sensed his thoughts. She glanced at the manuscript. "I suppose you rifled through Teddy's desk for the gun?"

"Yep."

"Did you read his poems?"

"I did."

"And?"

He was a pinhead who didn't deserve you. "A little gloomy for my tastes. Not my cup of tea. Speaking of which, how about I make you a cup? And then you ought to get into bed." He rose, offered his hand. "Technically, I guess it's morning, though it looks more like night to me."

To his surprise, she slid her palm into his. They stood together in the dim light. The energy between them was thick, tangible, tingling. The rain was tapping at the window like a Mozart fugue, orchestrating the moment. It was a sound he would remember all his days. He longed to kiss her again.

"Ah, but I am tired." She let go of his hand, took the lamp, and headed toward the stairway. "I'll make the tea."

"No. I will," he said.

She moved ahead of him down the steep stairs. The light illuminated her figure, her brown sweater skirting her hips, their sway stirring his imagination.

"Are you sure you know how to boil the kettle?"

"I can fly a Wellington bomber. I think I can handle a teapot."

"Don't be so sure. It's an Irish teapot."

The main room downstairs was dark and cold. Nan set the lamp on the mantel. She bowed her head to the picture of Jesus and muttered a prayer that Dutch couldn't quite make out. "I'll start the fire," she said, reaching down into the basket for turf bricks.

"You'll do no such thing. Sit." He led her to the overstuffed chair and pulled up a stool for her feet. Arranging a blanket over her, he said, "Rest. It'll be toasty in here in no time."

"You know how to build a fire?"

"I'll manage. I used to take my nephews camping every summer."

"Tell me about camping."

"It was fun. The kids were troupers, hauling up the mountain with heavy backpacks. Not a word of complaint. I used to take them because my brother has a bum leg. Couldn't manage jumping the streams."

The turf bricks smelled like autumn leaves. He stacked them under the grate, upright like dominoes.

"What's wanting with his leg?"

Dutch shrugged. "Birth defect. His left leg is shorter than his right, and it barely moves. He walks lopsided, but he gets around. Didn't stop him from excelling at school. Top of every class." He stacked the turf bricks in a circle, found a few twigs, and lit the fuel. Then he fanned it with a rolled-up *Irish Times* until the flames licked the turf.

"See?" This was the first turf fire he'd ever built. Proud of the job he'd done, he turned and smiled.

She was asleep. Her snore made him grin.

Once the tea was made, the bread sliced, and the jam ready, he sat across from her, wondering if he ought to wake her before the tea got cold or just let her sleep.

She woke to his stare, blinked several times, and then the sweetest smile he'd ever seen crossed her lips. It was innocent and childlike. She blinked several times, and the weight of reality darkened her features.

"Hey," he said. "You hungry?"

"Starved." She started to rise.

"No, you stay. I've already made the tea. I'll pour. Milk, no sugar, right?"

"Yes. You noticed. What else have you noticed?"

Pouring the tea into a cup, he hesitated. "A lot of things."

"Like what?" Her gaze nearly stopped his heart, the sadness that lay inside those eyes.

He gave her a cup of tea. "You prefer a thin layer of jam on your bread. When you're mad, the left side of your mouth darts downward."

"Ah, you've seen that now, haven't you?"

He grinned. "A few times. You sometimes favor your right foot when you walk. Did you injure it?"

She glanced down. "No. Can't say that I have."

"And you're fierce. Gutsy. Brave."

"You have to be, in my line of work. Babies and mothers are tough." She sipped her tea. "Delicious. Maybe after the war you can run a café."

The mischievous sparkle in her eyes made his stomach do loops. "Only if the café is on an airplane."

"Ah. Makes sense."

For a while, they sipped their tea and ate their bread, the plates balanced on their knees. They exchanged fleeting glances at each other, then looked away quickly to the blazing turf fire. The cabin had turned from darkness to gray. Only occasional raindrops tapped on the windows.

He took their empty plates to the kitchen sink, poured two more cups of tea, then set the full cups on the tables beside their chairs. He returned to his seat. She was staring into the fire, lost in her thoughts.

It was dangerous ground, but he had to open the conversation with her. "Tell me. How long since your husband passed on?"

He heard her breath catch. "Three years."

"Why, after three years, haven't you moved on?"

"From here? And where would I go?"

"I don't mean 'here.' I mean"—he placed his hand over his heart—"from here."

"What are you talking about?" She wouldn't meet his eyes.

"It's been three years. Why haven't you moved on from your grief?"

"I just can't. That's why."

"Can't what?"

"Forget."

"You don't have to forget. No one forgets their loved ones. But the living start to live again."

"Isn't that a strange thing for you to say? What do you know about losing a spouse?"

"True, I've never been married, but I've lost people I've loved. And I know one must start living again."

"It's not that simple."

"Yes, it is."

"Not for me." She still would not look at him.

"Why? What makes your grief different?"

"I can't forgive myself."

"Forgive yourself? For what? Did you push Teddy off the cliff?"

She blinked. "Maybe."

"Really? Gave him a shove?"

"No. Of course not. But . . ."

"What?"

"I couldn't stop him. It's what I couldn't do that matters. And what I didn't do."

"How could you stop an accident?"

She placed the cup on the side table. "I really don't want to talk about this."

"Maybe you should. If not with me, then with someone else. Tuda, perhaps?"

"She knows. Suspects."

"What?"

"It wasn't."

"Wasn't an accident?"

She shook her head. "I can't talk to you about this."

They were silent. He flicked his gaze to the picture of her dead husband, and his anger grew. He'd love to wring Teddy's skinny neck.

"Nan."

She jerked a shoulder back but wouldn't look at him. "No. I'm not discussing this."

"Whatever happened, give yourself a break. You're not responsible for his actions."

"You don't understand. He slipped into a dark place, and there was nothing I could do to reach him. I failed to save him."

"Yeah. Really dark. I read his poems. He made Edgar Allan Poe seem like an optimist. No one could have dragged him from a pit that deep. I bet you tried, though."

Her frown confirmed it.

"You have to let him go, Nan. He's dead, you're not."

"How could you say such a thing?" She finally looked at him.

"Because it's true. You'll never love another man if you don't let Teddy go and allow yourself to get on with your life."

"I couldn't bear to love another. Look what Paul is going through. He'll have to cope with losing a second spouse. I just couldn't. I don't want to have another grave to visit."

"What's that expression you use? *Don't be daft.* Teddy isn't worth throwing your life away over."

"Throwing my life away? By mourning my husband's passing? You're a coldhearted man."

"Not by any stretch of the imagination. Grief takes as long as it takes, but you've decided to jump into the grave with him."

Nan's jaw moved as though words might come out, but for a second or two, none did. Finally, she said, "You don't know anything about me. About my life."

"Maybe, but I know this. Mourning Teddy the way you do is unhealthy. His death had nothing to do with you. He was mental."

"How could you say such a horrid thing? You don't know that."

She looked as if she might jump from her seat in outrage, but he had to keep going. "As an outsider reading that rubbish . . . his poems." He paused, pointed upward. "Yes. I can tell you he was off his rocker."

"He was brilliant," she said. Her voice was high-pitched, and her eyes were edged with tears.

"Stop making excuses for him. He was off his head." Dutch was relentless. "Until you put him to rest, love will never come your way again."

"I'm okay with that."

"Because it's safe?"

"Yes."

"So you'll have a safe, lonely journey to your grave? Is that what you imagined for your life?"

"None of your business."

"You're a comfort to so many, Nan." He softened his voice. "Allow someone to be a comfort to you."

She shook her head. "No one can take Teddy's place."

Let's hope not. "Look around the room. On every wall you have a portrait of Jesus or Mary or some saint. Don't you get it?"

"Get what?"

"You need faith. Faith that there's life after Teddy's death, no matter how awful you feel about what happened. We all despair; we all have regrets. We all lose someone we love. That's when we need our faith in God to bring us through."

Nan scanned the room, stopping at each religious relic until her gaze settled on the portrait of Jesus, above the mantel. Tears were pouring out of her eyes. "I'm tired of grieving for him, I am. Of always thinking of him. I loathe this unending grief. I hate myself for indulging in it." She tried to wipe away her tears. "I don't know how to stop."

"That's the devil coming against you, robbing you of peace."

Her gaze lifted to his. "The devil? Yes, you're right. He knows how to pick at our wounds."

"He infests us with condemnation. Makes us hate ourselves. Sometimes I struggle, too." He didn't want to share this. Didn't want to dig up the regret and the hurt.

"With what, Dutch?"

If talking about this could help her, he would do it. "Late at night, when I can't sleep, the devil whispers to me. My mind goes to the day my dad died. I was sixteen. I'd ditched school that day, with my friends. Across town, my father had a massive heart attack. He was dying, asking for me. Everyone tried to find me. The school. My mom. My brother. By the time I got to the hospital, it was too late. Dad was gone, and I hadn't said good-bye."

"Oh, Dutch." She slid to the edge of the chair. "I'm sorry."

"If I hadn't broken the rules, my father would have said his good-byes."

"You'll say your hellos in heaven."

A smile came across Dutch's face. "That's what my mom said. But I had to come to terms with what had happened. Had to stop the devil from stealing my peace, because, boy, did he lay into me."

"How did you combat the devil?"

"Prayer. My pastor told me the only way to get the devil off my back is to pray, send him packing each time he whispers into my ear. Just as you need to do."

"But I've prayed season after season after season."

"There's a second part. You must accept His forgiveness. He died for our sins on the cross so that we would be made free."

"I don't know, Dutch. I don't know. It's a terrible thing, all the doings that day."

"What happened?" His tone was as gentle as he could make it. "You can tell me."

"I . . . I've never told anyone before. Not the whole story."

He bent forward. "You're safe with me. What happened on the cliff that day?"

She seemed to be on the verge of letting him in, but suddenly she stopped. "I'm sorry. I can't talk to you about this."

She didn't trust him yet. *Fair enough.* "Okay. I'm here if you want to unburden your soul."

"That's Father Albert's role."

"Then talk to him. Let him help you."

"Maybe." Her voice seemed unsure.

He touched his hand to her knee. "Have faith that you are forgiven. Give your cares to Him. Let it rest in His hands."

She stared at the portrait of Jesus.

Dutch reached for her hands and squeezed them. "Your time for grieving needs to end. You'll have no room for me until you let Teddy go."

"Room for you? Aren't you the bold one? You're off to fight a war. You really think you'll give me another thought after tomorrow?"

"I'll never stop thinking about you."

Palms together, fingers lacing, they were inches from each other's lips, yet worlds apart. Dutch thought she might drift closer, maybe even kiss him or say something. The sound of the gate opening stole the moment.

"Who could that be at this early hour?" Her hand slipped from his as she stood. "The sun hardly up."

Dutch sat back. "You've got more visitors than Grand Central station."

"It's probably Tuda with . . ." She parted the curtain a slice. Her profile gleamed from the morning light. "Finn."

"Tuda's here with Finn?"

"No, just himself. Best you get into your hiding place."

Dutch stood. "Here we go again."

For the last time, he hoped, filled with a brew of relief and sorrow. The thought of leaving her now tore at him. For both of them to be free, they needed one another.

CHAPTER 21

The insistent fist pounding on the door shook the wood and strained the hinges. Nan looked around the room. Everything needed dusting. She couldn't remember her house being this dirty before, not even after Teddy's death, when she'd cried for two weeks.

She kicked the box from the doctor under the table.

Dutch was right about Teddy, she knew, but she couldn't deal with that right now.

"Who's there?" she called, as though she didn't know, but she had to delay answering the door for as long as she could.

"Officer Finn."

Digging her fingernails into the door, she gouged out a speck of red paint. She heard the hiding-place latch open and then close. Dutch was tucked away, safe for a while.

"I said, who's there?"

"Officer Finn. You'd best open the door. I'll not go away until I get what I'm after."

"Coming." Nan positioned her foot an inch behind the door. Fingers on the latch, she looked behind her at the wall where Dutch hid.

She cracked open the door, cold air swirling around her ankles and finding its way up her legs.

Fog, thick as sea foam, slithered into the courtyard, shrouding the outbuildings. Finn's smell radiated toward her. Sweat. Pig muck. Cheap cologne. He was tucked into his uniform like something the bog had spat up.

Finn tipped his cap. "Morning, Nan."

"Ah sure. Good morning to ya." She ignored the nausea swimming through her. She mustered up a sweet smile. "What's wanting on this fine, soft day, Officer Finn? Your ma? Is she well?"

"She's grand. I'm not here for Ma. You and I have official business."

Nan's toes curled. "Have we?"

"Yes."

He waited a beat, sized her up with a gaze that started at her boots and ended on her eyes. She willed herself to appear calm but couldn't stop the tremors racing up her legs.

"What about?"

"Thomas Carlow."

Nan let out a breath, cut the sign of the cross over herself, and said, "May the Lord welcome him into heaven."

"Unlikely given his sinful nature."

Who is he to judge? "Aren't we all sinners?"

"Some more than others." His focus dipped back and forth between her breasts and below her belt.

A shudder quaked through her. Once she got rid of Finn, she'd need a bath. Maybe Dutch was right; eventually she'd pay for her flirtations, but not today. No matter how belligerent Finn might get, she'd add to her debt by remaining charming.

Rubbing one hand over his double chin, he shifted his other to the gun at his side. "Since Sergeant Halpin is still at hospital with his wife, he's assigned me temporary Garda."

"Lord have mercy." *On us all.* "Any word on Kelly?"

"None a'tall. Halpin's by her side, and the doctor has agreed to remain nearby, but I gather the situation is grave."

"In the hands of the Lord, then." Everything, always and forever, including this encounter. "We'll need to pray for them both. You best be on your way." She started to close the door.

One fat hand held it open. "Not yet. I must make an official report on Carlow's death. Let me in, Nan. It'll only take five minutes."

"Let you into my house? Ah now. It wouldn't be right. Me a single gal and you—"

"Willing to change that."

Her stomach churned. "I'll stop by the station later and give you my statement."

With his meaty paw on the door, he grinned. "If you prefer. But if you have things to do today, it's best we take care of this official matter now. Five minutes, Nan. Or two to three hours at the station. And if you don't show up today, I'll come back tonight and arrest ya."

Nan lifted her chin. "Why so long at the station?"

"Because I can make you wait."

Of course. He's being strong on me. "And you'd do that, would you?"

"I would. I'm an official member of the Irish government on a mission. Let me in. You can trust me."

Knots formed between her shoulder blades. *Trust* and *Finn* were two words that did not mesh. Something about his smirk was so downright arrogant, it unnerved her.

She weighed the options. He would drag her through hours at the station, or he'd show up tonight to arrest her. That wouldn't do a'tall. Best to just let him in now and get rid of him for the rest of the day.

She hesitated. Something was different. Didn't feel right. The way he licked his lips, tugged on his jacket. Dutch's warning about Finn rang through her mind.

Tuda will be here any second, she thought, pushing down the warning. Best to get this over. Finn wouldn't take no for an answer this time.

"All right, Officer Finn. I'll leave the door open. And your gun— park it outside. No one comes into my house with a gun."

"Sure then, if that makes you more comfortable." He set the weapon into a leather bag at the side of his bicycle. "In case your cat gets a notion to steal it."

"You never know with Mr. Dee." She opened the door, and the cold morning air rushed in. "Let's make this quick. I've rounds to start."

"That all depends upon you," he muttered, not bothering to wipe his feet before he stepped inside.

Finn strutted toward the burning turf fire. He swaggered around the room and sniffed like a dog in search of a buried bone. She crossed her arms over her chest, thinking of the "bone" that was safely hidden behind the wall. She resisted the urge to glance in Dutch's direction. Mother had always warned that even a mere glance would be a dead giveaway.

Finn settled onto the cane-back chair and stretched out his legs.

You'd think he was here for Sunday supper, the relaxed way he acts, sitting there as though about to be served.

"I fancy a cup of tea, Nan."

"Do ya? Lucky for you, I just made some." Or rather, Dutch had. There was enough for one cup. "Sugar? Milk?"

"Black. Why do ya have two dirty cups out here? One beside each chair?" He touched the cup. "Still warm?"

Nan set the cup beside Finn, reached for the one Dutch had used, and shrugged. "I'm a terrible housekeeper lately. Are ya here to discuss my lack of cleaning skills or Thomas Carlow's death?" She sat across from him, her nerves raw.

He noted the multitude of dishes on the sink board. "Seems there's two of everything." Picking up his teacup, he stared over the rim as he sipped. "Things in pairs."

"My dirty dishes are piling up. What of it?"

"Just an observation." Finn pulled a notepad and pencil from his inside jacket pocket. He licked the pencil's sharp point several times, his wet tongue glistening in the glow of the fire. "All right then, Nan. Let me hear your account of what transpired last night."

Nan related the full story with as many details as she could remember. Finn took it all down, glancing up at her breasts as though the words were emanating from there.

He finally set his eyes on hers. "Do you suspect foul play?"

"Why would there be foul play? He was a bachelor without any relatives. Barely a pence to his name, I'd reckon."

"I'm being my thorough self is all. I'll ask ya to answer the question. Do you suspect any foul play?"

"None a'tall. It was the drink. The ruin of many a good Irishman."

"I don't drink that much," he blurted.

"I wasn't accusing you." *And you're not a good Irishman,* she thought.

"Grand, then. That should do it."

"Good. You'll be on your way." She started to rise.

"Sit." He tucked the pad and pencil back into his inside pocket. "We have another matter to discuss."

"What might that be?" She slid back against the chair, wishing she could wrap it around herself for protection.

"I could be a hero right now."

"Oh? Is that so?"

He nodded, his jowls jiggling like a gelatin pudding. "I could have the Garda, the Irish Army, and my fellow LDF officers here, pulling your house apart."

A rush of panic sparked through her. "Why would you be wasting everyone's time with such an altogether useless pursuit? I told Father Albert, I do not have any literature on birth control."

His blush turned into an angry glare. "That's not what I mean." He kept his focus on her. "I'm knowing he's here. If not in the house, then in an outbuilding."

The cat jumped onto Nan's lap. She snuggled him to her chest. "I have no idea what you're talking about. How about you, Mr. Dee? Have you a clue what he might be after?"

"Officer Christopher Whitney." Finn's voice carried through the room and torpedoed through her. She continued to pet the cat. "Who?"

"'Dutch.' I know he's here."

She rolled her eyes. "Where did you get a daft notion like that?"

"My ma."

"Your ma? Is she hearing the voices again?"

Finn leaned forward, his belly pressing into his legs. "She is. She overheard a conversation between Margaret, Mrs. Odin, and Mrs. Norman in the shop. They didn't know she was listening, but she heard it all. How he came to your door. How the doctor helped. How Tuda helped, too. You'll not get away with this, none of ya."

Stroking the cat, she shook her head. "Snooping, is it? Your ma got things wrong."

"She didn't."

"Then you must have misunderstood her."

He snorted. "If you want to keep a secret, don't tell the likes of those old biddies. You might as well have announced it over the wireless."

Nan looked skyward. *If ever I needed Your help, it'd be now, sweet Jesus.* She leveled a glare at Finn. "The RAF pilot is not here, Finn. I resent your accusations. Get up and be on your way. And tell your ma to keep her nose in her own business."

The buttons on his jacket pulled as he puffed up his chest. "I'll not ignore the information."

"Officer Finn, what you heard is gossip."

"I can have the Irish Army here with one word and, by doing so, secure my Garda position after the war ends. I'd be a hero, I tell ya. A hero."

"You'd be a fool. There's no one here but me and my cat. So go ahead. Why don't ya call them in? Be a hero."

"Because I'd rather be your hero."

"My hero? Is that so?"

"On my word. If you agree to certain terms, I'll let the bomber boy go and turn a blind eye to you and your friends' involvement in this highly illegal activity against Ireland. Otherwise, you'll all go to jail. I'll see to it."

Her palms pressed against the cat's soft fur. "Just out of curiosity, what terms?"

"Marry me."

Acid bubbled up from Nan's stomach, but she remained outwardly calm. She squeezed the cat so hard, he shifted in her arms and gave her a questioning meow.

"Is that all?"

"And once we're married, you'll give up your practice and be a proper Irish wife. You'll take care of my ailing ma."

Nan laughed. "So I'm to be a pig-farmer's wife? A nurse to your mother? No, thank you very much."

"A Garda's wife. You'll have respect."

"I have respect now."

"You won't after I'm done with ya. And your friends won't, either. Women's prisons are ever so bad."

She clucked her tongue. "First of all, you're wrong about the bomber boy being here."

"He's here. I'll find him." His eyes shifted around the room, settled on the wall beside the fireplace as though he knew Dutch was there.

Impossible.

"And secondly," she said, straightening her back, "we are not getting married. Ever." She didn't mean for her voice to rise to such a high-pitched and piercing level.

His face hardened like ice covering the rain barrel. "That's a long time. About the same amount of time you'll spend in prison for your violations against the state. One way or another, I'll find that bomber boy. I can offer you freedom from prosecution. He can fly home, back to his own kind. Don't be an arse, Nan. I'm willing to marry you, not just bed you." He reached over, placing his hand on her knee.

She slapped his hand away and pressed back against the chair. "Bed me? Are you mad? I'd sooner eat fungus sandwiches and drink bog water than let your lips touch mine. There's the door. Use it. I'm far too busy today to play games."

He rose to his feet and closed the distance between them, towering over her, his stale breath insulting her senses. "You'll do more than kiss me."

"I won't. Get out, you blaggard. I'll report you to Sergeant Halpin and all your superiors if you don't leave me be this instant."

"My word against yours. And who would believe you?"

His eyes darkened like two portals to hell. A vile energy oozed from him. Even Mr. Dee stiffened, matching the tension in Nan's legs.

"Last chance, Nan. I'll let him go if you marry me." Finn's odor was sending her insides into a boiling pot of protest.

"Never. Get out of my house!" She held Mr. Dee closer.

"You'll marry me. You're lucky I even want you."

"Lucky? I'd sooner lick the devil's toes." Nan's heart was banging against her ribs.

His lips narrowed to a slash. "I'll have you, one way or the other."

His pudgy hand, fingernails jagged and dirty, reached for her. The cat growled and swatted Finn's thumb. A thin line of blood blossomed over his skin.

"Ouch!" He recoiled, shook his hand. When he saw the blood, his eyes blazed. "I've had enough of you, ya fleabag cat." Grasping Mr. Dee by the scruff of his neck, Finn tore the cat away from Nan.

"No. Let him be." She stood.

The cat clawed and hissed but couldn't reach his target.

Nan grabbed Finn by the arm. "Stop."

"This is nothing compared to what I'm going to do to that bomber boy once I find him." Finn flung the cat across the room. Mr. Dee slammed into the wall, dislodging a portrait of Saint Patrick. The picture hit the floor and shattered. The cat lay there, twitching. The splintered glass sparkled around the animal, blood spattering the shards.

"Mr. Dee." *Dead.* Her cat was murdered. Seething energy shot through her. "How could you?" Nan's fist smacked Finn's chest. He grabbed her by the waist and shoved her back into the chair. He was on top of her, kissing her throat, moving his mouth over her skin.

"Are you mad? Leave me be. I'll never marry you. Never."

"We're beyond marriage."

Pinned against the chair by his bulk, she fought to get free, but his weight wedged her into the cushions. He yanked the top of her pants.

"No!" She kicked at him, screaming. He was so heavy, she could barely move. "Get off," she screamed once more, pushing him away.

Then he was off, flung backward.

"I knew you were here," Finn cried in triumph. "I knew it. You're under arrest."

"Says who?" Dutch punched Finn's thick stomach. They began to wrestle, knocking over chairs and sending dishes to smash against the floor. They overturned the bookcase, hundreds of poetry books crashing to the floor.

"Stop!" Nan cried, uselessly. She stepped out of their way to avoid being trampled, then tripped on an upside-down chair and fell to the ground.

She scrambled to her feet and picked up a volume of Yeats's poems, circling around the men until she could land a hit on Finn's head. The blow did nothing to stop him.

Dutch caught her eye. "Poetry? Are you kidding? Get my gun."

"And do what with it?"

"Shoot him."

Dutch shoved Finn flat against the table, and Finn kicked back at Dutch, both grunting, groaning, growling.

She couldn't do it, shoot a gun. But she couldn't let Finn kill Dutch. She had to stop this. The gun.

She dropped the book and sprinted to the bedroom, to the secret cubby in the fireplace where she'd hidden the weapon. Counting down, she found the stone and yanked it away from the wall. She slid the gun into her hands and stared at it. It was heavy and cold, but it warmed in her grasp. *Guns.* She hated guns. What was she doing?

The crashing sound coming from the other room jolted her. *Saving the man I love, that's what I'm doing.* She had seen the look in Finn's eyes. He'd kill Dutch the same way he'd killed her cat.

Dutch was not going to die. *Not today.* She held the gun with both hands and hooked her finger around the trigger, then marched into the main cabin. The men were grunting between jabs, and something whizzed past her head.

Margaret stood at the door. She'd flung a jam jar at the men. It hit Finn's shoulder, then splintered against the floor. The next one she threw missed them and smashed through the window above Nan's sink.

"Stop, Margaret. You might hit the wrong man."

Margaret's scarf hung askew over her gray hair. "What about yourself with that gun?"

"Pray I don't." Nan pointed the weapon at the brawl.

The men were struggling, rolling over the glass. Finn was lying on top of Dutch, and she aimed. Then Dutch rolled on top. The two men kept switching positions.

Margaret was clutching another jam jar. "Ah, for the love of Mary, do something, Nan. Shoot."

Nan aimed at the ceiling, shut her eyes, and squeezed the trigger.

She stumbled backward from the force of the shot. Chunks of ceiling plaster fell, and the scent of gun smoke lingered in the aftermath. The men paused long enough to stare up at her. No matter how much she tried to steady the weapon with both hands, she couldn't keep the gun from shaking. Her ears were ringing, and she wondered if she'd busted an eardrum.

She pointed the weapon at Finn. "Stop. Both of you. On your knees. Hands on your head. I'll use it again, I swear on all that's holy, I will."

Both men climbed to their knees, hands on their heads.

"Not you, Dutch. Get up and take your gun."

Dutch rose, muttered something to Finn.

Finn gaped. Blood dripped from his nose onto his ripped jacket. "You're choosing England over Ireland? Shame on you, Nan O'Neil. Your ma and pa are spinning in their graves."

"I'm choosing the Allies over the Axis, you filthy article. You try any dirty Irish tricks and I'll shoot you. I mean it, I will."

Dutch took the gun from Nan and aimed it at Finn. "Well done, Nan. Guns trump poetry books."

"Only in this situation. Your lip—you're bleeding."

He wiped his mouth with his sleeve, leaving a trail of red. "I bet he looks worse."

"Even in the best light."

Dutch kept the gun pointed at Finn but addressed Nan. "You okay?"

"Yeah." *Sort of.* Nan straightened her sweater, brushed off her pants. Noticed a rip across the thigh. She was shaking so hard, she thought for a second she'd faint. She forced herself to make sense of what was happening.

"You'll not get away with this," Finn snarled. "I'll see you rot in jail. You, too, Margaret, you old biddy."

"Shut your trap," Margaret shouted. She threw a jar at him. It hit his chest, bounced off, crashed on the floor.

"You tried to blackmail me into marrying you," Nan said. "I believe that's against the law."

"My word against yours."

Margaret cradled Mr. Dee against her ample bosom. "I saw the whole thing. The whole thing. And look what ya did to the wee kitty. There's a special place in hell for blaggards that hurt animals. And the devil is making a bed for ya. Out of burning nails."

"Oh, Mr. Dee." Nan's heart nearly broke at the sight of her brave kitten. His eyes were closed, and blood oozed from his mouth. Nan wanted to kick Finn.

"Is he dead?" Dutch asked.

Nan pressed her hand against Mr. Dee's chest and felt a heartbeat. "Not yet."

"Let me make Mr. Dee more comfortable. Clean him up," Margaret said. "You and your flyboy figure out your next move."

Dutch kept the gun pointed on Finn and glanced at Margaret. "Who are you?"

She dipped a curtsy. "I'm Margaret. Nice to finally meet ya." She started toward the bathroom, cooing to the cat.

"God bless you, Margaret," Nan said. "But why are ya here?"

"'Twas the Lord's timing. Your jam jars came in." She looked at the broken jars, scattered around the room. "I'll have to order ya some more."

"She won't be needing them," Finn said. "She'll be in prison for betraying her government."

Margaret's expression tightened. "She won't. I'll testify against ya. You're the one who won't get away with it, Finn. Blackmailing the lovely Nan O'Neil into marrying you. Attacking her. Trying to have ya way with her. Trying to kill her cat. Your sainted mother will be so disappointed."

"I did it for her. My ma."

Margaret shook her head. "For ya ma? That makes about as much sense as going to Mass naked."

"My ma needs a nurse. I need a wife, and Nan needs a husband. I had it all planned. It was perfect. Until this English bomber boy showed up and ruined everything."

"He's Canadian." Nan placed her hand on the small of Dutch's back. "And you've made a perfectly ridiculous assumption." As repulsed as she was, she felt a wee bit of sympathy for the eejit. He loved his mother.

"I'm glad I discovered ya true colors," Finn said. "You're nothing but a tart. Giving me signals that you cared about me. Wanted me. I've always suspected you drove your husband over that cliff. You're nothing but a witch."

Sympathy gone.

Nan's stomach kinked. She had misled him, but only to protect Dutch. Dutch had been right; she'd underestimated Finn.

"Shut up, Finn." Dutch raised the gun and aimed.

"Go on, shoot me, then, ya coward. Hiding under Nan's skirts. I'll see y'all in jail. And you, bomber boy, to internment camp. And the rest of you old biddies who helped this combatant, you'll get yours. I've made a list of all who helped."

"That'd be half the women in town." Tuda stomped into the house, her boots crunching over broken glass.

Finn let rip a string of curses so loathsome, Margaret winced—this from a woman who ran a pub in the back of her store.

Dutch raised the gun. He had that focus, that harshness about his eyes that made Nan shiver. "Dutch, don't shoot him, ya hear me?" She cupped her hand over Dutch's elbow. "Please."

"It's tempting." His arm relaxed beneath her grip. "Let's tie him up. Do you have any rope?"

Nan looked out the broken kitchen window. "My clothesline."

"I'll get it." Margaret handed Mr. Dee, now wrapped in a towel, to Nan. "I think he needs some nursing," she said, going toward the back door.

Nan's heart tore into pieces. "Ah, you poor wee thing."

"You're some piece of work, Finn," Dutch said. Keeping a steady aim, he glanced at Tuda. "Did you get the part?"

"Maybe." She pulled a hose out of the back pocket of her overalls. "I got this from your car, Finn. What do you think of that?"

"I think you're a disgrace to your husband."

The corner of Tuda's mouth lifted. "You would," she said, striding over to Dutch. "The real part we need won't get here until the evening train, but this might work."

Dutch nodded. "Get the car started, Tuda. The sooner I'm on my way, the better."

"I'll do my best." With a nod, she turned and disappeared into the misty morning.

"You shouldn't have come out of hiding." Nan rocked the cat in her arms. His eyes opened, and he looked up at her.

"And let this scum touch you? Never."

"But now you have to leave, ready or not."

"I'd do it again," he said.

Her insides sparked. He'd jeopardized his mission. He'd chosen her over the war. It hadn't been wise, but she loved him for his rashness.

"And I'd go to jail for you, I would, Dutch." They exchanged a gaze so binding, it brought tears to her eyes.

"Glad to hear it." Finn sat on the heels of his boots. "'Cause that's where you're headed. You'll not get away with this. Any of ya. I'll see to it. I'll see that you get your just rewards, Nan O'Neil."

"I'll give you some just rewards." Dutch aimed the gun at Finn's head.

Nan's heart grew heavy. Gone was the lover; the warrior had returned.

CHAPTER 22

Gun tucked inside the waistband of his pants, Dutch limped in front of the fireplace, his knee aching from Finn's kick.

"Don't ya look lovely in pink?" Margaret laughed, and then continued sweeping the wreckage around Finn's feet. He rocked back and forth, yelling into his gag.

The ladies had bound Finn to the cane-back chair. After he'd tried to bite Nan as she bandaged a cut on his face, Tuda had stuffed a napkin in his mouth and secured it with a pink scarf.

"Ah, Dutch, be a dear and boot that bit of cup toward me," Margaret said as she swept.

He kicked the dish toward her. He'd been considering the options. Finn wasn't going anywhere for a while. Eventually, though, he'd get free, but by then, Dutch hoped to be over the border and on his way back to base.

But what would happen to these brave women? He'd turned them into outlaws.

He remembered his advice to Nan and raised his eyes heavenward.

Lord, You say all things are possible in Your strength. If ever there were a time I needed Your help, it's now. Please, do not forsake me in my hour of need. And please, Lord, protect these brave women who have come to my aid, especially Nan.

Nan came in from the bedroom, cradling the cat. A bandage covered his back leg.

Dutch stroked the cat's head. "How are you?"

Mr. Dee seemed to wink at him.

"I think he spent another of his nine lives, but he'll be grand. Shook up and a few cuts is all." She added in a whisper, as though the cat might hear, "I'm a bit worried about internal injuries. We'll have to wait and see about them."

"Ah, ya poor wee thing. Come have a sip of milk." Margaret placed a bowl on the hearth. She accidentally on purpose stepped on Finn's foot as she returned to the kitchen sink. Finn rocked from side to side, tipping the legs of the chair.

"If ya fall onto ya side, I'm leaving ya there," Margaret said.

Letting Mr. Dee down, Nan gave him a long stroke along the back. "You're a good cat. Better than any dog."

Dutch grinned. No truer words had been spoken.

Nan surveyed the room, frowning. She looked up at the hole in her ceiling, then shut her eyes.

"I'm sorry about this," came Dutch's weak response.

"Ah, 'tis only stuff." Nan noticed the bulging knapsack on the counter. "Margaret, what are you packing for Dutch? It's a six-hour drive to the border, not a four-day journey."

"Well now," Margaret grinned, "the bottle of whiskey might come in handy should he need to soften a Garda. And bread is the staff of life. And since ya won't be getting new jars anytime soon to make your famous apple butter, I think these apples will do him."

Tuda opened the door, letting the cold mist inside. She gave Dutch a thumbs-down. "The thing won't turn over. I need that part from Limerick. Even if I had it, there's not a drop of petrol in town until late this afternoon. That makes the car about as useful as a chocolate teapot."

She walked over and picked up the broken picture of Saint Patrick. "When you chased all the snakes out of Ireland, you missed one, Saint Pat," she said, glowering at Finn.

"I've got to get out of here," Dutch said. He rubbed his forehead and paced in a circle.

"We'll think of something." Nan went to him with determined steps, an anxious expression on her face. He opened his arms for her. Why wouldn't she come with him? Even in front of her friends, Nan seemed to submerge herself into him, wrapping her arms around his waist, pressing her head against his shoulder. He wanted to keep her from harm.

Yeah, right. 'Cause I've been so good at that.

"I can take Finn's bike to the border."

Nan looked up at him. "Are you mad? It's six to eight hours by auto. You'll never make it with your knee. You need a car or a van or a lorry."

"Does someone have a car I can borrow? The doctor?"

"She's at hospital with the Halpins," Nan explained.

His cheek rested on the top of her head. These were the last minutes they'd have, unless she left with him. Her life here was in ruins, and it was his fault. He wished he knew how to make things right, for all of them.

"There has to be someone with a car. Let me think." A sudden smile lit Tuda's face. "Lord Harry. I finished restoring his Silver Ghost. He still owes me money on the bill."

"Then that's the ticket." Nan held her hand over Dutch's heart. He wondered if she could feel how hard it was beating as he closed his hand over hers.

With eyes as blue and clear as the horizon on a sunny day, she said, "I'll take you over to Gilmour House."

"Will ya?" Tuda straightened her back. "And say what to Lord Harry?"

"Ah . . ."

"Exactly. Nope. I'm coming along with ya to twist his arm. I told him I'd repossess the car if he didn't pay me. And six weeks later, not a penny toward his bill. You wait at the gate, and I'll get the car."

Dutch nodded. "Yeah, okay, but it's dangerous. If you get caught, you tell the Garda I made you do this at gunpoint. Understand? This has to be the story each of you must tell. Don't stray from it."

"We won't get caught. Not now, anyway. Count me in." Tuda opened the door. "Shall we?"

"Yes." Nan released her hold on Dutch and ran to the counter for the knapsack. Finn was struggling as she passed him, but she ignored his grunted pleas.

"Margaret, you best be going. Don't say a word about any of this to anyone. Promise?"

"Promise, but count me in, too." Margaret swept the last bit of broken plate into a pile. She set the broom beside the cooker. "You'll not have all the excitement without me." She swung her coat over her shoulders, looking as if she were about to board a ship.

The Titanic, Dutch thought.

He held Margaret back by the shoulder. She reminded him so much of his great-aunt Millie, a suffragette who had chained herself to the courthouse during a protest. "Margaret, I don't want you involved. It's too risky."

"Not involved?" She pointed with her chin to Finn. "Wasn't it myself who gagged that one over there? Threw jars at him? I'm already involved. And what do ya think Lord Harry will do if things go awry? Throw a hothouse tomato at me? I'm going with you all."

Just like his grandaunt; no one could stop her, either.

Nan asked, "What about Finn?"

Dutch found the map from under the table. "You ladies will have to release him at some point, or someone will eventually come along. Get your stories straight. I mean it. I made you all do this at gunpoint."

Margaret nodded. "Okay, but I gotta tell ya. Sergeant Halpin will sooner believe the Tinkers sold us a pooka."

"Regardless." He studied each of them. "If you stick to the same story, it'll fly." He stuffed the map into the knapsack along with everything else the doctor had brought.

"Don't worry, Dutch." Nan handed him the tweed jacket. "We'll make Halpin believe us."

He and Nan were facing each other. He was overcome with regret for knocking on her door, bringing the war inside her home. He had ruined her life here. But there was a stronger feeling fighting his fears. He'd never want to change the fact that he'd found her. Sighing, he thought how it might be if the circumstances were different.

Tuda nudged Margaret. "Come on, Margaret. Let's get Nan's bike from the garage."

"Hey, Mr. Dee," Margaret called. The cat was on his pillow beside the hearth. "You watch over Finn. Scratch his eyes out if he tries anything."

Finn's face turned red. He rocked the chair back and forth. The cat hissed at Finn's muffled shouts.

Dutch followed Nan outside, dropping the knapsack into a basket on the back of Finn's bicycle. As Nan was closing the door, he heard Finn's continuing muted rant.

"You going to lock it?" he asked.

"No. As much as I hate him, it's better if someone finds him. I prefer he's gone when I get back."

Dutch pulled her into his arms. "I've ruined your life here. Will you come with me?"

"To England?" Her breath warmed his neck.

"Will you?"

She lifted her face to his. "And what would the women in town do without their midwife?"

He inhaled her scent of rosemary and lilac. "They have a female doctor."

"One who never seems available? I'm sorry, Dutch. I can't."

Her answer drained the hope from his heart. He cupped his hand under her chin. Studying those strong blue eyes, he lowered his lips to hers. "Can't? Or won't?"

"Both, I'm afraid. Come on. No time for this now."

"We're almost out of time, Nan." The kiss was near, but she stepped away.

"I can't leave my home," she said, her voice husky. "What's left of it."

"Or maybe you can't leave your husband's grave." As the words came out, he wished he could take them back, but that was impossible.

"No," she repeated, "my home. I can't leave my home."

"You *won't* leave your home. And there's a cost to you staying, even if it's my fault. Come with me. Start a new life with me."

"It'll cost more to leave," she whispered.

"Will it? Why?"

She wouldn't answer him, wouldn't look at him.

"Are we interrupting something?" Tuda wheeled the bike out of the calf house, Margaret on her heels.

"Yes."

"No," Nan replied at the same time, grasping her bike's handlebars. "We're done here."

"Ya sound like a married couple already." Margaret mounted her bike.

Dutch punched his hand into his pocket. *Fat chance of that happening.* He felt sudden sympathy for Finn. Rebuffed, they both were.

"Stop mooning, you two. Let's get a move on." Tuda got on her bike and glided toward the gate with Margaret behind her.

Nan buttoned her coat and pulled on her beret. "Go on. Take Finn's bike."

Dutch went over to Finn's bicycle. It was a fine machine, apparently well maintained. A glint of steel from inside a leather saddlebag caught his eye. He reached in and found Finn's gun. *Bonus.* Running his hand over the cold metal, he hoped he wouldn't need to use it.

Tuda and Margaret were riding ahead of Dutch and Nan. The arching trees formed a leafy tunnel, with drops of water splashing him as the leaves grew too heavy with mist. The Irish air smelled of earth and musk.

With every pump of the bike pedals, his knee ached. He was struggling to keep up with the three women. He realized that Nan was hanging back with him, the haze curling her red hair, her cheeks a sunset pink.

She looked over her shoulder at him. "How's your knee holding up?"

"Peachy."

"We're almost there. Just around the corner." Her smile filled his heart.

The shriek of brakes and the roar of an engine came around a twisting bend in the road. A silver Rolls-Royce was bearing down on them.

Dutch's heart stopped.

He was going to die here after all.

Dutch exchanged glances with the wild-eyed woman behind the wheel.

"Hit the ditch!" he screamed.

Inches from striking him, the driver turned the wheel. As though in slow motion, the four bikers moved into the bushy hedge and the car roared past them, scraping against the stone wall on the other side of the lane.

Dutch felt as if his legs would not support him, and his heart was threatening to explode. He dropped the bike and sank to the side of the road, gasping for air, trying to lower his blood pressure. The knapsack had opened, and the contents had spread across the lane. "Is everyone all right?"

The women, stunned, only nodded. Their bikes lay in the lane, half in the hedge. The three ladies joined him on the ground, each holding her chest and trying to catch her breath.

Margaret picked up the whiskey bottle, which was rolling away from the bag. She pulled off the top, took a swig, and then handed the Jameson to Tuda.

"Ah now, what do ya think was so important that Lady Margot would almost run us over?"

Tuda lifted the bottle to her lips. "I dunno, but I'm glad she had the sense to miss us. By an inch. Isn't she expecting, Nan?"

Nan refused the bottle. "She probably had a craving for pastry."

Still holding the bottle, Tuda sloshed the liquid around. "She's gonna have to do a wee bit of explaining to Lord Harry about his car."

Dutch understood the significance of her words right away. "Was that the Silver Ghost?"

"'Twas the Silver Ghost that almost made a ghost of us all," Margaret said.

"Ah, for the love of Mary," Nan said. "There goes your ride to the border."

"Great." Dutch rubbed his throbbing knee. "There's a train, right? Coming into town? Didn't you say that, Tuda?"

Tuda shrugged. "Seven o'clock. We could hide you."

Nan stood and picked up her muddy bike. "How will that work? Dress him in ladies' garments and sneak him on the train?"

"I'm not wearing a dress," he said, beginning to retrieve the contents of the knapsack.

Nan stared at Finn's gun as Dutch stuffed it into the bag. "How are we going to get you across the border now?"

He crammed the map back inside the bag and shrugged. "I'll ride the bike."

As if any of them thought that was a feasible option.

Tuda shook her head. "The crows will stop picking at the rubbish heap behind the pub before that happens."

Margaret's eyes opened wide, and she elbowed Tuda. "The pub. Mrs. Odin. Of course."

Tuda's mouth opened into a smile. "Yes. I like where you're going with this."

"Where are we going?" Dutch asked.

"What about Mrs. Odin?" Nan poked a finger into her ripped pant leg.

"I happen to know Mrs. Odin is entertaining a certain man who has a Guinness lorry full of lovely petrol," Margaret explained. "He's there right now, like he always is, two times a week. He's in the kitchen, eating another one of Mrs. Odin's fine Irish breakfasts."

"And after, if all goes as it usually does," Tuda chimed in, "he'll be heading up the stairs for a wee bit of dessert."

"Ah, the cheek on ya," Nan huffed. "What would Father Albert say?"

"Get on your knees and give me five Hail Marys," Tuda laughed. "Nothing Mrs. Odin doesn't hear after every confession. If she bothers to confess about Brian."

"I dunno. That's a brazen plan." Nan wiped a splatter of mud from her face.

"'Tis. What do you say, Dutch?" Tuda asked.

"I don't understand what you're talking about." He lifted Nan's bike. Their hands brushed together as Nan took it.

She let her fingers linger there. "What they're trying to say is that the driver won't have his mind on the business of delivering the Guinness. His lorry might just slip away."

"Are you suggesting I steal a truck?"

Margaret's mouth pursed. "Steal? Never. Who said anything about 'stealing'?"

"No, that'd be a sin," Tuda said. "Let's say you borrow it for a few miles."

Nan grasped his hand, sending shivers up his arm. "Dutch, can you think of a better option?"

He pondered the idea. "I'll take the risk, but I don't want you ladies to be burdened with the crime. If I steal—"

"Borrow," Margaret corrected.

"If I take the truck without permission," he continued, "it's not 'borrowing.' And I can't control what the Irish authorities will do to all of you."

"They won't do a thing. After all, you held us at gunpoint, didn't ya?" Tuda reminded him.

"That's right, isn't it, Nan?" Margaret pushed the cork back into the whiskey bottle. "And what will it matter when the Garda discovers the abandoned lorry still full of its cargo? You will be safely in England, after all."

Dutch could hardly believe what he was hearing. These women were sacrificing their safety and freedom for him. "I can't ask you to do this."

"Listen." Tuda flipped a wayward curl from her forehead. "If my boys were behind enemy lines, I'd hope some brave women would do the same for them. So yes, we can."

"And we will." Nan's voice was strong and clear, as firm as that of any RAF crew member before a mission.

A couple seconds of silence passed before Dutch said, "Excellent plan. Carry on."

CHAPTER 23

Nan stood arm in arm, chest to chest with Dutch in the alley behind the pub. They watched Tuda and Margaret approach Mrs. Odin's back door, sidestepping the piles of discarded boxes and overstuffed rubbish cans.

"What if she doesn't answer the door?" Nan asked, leaning into Dutch's chest.

"We'll think of something else," he said, holding her closer.

She felt the heat of his body and squeezed her eyes shut, trying to force down the longing, the desperation for him. But the ache was undeniable. She wanted to tell him what had happened on the cliff. But what if he withdrew his tenderness when he saw the darkness and deceit inside her?

Mrs. Odin, dressed in her flowered bathrobe, opened the door and greeted Margaret and Tuda. They talked for a minute; then Margaret glanced over her shoulder and gave a nod.

"My two best friends in the world," Nan said. "They've proven their loyalty beyond what I'd ever ask."

"I suppose I'm your worst nightmare."

"Not a'tall." She had to tell him how she felt. "You've awakened me, and I'll not forget you."

That connection to him, that yearning for him, overwhelmed her. Dutch held her more tightly, then led her to the moss-covered stone wall beyond the gate. In this private place, he kissed her with such a gentle touch, it could have been a whispering breeze. Then she met his intent look, and he unleashed what they'd been holding back. The wildness of their souls. Everywhere he touched left a burning trail. His kisses deepened, and she grew dizzy.

"Come with me," he whispered.

Her body turned to liquid gold at the mere thought. She shook her head. "I told you. I can't."

"You can." He brushed his thumb along her cheek. "Come with me."

She fell into his blue-eyed gaze, and all the reasons not to leave with him tumbled through her mind. *Her home. Her practice. Her friends. Her country.* Her insides looped and swayed and pitched in every direction. "I can't."

He rested his forehead against hers. "All right. I'll pray for you every day."

She cupped his jaw and kissed him again, wishing with her whole heart that they could stay together.

"Look what I have," they heard Margaret call out. "Where are ya two?"

Dutch released a deep breath and stepped back. Nan felt cold, empty air filling the space between them.

Margaret came through the gate, holding the key in front of her. "I've got the lorry's key, and he has no idea it's been pinched from his pocket." Tuda followed.

"Well done, Margaret," Dutch said. "Bravo."

"'Twas Mrs. Odin's doing, not mine." Margaret placed the key into his palm. "She knows his pants inside and out. I'm sure Father Albert has told her she's got a one-way ticket to hell. Of course, she'll be grinning the whole way."

"And Brian beside her," Tuda added.

Nan felt her face grow hot. "Such boldness, you two."

"When ya our age, you've earned it," Margaret said. "Okay, here's the deal. We're to wait until Mrs. Odin closes the upstairs curtain. That's our signal. Then we have five minutes while they rumple the sheets and you get the lorry out of town."

"Only five?" Dutch said.

"That's all we get. He's no spring rooster like yourself."

"Five is probably optimistic." Nan cooled her cheeks with her cold fingers. "We better plan on three."

"Two," Tuda muttered.

"If he's anything like my Mikie, one."

The upstairs curtain closed. Nan lifted the knapsack from Finn's bicycle basket. She hesitated. The side pocket gapped open, and she could see Finn's gun inside.

"Come on," Dutch said. "We have to go."

"Do you really need a second gun? This is Ireland, not occupied France or Nazi Germany."

"Just a spare. For intimidation only."

Tuda led the foursome down a narrow alley between the pub and a tailor shop. At the edge of a building, they pressed their backs against the wall, the bricks cold and rough against Nan's hands. Something snagged her trouser. She yanked her leg away and heard a rip.

"There it is," Dutch whispered.

Peeking into the fog-cloaked street, Nan saw the Guinness lorry parked in its usual place. They were about to step out of the alley when they heard horse hooves and squeaking cart wheels.

"Get back," he said.

A horse-drawn cart filled with vegetables was coming down the street. The driver sang above the sound of the wheels.

"I was grateful last night for the clear, moonlit sky, and today I'm thankful for the fog." Nan's voice, a notch above a whisper, seemed to disappear into the mist. They listened to the clumping and clapping of the hooves on the cobblestone street.

She gazed at Dutch's profile, at the determined set of his eyes and jaw. Nothing would stop him from crossing the border.

This is it, she thought. The last time she'd see him. Dutch was leaving Ireland. Forever. The realization made her question her decision; could she stand to watch him disappear toward his escape and back into the war?

She'd have to. That was all there was to it. She'd manage, she would.

When the cart turned the corner, Dutch said, "Okay. Now's my chance."

"Mind you don't take the lanes too fast or the turns too hard," Tuda warned. "You'll tip the thing over."

Margaret paced to the back of the lorry. "And if you lose a barrel, let it be. The fairies will soon roll it away and have it for their tea."

With the door wide open, he looked at Nan. "Pray for me." He reached for the knapsack she held. His lips touched hers. Electricity sparked between them, hot as burning turf.

Dear Lord. How can I let this man go? After he opened his heart to me?

Deep inside her, a quiet voice answered. *I can't. Not yet, anyway.* Nan climbed into the lorry, pushing the knapsack to the other side of the seat and sliding across to the passenger door. She tried to smile but couldn't quite pull it off. "What are you waiting for? Get in. We haven't got all day."

His mouth parted, yet no words fell from his tongue.

"Don't look so surprised. Didn't ya just invite me to come along?"

What if he made her get out? How would she ever carry on?

The smile he gave her confirmed his desire for her.

"Are you mad?" Tuda said. "You're going with him?"

"Only to the border."

Dutch frowned. "You're not going to England with me?"

Tuda glared at him. "Are ya daft? She's not going to England." Her expression turned motherly as she faced Nan. "Don't ya think you've done enough for your secret flyboy? It's your freedom we're talking about now."

A stab in her gut confirmed that Nan had the same fears, but the pull toward Dutch overrode the urge to run home to the safety of her hearth. "I'll get him to the border. Just look at him. He still needs my help. Have you heard his brogue? As soon as he opens his yap, it'll be over for him. Besides, if I stay here, I may still end up in jail."

Tuda shook her head. "Are you sure about this, Nan?"

"Of course she is. Where's ya sense of romance, Tuda?" Margaret grinned. "If ya get caught, we'll say Dutch took ya at gunpoint. Isn't that so, Tuda?" She elbowed Tuda, who did not look convinced.

"We're good at lying," Margaret continued. "Haven't we had eight hundred years of practice from British oppression to keep our stories straight? Finn has no idea what he's up against."

"We'll keep the fib afloat," Tuda allowed, "but you're absolutely mad, Nan O'Neil."

"She's mad in love. The two of them." Margaret winked. "Don't you remember what that felt like, Tuda?"

Tuda's face softened. "I do. May the Lord be with you."

"Also with you," Nan said, glad to get the blessing.

"Thank you, both." Dutch gave the two women quick hugs before he climbed into the lorry.

Tuda shut the door. "Mind you take good care of her, or we'll find ya and tie you up like we did Finn."

"I will, with my life." Dutch inserted the key, and the engine thundered into operation. He ground the gears a couple of times before the lorry lurched forward. Soon they were going over the bridge, out of Ballyhaven, and into their future.

Nan picked up a flat cap—Brian's, no doubt. With trembling fingers, she passed the hat to Dutch. "Here, put this on. Try to look Irish."

"That's easy. I'll sit on my hands and pretend to care about what happens to the Allies."

"I ought to slap your piehole for that comment."

He swung the cap on, pushed it down over his forehead, and grinned. "I'd prefer if you kiss it."

She'd prefer that, too. "If we're stopped, promise me you'll let me do all the talking. None of your Irish brogue. Did I ever tell you that you sounded ridiculous?"

"Ah sure now, ya didn't have ta, lass."

"It hasn't improved," she observed.

"But my health has, thanks to you." He reached over and ran his hand along her thigh.

"Look out!"

Two barking dogs ran out into the lane in front of them. Dutch gripped the steering wheel and swerved to miss the mutts. The lorry scraped the stone wall, bounced back.

"Slow down. You're driving like Lady Margot." She glanced behind at the barrels knocking and bouncing. The dogs scooted away, unharmed. "I hope you fly better than you drive."

His cheeks bloomed with color. "You're a major distraction."

"Oh sure. Blame it on me."

"Get out the map. Where's our first turn?"

"At least ten miles north. Let me see."

Nan unfolded the map. A red-penciled line wove a complicated path to the border. She studied the roads—some familiar, others she barely knew existed. "Who do you think plotted this course?"

He shook his head. "Not the doc. Whoever gave her the map. Great details, right down to checkpoints and petrol stations. Have you been to this abbey?"

"Can't say that I have. There're hundreds of ruins in Ireland. Cottages, castles, abbeys." She glanced at the lorry instruments. "But not that many petrol stations. We'll have to stop, won't we?"

He nodded, his hands gripping the steering wheel. "There's a place marked on the map. And there's money. See it? And a ration book and fake ID."

Nan peeked inside the envelope. "She thought of everything, didn't she? Wait. I don't see a ration book. Some money, but I don't see an ID, either."

"What? Look again; it has to be there."

She rummaged through the envelope, took everything out. "Not here."

Dutch smacked the steering wheel with his open palm. "It must have fallen out when Lady Margot ran us over."

"Maybe we won't need it. I mean, we have money."

"Maybe."

It was possible. She opened the glove compartment and searched through the contents. Rags, a leather-bound ledger. Her heart skipped a beat. "A ration book. And Brian's ID."

"Thank you, Jesus," Dutch said, flicking his eyes upward.

"Amen to that."

Nan opened the map and studied it. "I wonder how Dr. Mann got this?"

"I reckon the same way she got the penicillin," he said.

Recalling the story of how Dr. Mann had come by the medicine, or rather charmed it off a research scientist, now Nan wondered exactly what the doctor had done, and with whom, to get this map.

How magnificent Juliet Mann was in her formfitting suit, Nan thought, picturing the woman's shoes, which never seemed to acquire mud, that perfect skin with perfect makeup, the hair in gorgeous waves, that brilliant lipstick and matching fingernail polish.

Nan stared at her own rough fingers and short nails, the ripped trouser material coarse under her touch.

"The doctor." Nan paused.

"Yeah? What about her?"

"Who do you think she really works for? Do you think she's MI6?"

"I don't know." He shrugged. "Maybe some sort of American intelligence organization."

"In Ireland? Why?"

"Nazi spies."

"What? Here? You must be joking."

"I'm not. They're everywhere, including Ireland. The Nazis are up to no good, and we have to stop them."

His knee moved to touch hers. "It's called a world war for a reason, and it's here, like it or not. The internment camp is real. Consequences for what you and your friends have done to help me, that's real, too."

"I'd do it again, any day. You're on the right side of this awful conflict." She glanced at the map. "There's the crossroads ahead. Take a left."

The lorry's wheels spun in the mud as he made the turn.

"What is the RAF concept of 'slow down'?" she asked.

"Don't crash."

The road became rocky and bumpy for the next couple of miles, and then they passed a farmhouse with a score of chickens plucking at the ground. A few yards away, a flock of sheep mobbed the road. Dutch stopped the lorry amid the loud sounds of bleating.

"Great. Just great."

"Well now, it wouldn't be a journey without an Irish traffic jam."

"How long is this going to take?" He drummed his fingers on the steering wheel.

"Patience, city boy. You'll have to ask the sheep."

"Fine." He rolled down the window. "How long are you going to take?" he yelled.

"Dutch, are you daft?" she laughed.

"A little." He placed his hand on her thigh. "I can't believe you're here."

"Only to the border. You obviously need my help."

"I do. How are you doing?"

She hesitated. There seemed no end to the slow-moving lumps of baaing wool blocking the road.

Pressing her hand against the cold window, she stared at the cloudy impression forming around her fingers. *Ah well, isn't this a grand time to tell Dutch he was right about Teddy?*

"Nan? You okay?"

She turned to face him. "I am, now. I want you to know something. You're right about Teddy, about my needing to let him go. I've been hiding in his shadow, cloaking myself in sorrow and fear. You showed me that. You've taken me out of the murky gloom."

There. She'd said it.

"Teddy wasn't worthy of you." His voice was soft. "You deserve much more. What happened that day?"

She shook her head. "It was shameful."

"You can tell me, no matter what. Go on. The truth will set you free."

His eyes, kind and openhearted, and the slight nod of his square chin urged her toward the truth.

"That day. I came home from a birthing to find Teddy had been up all night, drinking. He was inconsolable, crying. And then he, I don't know, went crazy. He pushed me away, grabbed the gun, and ran out of the house. I followed him, screaming for him to stop. When he did, it was at the edge of the cliff."

The scene bore down on her, and she shuddered. She relived the feel of the wind on her face, the wet grass on her calves. The horrible grimace on Teddy's face.

Dutch wrapped his arm around her. "I can't imagine how terrible that must have been for you."

"It gets worse. He held the gun to his neck. 'No, Teddy,' I yelled. 'What are you doing?' I tripped, gashed my hand on a sharp rock." She looked at her palm, at the scar on the fleshy side of her hand, a reminder of the day.

"He stared at me with eyes so bitter, so dark, I almost thought he was a different person. 'I'm ridding myself of you,' he shrieked. And then he shot himself in the neck."

Dutch pulled her into his chest. She threaded her hand inside his vest, felt his heart beating beneath her fingers. "I can still hear the sound of the bullet. The smell of gunpowder. He fell backward into the sea. The gun stayed behind. I crawled over the wet grass until I reached the cliff. Teddy was facedown on a boulder, his blood spilling into the sea, turning the ocean red, then pink, until a wave picked him up as though he were a piece of driftwood. Under he went, out to sea. The gun was stuck in the dirt, so I picked it up and threw it into the ocean."

"He'd taken his life and blamed you," Dutch groaned. "It wasn't your fault."

"I've told myself that a million times, but I should have stopped him."

"You couldn't stop him. No one could. There was nothing you could have done to change the outcome. He was sick. Mentally."

"There's more." Nan hesitated for a second, but she'd told most of the story, and now she had to finish it. "Teddy's body washed up onshore the next day. There was no gunshot wound. He must have nicked his neck artery, I guess. Halpin declared Teddy's death was accidental. My biggest sin . . ."

"What?"

She tasted the salty tears that streamed down her cheek. "I said nothing to Father Albert about the suicide. I watched my husband be buried where he did not belong, in hallowed ground. I knew it was wrong from the second the first shovel of dirt hit Teddy's coffin."

"Nan," Dutch whispered. "He is the potter and we are the clay. We're a work in progress. None of us is perfect. We don't always make the right decisions or do the right things. And unfair situations come against us. What happened to you was beyond the pale."

"I should have demanded Teddy see a doctor. I should have spoken to the priest about him. I shouldn't have kept silent when he took his life."

"You can ask for forgiveness. Ask right now. I'll stand by you. No matter what. Go on."

She shook her head. "I can't."

"Of course you can. He's ready to listen. Close your eyes and seek forgiveness."

Nan closed her eyes.

Sweet Jesus, have mercy on me. Wipe away my sins. Make me clean again. Forgive me. Please forgive me.

She waited for a beat. An answer came with a warm sensation that started at the root of her soul and flowed and bubbled and rose within her. The Holy Ghost. She could feel God granting her forgiveness. *Peace.* A burden seemed to lift from her shoulders. The sound of waves crashing, that only she could hear, made her flinch. She was forgiven, yet the Holy Ghost prompted her that there was more to be done. And in that instant, she knew what He required her to do if she truly wanted to find peace.

She opened her eyes. "Oh, Dutch. I've been forgiven."

"Of course you have. Have you accepted the forgiveness?"

"Yes. But there's more work to be done. I need to fully reconcile."

"What do you mean?"

"Father Albert. I lied to him many times about Teddy's condition. Then about his death. I'll not rest until I've confessed and asked Father Albert for his forgiveness."

"If you feel it's necessary."

"Yes. The Holy Ghost is prompting me."

"Then you must follow." He kissed her forehead. "I love you, Nan O'Neil."

This aching in her heart. She knew what it was. It was love for Dutch.

"I love you, too. The Lord sent you to my door. I may have healed your wounds, but you've helped to heal my soul. Thank you."

"No, you set yourself free by facing the truth. I've never been more proud of anyone." His smile lit his features. "I guess the Holy Ghost led us to each other. Think He intended us to become the Irish Bonnie and Clyde?"

"Who are they?"

"American gangsters. After all, we tied up an LDF officer and stole a truck."

"Borrowed." Nan laughed. "Ah, you've ruined me, all right. Turned me into a desperado."

The final sheep crossed the road, and a weary old man with a cane followed. He tipped his flat cap to Nan and Dutch before he closed the gate. An old woman stood in the doorway of a cottage, with a steaming cup of tea. The scene touched Nan. Would that ever be her? Waiting with a warm greeting for her husband in the twilight of their years? Dutch, maybe?

"Kinda sweet, huh? Will you be there with a cup of tea for me when I'm old and bent over?"

Fear of losing him spiked through her again. *Please, Lord. Watch over him. Keep him out of harm's way.* "Sure, I will. You plan on being a sheepherder?"

"Only if you insist." They waved to the old couple before continuing down the bumpy lane, the beer barrels rumbling behind them. Funny, she marveled, how the scent of freedom would be that of sheep and rain, but wasn't He the shepherd and herself a lamb?

Here she was, running from the law with a sackful of sins to declare; still, she'd never felt so free. And, she vowed, she would confess the entire Teddy affair to Father Albert. Right now, she needed to get her secret flyboy over the border. She sighed. Which meant delivering him back into harm's way.

CHAPTER 24

Nan focused on the map with all its notes and arrows. She felt as if she were going cross-eyed. "Wait. We missed a turn."

He slammed on the brakes, sending the barrels knocking against the sides of the lorry bed. "I'm going to fire you as my navigator."

"You should have fired your Wellington navigator. Then you wouldn't be in this situation a'tall."

He grumbled, backing up the lorry a few feet.

"Stop." She rolled down the window and leaned outside. A few feet behind them, a pile of rocks spread across a lane. "I think that must be the turn. Looks like a mudslide washed out the road."

He popped open the door, slid out, and walked to the debris blocking the road. She watched him, standing there tall and lean, scratching his head. Ah, but he was a warrior. He kicked the pile before he turned on his heel. Even with the scowl, he looked incredibly handsome.

"Impossible," he said, climbing back into the lorry. "Let me see the map."

She passed it to him. He stared at the chart for a few seconds, then handed it back. "It's okay. We'll take the next northbound road. Start praying it's not washed out, too."

For the next few miles, she prayed.

"There. The boreen. Lane. There." She pointed to a slit of a road wedged between two overgrown hedges. "Slow down."

He braked hard. The lorry swayed from side to side, and he struggled to keep it straight. "Next time, give me more warning."

"It's not like I know the roads. Why don't you try slowing down?"

The lorry barely fit between the narrow hedges. The branches whacked the sides of the vehicle and rattled the beer kegs.

He uttered a sigh of relief when they emerged through the tunnel of foliage and into the open, bare landscape. A few falling-down homes, their walls reclaimed by nature, stood neglected. Fog descended around them, consuming their vision of the horizon.

The lorry chugged up a hill. A car was parked at the bottom of the other side, blocking a humpbacked bridge. Her heart leapt. She dug her fingers into his arm. "A roadblock."

Two men with rifles stood in front of the car, with another man behind the steering wheel. "Oh, for the love of all things holy. LDF."

He stopped the lorry. "Was that on the map?"

"No, but it wasn't our route, either."

Dutch pulled the cap down over his creased forehead. "Should I plow through them? Or brandish my gun?"

"Don't be daft. You might kill someone. I'll get out. Let me do the talking."

"Fine. But I have a gun, and I'll use it. The truck's a weapon, too, you know."

"You won't use either. If you did, which man would you pick off first? The fat one who probably has a wife and seven children? The old one? Make his wife a widow? The young man behind the wheel, who doesn't look old enough to drive? Which one, Dutch?"

"The one who threatens us." Dutch gripped the steering wheel with one hand while the other went to the gun tucked against his side. He revved the engine. What was he planning to do? she wondered, terrified.

"You don't need brute force." She touched his fingers. "Promise me you won't use your weapons. It'll do only harm in the end."

A man with a fedora took off his hat and waved at them. Nan sat up. She gazed skyward and whispered, "Thank you, Lord Jesus. I know him."

"Who? Christ? This is no time to be evangelizing to me. This is war. People die."

"The man with the fedora, I delivered his grandson last year, the first after a dozen girls. We had a grand time at the christening. He sang many of the old tunes and, after a few pints, got up on the table and did a jig in honor of his first grandson." She reached into the knapsack for the bottle of whiskey.

"You getting out the other gun?"

"What did I just say to you?" She pulled the bottle of whiskey from the knapsack, her nose twitching at the powerful scent. Ever since Teddy had started drinking, she could no longer tolerate liquor.

"What are you going to do with that? Hit him on the head?"

"Don't be an eejit. He has a weakness for the drink." She let the knapsack fall back to the floorboard.

"Be careful. There's a loaded gun in there. You're gifting him a half-gone bottle?"

"A bit of whiskey on a cold day will always warm an Irishman's soul. Unless he's taken the pledge, like he promised his wife he would do that night." She straightened her jacket, combed her fingers through her mass of curls. "I must be a sight. Do I look all right? Presentable and all?"

He rubbed a spot on her chin. "Like an angel straight from heaven."

A chuckle rattled her throat. "Ah, that flat cap has infused you with more of the blarney." She opened the door, dropped to the muddy road. "Hello, Mr. McClare. How grand to see you again. What a strange, small world we live in." No truer words had ever left her mouth.

Dutch pulled at his collar and shoved the cap farther down his forehead. The joy he'd felt when Nan had slipped into the truck had gradually turned to fear. This could be very bad. He looked toward Nan, who was a few feet away, conversing with the men as though she were the heroine in some light opera, her musical laughter ringing over the barren hillside.

She'd been chatting for only a few minutes, but it seemed like an hour. The men spoke with such heavy brogues, Dutch couldn't understand what they were saying. They were getting toasted, taking turns, swigging on the whiskey. Nan said something; the men looked at Dutch and then roared with laughter.

"Glad you think I'm so funny," he muttered, wondering what she'd done to elicit such a response. Didn't seem right, those guys in uniform boozing before noon. Reminded him of Teddy. His chest warmed when he looked at Nan. She could move on now. *If only she'd move on with me,* he thought, yet he was glad to have played a part in her healing. She deserved the best in life.

His foot was poised to engage the gas pedal if she looked as though she were in trouble. He wondered which man he would pick to shoot.

Then her words carried back to him, making the uniformed men human, not merely enemies or obstacles to his escape plan. The fat one could be Margaret's husband—one-minute Mikie. The boy could be Tuda's son. And the old man chatting with Nan was a grandfather of thirteen children.

Dutch rubbed his eyes. Over the last few days, the war had developed faces. The realization knotted his stomach. He'd never given it much thought, sailing above the fires after his crew had dropped their arsenal on the Germans.

It was them or us—that was the motto, the way to get around thinking or feeling or questioning their mission. Until today on this lonely Irish road, he'd never allowed the war to get personal.

No. He could not . . . would not shoot these men, unless they threatened to hurt Nan. He slipped the gun from his belt and shoved the weapon into the glove compartment.

What if the officers have a radio? he suddenly thought. *What if Finn has been found or the rightful owner of this truck filed a police report?* He closed his eyes. The gun was merely a reach away if he needed it.

Get back in the truck, he wanted to scream. Instead, he banged on the door for her attention, and then motioned with his hand to return, something an impatient husband might do.

"Ah, there's himself, getting all worked up. I best be going," Nan said. "We have a long journey."

"All right then, Nurse Nan." McClare kissed both her cheeks.

"You give that grandson a hug for me, will ya?"

"I will. Promise me you won't tell me missus about this." He lifted the near-empty bottle.

"Now, why would I get you in trouble?"

"You're altogether a grand lass, Nan. Take us up on a poker game sometime, will ya? And good luck with the new mister and his legs." He lifted his chin toward Dutch, who nodded in response.

Legs? His fictional ailment was his throat, not his legs. What had Nan told them?

She stepped to the lorry, swinging her hips. The men were looking at her backside, the gleam in their eyes sparking a fury in Dutch. She wasn't enjoying the folly, though. Her beautiful face was pinched, her lips drawn down.

"Go. Now," she said, getting back into the truck. "They're not going to ask for your papers."

Dutch started the vehicle, and the car blocking the road slipped backward to let him pass.

"Slow down," she said, leaning out the window. Her bright smile returned. "Give my love to Mary and the baby."

"I will. And congratulations, young fella. You got yourself a proper Irish wife."

"Yeah," the fat fellow added. "Keep them legs good and strong."

Dutch glanced out the rearview mirror at the three men, still laughing.

"What line did you feed them?"

"The lorry driver is my uncle. And he's under the weather, so we agreed to make the deliveries. You have a bad throat infection, can't speak, so I'm helping with the rounds. Then I bedazzled them with my charms."

Her shy grin filled his heart. "It worked. You're an expert liar."

"I'm not proud of the fact. Father Albert is going to get an earful when I finally confess."

"What was so funny back there?"

"I don't really know."

"What did you say? You tell them I have a bum knee?"

"No," she shrugged. "They asked why you didn't get out of the lorry and come say hello. I told them you had a bad throat and couldn't talk. McClare asked about your legs. So I said, 'Yeah, they're all in working order.' And then the fat one goes, 'That's grand. It's the third leg that matters to a man.' They all laughed and I laughed, too, but I don't understand why. What did they mean by a third leg?"

Dutch let out a snort. "How many years were you married?"

"Two, almost three." She looked at him, confused, until he glanced at his lap. Hands on her mouth, pink bloomed over her face. "Ah, those cheeky lads. Oh! And me an unwitting part of it."

Dutch laughed as he shifted gears and sped over the roller-coaster hills. His smile evaporated when he noticed the gas gauge. The needle flirted with empty. At the crest of a hill, there was a fork in the road. He slowed. One way led north, the other downward to a village set in a valley between steep green hills.

"We need a gas station."

The map rustled as she studied it. "There's a safe one when we get back to the regular route."

"How soon?"

"Twenty miles."

He tapped the fuel gauge, but the needle remained on "E." "We won't make it. What's that town down there?"

Nan ran her finger along a line and said, "Cliffside."

"Cliffside it is." He veered to the right and glanced at her. "Maybe you can pray for us to have an uneventful, quick stop?"

"I can and will." She made the sign of the cross over herself, closed her eyes, and began fervent prayers.

CHAPTER 25

As they crept toward Cliffside, Nan's heart sped up, pounding against her rib cage in a million warnings.

Dutch downshifted, slowing as they left the twisting mountain road. The lorry crossed over the narrow bridge that led into the village, a turbulent river racing beneath them.

"I just had a terrible thought," Dutch said. "You think this town might be on the truck driver's route?"

"Maybe." Her stomach lurched.

"See if you can find the driver's delivery book. Perhaps Cliffside isn't one of his stops."

Nan opened the glove compartment. She sucked in a breath. *Interesting.* Dutch had stuffed his gun in there. From under the weapon, she pulled out a leather journal. Thumbing through the register, she found the town.

She bit her lip. "Cliffside is on his route. Two pubs. So, we make the deliveries?"

"No way. Let's get our petrol and blow out of town before we draw any attention. We have to get to the abbey before dark, or I'll never get across the border today. We'll get stuck. Together. Alone. In the abbey."

"Heaven forbid," she said, although the thought intrigued her. One more night with her secret flyboy. Ah, but she had a sinful nature.

"What will the locals think when they don't get their deliveries?" she asked.

"They'll think it's fishy, and they'll be mad. But if we're lucky, we won't see anyone. It's only, what? Nine o'clock?"

Nan looked at her wrist. She'd left her watch behind, along with the rest of her life. "I think so. But we can't go through town and not make Brian's deliveries."

"Of course we can."

"You want to avoid the Garda? Then make the deliveries, or you'll have the pub owners screaming at the injustice of it all."

He seemed to be considering what she'd said.

"Besides, if we don't deliver the Guinness, there's no telling when a lorry will be back here."

"Why is that a terrible thing? Don't you Irish drink too much?"

"Once again, you don't understand us. The pub is the local gathering place, the living room. It's more about community. Most people go there for the craic, not to get drunk."

"The craic? What's that? Some kind of food?"

"The talk. The gossip. There's a lot you don't know about Ireland."

"There's a lot I don't know, period."

He slowed as they approached the church with its uninspired steeple. The clouds parted, and the sun sparkled on the town's wet slate roofs. For once, Nan wished the rain would return.

A man with a red beard, wearing a brown vest, stepped out from a storefront. He stood in the middle of the narrow lane, waving.

"Don't you dare run him over."

"What do you take me for?" Dutch slowed to a stop.

"Men do irrational things when they're desperate."

"Relax. I tucked the gun away. I'm not about to use the truck as a weapon. At least, not in this situation."

He parked outside the spirit grocery. A hinged sign swaying in the breeze read "Keatings."

"Ah, good day to ya both. You're early. Don't usually get my order until late afternoon, but I'm glad to see you." The man hooked his thumbs into his vest pockets. "I'm Clancy Keatings, owner of this establishment. And who might you be, driving Brian Monaghan's Guinness lorry?"

"No names," Dutch muttered.

Nan leaned out her side of the lorry. "My uncle Brian is having a bit of a lie down today. We're taking his route. A favor, you see. This is my husband. Sorry, he can't talk on account of a terrible throat infection, but his legs are fine."

The man scratched his scruffy beard and gave her a questioning look. "Well, isn't that grand for him?"

Dutch rubbed a hand over his mouth, but Nan still heard his chuckle.

"My uncle's notes say you take four barrels?"

"I do, and I will. Just pull up alongside the front door, so. Mind ya don't slip on the wet floor. And be careful around the potato bins."

Clancy strolled back toward the pub and propped the door open with an old iron.

"Now what?" Dutch asked through clenched teeth.

"We make his delivery. But don't talk."

"That's easy. You've left me speechless."

"Good. Can you lift the barrels with your bad arm? That bum knee?"

"Piece of cake. Why did he warn us to watch out for potatoes? Is that some sort of code?"

"Keatings is a spirit grocery. Pub and general market. Like Margaret's."

"You can get drunk and pick up your potatoes in one trip? Convenient. What will the Irish think of next?"

Nan shot him a glare.

Dutch slid out of the lorry at the same time as Nan. He walked to the back of the vehicle, and Clancy strolled around the other side with Nan.

Mr. Keating made a sucking sound. "Now, that must be a burden."

"What's that, Mr. Keatings?"

"Call me Clancy. Himself not talking."

"It's more of a blessing."

Clancy laughed, revealing stained bottom teeth. Dutch shot Nan a look somewhere between admiration and frustration. He studied the lorry's gate for a few seconds, and then, as though he delivered Guinness for a living, he opened the back and began dispensing the barrels to the pavement.

Once the kegs were inside the pub, Dutch retreated to the lorry. Nan stood in the back of the grocery, at the bar counter, thumbing through the ledger book for Clancy's name. Once she found it, she sat on a stool and waited for Clancy to return from the back room.

She looked around the pub. The dark walls were filled with pictures of saints and hurling stars. A photograph of de Valera shaking Clancy's hand hung over the bar. Rows of glasses and whiskey bottles graced the shelves above the sinks. A fire smoldered in the fireplace, where several chairs were pulled up to the hearth.

Clancy strolled in and took his place behind the bar counter. "What do I owe ya?"

"My uncle will square up with you next time. Just sign here for today."

"What? That's highly unusual. Brian is a man who keeps his money tight."

"Those were his instructions. Please just sign." Nan acted as though she knew what she was doing, as though she'd done this a hundred times. After he signed, she smacked the ledger closed in hopes that she'd appeared efficient. "Thanks. Tell me, Clancy. Where is the petrol station?"

With a crooked finger, he pointed. "You take the lane down a bit, turn to the right when ya come to the shop with the red door. It'll be down there, across from Dirty Mary's Pub. She'll be glad to see ya. She went dry last weekend on account of John Dumont's funeral. She's got the funeral home in the back of her pub, so."

Guinness and funeral parlors were not an uncommon mix in Ireland. The drunk and the dead. *They have a lot in common,* her ma would say as they strolled past such establishments in Cork.

"She's been waiting for her delivery every day since the wake. Mind you, I enjoyed having her patrons, but she's a grand old gal, and I only want the best for her. Plus, she's my aunt by way of a third marriage, to my uncle, dearly departed ten years ago on account of the gout."

More information than Nan needed, and if she didn't leave now, he'd surely continue. "Thanks. We've a long day ahead. We best be off. And my cousin will be back next time."

"Ya cousin? I thought you said he was your uncle?"

Nan stilled her expression, but inside her pulse pinged. Pasting on her convent-school smile, she said, "He's my cousin, but we all call him Uncle Brian." Her heartbeat pounded right down to her fingertips. He gave her a questioning lift of an eyebrow.

Backing toward the open door, she nodded. "Nice to meet you."

"Wait. Don't move."

Nan's legs shook, but her feet remained planted. The man reached for something behind the bar. *A gun.* He must be reaching for a gun. She blinked, following his movements. It was over. No need to run. He had her caught in the lie. My uncle, my cousin. *My foot.* Now, because of her slip of the tongue, Dutch would be on his way to internment camp.

She was bound for prison.

"Ya look famished. Take these."

Nan near melted at the sight of two boiled eggs. "You're a sweet, sweet man, Clancy." She paced back to the bar, took the eggs, and shoved them into her pockets.

"That I am." He winked. "All the girls around here are mad for me. Maybe I've been a bachelor for too long. Too bad ya already taken, 'cause I'm thinking you'd be a grand wife."

"Ah, go on with ya."

She tried hard not to run, but if her heels had lifted any faster, she'd have stepped in time with the horse and rider who trotted past her out on the street.

She slipped into the lorry, her body trembling, and emptied her pockets. "Go. Please."

Dutch glanced at her. "You talked him out of eggs, too? You ever think of taking up crime as a career?"

"Sure, you and me. The Irish Boney and Clive."

"*Bonnie* and *Clyde*."

"Off with ya, now." She dropped the eggs into the knapsack. "I'll have to admit, outsmarting the authorities runs in my Irish blood, but pub owners are a mite harder to fool." Nan continued, "The petrol station is across the street from Dirty Mary's Pub. She's waiting on a delivery, too."

"Let's hope Dirty Mary doesn't see us, 'cause I'm not stopping after we get gas."

"Dutch, we have to. She's been dry since last weekend. This is her livelihood."

"This is our life."

"We must."

"Not."

"Yes, we have to."

"I'm not stopping, Nan. I'm sorry, but your safety is more important to me than Dirty Mary's beer delivery."

The sun disappeared behind thick clouds, draining the town of color. Now everything, even the surrounding mountains, was gray.

The petrol station was painted black, with white trim around the oversized windows and door. Dutch pulled up to the pump. "I need Uncle Brian's ration book."

Nan laid her hand on his. "Where you going? Remember? You can't talk. I'll handle this."

She grabbed the ration book, stuck it in her coat, and then scooted to her side of the lorry. No sooner had her feet touched the ground than a tall, stooped man smoking a cigar strolled out from the office.

"You 'tain't Brian." His eyes seemed to nail her.

"No, I'm . . ." Who did she say she was? Her mind drew a blank. *Wait.* She hadn't given him a name. "I'm Brian's uncle. Cousin. He's out of sorts today, so my husband and I are doing his route. We need petrol, please."

"Have ya got a ration book?"

"Sure I do." She pulled the book from her jacket pocket, her heart pounding. The man squinted at it.

"Ya got a note or something from Brian saying who you are?"

"Why would I be needing that? I know who I am." If her heart beat any faster, she was going to pass out.

A woman in her seventies scurried across the street, toward them. She wore a flower-printed scarf around her head, with white curls peeking out at the sides. Her tweed coat gave her the round appearance of a walking teddy bear.

"Ah, brilliant. My Guinness. You're early. Good thing I caught ya. I was on my way to press the father's vestments." She looked around. "Where's Brian? And who's that handsome young fella where Brian usually sits?"

"That's what I'm trying to find out." The station owner held the ration book. "'Cause I won't sell petrol to just anyone."

"The young fella is my husband." She coughed after the word "husband." "I believe I told you who I am. I'm Brian's cousin, making his rounds for him today. He's tied up." Almost as tightly as Finn, except she suspected Brian was having a better time of it.

The woman slapped the man's arm. "Ruari, don't be an eejit, and stop playing LDF. They're who they say they are. Who else would they be?"

He flicked cigar ashes over his boot. "How do we know?"

"We just delivered Clancy's Guinness," Nan said. "You can ring Clancy. Ask him."

"Ya see? If they weren't who they say they are, why would they be making Brian's deliveries instead of drinking them?"

Ruari scratched his neck, the skin rippling like a turkey's. "You've got a point there, I suppose."

"They're going to deliver mine next, so get a move on. If I'm late again, Father James will be cross, and he'll give me extra penance for being lazy."

"Dirty Mary, ya keep your nose out of this." Ruari tilted his head. "I just want to know who they are."

Dirty Mary stomped her foot, sending a splash of greasy water over the man's worn boots. "I've enough of you, always snooping. Making trouble. They told you, you big lout. Now, get them their petrol so I can get me Guinness and be on my way to the rectory."

Ruari grunted, then unscrewed the cap to the petrol tank. He lifted the nozzle and began filling the lorry. Nan smiled at the old lady. Angels came in all shapes, sizes, and ages.

"Thanks for your help."

"Not a'tall." The woman extended her knotted hand. "I'm Mary. Dirty Mary. They call me that on account of when I was young and beautiful like yourself, my blonde hair had muddy-colored streaks through it. These days, it's white. They should call me Snowy Mary, but ya can't teach old dogs new tricks."

"I'm pleased to meet you." *No lie.* The women shook hands, and Nan was amazed at the strength of Mary's grip.

"So what's wanting with your husband? Why isn't he out here, helping ya?"

"Ah, he's doing poorly today. A throat infection. He brought me along to do the talking."

"And the thinking, too, if he's anything a'tall like Ruari, here. Now, how will he get the barrels down, feeling so poorly?"

"He can do that, no problem."

Mary stepped closer to Nan. The older woman smelled of turf, bacon, and bread. "He's a looker, isn't he?"

Nan nodded. "Yes." Her stomach flopped like salmon jumping upstream.

"He does look ever so pale. The poor lad needs his rest. He ought to be home in bed. With you." A sharp elbow to Nan's arm was followed by a cackle.

Dirty Mary turned to the petrol-station owner. "Ruari, when you're done here, we need ya help getting my Guinness down. The lad inside is doing poorly."

He hissed at her. "You had three husbands, Dirty Mary. You overworked them all and sent them to early graves."

Mary gritted her teeth and shook her fists. "Keep it up, Ruari. Just give me a reason to pop ya one, again."

A few minutes later, after unloading five barrels of beer, Nan and Dutch were on their way, the lorry chugging uphill toward the north. Dirty Mary had made them sausage-and-egg sandwiches, which they'd gobbled up along with a shared bottle of milk.

"The petrol-station owner, Ruari. Do you think he might call someone about us?" She rolled the sandwich papers into a wad.

"Maybe. I don't think he bought our story." Dutch glanced at her. "You see a Garda station in town?"

"No. Cliffside only comes alive on the weekends, when the market is in town, or when the races are held a few miles away. There's probably a Garda in the next town."

She felt uneasy about Ruari, but rather than feeding the unrest, she kept her mouth shut.

The wide-open landscape left nowhere to hide. They rambled northbound, the road twisting and coiling over the barren land. Green hills sloped gently up and down. Rock walls sectioned off forgotten patches of green. A ruined Viking tower dominated the landscape for miles.

Nan studied the map. "It's not far now. We'll take the mountain pass, and at the bottom we'll be back on track to the abbey. And the border."

"The sooner the better." Dutch slowed down. "What's that?"

Nan sat up, fixing her hands against the dashboard. In the distance, like lumps of clay on the horizon, several men and a car blocked the road. "Ah no. Another checkpoint."

"Aren't we in the middle of nowhere?"

"Only seems that way. Over the other side of the mountain, there's a big lakeside fishing community. You think Ruari called someone? Got word to them?"

"Perhaps. Stay calm."

Knots gripped her throat. She struggled to swallow. "Maybe I'll know them." Her voice shook, not confident in that statement.

"When we get close enough, tell me if you recognize them."

"If I don't?"

He glanced at the glove compartment, where the gun was stashed. "You'll have to fake it again."

Dear God, please let me know them. Please.

Rubbing her hands together, she searched their features. Two men in their forties or maybe fifties, wearing LDF uniforms, sat on the car's bumper. They held guns at their sides. Another man was stationed inside the vehicle.

"They're LDF, but I don't know them."

"Think you can talk your way through?"

"I'll try. And if I don't, no one gets hurt. Promise?"

"Sure." Dutch slowed the lorry to a full stop. One of the men approached them.

"Over here," Nan said through her open window. "My husband can't talk. He's ill."

The officer frowned, stared at Dutch, who stared back.

"All right, miss. What brings you this way on such a fine day?"

Nan laughed. "I'd think it be obvious. We're delivering Guinness."

"Are ya, now? Have ya any papers?"

"Ah sure, we do." She offered him the pack of cigarettes along with Brian's ration book. "Are ya lonely out here?"

"A bit boring sometimes, yeah." He pocketed the cigarettes. "What's this?"

"Our papers."

"This is a ration book. How about some identification?"

"Ah, Brian dear," she said to Dutch, "will ya give me your identification papers?"

Dutch reached inside the glove compartment. Fortunately, the gun had shifted to the very back of the cubby. He handed her Brian's driver's license.

"Here ya go, Officer." Nan smiled. "Getting cold. Do you think it'll rain?"

"It always rains in Eire." He flicked the license against his rough hands. "How about yours?"

"What about mine?"

"Your papers. I'd like to see them, miss."

This officer was no pushover. Her charms weren't going to work. "Ah sure. I don't have them on me. I wasn't aware the Emergency Act requires that passengers carry their identification cards."

"You should carry it always."

"Next time I will." She grinned at him.

The officer was inspecting Dutch, who had pulled the cap down so far over his head that his eyes were barely visible.

"All right. Let me just take a gander at this." He patted his pockets. "Ah, for the love of Pete. What did I do with my reading glasses? You wait here." He strolled over to the car.

When the officer got back to his vehicle, Nan squeezed Dutch's hand. "What are we going to do? He's bound to see you're not a fifty-five-year-old man."

The two officers outside the car inspected the license. The taller of the two men frowned. They looked at Dutch, back at the license, and back at Dutch again.

"They made us," Dutch said.

"What are you doing?"

"Getting away. Hang on."

Nan grabbed the lip of the seat. The lorry lurched forward, increasing speed, skidding up an embankment and around the officers' parked vehicle. The truck spun to the left and clipped the front end of their Ford. The lorry shook, swaying from side to side, Nan along with it.

Nan looked out the back window. The officers were taking aim with their rifles. The blast sounded, and a shot banged against the lorry's gate.

"We're hit." Her surprise outweighed her fear. "I can't believe they're firing at us. What a dirty Irish trick."

"Keep your head down." Dutch shoved her, slamming her face against the seat.

Pain radiated over her cheek. It felt as though the vehicle was coming apart, piece by piece. Dutch struggled to keep the steering wheel steady. The lorry pitched and shook along the road, as Nan bounced up and down on the seat.

She found herself praying out loud. When she finished, she reached into the knapsack for the gun and flipped onto her back. "You need this?"

He gaped. "Put that away before you accidentally shoot yourself. Or me."

She shoved the gun back inside the sack and remained down on the seat, the scent of beer and motor oil making her stomach protest.

He let out a laugh.

"What's so funny when we might be dead in a few minutes? What?"

"Sit up and take a look."

Nan sat upright and peeked out the back window. A lone barrel bounced and rolled off the lorry bed. It skidded down the lane and joined the pile of barrels blocking the road. Dark liquid spilled over the landscape.

"Thank you, Lord," Nan said.

"That's probably what the LDF officers are saying, too."

A giggle and then uncontrollable laughter took her over, tears running down her cheeks. Within a moment, Dutch joined her. They rambled along the country lane, both of them shaking with hysteria.

Their mirth gave way to sobriety once they turned onto a road that led to the ruined abbey. If the map was correct, they'd be there in three to four hours. There, they'd part. He'd make the rest of the journey on foot, and she'd drive the lorry home, armed with another lie about being kidnapped.

They didn't speak much for the next few hours. Nan stared ahead at the winding road. The hills became steep, rocky, jagged. Trees crowded either side of the route, turning the path cold and dark. Through the gaps in the forest, Nan spotted a lake. "According to the map notes, we're getting close."

The lorry sputtered up a twisting road, into a cloud of gray drizzle. The windshield wipers arched back across the glass, providing a steady clicking sound. Time ticked down to this moment, this one shot at freedom for Dutch.

She looked at him. Eyes focused ahead, he squinted at the rain hitting the windshield with loud taps. "It's really coming down."

"And it's getting dark."

In the distance, the abbey rose from the ground, a skeleton of its former self. Window openings minus their glass allowed the rain to slant through, slashing against mossy stone walls.

He downshifted, the gears making a grinding sound as the lorry putt-putted toward the crumbling structure. The right wheel pitched forward, and Nan slid along the seat to smack against him.

"Hang on," he said.

"To you?" How she wished she could.

"If you'd like. I think we blew a tire. I'll pull the truck inside the abbey and change it before I hightail it for the border."

"No, you can't go yet. The night is coming. It'll be too slippery and dark to make the crossing. The map notes say there are drop-offs and deep crevasses. 'Don't attempt during night.'" She found the paper crumpled on the floor, picked it up, and showed him the hand-printed warning, as though he hadn't read it already.

"There must be a flashlight in the truck somewhere" was his only response.

"Don't be an eejit. You didn't come this far to slip off into the abyss. You have to wait until morning."

The lorry's headlights lit the cavernous abbey like ghosts dancing around the masonry. "You can't leave until morning, either," he said this time. "The roads are barely passable even in sunshine. And you need the daylight, too."

"Spend the night with you? Alone?"

"Why is this any different from your cottage?"

"Because I never shared a bed with you."

"Yes, you did."

"That was different. You were unconscious."

"Not completely."

She poked his arm. "Will you stop teasing me?"

The lorry limped inside the roofless structure and came to a stop. "Nan, your virtue will remain intact. I'll find a dry spot outside the abbey somewhere."

"Thank you." She was a good Catholic girl, and hell wasn't the place she wanted to spend eternity. Yet she added, "I'll be massively cold tonight. It's your turn to keep me warm."

He looked pleased at the prospect, and didn't she agree, sinner that she was?

CHAPTER 26

Dutch found the abbey spooky in the waning light. The mist hugged the black walls, and the faces carved into stone above the multiple arches gave him the willies.

The wind circled the top of the highest wall and then cascaded down to surround him. He turned up his collar. The sickeningly floral scent of dirt and moss did nothing to settle his nerves. Beneath his feet, the ground went from spongy moss to cold slate. *There sure isn't anything like this in Canada,* he thought.

Nan seemed perfectly at home, and why wouldn't she?

"Be careful," he called as she scurried around the abbey like a mountain goat. She climbed the steep steps that hugged the walls of the ruins.

As she neared the top of a stairway, she slipped, and his stomach lurched. "Will you be careful? The map is wrong. It's been wrong all along. There couldn't possibly be a box of supplies up there. Come down. It's not worth it."

"The map wasn't wrong. We took a wrong turn. Aren't you the least bit curious?" She poked a stick between the stones.

"No. Watch out for spiders."

"Why? You afraid of them?"

"Would you come down already? You're making me nervous."

"I'm not nervous."

"Come down. You're not going to find anything up there but a sprained ankle." She was in enough danger already, without adding a self-inflicted injury in this death trap. "Nan. I mean it. Come down. I don't want this to end like some stupid ballet. You haunting the abbey in search of your lost—"

"Brains." A tinkling sound echoed through the ruins. "What's this?" Beaming as though she'd found a diamond necklace, she held a tin container the size of a cigar box. "Can't wait to see what's inside."

"Be careful." Dutch bit his ragged thumbnail as she descended the stairway. It was as if she climbed ruins every day.

Strange how things had turned out. A few days ago, jumping out of the Wellington, he thought he was good as dead. He never imagined he'd be rescued by a beautiful Irish woman. He peered upward through a lancet window at the darkening sky.

Dear Lord, you brought us this far; please be with us the rest of the way.

Nan approached him, slipping over the moss-covered rocks. Righting herself with graceful movements, she glowed. At every step, something rattled inside the box. "What do you think it is?"

"Another gun?"

"I hope not."

"Bullets?"

"You have a one-track mind. We don't need another weapon or more bullets."

She stood beside him, her sweet scent of lilac and soap surrounding his senses, her hair curling even more in the gathering dampness. The beret plastered on her head reminded him of soggy pancakes, and the thought of food made his stomach grumble.

"I can't open the lid."

The contents again rattled inside, echoing through the abbey like dead monks shaking their rosaries.

"Weakling," he muttered, taking the box. After a few tries, he popped the lid. "Here you go. Have fun."

"Some bandages," she said, picking through the tin. "A tube of ointment. A tin of sardines."

"Yuck." Although right now the smelly fish sounded good.

"Candles. Matches. Ah, but didn't they think of everything?"

"An escape tunnel to the north would have been better."

Nan smiled brightly enough to light the night without the aid of candles. But around her, the wind howled through the drizzle.

She shivered. "Not exactly romantic, Ireland, is it?"

"I don't know," he said, sliding off his jacket and draping it over her shoulders. "Reminds me of *Wuthering Heights*."

"You read the book?" She cozied herself into his jacket, clutching the edges together for warmth.

"Forced to in school. Then I took my mom and sister-in-law to see the movie. It was the last gathering with my family before I left for England and the RAF." And then too many hugs. Too many tears. Promises he hadn't known if he could keep.

Her finger traced the back of his hand. That act alone made him tremble.

"You're a good lad."

He wasn't sure what "good" was anymore.

"Let's get out of the dampness," she said, leading him to the truck.

They settled in the cab, one on each side of the seat, the candle lit and stuck to the dashboard. They ate the sardines, which tasted better than he'd imagined, the apples from Nan's trees, and the eggs from the pub.

With total darkness came moist cold, the kind that stung through clothing. Rain was pouring down as though God had turned on a faucet and forgotten to turn it off.

When Nan could no longer hide her shivers, he said, "Come on. Lean into me. I won't bite."

With her back pressed into his chest, they shared their warmth. The candlelight flickered in the breeze that crept in, the wax dripping onto the dashboard. He held her around the waist, his cheek resting on her head.

"When did we crack the windshield?" she asked, positioning her arms over his.

Dutch squinted at the glass. The dancing light glinted on the web of crazing that rose from the left side to the top of the windshield.

"I don't know."

"We managed to make a wreck of the lorry," she said. "That alone will send me to prison."

With arms tightening around her, he inhaled the scent of her hair. "I'll pay for the damages."

"How will you do that on a flyboy's salary?"

Should he tell her? He hesitated. "My family has money."

"Well, isn't that nice. But I won't have them spending their nest egg on an old lorry."

"No, I mean a lot. My family won't miss a few hundred dollars."

"Are you telling me you're one of those hoity-toity rich people?" She laughed.

"We're not hoity-toity."

Nan lifted her face to his. "What would your mother say if you come home with an Irish peasant girl?"

"She'll love you because I love you."

Nan's eyes glistened. "Would she?"

"Can't wait for you two to meet." He caressed her cheek with his own. "Will you change your mind? Come to England with me?"

She shook her head. "My life is here. I can't go with you now. I've created a mess for my friends."

"I've created the mess for all of you."

"Well, you helped, but we'll stick to the story. You made us do everything at gunpoint. All of us will say so."

"I hope the story sticks."

"Don't worry about me. Know what I think?" She fidgeted with her wedding ring.

"What?"

"There are no accidents, only divine connections. The good Lord sent you here to heal my heart."

He thought about it for a minute. "Yes, maybe He sent me to find you. And for me to see the face of war. I always viewed it from above, not down here on the earth. I don't understand how those infantry soldiers do it. They have to see the dead."

"Guess we saved each other." Crawling to the other side of the truck, she rolled down the window a crack. "Good-bye, Teddy. Ya blaggard." She threw her wedding ring out the window.

Dutch sat up. "Nan. What have you done?"

"Closed an awful chapter in my life. Almost. I still need to confess my sins to Father Albert and receive his forgiveness. And do a boatload of penance."

"You're truly free to be with me?"

"Yes. And I want to be, Dutch."

"Will you marry me?"

She smiled. "I will."

"Cross the border with me tomorrow. We'll get married on base. Come with me to England. Live nearby." He slid closer to her, reached for her, wanting to hold her tight. His leg pressed against hers, her warmth sending waves of tingles up his back to rest between his shoulder blades.

She stopped him with a hand to his chest, her eyes searching his face. "I'll go with you. Cross the border. Be happy to marry you. But . . ."

"What?"

There seemed to be a battle raging behind her eyes. "But I must return to Ballyhaven."

"Why?"

"You know why."

He let out a sigh. "Father Albert."

"And I can't abandon my friends to deal with the mess we've made. When all this gets sorted out, I'll find a way to join you. Dutch? Please?"

Her loyalty astonished him, though it shouldn't have. This was why he loved her so. "But I want you with me." He must have sounded like a whining child.

"Once we're legally married, can't I travel to Belfast and meet you on base? Or go to England for a visit?"

He shrugged. There was logic to her reasoning. "I suppose that's possible. How will we manage that? How—"

She glided her hand up his throat to cover his lips. "We'll pray. Put our trust in God. Figure out the details tomorrow. And like all war brides, I'll be waiting for the war to end so we can be together for all time."

If he pushed her too hard, she might back away. He couldn't bear losing her over his stubbornness. "I . . . it's not ideal."

"Nor is you getting back into a bomber. But this is war."

"You have a point. If that's the way it has to be, okay."

"'Tis. And I love you." She fell into his waiting arms.

"I love you, too." The wind rocked the truck, or maybe it was only the dizziness he felt for being with her. Now more than ever, he prayed he'd be spared in combat.

"Your cheek. It's bruised. Did I do that when I pushed you to the seat?"

"I must look a fright." Her fingers trembled over the dark patch.

"You look incredibly beautiful."

"Go on with ya. Me? An old mud hen?"

He touched her cheek, her skin silky under his palm. With shaking fingers, her hand covered his. They locked gazes as their lips found each other's. The kiss began tentatively, then deepened. They were connected by touch and spirit. A forever kiss in a wrecked Guinness truck. A story for their children's children.

He had no doubts now, he realized. This was the woman God had chosen for him.

"Close your eyes," she said, her voice soothing. "We've got to rest. It's a treacherous journey in the morning."

Dutch closed his eyes and drifted into slumber, holding on to Nan and to the hope that by this time tomorrow, they'd be married. Yes, he'd head back to England, but he'd see her soon. And she would be waiting for him when the war was over.

Lord, he prayed, *thank you for this precious woman. Please make a way for us to be together sooner rather than later.*

CHAPTER 27

Dutch's mechanic tapped on the wing of his Wellington bomber. The steaming afternoon sun, more like a hot day in Toronto than a typical day in England, burned, blurring Dutch's vision.

He stared at the pristine bomber. "I thought this old gal went down in Ireland."

"Yep, but it'll fly again." The kid's smile sent wrinkles around his eyes. "Take us right out of here, sir. Take us home. Say, didn't you go down with your crew last month?"

The kid tapped the wing again. And again. Dutch woke, this time turning his head toward the tapping sound.

His stomach lurched. Outside the truck, a line of soldiers had their rifles set on Dutch and Nan. A man wearing a green uniform grinned. "Ah, did we wake you, then? Top of the morning to ya, Flight Officer Whitney."

Dutch jolted upright, rousing Nan. The doors swung open. From either side, uniformed men grabbed the couple.

"No, no." She kicked the soldier climbing in, but the trooper managed to seize her legs. "Get off."

She held on to Dutch, but they were yanked out. They stumbled, struggled to stay together, found their footing. Her eyes, so wild and afraid, tore at his soul.

The Irish Army officers wrenched Nan from his arms, and a soldier grabbed her around the waist. Nan reached for Dutch with arms and legs as they were dragged away from each other.

"No, no. Let him go. He's a hero."

"He's a combatant," the man with a too-tight uniform said. "He's off to internment."

"She's not involved," Dutch protested. "Leave her be. You're hurting her." He struggled to free himself from their grip, and one of the officers struck Dutch in the stomach while another punched his face.

"Stop. You're killing him." Nan's struggles were met with tighter holds.

"We're doing no such thing. Hands on your head, miss," a soldier instructed. He patted her down with a smirk.

"Don't you touch her!" Dutch yelled.

"Shut up, you." The butt of a rifle struck his ribs.

Pain from the hit stabbed through him, and he grasped for breath.

"Ah, would ya look at this. Not one gun, but two." A trooper with missing front buttons on his uniform climbed out of the truck, holding the weapons.

"That's evidence. Take it along."

Handcuffed and thrown into the back of an army vehicle, Dutch fell against the dirty floor. He tried to stand, but a booted foot slammed him back down. "She's innocent. I made her do everything at gunpoint. Let her go."

"We can't do that. The Garda will determine her fate."

Soldiers yanked him up to the bench and wedged him in on either side, their bulk restraining his movements. All he could do was crane his neck to gaze out the back window.

"What are they doing to her?"

"Ah, don't ya worry."

"What are you going to do with me?"

"What do you think, lad? You're off to the K-Lines. Curragh Internment Camp. Where the Brits used to imprison the IRA. Ironic, isn't it?"

Dutch didn't care about internment anymore. All he cared about was what would happen to Nan. He'd failed to protect her. Failed to keep her from being arrested. In the distance, she grew smaller and smaller as troopers walked her out of the abbey and onto the tree-lined lane.

◆ ◆ ◆

Hands on her head, Nan no longer fought the urge to cry as two Irish Army soldiers escorted her down a muddy road.

One of the men handed her a handkerchief. "If you promise not to run, you can put your arms down."

"Thank you," she said, wiping her tears.

"Not a'tall." The young man kept his gaze ahead.

Where would she run? Only back to Dutch. There was no fleeing from what she'd done, from the sins she'd racked up. But this was serious. It was God's will, or their plan would have worked. He must have something else in mind. *Trust in the Lord,* a still, quiet voice rose from deep down within her. She did, but He wasn't making it easy.

They continued down the lane about a half mile until they came to a Garda van, its back doors open. Inside, a man with sloped shoulders and drooping eyes sat on a bench. He flung down an *Irish Times* newspaper.

"Ah, there ya are. Thanks, fellas. We'll take her from here."

The two soldiers nodded and strolled back toward the abbey.

The Garda from the van hopped out. "I'm Officer Dunn. And this here . . ." He looked from side to side. "Johnny, where are ya?"

A man with a red nose slunk around the side of the van. "Hello, miss. I bet you're famished. Fancy a cup of tea and some breakfast?"

"I dunno, Johnny. Don't you think we ought to pat her down first? For weapons?"

"Brilliant, Dunn. Brilliant."

"They did that to me already." A blush spread over her cheeks. She thought the army officers might have enjoyed their task. Hands everywhere, touching her. Making her skin crawl.

"It's procedure." Johnny closed the distance between them. His breath could kill a cow. "Do you have a gun, miss?"

"I don't."

"Okay." He stepped back.

"Ah, but that's not procedure, Johnny. She might be a dangerous criminal."

Nan stomped her foot, although in the mud, the only sound it mustered was a squish. "I am not. I'm just a midwife. The Irish Army pawed me already."

"Ah, the brutes."

Officer Dunn folded his arms, looked her up and down. "Ya see, miss. You might look as innocent as a lamb at Easter, but someone tied up Officer Finn. Someone stole a Guinness lorry. Used false papers to get petrol. Mowed down an LDF checkpoint. Last time I checked, all that was against the law, and you and the RAF pilot are the prime suspects."

"He kidnapped me."

Both men laughed.

Her face flushed. "I'm innocent until proven guilty in a court of law." Nan focused on the ground. She was so guilty, it wouldn't be worth hiring a lawyer to plead her case. She'd spend the rest of the year, maybe the rest of the decade, in jail. She might never see Dutch again, she thought with dread. How could they have hit him? How could they have harmed him?

And what would the women of Ballyhaven do without their midwife? Dr. Mann, while brilliant in every way, didn't seem committed to her physician duties.

"Go on then, Johnny. Pat down the missus."

"I don't have any weapons."

Officer Dunn perched on the edge of the open van, poured tea into a cup, and crossed his legs at the ankles. Steam looped upward from the beverage. "How will we know unless we pat you down?"

"Maybe she can pull her sweater tight? Give us a bit of a turn around?"

"Brilliant! Do ya mind, miss? 'Cause we really don't want to put our hands on ya."

"Oh, fine." She took off her jacket, tossed it to Dunn, and then pulled her sweater tight in every direction, revealing her curves. After a slow turn, she lifted her eyebrows. "Once enough?" From their gaping mouths, it seemed her figure was weapon enough to leave the men stunned.

Dunn licked his lips and offered a lopsided smile. "All right. You remind me of my daughter. Take ya coat, miss. It's powerfully cold this morning."

"Really, Dunn? She reminds me of a Hollywood star. Climb inside. Have a cup of tea. Sit down. There's a bit of paperwork; then we'll be on our way."

"To where?"

"Ballyhaven. Our orders are to deliver you to the Garda. He's waiting for you."

Her hand covered her mouth. She was doomed. A bolt of panic soared through her as she pictured Finn. What if Halpin, God forbid, was mourning his dead wife? Finn would be in charge. Oh, what would he do to her now? She remembered him on top of her, pawing her, trying to get her belt open.

She straightened her shoulders. She'd gladly go to jail if it saved her from the likes of Shamus Finn. "What about Dutch? Officer Whitney?"

"Himself? Off to internment camp."

"They should let him go," Nan said. "He's on the right side. He's so close, just a walk away from freedom."

"We can't very well pick and choose which belligerents we intern if we have any hopes of staying a neutral nation."

Nan sighed with defeat. The image of Dutch, doubled over from the punch to his gut, blood trickling from his nose, turned her stomach. For the first time in her life, she was ashamed of her country. They needn't have roughed him up, all the while pointing their rifles at the couple.

Nan settled on the wooden bench inside the van. Dunn poured her a cup of tea, gave her a slice of soda bread smeared with butter, and then closed the door. The sound of the lock clicking shut vibrated in her ear. So final a sound, it made her cry.

Through the back window, gray light illuminated the interior of her prison. She stared into her cup, the contents of her stomach turning to acid.

I have faith, but where are You in this, Lord? Please, dear heavenly Father, protect and save Dutch.

A few hours later, the landscape grew familiar. Ballyhaven, with its lopsided church steeple and gray, tile-roofed buildings, came into view. They rode on the narrow path beside the graveyard. This wouldn't be home for long, though. She'd be off to prison, to some dark, lonesome place where she'd rot away and pine for Dutch.

"What do ya make of that, Dunn? All those women following that lad down the lane, poking him with their brooms?" The van came to a screeching halt outside the churchyard.

"Ah now. Are they throwing vegetables at that poor bloke? Where would they get them tomatoes this time of year?"

"I dunno, but we'll have to wait. They're blocking the road."

Nan went to the barred window, shaking the van from side to side. With a sharp gasp, she watched Finn hurry across the street, holding a suitcase. A crowd of womenfolk, her friends, marched after him. Two gals snarled and shouted at him, prodding him with the ends of their brooms. Tomatoes flew through the air from the crowd, some hitting Finn, others splatting on the road, leaving bright-red marks on the gray pavement.

Nan threaded her fingers through the open bars. She recognized the walking ball of yarn. "Margaret," she called. "Margaret."

Her friend looked in her direction.

"Margaret. In here." Nan stuck her fingers through the grate.

"Nan! It's Nan!" Margaret broke from the mob and ran to the van. "Ah, what have they done to you?"

"Arrested me."

Tuda appeared next. "Are you all right, aside from being locked up?"

"Yes, but my heart is mashed potatoes. They took Dutch away. Ripped him from my arms. Beat him."

"The blaggards." Margaret pressed her hands together. "But isn't that romantic?"

"Are you daft? It was horrible. He's on his way to internment camp, and I'm on my way to prison." Nan felt hot tears run down her cheeks.

"Ah now, we'll see about that." Tuda handed Nan a handkerchief. "Did ya see the doings with Finn? He's getting run out of town. And about time."

Nan took the linen tissue and wiped it over her wet cheeks. "Why?"

"On account of slapping Lady Margot."

Nan placed her hand over her mouth. "What?"

"'Tis true. After Finn got free—"

"How?" Nan asked.

"The Tinkers. Ah, I'm sorry, Nan. They helped themselves to your stuff before they untied Finn."

"I don't care about my stuff. What happened next to Finn?"

"He must have heard us talking about the Silver Ghost, because he went to the manor house and confronted Lady Margot as she stepped out of her lovely car," Margaret said.

"She was holding a cake," Tuda said. "When she told him she had no idea who or what he was talking about, he grabbed her arm and shook it."

"No!"

Margaret nodded. "She flung the cake at him and hit him in the face. Then he slapped her. Lord Harry saw the whole thing, the whole thing. They got into quite the shoving match. His lordship had him arrested and stripped of his uniform, and then his lordship said he'd drop the charges if Finn would leave town. Immediately. That was a bit of God fighting our battle, don't ya think?"

"I do," Nan said. "I'm glad to see the back of that man."

"Ah sure, we all are." Margaret adjusted a stray hair from her messy bun. "All us women, anyway."

The last of the ladies crossed the street, and the Garda wagon shook into gear. "We'll see you at the station. Come on, Margaret. I still have a basket of rotten hothouse tomatoes, and the target has a backside the size of a barn."

"Throw one for me," Nan shouted, glad that Finn would no longer wander the streets of Ballyhaven in pursuit of mischief.

The vehicle rumbled over the cobbled street. Still standing at the window, Nan peeked over the stone fence at the graveyard. Wind parted the mist long enough for her to see her husband's grave, covered in moss and wet from the morning shower.

Her heart sank, as her biggest sin seemed to stare back at her. She had to confess to Father Albert, make her slate clean. He would need to know. She wondered if Teddy would be dug up, removed from the graveyard. The church was firm on this issue—suicide was a mortal sin.

She slumped onto the bench. Soon, she'd be formally charged. Sent to prison. Set apart from a life she'd so carefully built. But at least Finn would no longer torment the women in town. Something good had come from all this.

"What the heaven is going on here? Why are all those men standing outside the pub?" Nan heard Johnny exclaim.

"Looks closed. What do ya think of that, Dunn?"

"I think there must be something powerfully wrong to close down a grand pub like that."

She returned to the window. Sure enough, the town's men milled outside Mrs. Odin's pub, their facial expressions ranging from confused to lost. The pub door was closed, and the window shutters were latched shut. It was strange; Mrs. Odin always opened the pub by this time in the afternoon. Dread raced through Nan. Maybe Mrs. Odin had been arrested, too.

But that didn't make any sense. Tuda and Margaret were free, but perhaps Halpin hadn't caught up with them yet.

A few minutes later, the van pulled to the curb. So this was it. The end of the line. The end of freedom. Nan let out a sigh as the Garda opened the wagon's door. They led her into the station, down the hall, and presented her to Officer Halpin, who sat in his office, behind his desk.

Thank you, Lord, that it's not Finn, she thought.

"Ah, Nan. You've been a naughty girl."

"I have." Heat surged through her. "Kelly. How is she?"

"Still in hospital. Resting. Dr. Mann insists your quick thinking saved her life. For the most part, she will fully recover."

"I'm so glad." Nan crossed her hands over her chest. At least she had done something right over the past few days. "The baby?"

"Growing like a weed. We'll love her even more dearly now, if that's a'tall possible. You see, we won't have any more children."

"I'm so sorry, Paul."

He toyed with a fountain pen. "You needn't be. I have my girls. That's enough."

There was a wistfulness in his eyes, and then, as though an actor in a play, his demeanor changed. He straightened his shoulders, and his expression turned serious. "You've been quite the active girl." He opened a file. "Sit."

Nan lowered herself to the chair. The scent of turf burning in the fireplace filled the room but failed to take the chill from her bones.

A shuffling noise came from the hallway. Halpin glanced above the file to the closed door. "Mrs. Norman," he called. He waited a beat. "Mrs. Norman, I know you're listening at the door. Would you mind terribly bringing Nan a cup of tea? And a biscuit?"

Through the closed door, they heard the woman say, "Right away."

A last meal before imprisonment, Nan thought. "Why is Mrs. Norman working here?"

"She's filling in until things get back to normal. All right, young lady. Let's sort this out." Halpin returned his attention to the police file.

Nan's throat tightened. She had a police file. She'd never work in this or any other town again. She was ruined. And Dutch was ruined. Both of them, ruined.

"How did you find us?" she asked.

"It wasn't very hard after a petrol-station owner in Cliffside tipped off the Garda. He reported suspicious behavior by a Guinness lorry driver and his wife. Figured it was you and Whitney, heading to the border. After we got the report that someone had run an LDF checkpoint on Cecile Road, we figured you had to be headed to the abbey. It's the last place to hide before crossing to the north."

"*You* called the Irish Army?"

"I won't lie to you. I helped them work this out."

Nan slumped against the chair. He was only doing his job, and she knew she shouldn't feel betrayed, but she did. "The Irish Army officers, they beat Dutch when they took him."

Halpin looked surprised. "Why?"

"He tried to get away. To rescue me, I suppose."

"I see. Resisting arrest. Probable cause, then. But that was wrong of them. Unnecessary." He turned the pages of the file. "Deep-seated hatred for the English comes out sometimes."

"He's Canadian."

"He's RAF. They've taken him to Curragh Internment Camp. It's a military base outside of Dublin."

"I know. Will he be charged with any crimes?"

"We're cooperating with the RAF, so no. But you will." He held a steady gaze on her.

Her mouth went dry. "With what?" Her voice squeaked out the words.

"Tying up an LDF officer. Stealing a Guinness lorry. Using stolen identification and running a checkpoint. There's also the matter of the wrecked lorry and the loss of the inventory. Plus, you aided a combatant trooper, which is clearly in violation of the Emergency Act."

The blood seemed to drain from her head as he read out the charges. "That's a long list."

She would be going away for quite a while.

He sat back, folded his arms over his chest. "There's also a charge of false imprisonment."

"What?"

"Didn't you and Whitney hold Tuda and Margaret at gunpoint? Make them help you do all these things? Isn't that true?"

Her gaze shifted. Talk about backfiring, but if she didn't admit to the charge, Halpin might arrest her friends. She was going to jail, but she didn't want to drag her friends along with her. "Yes. We held them at gunpoint, made them help us escape."

"Right. Have you anything to add?"

Nan squeezed her eyes shut, then opened them. "Dutch is on the right side of this conflict."

"I suspect he is, but that doesn't change anything, and it's no defense. Speaking of which, I highly recommend you engage a solicitor."

313

He leaned over the paperwork and wrote something. The sound of his pen scratching on the paper grated in her ears.

A ruckus came from outside the office. The door swung open, and Mrs. Norman stepped in. "I'm sorry, Officer Halpin. I couldn't stop them."

A dozen or so women crowded into the room, pressing forward, filling every space. An acidic smell of tomatoes lingered in the air. Nan knew them all, had attended to their female needs, and her spirits lifted at the sight of them.

Mrs. Kennedy, dressed in a black wool coat, her face splashed with a crimson glow, carried her infant son and placed him in Nan's arms. "The seventh son of a seventh son. He'll bring ya luck."

"I could use that." She looked down at the bundled-up infant, and he smiled at her. "Hello, little Thomas."

"What is the meaning of this?" Halpin demanded.

Tuda and Margaret pushed to the front of the crowd. With hands on her hips, Tuda said, "We are here to ask the same question. What's all this? What do you think you're doing to our Nan?"

Halpin dropped his pen on the open file. "Not that it's any of your business, but I'm arresting Nan on a multitude of charges."

"Are you? Such as?"

"Tying up an LDF officer for one."

Margaret huffed as she pounded her forefinger on the Garda's desk. "That was self-defense. I saw it all, every bit of it. Finn attacked Nan."

Grumbles and shocked intakes of breath rose from the crowd, along with murmurs of "Blaggard . . . disgraceful . . . the lard-arse . . ."

"Ah, ya poor dear," Mrs. Kennedy said. The baby's tiny hand squeezed Nan's finger as though in solidarity with the ladies.

Margaret pounded her fist on the desk and leaned forward. "What was she going to do? Just let Finn have his way with her? The big lard-arse had been harassing her for weeks. You should have put a stop to it long ago, 'cause you knew about it, didn't ya?"

Halpin pulled his collar. "Nan indicated she had the situation under control."

"That animal? Ya should have protected her. All of us."

The crowd shouted out their agreement.

Tuda crossed her arms and glared down at Halpin. "Nan should sue you and the LDF."

Nan shook her head, acknowledging that she'd underestimated Finn's vile temperament. "No. I want no part of that. What Paul said is true. Finn's gone now, and let that be the last of him." She repositioned the baby against her shoulder.

Halpin cleared his throat. "Is that so, Nan? Did Finn attack you? And then you acted in self-defense?"

"Yes, it's true. I did. And if Dutch hadn't come to my aid, I shudder to think what would have happened." She felt Margaret's hot hand on her shoulder. The crowd mumbled sympathetic words of encouragement. Turning to them, she nodded in gratitude.

Halpin looked Nan up and down. "Considering we now have an eyewitness to the altercation at your home, and you and Dutch acted in self-defense, we'll let that one go."

"Thank you." Nan began to rise.

"Not so fast." Halpin signaled with his hand to sit. "There are other charges. You stole a lorry."

"Wait one second, there." Holding Brian's hand to drag him along, Mrs. Odin weaved through the crowd.

"'Tis himself, lover boy," a woman said with a smirk. A chorus of kissing noises turned Brian's face red.

Mrs. Odin nudged Brian forward until his legs were against the desk. "Go on. Tell the Garda."

The muscles in Brian's face tightened. "No."

"Tell him." Her voice was as sharp as the poke she gave his back.

"Ouch. No. I'll lose my job," Brian hissed through clenched teeth.

"And I'll close my pub forever. The men in town will tar and feather ya." She moved closer to him and whispered into his ear. "You'll never, never taste my . . . blood sausage . . . again." She licked her upper lip and arched an eyebrow.

Brian trembled and let out a sigh. "Fine." He squared his shoulders, looked at Halpin, and said, "I let them borrow the lorry."

Applause broke out in the room.

Halpin's lips narrowed to a slash. "Did you? Really?"

When Brian hesitated, Mrs. Odin kicked his ankle.

Brian slanted a look at Mrs. Odin. "I did."

"You'll have to drop that charge, too, won't you?" Nan tried hard not to smile. The baby against her shoulder seemed to giggle, but of course that was impossible for such a wee babe, even the seventh son of a seventh son.

"Ah for the love of God," Halpin said, scribbling something in the file. "Since the Guinness driver won't or can't seem to bring himself to admit you stole his lorry, I have no choice, but there's still a charge of you running the LDF checkpoint."

Nan knew she was guilty. "I, ah . . ."

"Stop. Not another word, Nan. Out of my way, let me through."

Nan turned toward the voice to see Siobhan emerge from the crowd. The teenager's freckled face was pink, and she held her hands in fists at her waist. "Nan, I'm not a solicitor yet, but I've worked for my da long enough to know when the Garda is out of line and treading a position that's tenuous at best. And he's trying to weasel a confession out of ya. Will you let me represent you?"

"Yes. Please." New hope rose in Nan.

Siobhan rose to her full diminutive height. She turned her focus on Sergeant Halpin. "What are the charges you're thinking of pinning on my innocent client?"

"I'm not thinking about it. I'm doing it. She ran a checkpoint with the stolen . . . borrowed lorry."

"Did she? Alone? Was she driving the said lorry?"

"Yes. No. She and her companion."

"I see," Siobhan said. "Nan, were you driving said vehicle?"

"I was not."

"So you were merely an innocent passenger, with no say in what your companion's actions might be?"

Nan felt a grin. "Yes. Exactly."

With palm open to the sergeant, Siobhan said, "I don't see how you can hold my client accountable for that action, do you?"

The crowd's voices rose in agreement.

Halpin's eyes narrowed. "What about the false identity papers? Well, Nan?"

"What false identity papers? I never presented any such article." Which was true. Only Dutch had.

"I read it right here. In the report." Halpin shuffled through the report. He let out a deep breath. "Fine. Nothing in the report about you exactly having—"

"Then you can hardly charge her for something her companion allegedly did, can ya?" Siobhan placed her hand on Nan's shoulder. "Well then, she's free to go, isn't she?"

"Not so fast. There's the matter of the damages to the Guinness lorry and the loss of their inventory. If you can't pay the damages, I've no choice but to lock you up."

"Wait, I have something for ya. Let me through, let me through." The crowd parted, and Mrs. Norman arrived at the edge of the desk with an envelope. "Here's an anonymous payment for the wrecked lorry and the lost inventory, from Dr. Mann. Oops." She covered her mouth with her hand.

"Give it over, Mrs. Norman." Halpin opened the envelope, counted the money. He slapped the envelope onto his desk.

"Have ya anything else? Are we through here?" Siobhan asked.

Halpin stared at Nan for a moment. "No. You aided a belligerent. That is a violation against the Emergency Act."

Nan's heart beat so hard, she was sure everyone in the room, all her dear friends, could see her rib cage move. The baby began to wail.

"Are you mad?" Tuda asked. "She's a nurse. It's her moral obligation to help the wounded. She couldn't send the poor lad away."

Halpin leaned an elbow on his desk and, over the baby's crying, said, "She should have turned him in. It's the law."

"And let him die? Isn't she responsible for saving your wife?" Tuda turned to the crowd, and over the increasing sound of the baby's wailing, she shouted, "Who here has been helped by Nurse Nan?"

A wave of hands went up. The baby screamed louder and louder.

"Oh, all right. I give up." Halpin closed the file and scribbled something across the front. "After closer examination of the evidence, this case is closed. You're free to go. And get that screaming baby out of my office."

"I'm free to go?"

"There's the door. All of you out."

The crowd erupted into applause. Mrs. Kennedy took the baby from Nan's arms. "I told you he'd bring ya luck."

"Come on, everyone," Mrs. Odin said. "Time to open the pub. First round on Brian."

"What?" he asked.

The sound of shoes trundling out of the room mixed with laughter.

After exchanging hugs with Tuda, Margaret, Mrs. Norman, and Siobhan, Nan lingered behind. "What about Dutch?"

Sergeant Halpin shook his head as he dropped the file into a drawer. "I'm sorry. That's completely out of my control. One more thing, Nan."

She stepped back. "Should I call Siobhan?"

"No. We want you to be Maeve's godmother."

Nan pressed a hand over her heart. "Of course, I'd be honored."

"Go join your friends." He picked up the ringing phone. "Officer Halpin." He glanced at Nan.

She smiled and nodded to him before leaving the room. Dutch might have complained about the Irish, how they didn't see things as cut-and-dried, but didn't that just work in her favor?

Within moments, the relief she felt at being freed began to dissipate, and she allowed herself to feel the deep longing for the man she loved. When would she see him again? Hold him in her arms? Her heart hurt at the thought that she might never look into his eyes again. The way the Irish Army had treated him, she feared for his life.

Outside the office, Mrs. Norman was dusting a picture of de Valera that didn't need dusting.

"Ah, there ya are. I knew none of them charges would stick. Going down to the pub to celebrate?"

Nan looked at the clock. She still had time. "Going to confession."

"Aren't you the good Catholic girl."

"If I were, I wouldn't be going to confession."

Mrs. Norman looked both ways before she spoke. "Spending the night in the arms of the man you love is worth the penance."

"Maybe. After confession, I'm going home to feed my cat. He must be starving. And take a bath." Somehow, she'd sort out her life and get it back together. Find a new normal. Wait for the war to be over. Then she and Dutch could get married. Tonight, she'd find comfort in a cup of tea and a cuddle with Mr. Dee.

"Ah, your cat. I'm sorry about your cat."

Her arms fell to her side. "When did he die? Where is he buried?"

"He's not dead a'tall, but he's not yours anymore, either. Margaret has him. Seems he's taken a liking to the hearth in the shop. Prances around like he owns the place. Oh, that's the kettle whistling for the sergeant's tea. Gotta go."

So the cat had abandoned her. Her cottage would be a cold, empty mess when she returned.

As Nan stepped out into the misty afternoon, Tuda approached her with open arms. "There's herself. You're free. We're all free. Especially free from that blaggard Finn."

"And I'm free from Teddy, too. Dutch helped me through."

"Finally. I'm so glad." Tuda pulled her close, and the warmth of the embrace sent tears to threaten Nan's composure. "Ah, look at yaself, crying."

With an arm around her friend's shoulder, Tuda guided Nan to a bench outside the Garda station.

"I never set out to fall for a flyboy, to break the law, to have my heart torn in two."

"That's life, Nan. Surely you know that. Would you prefer to be safe in your little house, not having had the adventure of your lifetime?"

"And still churning over Teddy? No."

"You have Dutch to look forward to."

Nan thought about Dutch. His smile. His dazzling eyes. His touch. Their kisses. The memories would always warm her. "Why does it have to hurt so much?"

"Because there's no heaven on earth. Now dry your eyes. Your journey is far from over. In time, the war, like all wars, will end. You'll see your flyboy again. At least he won't be up in the air, being shot at by the Nazis."

"He's a trapped bird. I hope his heart won't die." Nan wiped the hankie under her nose. "Maybe he'll forget me."

"Forget you? Not a chance. The way he looked at you? Come on, let's go down to the pub."

"No. I'm going to confession. One last thing I have to do. But will you take Mrs. Odin aside and thank her for me?"

"Of course I will."

Nan adjusted her jacket and squared her shoulders. "I'll walk with you. Oh dear. I need a hat or a scarf for my head." She patted her pockets, wondering what had happened to her beret. "Do you have a scarf I can borrow?"

Tuda reached around her neck, tugged off a brown scarf, and handed it to Nan. "Father Albert is in a beastly mood. Seems someone slipped a rhythm-method pamphlet under his door."

"Now, who would do a thing like that?"

"Someone bold. And I applaud her, too."

Nan wondered if Tuda might have been the person. Or maybe the doctor. *The doctor.* She owed the doctor so much.

The clouds parted as she and Tuda walked down the hill toward the village. *Life is a series of contradictions,* Nan thought, tucking her cold hands into her pockets. Mr. Carlow gone, Maeve Halpin born. Nan free, Dutch interned.

"I have to tell you about your house," Tuda said, stopping in front of the pub. Fiddle music came from inside, along with loud singing and laughing.

"Yes. I know. The Tinkers helped themselves to my things."

"Did they ever. We tried to clean up the mess, but I'll warn you, it's still in shambles."

"Just like my life. How appropriate."

"Why don't you stay with me tonight?"

"Thanks. No. I prefer to be alone." Lick her wounds in private. "See you, Tuda." She hugged her friend, then set off for the confession booth.

Nan tied on the scarf before she walked into the church. It was nearly vacant, and a sliver of light lit the stained-glass window where the Virgin Mary held the Infant Jesus. Rows of offertory candles sent a reddish hue over the Virgin's white dress.

The familiar scent of lemon oil and frankincense calmed Nan's soul. The rituals, the expected, the same old same were a comfort. She slid into a pew as quietly as she could, found an abandoned rosary, and picked it up.

She gulped when the confessional opened and Finn's mother limped out, taking no notice of Nan. The withered, slumped-over woman staggered to a pew at the front of the sanctuary. Her rosary beads draped around her knotted fingers, and she sank to her knees in prayer.

Guilt washed over Nan. It had never been her intention to hurt Finn's mother. How would the old woman get on without her son? Even such as he was, he did take care of his mother. And the pigs. Dirty animals, but they were God's creatures and deserved to be cared for as well. Nan let out a sigh and headed to the confession booth.

She kneeled inside, the way she'd done since before her first Holy Communion. "Bless me, Father, for I have sinned."

Father Albert listened without comment until the end, when Nan stopped short of the one that might stop the priest's heart.

"Is that all, my child?" His tone indicated he had a lot of material to work with.

"No, Father. I have to confess something else. Something altogether terrible. Something about Teddy."

"And what might that be?"

Nan squeezed the rosary beads she'd laced between her fingers. "It's like this, Father. Three years ago, when Teddy died . . ."

"Yes. Go on."

"He didn't just die. He killed himself."

Nan heard the priest suck in a breath. "Go on."

She continued, telling him the entire story. At the end, she said, "I'm sorry that I wasn't completely honest with you. And that I didn't seek your help. We've had our differences, but you deserved the truth."

"Are you done?" he asked when she'd finished.

"Yes, Father. What will you do? Will you remove Teddy from the church graveyard now that you know?"

"We'll let the dead be," he answered. "Tell me, Nan. How are your knees?"

"They're fine, Father. Why do you ask?"

"Because you'll be down on them, doing penance, for a very long time."

CHAPTER 28

Nan trudged through the graveyard, her knees aching, but her soul healing. There was one last step. She had to confront Teddy and tell him she'd no longer allow her heart and soul to be his. She stood at his grave. The Celtic cross, once the color of Irish sea salt, was now gloomy gray. Moss and lichen and mold were winning the battle to claim it as their own.

"Teddy," she said, touching the cold gravestone. "I gave you my love. Only our heavenly Father understands the why and what of your actions. I harbor no bitterness toward you. I forgive you. I pray your soul finds peace."

With that, she turned away. The sun broke through the clouds and washed the church steeple in gold. The beams stretched down to dance over her. Closing her eyes, she opened her hands, invited the Holy Ghost to seep in, to fill her with His amazing grace. She basked in His radiance, which made her feel so light, she thought her feet might lift and carry her up to meet Him.

She was free from her bond of shame, regret, darkness, and sorrow. Free of Teddy. Truly forgiven.

"Thank you, Lord." She opened her eyes. For a brief second, a rainbow spread across the sky. Then it disappeared as though she'd imagined it. Or perhaps it was the Holy Ghost winking at her.

Her steps were light until she neared the church gates. She'd put Teddy to rest, but her longing for Dutch pulled her down again. *Trust in the Lord.* The thought rose up from down deep. Yet, she couldn't see how to be with Dutch until after the war.

She stood on the cobbled street, looking up the hill at the row of attached buildings. The sound of laughter and music drifted toward her on the wind, along with a whiff of burning turf. She was supposed to join everyone at the pub, but her heart ached for Dutch, and she'd only cry if she had to retell the agony of the past few hours. *No.* She'd walk home now. Try to make sense of what had happened between them. And what hadn't happened.

They could have been across the border by this time. Safe. Married. Instead, she was alone, wondering if her man was injured and rotting in a dirty POW cell. *Dear God, no. Please take care of him.*

Nan had crossed the bridge when Dr. Mann's Ford Model A pulled up alongside her.

"Hey, kid," Dr. Mann shouted through the open window. "Climb in."

"Thanks, Doc. Thanks for all you did. I can't talk right now. I prefer to walk."

"Not a request." Juliet swung the door open. "Get in." Her eyes had the hard precision of a cold military officer, rather than the softness of a kind country doctor.

Nan owed the woman. She could hardly justify refusing this order. "If you insist." Nan climbed into the warmth of the sedan. She had a feeling she was about to give the doctor a debriefing.

Dr. Mann's expression could freeze tea leaves. "Holy cow dung, O'Neil," Juliet said. "What happened? How the heck did you end up in Cliffside?"

"We had to take a detour."

"Why?" Juliet barely slowed down enough to make the hairpin bend on the road. The car's back wheels hit a patch of mud. The sedan slid right, left, right. The doc calmly regained control of the vehicle.

"One of the roads was washed out. We couldn't pass. It put us off the route—"

"What happened to the map I gave you?"

They sped down the lane, toward Nan's house. The sunset painted the sky with orange, gold, crimson, and pink hues. The big, puffy clouds were cheerful. So unlike Nan's mood. Or the mood of the gal next to her. "We followed it, but once we—"

"I know that. What happened to the *actual* map?"

Nan frowned, tried to recall the craziness of the morning. "Honestly, I don't know."

"Did the Irish Army get it?" The doc seemed to have aged since the last time Nan had seen her. Lines darted down from her lips to her chin. Dark under-eye circles stood out against her pale skin.

Nan shrugged. "They found the guns. I'm sorry. I don't know if they nabbed the map."

"I don't give a fig about the guns. What did you do with the map? Where was it the last time you saw it?"

"On the floor of the lorry."

Juliet wiped a hand over her mouth, smearing her lipstick onto her white glove. "They probably found it." She smacked her hand on the steering wheel. She swung the car around a corner.

"Look out," Nan shouted.

Juliet careened out of the path of a wayward cow, barely missing the animal. The car rode up an embankment, and for a second Nan thought they'd capsize, but the doc righted the vehicle as though this happened every day.

"Wowza. Steak tartare, anyone?" She zoomed back into the middle of the lane. "How about the fake ID?"

"We lost that somewhere. Along with the ration book."

"Where?"

"Probably outside the Gilmour House gates. When Lady Margot almost ran us over."

"So you never used it?"

"Never."

"Okay, good. I'll head over there and try to find it."

"Was the map important? The ID? I'm sorry. We didn't mean to lose them."

Juliet shook her head, and the serene expression returned to her face. It was as though she'd turned a switch and the glib doctor was back. "Don't be. I'm the one who's sorry. Too bad you didn't get your flyboy across the border."

"Without your help, Dutch would be dead. And thanks for paying for the damage to the lorry."

"You're not supposed to know about that. Who told you?"

"I'd rather not say."

"Mrs. Norman." Juliet downshifted, grinding the gears. "That woman and her big ears and even bigger mouth, she's going to get me killed."

Nan grinned until she saw the tension in Juliet's face. The doctor wasn't kidding. Dutch was right. She must be with American intelligence. "Doc, are you a spy?"

"Spy? Me? What a hoot."

"Are you?"

She glanced at Nan. "I could tell ya, but then I'd have to shoot ya. Listen, kid, I am sorry about the loused-up escape. Paying for the Guinness Company's damages was the least I could do. I hear the Tinkers did a number on your house. What's next for you?"

"Carry on, I suppose." The old Nan would have gone back and sorted through her damaged home and attempted to reconstruct her former life. Hide away from adventure. But that life was over.

They approached Nan's house. Dark. Silent. Abandoned. There were neat piles of debris lined up outside. A tarp covered the hole in the roof. This empty shell didn't feel like her home anymore. Especially now that Dutch wouldn't be there. Or Mr. Dee.

There was nothing inside she cared about except for a few books, her rosary beads, the portrait of Jesus, and the statue of the Blessed Virgin Mary her mother had given her at confirmation. She hoped the Tinkers had the decency to leave those items alone, but she wasn't hopeful.

"Wow, kid. Your house. It's in shambles." The doctor pulled into the courtyard and parked the car, engine still running. "You want me to go in with you?"

Nan shook her head. "No."

Juliet reached into her boxy leather purse and pulled out a tube. She ringed her lips with the Tangee lipstick. "Okay. You getting out?"

Nan didn't move, mulling over what to do next.

The doctor stopped applying the lipstick. "What? You need money? Just ask."

"Thanks. I don't. I need to put my life back together. Ah, I can't believe I'm back."

"That's a good thing, isn't it? Beats jail."

"That's true. This could have turned very ugly." Nan let out a groan. "I thought I'd be back. But . . ." Nan glanced at Juliet, trying to decide if she ought to confide in the doctor. "I was going to flee across the border with Dutch. Get married on base. See him off to England. Then I'd return home. We'd see each other when we could."

"I thought from the second I saw you together that it was the real deal. You two make a great couple."

"Did you? Now we'll have to wait until after the war to get married." The uncertainty of how long it'd be before she held Dutch in her arms again stabbed through her gut. The memory of his lips, his scent, his gaze turned her heart upside down.

"Invite me to the wedding. If I'm around." Juliet huffed. "And I probably will be because I'm not getting assigned to London anytime soon. Say, you okay, kid?"

Nan hadn't noticed she'd been wringing her hands. She stopped, folded them in her lap. "Other than feeling as though I just lost the love of my life—"

"He's not lost. He's interned. At least you know he won't get shot down again. And you know where he is."

"What do you know about the internment camp? Is it horrid? The Irish Army yanked him from my arms and beat him before they threw him in their lorry."

"Did they? The cretins. The K-Lines is thirty miles southwest of Dublin. One side of the camp houses the Allies. The other, the Axis. That's about all I could ferret out."

"I hate to think of him locked away in a cell. His injuries not being cared for."

"I want to help you, but I'm not exactly in a position to do that right now."

Nan squeezed her left finger, longing to wear Dutch's wedding ring. "If I were married to him, I'd have legal rights." Nan shifted, tapping her feet. "I have a good mind to go up to that camp and bang on the manager's door. Demand to see if Dutch is being treated right."

"The camp commandant, not the manager. What's stopping you? You don't strike me as timid. Maybe use your charm instead of brute force, though."

A bead of hope sprang up in Nan. *Yes. That's right. Why not?*

"They must have medical staff. Maybe I could worm my way in. Maybe I could sweet-talk myself into a position. Or volunteer. Not much call for a midwife, though."

"You're a top-notch nurse. I've seen your stitches."

Nan looked at the empty house. It would mean leaving her friends and patients, though. But Dutch. *Dutch.* She had to be with him.

Nan grabbed Juliet's arm. "I'm going to the K-Lines. But you have to promise me you'll stay here. Look after the women of Ballyhaven."

Juliet put her hand on top of Nan's. "I can't promise that. But if I leave, I promise there'll be a doctor and a midwife here. I can do that with a snap of my fingers."

"What time is it?"

Juliet looked at her watch. "Four forty-five."

"Will you wait for me for a few minutes? I'll throw whatever's left into a suitcase. If I hurry, I'll make the night train."

"Sure, I'll drive you. Don't you want to stop by the pub and say good-bye to Tuda and the girls?"

"I think I best just be on my way. If I go by there now, I may never leave. Tuda and the girls will understand. They can visit me."

"Okay. Get a move on." Juliet closed the lipstick. "Here, take it," she said. "You'll want your lips to be silky smooth when you finally get to the Curragh, then you can kiss your man silly."

❖ ❖ ❖

After an agonizingly slow train ride to Dublin and an even slower bus ride to Newbridge, a town near the Curragh where Nan found a room at an inn, more than twenty-four hours had passed. It was already afternoon. She stood outside the K-Lines, closer to Dutch, but not close enough.

Nan gripped her medical bag and entered the POW camp. A rectangular perimeter fence made of barbed wire enclosed the compound. Inside, a vast collection of barracks seemed deserted. Only a fierce wind howled between the rows of buildings. The area was divided into two compounds by a corrugated-iron fence. The barbed wire ran the length of the separation.

Ironic, she thought. Until yesterday, her heart had been surrounded by barbed wire. Dutch had clipped the wires, released her heart to love again. He'd freed her. Now Dutch was behind barbed wire. And God help her, Nan was going to cut him free.

She swallowed against the knot in her throat. Elevated gun posts marked each of the four corners of the perimeter. Armed guards, stationed in the towers, pointed their weapons into the yard. There were two pedestrian gates to enter the camp. Nan figured the sign marked "B" must be the British side, and "G" indicated the German side.

She sucked in a breath, reminded herself of the doctor's instructions. *Use your gorgeous eyes and smile to disarm the guard and get past him to see the commandant.*

Nan walked through the British pedestrian gate with her lips pouty—and hopefully alluring with the many layers of Tangee—plus enhanced eyebrows, eyelashes, and cheeks, all provided by the magic of Dr. Mann's makeup, a last-minute gift from the doctor at the train station.

A young Irish Army soldier battling acne gaped. "Good day, miss," he said.

"Ah, how you keeping?" Nan spread a slow smile, and the soldier responded exactly the way she wanted him to.

"Ah. Fine, miss. What can I do to you?" He shook his head. "For you."

"I'm here about the nursing position. I have an interview with the commandant."

He looked at his papers, shuffled them around. "I'm sorry. I don't have any interviews listed."

"Must be some mix-up. Can you please see if the commandant is ready for me now?" She leaned toward him, making sure he got a glimpse of her cleavage, where she'd intentionally left open a button.

Lord, I'm going to hell. Or at least spending a few centuries in purgatory.

But it worked. The soldier's gaze stayed on her chest. He picked up the phone. He said something into the receiver, then lifted his gaze to hers. "What's your name, miss?"

"Nurse Nan O'Neil."

He repeated it into the phone. "And where might you be from?"

"Ballyhaven." Nan's pulse pounded, drumming in her ears. That might have been daft, to give her real name and town. The doctor hadn't instructed her on that part. She should have asked Juliet. *Well, too late now.*

The soldier put down the receiver. "Commandant McGann will see you. Please wait a tick while someone from his office comes to fetch ya."

A few minutes later, Nan sat at a long table in a conference room. She was given an application to fill out, which took her less than five minutes. She pushed the fountain pen back and forth between her hands and took in the room. A potbellied stove warmed the space. Maps of Ireland hung on the walls. Bookcases, crowded with binders, stood under a row of windows.

Outside, the camp was still and vacant. Tan. Dull. Monotonous. Inside and out. Where were the prisoners? She hated to think of them locked away in cold cells, especially Dutch. How could men be so cruel?

The door opened, and a middle-aged man walked in, wearing a khaki-colored uniform. He reminded Nan so much of Paul Halpin, she decided the commandant would immediately see through her lies and half-truths.

He nodded to her, his dark eyes evaluating her. "They tell me you're here about the nursing post." He pulled out a chair and sat across from her.

"I am." She straightened and slid the application toward him. *What luck.* There apparently was an opening.

"The one that doesn't exist?"

Or maybe not. Nan folded her arms, crossed her legs, managed a thin smile. "Please don't tell me I've come all this way on a false promise."

"Now, who might be promising you such a thing?"

It was evident to Nan her physical charms would be useless with this man. "My parish priest. Father Albert." *Another lie. Oh dear, oh dear. Oh dear.*

"From Ballyhaven?" He wrote the priest's name across the top of her application.

"Yes." Her answer came out high-pitched, sharp. More like a yip.

"Ah well, but I don't know where he'd get that notion." The commandant studied her application. "Tell me so, Nurse Nan. Why are you leaving your last post?"

"I have relations nearby."

"I see. I see. Tell me. Have you ever been convicted of a crime?"

"No, sir." She hoped her voice hadn't sounded too wobbly.

"Arrested?"

Her knees began to shake. It took all her effort to stop the quaking. "Why is that important? I thought only convictions counted."

"Ah no. You're right. Your name just seems familiar."

"Does it? It's a common-enough name. If you don't have a post right now, I could volunteer until one comes open."

"Are you sure about that?"

"Of course. I want to do my part for the Allies."

"How about the Axis troopers?"

"If they're injured, 'tis my duty to heal them."

"I see, I see." He picked up her application and stood. "Let me check on a couple of things. And you look like . . ." He paused. Nan bit her lip. She fully expected him to say she looked like a liar. "A lady who could use a cup of tea."

"Thanks. That'd be lovely."

"You wait here. Be back soon."

Nan got up, started pacing. This had been a bad idea. He was probably calling Father Albert right now to verify her story. She'd be thrown out on her rear end. Or worse. Arrested on some charge that would land her in prison.

The door swung open and Nan pivoted.

Commandant McGann nodded to her, blocking the exit. "I've some bad news for you."

Nan's eyes darted left and right. She felt as though she were a fox, the hunters had cornered her, and she was about to be set upon. "Do you?"

"Yes. I'm afraid there's no open post for a nurse. There never was one a'tall. That, I suspect, you already know."

She gulped.

"But I've good news for you, too. Tea will be here in due course. In the meantime, perhaps you can give this young pilot officer an exam." He stepped aside from the door.

"Dutch?" Nan thought she was seeing an apparition. "Dutch. Is that really yourself?"

Dutch didn't talk. He didn't hesitate. He rushed to her, took her in his arms, and swung her around and around and around. Their kisses sent an earthquake through her from head to toe and back again. Electric currents were sparking up and down her spine, circling her brain. Toasting her cheeks.

They finally sat at the table, holding hands. Then the situation sank in.

"It was awfully nice of your commandant to let me see you," she said. "Ah, that's a nasty bruise on your handsome face." She touched the back of her hand to his discolored cheek. "Have you a salve for the scrapes along your jaw?"

"Don't worry about me. How did you get in?"

"Ah, I bluffed my way. Said I was applying for the nurse post." She hadn't even noticed who had brought in a tray with tea and biscuits. She poured two cups of tea from a Brown Betty teapot.

"You're a woman with guts of steel, Nan O'Neil."

"Early training."

"What happened in Ballyhaven? I've been worried sick about you. And the ladies. I couldn't get a straight answer from anyone."

"All charges were dropped. Dr. Mann paid for the damage to the Guinness truck. And best of all, Finn was run out of town by a rotten-tomato parade."

"Good. Good. And?" He squeezed her hands. He didn't need to expand the question.

"I reconciled with Father Albert. And Teddy."

"Thank heaven."

"Yes, we can get on with our lives." In a low tone, she said, "How can I help you escape?"

"That's a bit tricky. But now that you're here, I don't think it's necessary."

She straightened. "Why? Are they going to let you go? That's altogether grand."

He let out a gentle laugh that warmed her. "Not quite. You see, this internment thing here, it's very strange."

"Ah, Dutch. Are they beating you?"

"No. Not at all. Let me explain the situation. First, I can get a parole to leave the camp as long as I agree to not try and escape."

"You can?" She shook her head, the words not making a lick of sense. "They let you out of here?"

"Yes. A day pass. All of us. The Germans, too. We all promised to patronize different eating and drinking establishments. It's the Irish attempt to keep the conflict at bay. They see us as 'guests of the state' rather than 'prisoners of war.'" He sipped his tea. "I get full pay plus a clothing allowance."

"If you can leave the camp, why don't you escape over the border?"

"Not allowed. When I accept parole, I give my word as an officer of the RAF to honor the terms of my conditional release. I must return to camp. Of course, once I'm back at camp, it's my duty to try to escape. But while on the outside, the official word is"—he paused, sipped his tea, then continued—"I shall not talk about or enlist any help from the locals for an escape."

Nan could swear she was Alice down the rabbit hole. "And if you do escape while on parole?"

"It's against the RAF code," Dutch said flatly. "I'll be returned promptly. And deemed an insubordinate troublemaker."

"Are you joking?"

"Nope. The RAF will court-martial me." He took her hand, kissed each finger. "You look confused."

"A wee bit."

"They tell me life's not too bad here." Dutch planted a kiss on her palm, sending a shiver through her. "The golf is supposed to be great. We're sort of celebrities around town. Lots of excellent horseback riding, too, they say."

Nan slapped a hand on the table, rattling the teacups. "I don't understand my country. The Irish Army combed the countryside to find you, beat you up, drag you to this POW camp, and now they'll let you roam around free in town?"

"Temporarily free. I know. It's crazy. But listen. I can be with you."

She gazed into his eyes. "You're interned but you can leave camp? I don't understand."

"That's the Irish government for you." He shrugged one shoulder and grinned. "I do understand one thing."

"What's that, Dutch?"

"I never want to be separated from you ever again for as long as we live. Do you still feel the same?"

"Why would I be here if I didn't?"

"Then let's get married. As soon as possible. In town."

"Oh yes, Dutch. Yes."

◆ ◆ ◆

A fortnight later, Nan wore a wedding dress made of delicate lace and satin. Juliet fluffed the long veil that flowed to the floor of the Newbridge church. The parish priest was the kindest man Nan had ever met. The father had welcomed her and had knitted her immediately into his flock and the church activities. At the priest's recommendation, she already had several patients.

"You look like a million bucks, kid," Juliet said, adjusting the veil's crown. "Don't you agree, Tuda?"

"Ah, she does. She does. Where did you get such an altogether gorgeous dress, Juliet?"

"We probably don't want to know," Nan said, taking a bouquet of white roses from Margaret.

Margaret nodded. "And wasn't it nice of the lovely Commandant McGann to allow Dutch to get married in the church?"

"He's been very kind."

"I'll say." Juliet poked Tuda with her elbow. "McGann gave Dutch parole for two nights to be with his new bride."

Nan felt her cheeks grow hot. "Dutch calls our little cottage on the river our 'sugar shack.' But I call it 'heaven on earth.'"

The ladies giggled. Margaret gave Nan a hug. "Aren't you the cheeky one?"

Dutch's entire crew and a few other interned RAF officers were waiting in the pews for her to walk down the aisle. Along with Paul and Kelly Halpin. She could hear their baby wailing.

The organ music started. "That's the cue to take your places," Nan said. "And thank you. Thank you all for coming to my wedding. And for all you did for Dutch and me."

Margaret opened the heavy church door. "We wouldn't miss it for the world."

Nan was glad Tuda had agreed to walk her down the aisle. She needed Tuda to lean on. When Nan spotted Dutch standing at the altar, her breath caught in her throat. He wore a dark-gray suit, and his smile nearly caused her to swoon.

"Don't faint now, love," Tuda said. "Wait until you see what's in store for ya tonight."

Nan was completely ready for this man to be beside her. This man who fell from the sky and into the bog. This man she nursed to health. This man who turned her life upside down and her heart right side up. This man was hers forever and evermore.

ACKNOWLEDGMENTS

Thank you, Sheryl Zajechowski, Faith Black Ross, and the team at Waterfall Press for all your expert insights and for bringing this book to life. I'm thankful to my agent, Victoria Skurnick, who never gave up on sending out this book. For encouragement along the way, thank you, author friends Judy Duarte, Susan Meissner, Linda Thomas-Sundstrom, and Carlene Dater. Thanks also to Romance Writers of America for providing a place to learn and to find like-minded authors, and to American Christian Fiction Writers for providing a place for Christian writers to gather.

Thank you, Scott. Your patience is astounding. And to Hayley and Hannah for just being there.

Many thanks, hugs, and kisses to my dad. His stories of neutral Ireland during World War II, and of what his generation endured, provided the seeds for this book.

ABOUT THE AUTHOR

Photo © Holly Ireland

Jeanne M. Dickson was born into an Irish American family, the only girl surrounded by four brothers. Her grandmother lived with them and was a constant source of stories about life in Ireland and about saints and ancestors long gone from this earth. Jeanne credits her mother, her aunts, and her grandmother for her love of storytelling.